TWILIGHT WHISPERS

"Stay with me, sweetheart. It's been a hard day. Don't make tonight harder."

"Oh, Blake . . ." Dani whispered.

Giving her no time to formulate a plan, Blake put his arms around Dani's waist, pulling her up toward him. She came easily, her lips protesting, her body melting into his as it should, and he kissed her.

Their mouths met so tenderly that, when her eyes closed, Dani thought she might be dreaming. But it was no dream because her hands, instead of pushing Blake away, curled up into his shirt until she was pulling him into her as they sank back onto the couch.

"Blake," she murmured when his lips drifted from hers.

"Dani, just be with me. Please," he whispered, pulling her closer and closer.

"Just for tonight," Dani promised as she was lost in their lovemaking as she had been lost so many times before.

REBECCA FORSTER

VOWS

ZEBRA BOOKS
KENSINGTON PUBLISHING CORP.

ZEBRA BOOKS are published by

Kensington Publishing Corp.
475 Park Avenue South
New York, NY 10016

First Printing: April, 1994

Printed in the United States of America

Chapter One

1975—Chicago

"He's home, miss."

"In the house, Martha?"

Dani Cortland's head popped up, white blonde hair falling away from her young face, revealing an expression less Alice-in-Wonderland than David Copperfield.

"Just coming up the drive. Better hurry or *she'll* get there first." The maid shook her head and turned away, hiding the pity she felt for her young mistress. Ten was just too early to be competing for a man's attention. Especially if it was her father's.

"I will. I will," she called breathlessly though the woman had already disappeared. Whispering frantically to herself, Dani stuffed her rumpled cotton shirt into her pleated uniform skirt. "Be perfect, Dani. Never less than perfect," she admonished under her breath, almost enjoying the litany so painfully learned. One last tuck and she straightened her shoulders. Raising her voice, trying to sound confident like him, she said, "People judge you by how you look and what you do. Look perfect, act like you're the best. Be number one. Number one . . ."

Dani closed her eyes, trying very hard to see herself the way Papa wanted her to be. Failing, she opened her eyes, stopped her dreaming and resumed her incantation ". . . That's how you become someone, Dani. Start at the top. It's stupid to start anywhere else. Fight for what you want. Don't lose. That's very, very stupid."

Dani certainly never wanted to be stupid or weak. That's what her mother had been. Papa had had to fight tooth and nail to keep Dani. That's what he had told her, still told her when she asked about her mother now and again. But much as she tried, Dani couldn't hate her mother for not fighting for her hard enough. Sometimes fighting for something you wanted couldn't get you what you wanted. Didn't she know? She'd tried to get her papa's attention in oh-so-many ways and still sometimes she just couldn't manage it.

A brush through the hair. A tug at her necktie. She wouldn't think of her mother. Papa wanted her, Mama didn't and now Mama wasn't around anymore. Mama was no one. Not a winner. Nobody to be concerned with just like Papa said she would be if she wasn't perfect. Dani hoped she was not too much like her mother. She would hate to just disappear one day. Suddenly, Dani wondered where her mother's clothes had gone. Just like the woman herself her things were in this big house one day, gone the next. Then *she* came to live and all traces of Dani's mother were wiped away.

Shivering at how easy it was to make someone vanish, Dani slipped into the navy blazer with the gold embroidered "M" of Mariville Academy emblazoned on the breast pocket, then stood in front of the mirror only to wish she hadn't bothered to look. She wasn't right at all, and that sinking feeling crept back into her stomach. Dani Cortland. Geek. Long and skinny and pale. Skin so milky she could see the threads of lavender veins through it. Eyes so big and blue they were startling, not pleasing. No wonder her papa didn't want to look at her. She didn't look half as nice as the other girls at school. Some of them already had breasts. At the very least they had beautiful wild hair or full red lips. So unlike Dani's chiseled features, her wide mouth, her narrow, straight nose. An angled little face that Dani was sure would never be beautiful; an angled body that would never be like the other girls.

Sticking her tongue out at her reflection, Dani dismissed herself. Who cared if Papa thought her unattractive? She had something else that would make him proud. Finally, today, he would take proper notice of her. She was about to double check her work when, beneath her window, his car door slammed and her stomach lurched. Papa was too fast. She wasn't ready.

Heart racing, Dani dashed to the window. Lifting the lace curtain she peeked at her father. Powerful. Important. Rich. He owned things, bought things, and everything he touched made money or gave him more people to order about. This Dani knew from conversations she'd overheard. Someday, perhaps, he'd have time to explain to her why he wanted to own people, lord over so many places. The money was easy to understand. It gave all of them so much: the beautiful house, the lovely furniture, trips and Mariville school. But maybe if they didn't have so much of those big things they could have a few small ones. Like friends who laughed instead of made deals or primped at the mirrors. Like time to just sit on the sweep of lawn in the back, maybe have a picnic even though cook

7

would be in the kitchen and could easily make them any number of wonderful dishes. Maybe if Mama had wanted her more and fought harder in court they could still be a family . . .

Dani shook her head. There wasn't any time for wishing now. Papa was moving, speaking to his driver, looking at the house. Not up at her, but toward the entry. Dani's excitement evaporated like a puddle on a blazing day. He was looking for *her*.

"Darn! Darn! Darn!" Dani's fists hit at the sash. There was no time to lose. Grabbing the blue covered workbook Dani raced down the stairs: afraid, hopeful. But *she* was with him before Dani could reach the marbled foyer. Papa was talking; *she* was listening.

". . . Argentina. At least two weeks. Perhaps longer." Papa's voice was wonderful. Controlled. Assured. Sometimes soothing in its depth, usually judgmental.

"Sounds marvelous darling. I'd love to go . . ." *Her* voice was like a sleeping cat suddenly wakened. Stretched and soft and self-indulgent.

Dani's voice was almost lost as she stopped midway down the sweep of stairs. She worked hard to keep it at the ready as she continued to walk, ladylike now. *Don't yell. Go slowly.* Papa didn't like running. Fast talking yes; movement, no. Actions, he swore, should always be first calculated, then executed swiftly and without hesitation. Such a hard lesson for Dani whose very essence was that of impulse; so difficult for her to think things through. Shooting off like a star was far more satisfying. Today, though, Dani was careful. Reaching the bottom of the stairs unnoticed, she stood respectfully beside the two tall, beautiful people and waited. But the wait was interminable; they were so

8

lost in their conversation, Dani could stand it no longer. She cleared her throat and tested the water.

"Hello, Papa."

Slowly Peter Cortland turned away from his new, young, and third wife. He faced his daughter. By the time his swivel was completed, Peter Cortland had almost veiled his vexation with her. Dani flinched, hating that he never managed to hide it completely before they were face to face. If only he were a better actor, she thought, she might be a better daughter. But now his attention was hers and she had to say something before he vanished again: into his study, out for the evening, into the bedroom he shared with *her*. Papa was always disappearing.

"Dani, home from school already?" He seemed almost disappointed.

"It's Easter vacation, Papa." For a smart man he had to be reminded of a great many things.

"Yes, of course. Did you bring someone with you? Someone to keep you company?" Dani shook her head. Why would she want someone around? What if he wanted to keep her company? What if he were to find himself with time on his hands? What if he wanted to do . . . something with her? A friend would only be in the way. Obviously Peter Cortland hadn't thought of that. He looked confused and waved his hand as if the entire conversation was of little consequence. "Well, if that's how you want it, I suppose you'll amuse yourself."

"Yes. I'll try," Dani said and hung her head, her chin pressing down into her chest, pushed there by the weight of his voice. He wasn't pleased. She made a mental note to invite a friend home for summer vacation. A good friend. One he would approve of. Someone really great. Someone beautiful. Aware that her

9

papa's new wife was moving, floating quietly apart the way she did when she was bored, Dani pulled herself together because her Papa would follow as surely as if the two of them were tied together, as if that woman trailed a scent Papa couldn't resist. Forcing herself to look him in the eye, Dani made her move before it was too late.

"I've won an award, Papa," she said boldly, proudly. "First place."

The blue workbook was offered up. Peter took it, looked at it, and allowed himself a small, surprisingly sincere smile, and Dani rejoiced. His eyes had softened, she was sure of it. The hole in the pit of her stomach closed, and she glowed with the well-being that brought. Even the marbled foyer warmed, the scent of his wife obscured by Dani's achievement.

"You certainly have, Dani. Congratulations." He was reaching for her, touching her so lightly on the shoulder, but touching her nonetheless, in a way he had never done before. But the touch was brief and when it was over she felt lost, diminished. Breath held, Dani waited for more, for any sign that he loved her for all the work she'd done. Peter Cortland's eyes narrowed. He flipped open the book. He was reading it!

"Interesting topic, Dani. The effect of recycling on the U.S. economy. Impressive. That school must be teaching you something. An ambitious undertaking for someone your age. First prize. I'm proud of you."

Little though it was, it was enough, this praise from him. Dani's chest puffed up with pride. Her voice fairly boomed, she spoke then before she really thought, not wanting to lose him now.

"I worked so very hard, Papa. I would have won the grand prize, but Marianne Pleishner did her report on

10

the world market, and I think she had her father help her and . . . and . . ."

Her voice trailed off. Thrilled though she was, Dani was too schooled in the signs of Peter Cortland's displeasure not to notice them now. So subtle. So painful. His lips tightening and turning down. His eyes narrowing. The world became cold at his command and the coveted workbook, the key to his affections, was back in her hands looking less impressive than she had remembered.

"Then this is not the first prize, is it Dani?"

"Yes, yes," she assured him quickly, her voice eager. She hadn't explained this properly. "There was grand prize, first prize, second . . ."

"No, Dani," he cut her off ruthlessly, teaching her his lessons the only way he could. "No matter what the school says, no matter what their designation, there is only one first, only one top. To call it anything else is to mislead. You are lessened when you accept such nonsense. It is sugar coating, Dani, nothing more." Peter Cortland was already turning away. Dani was losing him. "There are no excuses for second place, Dani. If you had determined that girl was your competition, then you should have made it your business to know what she was planning . . ."

"But I couldn't snoop . . ." Dani objected. Peter looked over his shoulder, but he didn't turn back. Why should he? Dani had disappointed him. No. She had failed him. Again.

"I'm talking about doing your research, Dani. That's not snooping. That's what will keep you on top. Stay one step ahead of the competitor. Don't ever forget that. No matter what you have to do or who you have to do it to, be first. If you're not first, you're nothing."

A rustle of silk underscored the lecture. The new wife was moving in, staking her claim. He'd smelled the perfume and felt the electricity. Dani was forgotten. He belonged to his *wife,* that woman who was perfect, who was first in her father's eyes in a way Dani didn't quite understand. *She* wasn't smart. *She* hardly ever spoke. *She* touched. *She* looked. *She* won and Dani lost.

Trying hard wasn't ever enough but sadly, Dani knew she would never stop.

"Pretty and smart," she muttered to herself as she slowly made her way back up the stairs. There was a new word in the litany now. She had failed this time. But someday . . . someday . . . she would make her father proud. Someday she'd be the woman on top.

"Pretty and smart," Dani whispered to herself, "and first."

Chapter Two

1994—San Francisco

"I thought you liked me, Dani."

"I do like you, Sid."

They were talking quietly at the end of the day. Fading light and lengthening shadows made Sid Pregerson's office seem almost cozy. But in reality it was as cold and calculating in its opulence as its occupant was with his power. Neither the softening light nor the benevolence in Sid's voice fooled Dani. She kept her smile polite, her attitude casual as she waited for him to reveal his real—and undoubtedly not so pleasant—agenda.

"You should, Dani. Considering all I've done for you, you should have a great deal of affection for me."

Dani steeled herself. Here it came again. The recitation of his magnanimity, a speech that made her want to scream. Sid Pregerson had the uncanny ability to make her feel ten years old again, a child waiting for her father to pronounce her lacking. But Sid wasn't her father, and she wasn't a kid ready to be influenced by anyone's perceptions. Annoyed, impatient, Dani checked her watch. Sid needed to hurry along before

13

she forgot how very impervious she was to the opinion of an older, more powerful man.

"Affection is an interesting word, Sid." Dani laughed dryly, patting the cuff of her saffron-colored sweater neatly in place over her watch. "It's a word we might quibble over." Showing him a face arranged in its most confident expression, she tried to hurry things along. "I won't deny how much I appreciated your help when I was starting out, but that was a long time ago. I'm assuming you didn't ask me here to reminisce about my early days in advertising."

Sid's lips curled. It was neither an expression of pleasure or amusement. Dani had long since ceased to amuse him and she had never pleasured him. But all that was about to change. Smart and beautiful though she may be, he knew Dani Cortland was also imprudent and impulsive. She insisted on trusting instinct when she should use that brilliantly, creative—dare he say wicked?—mind of hers a bit more cautiously.

"No, Dani, memory lane isn't calling. The here and now is much more interesting. We mustn't forget that you are a vice president here at Pregerson Advertising, not an intern. A powerful position. But Dani, I'm afraid you've seriously overestimated your strength."

Sid fell silent, toying with a piece of paper on his desk. With a dramatic, rather than heartfelt, sigh he held it across the desk. Dani leaned forward, taking her eyes off him only when she had the paper firmly in her grasp. One look at it and her blood ran cold. Christ. How in the hell had he gotten a hold of this?

"If I had been you, Dani . . ." Sid continued quietly, a cruelly triumphant edge in his voice, ". . . if I had wanted to unseat the CEO, the man I owed my career to, I would have done something quite similar. Approaching the board with insightful suggestions on

14

enhancing the bottom line, running the agency leaner, is the kind of smart thing a professional person would do. Yet, while your thinking was sound, your execution was flawed. You didn't check all the angles, Dani, and the one you missed impaled you."

Sid wagged his finger and clicked his tongue, thoroughly enjoying himself as Dani felt the years fall away. She struggled to psychologically stand her ground while Sid made another frontal assault.

"Choosing Fred Holbrook as your partner for this coup d'état was your first mistake. I thought everyone knew Fred owed me his financial life. I kept his company afloat when everyone else abandoned ship. Though he may have an appreciation for your quick mind and your lovely physique, he knows which side his bread is buttered on. He told me about your campaign to unseat me almost as soon as it was begun. Actually scurried in here with the information as if it wiped out the debt he owed me." Sid's head swung from side to side. He chuckled at such absurdity, then raised his eyes slowly. Hard, glistening points of darkness that said Fred would be off the hook when he chose to let him off the hook. "Fred can be so childlike in his trust."

Dani offered a wry smile. *Oh, Papa, I'm still missing the boat.* Defeated—this time—she sat back, not yet beyond learning from the error of her ways. Instinctively she ran her hand, slick with perspiration, over her pants, but the butter-colored leather only made her feel worse. She clasped her hands in her lap.

"And the second mistake, Sid?" she prodded, wanting to get away and lick her wounds.

"The second mistake, my dear, was committing your proposal to paper. I thought that a rather fundamental faux pas. If your duplicity wasn't recorded you

15

could deny, deny, deny, Dani. It's as simple as that."

Sid was up, sliding out of his chair. Then he was around his desk and by her side, his hand resting ever-so-lightly on her shoulder, letting it linger. It felt like the weight of the world. She stared ahead focusing on Sid's desk, wishing he would get back behind it. Instead he leaned close, his breath on her ear, a finger trailing the base of her throat. His voice lowered, his intentions clear.

"It's payback time, Dani." Slowly, with great reserve, she turned her head, looking him in the eye. Disgusted by his touch, and all it implied, Dani responded evenly, "I don't owe you a thing. Not one, blessed thing, Sid. You're tired and you've forgotten what this agency stands for, what your father built. With you at the helm Pregerson's going to be out of business in ten years. The best, most creative agency in the United States, and you don't even care. I don't think you ever did. But I care Sid. I live and breathe this agency and I'm the person who should be nurturing it. You can't take this business any further ahead because all you care about is the bottom-line, and now you've started to ignore even that." Dani's jaw tightened, "You've never created anything here. You've never had a vision of what this place could be. You're way past your prime and you should step aside. The only thing you care about is you—I care about the agency."

To his credit, Sid barely started. "Insults, Dani? Beneath you. Selfless visions of service? Laughable." He chuckled gently, he spoke cruelly. "And you're so wrong."

While no longer touching her, Sid stood his ground, too close, towering over her, making Dani feel small like she had before her father died. Smaller than she

16

felt when she'd discovered that Peter Cortland had divided his fortune between his wives—ex and current—leaving Dani to live by her talent and wits.

God, how alone she'd felt. He was gone and there was no one to compete with, no one to work at being perfect for. Funny how his death had seemed almost comical at the time. Such a big man, a powerful man, a man who insisted on giving a bit of himself only to those who he deemed worthy, making them strive to be better than perhaps they should ever have been. This larger than life man had died quietly in his sleep. A heart attack. A classic case, the doctor had said. A grip, a pain, and the heart had stopped. A rather gentle passing really. Some would say it was a miraculous one since they were unaware Peter Cortland had a heart at all.

But Dani didn't believe that. She would always believe in his love for her. If her father hadn't cared he wouldn't have fought tooth and nail for her in the custody battle, a war waged so long ago she barely had a memory of it now. Only the belief that he had done a good and noble thing remained in her mind. A good and noble thing. Peter Cortland had fought for her because he loved her.

It wasn't his fault he didn't know how to show that love when he finally possessed her as his alone, mother and wife gone, never to be heard from again. And wasn't that exactly what she was doing now? Fighting for something she loved, something she needed and believed in. This was what her father had tried to teach her. She had failed once, not struggling hard enough for Blake. But this time she would succeed. This time she wouldn't give up. Besides, this small defeat was easier to take than the one she had experienced with Blake. This time she didn't have to look into a face she

17

loved and admit she wasn't good enough. This time it was a thing she was after, and someday she would have it, make it perfect, make it number one. Today obviously wasn't the day, so Dani stared ahead, arranging her face in a gorgeous mask, as icy and defined as cut crystal, accepting this defeat as professionally as possible.

"What, Sid? What is it I owe you that I haven't paid back in full? Take a look, Mr. Pregerson." Now Dani was moving, striding across the huge office toward the bank of windows that framed San Francisco's skyline. Perhaps distance would save her from his desire. Blinking back tears of defeat, shame, and embarrassment, Dani convinced herself that she was in control. Sid wasn't her father. She wasn't a little girl. She'd performed for this damned agency, earned what she had and Sid was going to admit it. Dani threw her arm out toward that incredible scene, pointing to the TransTam Towers that dominated the view.

"The TransTam account is one of the largest in this agency. Why? Because I convinced them that they needed a full blown, multimedia campaign. A measly trade-to-trade bank of print ads became television, radio, and billboards. Direct mail. Billings quadrupled because of me, Sid."

Dani moved away from the window, pointing to the framed prints on the wall. Pregerson Advertising's best work—her work.

"And what about the Ashley Cosmetics campaign? It was the only major marketing effort ever to be brought in on time and under budget in this agency. What about the Farmington campaign? Don't you think I know that the entire banking industry was talking about the work I did?"

Sid was as motionless as the air before a quake,

almost a silhouette in the light that was now so dim Dani couldn't tell if he was really listening. Through the gloom did she see him smirk? If he laughed now, she couldn't bear it. She forged ahead, running on with her logic, knowing in her gut nothing she could say could extricate her from this situation.

"Jesus, Sid, I'm not blind, and I'm not stupid. Sure I had an army of support, but it was me—I was the one who handled everything every step of the way. When it was important that things be perfect, I was there. No details were ever left to some assistant. I'm a vice president that works, Sid. You don't have many of those around here, and I don't think you're ready to lose this one."

Then she heard it. A chuckle. A minor response to her major accomplishments. He put his hands together and clapped once. Twice. That was all he would give her.

"Bravo, Dani. A fine speech." He took one step forward. It seemed menacing, but no more so than his words. "You have talent. I exploited it, and you got to show off. Not only have you had fun doing what you do best, you've been rewarded with titles and money. Unfortunately, neither compensation was good enough for you. You wanted my job and you tried to take it. I'm not just going to accept an apology and let you walk away. You've got to pay for this one, Dani."

"Really?" she drawled. "And what exactly is it you'd like me to do to make all this up to you, Sid? Sit in stocks in the lobby?" Dani rolled her eyes, raised her shoulders. Both gestures of acceptance rather than helplessness. "I lost. It ticks me off. I'm humiliated. Isn't that enough? Let's be realistic. What do the guys do when they screw one another?"

"I haven't the foggiest, Dani. I've always been the

most traditional of men when it comes to screwing." Sid smiled benignly. Dani glared. She was actually disappointed that he wasn't above a comment like that. "In fact, I think we might just have hit upon an appropriate method of restitution. Something that would prove how highly you regard me. Perhaps some quality personal time might be just what you and I need."

"Oh please, Sid." Her blue eyes flashed and she crossed her arms over the chest he so admired. This was too ridiculous to be discussed. But Sid's silence was eloquent. Dani eyed him warily as he switched on the desk lamp. She blinked. The dark had overtaken them and now he wanted to see her clearly. Beyond the closed door the office had fallen silent too. People had gone home but for a few diehards. For all intents and purposes, they were alone.

"Is it that distasteful, this suggestion of mine?" Sid cocked his head.

"It's that laughable," Dani spat back. "We won't even discuss the fact that you're old enough to be my father. We'll talk about the nineties, Sid. What you're doing is called sexual harassment. That's a no-no. My little coup attempt failed. So sue me for trying. But you don't own me, and you can't mess with me this way. Call me when you're ready to really talk, Sid."

Dani walked toward the door, her head held high, her stomach churning. She was scared, and ashamed that she felt this way. Sid Pregerson was nothing. She was strong. She had a reputation. He couldn't hurt her. Another litany to get her through a tough situation.

"Dani," he called softly as she passed alongside him. He reached out, touched her arm, let his fingers slide over her silk sweater until he was holding her lightly. She shivered.

"Take your hands off me, Sid."

He tightened his grip, somehow closing in on her without moving. She could smell his aftershave, see the silver in his hair and the fine weave of the wool of his suit. Even though Sid was a handsome man, he repulsed her.

"Consider this, Dani. I may not have you in my bed, but I have your career under my thumb. I press down just a bit, and I crush you. You're nothing."

"Hah!" Dani released a laugh, yanking her arm away. Her white blonde hair swung forward, a strand of it sticking to her lip. She pulled it away, leaving a smudge of coral lipstick behind, mesmerizing Sid. When she spoke angrily he watched that imperfection with fascination. Dani neither noticed nor cared that he breathed a bit quicker, moved a tad closer. She was up and ready to fight. "You are a piece of work. I'd have you up on sexual harassment charges so fast your head would spin. I wouldn't be hurt, you would."

"Really?" He couldn't stop himself. He had to touch her. His hands slid up over her shoulders, up her neck until he cupped her face. Dani tried to shrug him off. He tightened his hold, his thumbs wiping away her lipstick, his stroke hard and obsessive. Shocked, Dani was paralyzed as his face moved closer, his fingers slowly pulling her head toward him until they were inches from one another. He whispered, "And what would a court of law say about your little corporate fun and games? Compared to those, my invitation is nothing."

"I don't know what you're talking about. I don't play games, Sid." Allowing him to hold her, ever alert now that he was deadly calm, Dani became wary.

"The fact of the matter is, Dani, I've wanted you for a very long time." A ribbon of warm breath floated toward her with his admission. "I'm not a terribly passionate man when it comes to sex for the sake of having sex, but you've intrigued me and I want you. If you refuse, I will go before the board and confess that I've made a terrible mistake in advancing you to the vice presidency. I will have to inform them that I recently discovered you were part of a conspiracy to defraud one of our clients ten years ago."

As suddenly as he had grabbed hold, Sid released her. Dani stumbled, disoriented now that she was free to go. She watched Sid move to the window, his back to her. He spoke intimately as though they were already lovers.

"You don't have any idea what it's like to realize your usefulness, your potential for pleasure, is limited. Age and change are terrible enemies. I want to fight them. Having you will help me do that, and I will use this unfortunate situation to get you. But you will not have my position in this firm. You will not best me, Dani. Not now. Not ever."

"Fine, Sid. Fine," Dani answered quietly, calmly. He was rambling and she was no match for his dementia. Dani had no desire to be a confessor out of bed or his savior in. The door was only steps away and she wanted to be on the other side of it. She started for it, arrested only when Sid spoke a name softly.

"Charlie Carter," he murmured. "Yes, I think at the time you were working with Charlie and the account in question was Heritage Fixtures." Sid turned his head. His profile was exquisite for a man his age. Behind him San Francisco glittered. He could have been a model hawking fine wine, expensive cars. But

22

she knew he was really only an aging man with an ugly appetite.

"I believe you authorized overbilling on the media, then buried charges from other accounts resulting in a double billing to Heritage Fixtures. A highly unethical thing to do, my dear. You should have been disciplined years ago." He turned to face her. The look of delight on a powerful face was a subtle thing. Sid Pregerson had perfected the expression. "Unfortunately it was only recently I found out about this, when I was lunching with Charlie. He felt terrible he hadn't mentioned it sooner. His conscience had been bothering him." Sid shook his head wryly. "Advertising men have such fragile consciences—not to mention egos—don't you agree?"

Dani didn't miss a beat, reacting the moment she realized his strategy.

"This scenario is a damned lie, and you know it. You and I discussed the double billings. We made up for them by providing additional creative services at no charge. The agency was in trouble. We needed that money during the slump in eighty-four. I'll tell the board about our meeting. I remember it clearly. You specifically ordered me to complete the paperwork against my objections. You said that kind of paper manipulation was nothing unusual. You were the one who told me I better get with it, or I'd never make it in this business. Sid, you implied you would never move me to a full-time creative position. You forced me . . ."

Dani's voice broke, and she cursed her weakness. Sid was ever watchful, attentive. He saw her crumbling and it satisfied him immensely.

"Did I ever sign an authorization?" he asked quietly. "Were there any witnesses to that discussion?

23

Even if such a thing was considered acceptable, do you really think this agency would want it made public that one of their vice presidents had been involved in such activity? Certainly not. We, in the advertising business, value our standing in the community. Unlike other professions, we discipline those of our own who are out of line. We have, after all, an image to maintain."

Sid laughed, long and languorously, pulling it down to a chuckle, allowing himself a self-indulgent chortle. He spread his arms wide, his palms laying against the cool triple pane glass as if he could embrace everything that belonged to him, pull the tower of glass and steel and brick into his arms, enfolding Dani in the process. He controlled so much and he was sure Dani would be no different. Sid smiled, his lips curling up slowly. There was no need to hurry now. She was his.

"Between you and me, Dani, I think you are a hell of a creative mind and a highly effective executive." His arms slid down the glass until they were at his side. "Definitely more ethical than many of us, and as unethical as you need to be when called upon. It's an attractive combination—your mind, your lovely, lean body, your ethics. When you think about it, what I'm asking is only the culmination of the career you have so carefully cultivated. Not only would that career remain intact, it would flourish under my good will. Yes, flourish . . ." Sid reiterated, eyes narrowing as he tired of the rhetoric. Dani was wasting his time, being difficult. Sid held his hand toward her. "Come on, Dani, show me you understand."

"Look, Sid," Dani said calmly, trying to contain the situation, "mistakes have been made on both sides. Mine was a long time ago. Taken in perspective, it was hardly a miscalculation. The client remains loyal, the agency is solvent. Let's just forget it. We'll go on as though nothing has happened. What do you say?"

Calm, calm she ordered herself. Bluff. Don't throw it away just yet. The ball was in his court, and she had no idea which way he'd play it. He didn't hesitate. An overhead smash directed at her weakest spot came quickly.

"No, Dani," he answered sorrowfully, pushing himself from the window, raising one hand to smooth his hair. "I don't think we can forget what's happened here today. You're a fine advertising person, but you're timing is a beat off. You screwed up your take-over bid, you screwed around with the billing, you didn't cover your ass. It's a perfect time for me to ask a little favor. And it is a very little favor, compared to all the favors I have done for you."

He inched back toward her, eyes raking over her long, fluid body. She looked good in yellow, marvelous in silk and leather. Better in nothing, he was sure. A prize. So much more desirable than the woman who waited for him at home. His wife was beautiful but without challenge. Now Dani, she was complex, interesting, enigmatic. He wanted her and he whispered low inviting words that were meant to strike terror.

Dani, cool, smart, beautiful Dani, watched him come. Listening to him she knew a mistake had been made when she put her career in his hands so many years ago. But Sid was making an even bigger mistake now.

"I hold your future in my hands," he murmured. "You can play my way, or you don't play at all. And I mean you don't play anywhere, Dani."

Sound ceased and the silence enthralled her. She had never felt words before. She did now. Air could be heavy. A pause could be pregnant. There was a devil with whom one could bargain for one's soul. Amazing! Options were weighed. A decision was made. Dani acted quickly. Without thinking she spoke. Surprisingly her voice didn't quaver. She sounded sure, mighty, and proud. What an incredible liar she was.

"Go fuck yourself, Sid."

"I'll ruin you, Dani."

"In your dreams, Sid."

Dani was out the door before she could second guess herself. She headed toward her office and walked right by, unable to look at the awards, the furniture, the pictures. One glance and she would crawl back to that man and save her professional life. So she swore this was nothing to her now: Sid was only a man she knew at an agency she used to work for. No, her heart hadn't been ripped out of her, her reason for being was not inexorably entwined with what she did. Right? Sure.

Ten minutes later Dani was pointing her Mercedes toward home only to change her mind before she was out of downtown. At home she'd be alone. And just then alone didn't seem all that inviting. But where could she go? Who would understand? Dumb question. There was only one person and one place she could go now.

As she turned the wheel and gunned the engine, Dani saw that her hands were shaking. She wondered for an instant whether it was from anger or fear or the excitement of starting anew. Seeing an opening in the traffic she floored the pedal and didn't wonder anymore. She was scared to death.

Chapter Three

"Yo! Mr. Erskin! You can't go in there when Mr. Sinclair is working like this. I've told you that a zillion times, and I'm not going to tell you again. It's a very dicey shot and he wants to get it set up just right before he gets the cameras rolling, if you know what I mean."

The black-haired girl spread her arms wide, slipping between the door and the fat man who was paying Blake Sinclair's fee. Her arms were exceptionally long for such a short person, her legs amazingly unattractive. Her face, kabuki stark under her white make-up, was set in an expression of the utmost boredom. From that waxen countenance her inky eyes glittered, orbs distinguished by kohl lines and ebony shadow. Her head was all but shaved and she clearly thought she looked quite wonderful. She touched her nose ring for emphasis. The florid-faced man standing in front of her thought she looked like the creature from the Black Lagoon. Erskin was one angry guy and he wasn't going to be put off by this sad excuse for a broad.

"Get out of my way you little slut," he growled, " 'cause if you don't, I'm going to pick you up and throw you out of my way."

"Mr. Erskin, that's not very nice," she scolded with a snap of her gum.

"I'll show you nice," he fumed, his hands clenching at his side. "Nice is if I take my money and get the hell out of here. What do you think your boss would think of that, uh? Think he'd be real pleased if you just let a hundred and fifty thousand dollars walk out of here because you won't let me through that door to watch my own commercial being shot? I'd say, little missy, that you'd be out on the street in about two seconds if you let me leave."

The girl sighed. Rich, overfed, and thinking his bucks could make the world go 'round, Erskin, king of sheets and bedspreads, was nothing new. He made her want to puke, but she kept cool. After all, she had spiritualness on her side. She was calm and sure of her mission. Mr. Erskin was no match for that. Blake had said closed set and closed it would stay.

"You're not going in there, Mr. Erskin, no matter what you say. Now, if you want a cup of coffee, hey, it's right over there next to the magazines." She ran her hand over the stubble on her head and popped her gum once more before sticking her beringed nose in the air. Her filing awaited. "Mr. Sinclair said he wasn't to be disturbed and that's that. Not for you, not for the end of the world, not for anything will I let you go through that door. Got it?"

"This is just outrageous," Erskin sputtered. "What the hell are they doing in there anyway? This isn't a government secret. You know, I'm paying good money . . ."

But Regina wasn't listening anymore. She was grinning at the woman coming through the door and, a minute later, Erskin was leering, his demands completely forgotten when faced with a living, breathing beauty like her.

Behind the door Blake was doing what Blake did so well. He was mixing business with pleasure, fiddling with the lights as his model came out of the dressing room.

Her shoulders provocatively bared, Meg drifted toward the silk-covered lounge and, in one fluid motion, lay upon it, one long arm thrown back over her made-up eyes to shield them from the subdued lighting. Blake smiled. He loved a professional. Carefully he adjusted the pink gel on a light then went on to adjust the next one.

"Sorry it's so chilly in here," he commented. She peeked and saw his fine, tight rear move up the ladder, his well-muscled arms reaching for the light.

"I don't mind." She assured him sweetly and he believed her. "I always warm up with hard work." He could believe that, too.

Her purring parted her full, wide lips ever-so-slightly so the warm words could ease their way onto the cool stage. Meg wriggled her bottom and settled in. Blake's smile widened from a tipping of his lips to an expression of sheer enjoyment. He loved women and, though there was one he loved best, each companion was most appreciated.

Lights adjusted, Blake stepped back assessing the set, pleased that the designer had recreated a nineteenth-century Russian boudoir down to the last picture frame. Opulent damask were hung from skeletal plywood frames. Period knick-knacks were scattered over tables which were, themselves, covered with lavish cloths that fell to the ground in a wealth of folds.

29

And the ground, nothing but cold concrete just that morning, was now spread with oriental rugs hired for the day from an antique dealer on Melrose. A carved four-poster bed had been placed just off center set, leaving the chaise lounge on which Meg lay the focal point. Blake's final lighting adjustments bathed the entire scene in a gold-pink glow reminiscent of twilight on the Siberian Steppes. Perfect. Lovely. Blake ran his hand over his hair, patted the little ponytail he managed only when working, and went to the star of the show.

"Are we ready . . . ?" Meg murmured, her arm sliding away from her eyes and her eyes sliding over him.

"I should think so." Blake pushed a strand of long dark hair away from his forehead. It fell back again in insignificant, yet even more charming, disarray. Despite his sculpted features, the hawkishness of his countenance, Blake Sinclair's face exuded a gentleness. His worldliness, tempered by humor and kindness, created a disarming and irresistible mixture that delighted Meg as he lowered himself onto the chaise. The tremor that rippled over the swell of her breasts spoke louder than the knowing look in her eyes.

Blake laughed, sweet and so far from carnal Meg almost laughed with him. But this situation wasn't funny at all. It was delicious. Meg's eyelids fluttered half closed, her long lashes casting a deep sea shadow over her irises as she looked up at him. He was tending to something and it wasn't her so she amused herself by admiring the rise of his chest when he reached a certain way, his shirt opening just so. His chest was smooth and beautiful, his skin the color of almonds. She closed her eyes enjoying the scent of him, rich and exotic. She opened her lips and with nothing better to do with them she whispered, "They say you're very, very good."

Blake grinned.

"Is that what they say?" He laughed softly, pleased as his fingers curled around the sheet that covered Meg. Carefully he drew it away from her body, pulling it over her breasts, exposing hard little nipples. A reaction that had nothing to do with the chill in the studio. Inch by inch he bared her, exposing the length of her torso, the swell of her hips, until he uncovered a lovely little thing—a G string of purple silk barely covering what was most private to her.

"Nice," Blake murmured.

"Thank you." Unashamed. Proud. Teasing. Work didn't have to be tedious after all.

"I think you'll look well in our client's product." Blake leaned over her again, retrieved a package on the other side of the chaise and held up his prize. "Satin sheets."

"Very nice," she whispered.

"Glad you like it. Now," Blake muttered with mock abruptness, "as director and cameraman today it's my job to tell you what I want you to do while the camera is rolling."

Meg nodded, perfectly willing to acquiesce on all fronts. Blake drew the cool satin over her long, smooth legs, draping it until the folds pleased him, no longer looking into her eyes but aware she was watching him. He spoke, to himself and to her and to his creative muses while his hands worked.

"You make a marvelous, decadent Russian noblewoman. Naked in the middle of winter under a sheet that took ten peasants a year to weave." Blake's hands moved over the fabric and Meg underneath. "We'll pan from your feet, up your calves, thighs, hips."

Blake's hands followed his words, a tactile tour until he discovered something that displeased him. His fingers played over her hips, feeling the hardness of bone and the almost imperceptible welt of her G-string. He scowled and even that was a delicious expression. "This definitely won't do."

"It's hardly noticeable . . ." Meg protested without conviction.

"To the naked eye, perhaps, but the camera is another matter . . ." Blake smoothed the satin over the offensive piece of clothing, put his hand under the sheet and looped his fingers through the elastic. Slowly he eased the little bit of fabric over her soft mound, past her lean legs until he held the lavender silk in his hand.

"Much better," Meg murmured, her eyes glazing with desire as the titillation continued. "But I'm still cold and my goosebumps will show . . ."

Smiling, she took Blake's hands in her own, placing his warm palms over her breasts, her hard nipples nuzzling into his flesh. The color in Blake's eyes deepened; his half smile grew no broader, only more candid as he bent toward her, lips parting to meet her more than willing ones. He was thinking how much he loved his work when the door flew open and, in a rush of warm air, Dani Cortland whirled into the studio.

"God, Blake, there you are. I hate to bother you, but I can't believe what's just happened."

She was on the set before Blake could say a word, settling herself on the chaise. Meg spouted small noises of indignation.

"Excuse me. Sorry," Dani mumbled, taking Meg's ankles firmly yet gently in her hands and moving them to make room so she could get comfortable. Dani leaned across the naked woman, pecking Blake on the cheek before propping her elbows on her knees, burying her chin in her upturned hands, and muttering.

"We've got to talk."

With Regina chasing Mr. Erskin as he ran onto the stage, and Mr. Erskin hollering angry admonitions, and Meg piqued by the interruption, there was only one thing Blake, as director, could do.

"That's a wrap," he called, pulling the satin sheet over Meg, giving her rear end an affectionate pat before he offered his hand to Dani.

Chapter Four

Young and hungry, smart and beautiful. Dani and Blake. A natural coupling so long ago. She was an account assistant charged with finding a cut-rate director for a client that was cheap and a product that was decent. Blake was just starting out and more than available. Even if he hadn't turned on that killer smile, even if he hadn't touched her hand, pointing out an especially interesting shot on his spec reel, even if he hadn't asked her out for lunch—dutch—she would have fallen in love on the spot.

Dani hadn't a doubt that Blake Sinclair would be an advertising legend before he was thirty, just a blink after Dani would make it big herself. Her shrewdness in hiring him would be recognized, and she'd be dropping the "assistant" appendage of her title in a snap. And so it had been—sort of. The commercial finished, Dani and Blake bedded and in love, they began their rise to the top of Madison Avenue's ladder.

They married. They worked. And they grew apart as Blake's star rose faster than Dani's, when Dani found she couldn't live with him. Loving him more than ever, knowing her irrational resentment was ridiculous, she sadly acknowledged it was real. Blake so easily garnered fame and fortune; she worked so hard for every attainment and Peter Cortland's specter hovered in the background to undermine their marriage. With Dani's self-confidence near shambles they divorced over Blake's pleas and the breaking of her own heart. What Dani didn't know was that Blake fully understood why their life together had fallen apart. Dani had added a new dimension to love and it was called competition.

Funny, but one of the things Blake adored about Dani was her competitiveness, her ambition, her determination to succeed. What he didn't understand was why she seemed to want to best him instead of the world at large. Someday, when she was satisfied, when she had banished her father's disapproval forever, she would be back and he'd be ready. But today wasn't the day for reconciliations. It had taken an hour and a half to coax the story of her demise at Pregerson out of her. Now, calmer, she sat across from him in a shadowy lounge trying to figure out if she was more hurt than angry, or vice versa.

"It's okay to cry, you know."

Blake's head was a hair's breadth from Dani's. In the dimly lit bar they looked like two halves of a broken heart. Her white blonde hair a chin-length curtain over her face; his almost black, almost as long. Dani peevishly stirred her drink with a swizzle stick, determined not to shed a tear even though Blake, dear Blake, would allow her any show of emotion without judgement. Blake's hands were clasped in front of him. Every once in a while he would extend one finger and draw it across the back of her hand, taking satisfaction in the oh-so-familiar trembling beneath her skin.

"I don't want to cry, Blake . . ." She clipped her words as much from frustration as a reaction to the electric charge of his caress. How embarrassing it would be if her indignation turned into sighs of pleasure.

"Dani . . ." he warned, knowing when a lie came tripping from her tongue.

"All right." She shoved her swizzle stick at a hole in one of her ice cubes, and missing, complained, "I want to cry. I want to scream. But I'm not going to do either."

"Might make you feel better."

Another caress. She missed the hole in the cube again, trying to ignore his scrutiny. Dani did an admirable job, so lost was she in her self-pity, her ire at both herself and Sid. She abandoned the ice play and moved away from Blake. He smelled too good, looked too marvelous in the white light of the candle flame.

"I almost ousted that old crow, Blake. He can't see the forest for the trees. Pregerson is the top agency but there are signs that it's on a downturn. Sid's a money man he's not an ad man, and he's losing his touch at that. Damn, I was this close." She held up two fingers. They were long and slender and Blake remembered raising them to his lips each night just before he fell asleep next to her. He missed the little things. He wished Dani did. It was a skill that, once mastered, would make Dani a content human being. Nice thought; impossible objective so he paid attention to what she was saying. "I could have done it except for Fred. God, I was so stupid. My father always said I didn't do my homework. You'd think I would have learned by now."

"Oh please, Dani!" Blake laughed, abandoning his one-sided intimacy. He leaned back in his chair, bringing his wineglass with him. It sparkled clear and bright against his deceptive darkness: shirt and eyes and hair, lightened only by the golden tint of his skin. He was as beautiful as a country night with only a moon to light it. "Forget your father. Forget this nonsense that you're nothing unless you're on top. It's absurd. And it's just that attitude, my love, that broke us up if you recall." Blake wagged a playful finger at her, warning her against au fait accompli. "And that attitude has put you in the messy little position in which you find yourself."

Dani tilted her chin, tightening her lips into a defiant line. "Easy for you to say. You've been on top so long you don't even know there's a bottom."

Blake waved away such absurdity, knowing it wasn't him at all that she railed against but an ambition, an idea, a dead man's warped thinking.

"Dani, that's only your perception. No matter how much money or power one person has there's always someone else with more."

"Did I say I wanted to be the Sultan of Brunei?" she drawled with an exaggeration that bordered on a fondness for being put upon. Funny lady. If only she could laugh at herself. "For once I want to have the last word, to be the head honcho. I want to run the agency and make all the calls because I can do it better than Sid Pregerson. I know I can and I just want to prove it."

"I'm sure you're right." Blake allowed her whining knowing it was Dani's therapy. He, on the other hand, preferred more physical outlets for his frustrations. "In fact, you could probably run most businesses better than their CEOs. But Dani, ousting Sid isn't the way to get what you want. Just keep a high profile. The world will come to you if you just forget the intrigue."

"God, Blake. I work my behind off, and I'm still just a vice president."

"Hah!" he laughed, honestly amused. "Twenty-nine and a vice president doesn't add up to a 'just.' It's damned incredible."

"See," Dani shook her hair back, unwilling to accept any compliment she couldn't back up with a business card. "This is exactly why we broke up. We don't look at work the same way. We don't look at the world the same way."

"That's what made us so wonderful. Opposites attract," Blake whispered, cajoling her, teasing her with his voice and the look in his eyes. Dani let her eyes slide away, but back they went to him. She dipped her head, unable to hide her smile.

"All right. I'm a child," she acknowledged. How she loved him. Blake knew her, accepted her, loved her. If only she could *live* with him.

"You're just this side of masochistic you know." Dani abandoned her drink and propped her chin into her upturned palm. The other hand now rested in Blake's.

"You're right," he teased, half serious, knowing a solemn comment would get them no further than it had two years ago when they came to that most dreadful decision to part. "God help me, I'd run back to you in an instant, fury at the world and all, if I thought it would make you happy. I miss you, Dani. I'm not waiting for you, but I miss you."

"And I love you, Blake. Fortunately, I'm more practical than you are. Another time we could have made it. Maybe if we hadn't met at the starting line it would have worked." Dani cleared her throat, let her hand slip out of his. She'd heard the softness in her voice, the note of longing that crept in behind her observation. Thankfully, Blake had missed it. He was back on to the old arguments again.

"Maybe if you stopped letting those records of Papa play in your head, you and I might actually have managed to stay an us. Then you could be happy doing what you do best—working those gorgeous fingers to the bone creating fabulous advertising."

"Maybe. Maybe," Dani sighed. "But I can only deal with one thing at a time. The point is, I quit Pregerson. Walked out with my nose in the air and my honor intact. Was I crazy? The biggest agency in town. I'm sitting pretty and I quit because Sid makes a pass, throws around a few threats."

"Would you have slept with him?"

"Blake . . ." She drew out his name, batting her darkened lashes, as if to say "how could you even think that." He chose to interpret this flurry as a definitive no.

"Then there was nothing more you could do. So now it's time to put that marvelous brain of yours to work. Stop feeling sorry for yourself. Call in some markers. Stop crying in your scotch and go for it."

"You're right. It's not the end of the world. Maybe I should head for New York or Chicago."

"Dani!" Blake cried, horrified. "You wouldn't."

Equally adamant, Dani insisted, "Why not? That's where the big agencies are. They aren't exactly beating down the door to open offices in San Francisco anymore."

"But I wouldn't see you." Trying to pout, Blake succeeded only in looking far more delectable than any man should.

"Your mawkishness never ceases to amaze me," Dani quipped. "You're in New York shooting more than you're living in San Francisco. We'd probably see each other more than we do now. It wouldn't be any different."

"Yes it would. I wouldn't keep hoping that some night in the wee hours of the morning, you'd come knocking on my door and ask me to keep you warm."

"Right. And who would have to move over to make room for me?" Dani asked.

"Touché. But I'd throw the baggage out in an instant. Just because I like company doesn't mean that I wouldn't take those vows all over again if you asked me. I'd promise to love, honor, even obey, Dani. I'd even promise to fail," he teased.

She rolled her eyes. The little candle in the blue glass holder between them flickered, reflecting an affection that spoke of sincerity. At least he wasn't holding his breath until she came to her senses. Smiling, Dani pushed her chair back a bit and half rose as she wondered if she had any sense. Gently, she put her lips against Blake's, pulling away before the warmth in her middle became an eruption of heat a bit further south. Down again, she raised her glass acknowledging this exceptional man.

"I'll give you plenty of notice so you can rent a tux," she whispered.

"I bought one just in case."

"That's so sweet."

"That's so pathetic." It was Blake's turn to laugh into his drink. He pushed it away. Time for serious talk, then they would part. That was the way it was. Soul mates on so many levels. How they missed the ultimate tier was beyond him.

"Dani, think about the situation you're in. Take a break. Just for a while. Kick back until you can figure out where you want to be."

"Blake, I know where I want to be. I feel like I'm playing Chutes and Ladders. You know that really big one, the chute just before the end of the game when you have to slide all the way to the bottom? Well I've just been down it."

"Don't be absurd. You've got a reputation that's

dynamite. The minute the word is out on the street that you're a free agent, your phone will be ringing off the hook."

"You really think so?" Dani's sapphire eyes focused sharply on his dark ones, reading the level of honesty in them. Damn he could still do it to her. Those eyes that deepened and darkened and wound their way into those places that were so private only he knew where to look for them. Dani glanced away, sat back. Crawling into bed with Blake, no matter how delightful a prospect, was not going to help. Her mind would be on Sid's threats, her new titleless status, and her future. Believing what Blake said was equally dangerous. Dani tempered her optimism by envisioning herself on the unemployment line. It wasn't a pretty picture. She shrugged in answer to Blake's pat scenario. Saying nothing, he watched her stare into her empty glass. Time for a change of subject.

"You look great," Blake whispered.

"Thanks. I'm afraid this outfit cost me an arm and a leg though. Maybe I should have had more sense." Dani smoothed her leather pants lovingly.

"The day you regret a clothing purchase is the day the world will end," Blake muttered, drinking in the silence that followed. He broke it a minute later. "Thanks for calling."

"Blake," Dani breathed, so softly he couldn't tell whether she was pleading for him to say more, or to stop while they were ahead.

"Hey, it makes me feel good that you still need me."

"Always, darling." Dani allowed herself a moment of sentiment before pulling herself up, straightening her shoulders, and admitting in that no-nonsense way of hers, "Jesus, Blake you should probably ignore me. I'm glad you don't, but you should. You look pretty

41

great yourself, but tonight I'm going to be a good girl. I'm going home and letting you off the hook. You can have some fun instead of babysitting me while I fall apart."

Dani looked at Blake and hoped she appeared sufficiently in control. The last thing she wanted was his pity. Looking at his broad shoulders stretching the cotton of his shirt, his bared throat, she thought she'd never seen a man so desirable. She had always preferred men in suits. Odd that, at one time, she should have pledged undying love to a man who had to be wrestled into a tie. Unconsciously Dani tapped her fingers against the empty glass and wondered what would have happened if they had been celebrating her successful take-over of Pregerson Advertising. Would she finally have felt right about Blake and herself?

Dani shook her head. There was no going back. They had put their marriage away like an old reel, taking it out once in a while, fondly remembering the excitement of creating the campaign, but able to see the strategic flaws even as they viewed the film.

"So, you're about as far away as you can get." Blake's voice floated toward her, easily cutting through the noise in the bar as he sensed her mood changing.

Dani chuckled. That quirk in her inner ear was still there. She could hear his whisper in a tornado. She smiled, showing him a brave face.

"Tired, I guess. Drained. I'm going to head home. Do you mind?"

"Not at all," Blake answered, tossing money on the table as he stood up. "In fact, I think it's time we both got out of here. Come on."

They stood up simultaneously. The drink had done nothing to ease her concern, and he hadn't been able to convince her all would be right with the world. Sad, but not unexpectedly, it still hurt. He heard her take a deep breath and over her shoulder she gave him a fair interpretation of a bright smile. "I better run home and get on the phone before Sid does."

"Wrong." Blake shook his head adamantly. She wasn't such a tough guy and he was determined she understand that—for one night. "You're going to relax. You're going to regroup. You're going to heal your pride so you can move ahead." Blake had his hand on her back, guiding her gently toward the door. Oblivious to the heads that turned to admire them, Blake hailed a cab once outside and said, "3250 Pacific."

"Your place?" Dani objected, knowing it was the last place she should go.

"Dani . . ." She heard the unspoken directive and followed it without another thought. Gathering her into his arms he held her tight while the driver expertly dodged the California Street cable car, skirted a line of automobiles at a red light, and deposited them at their destination.

Neither Blake nor Dani spoke during the short ride. He paid the driver, helped her out, and took her arm, but Dani extricated herself from his gentle grasp and walked ahead. Once inside Blake settled her on the deep white sofa, his tall body bending, his arms spreading around her until she was imprisoned by a living, breathing, heavenly man.

"Stay with me, sweetheart. It's been a hard day, don't make tonight harder. Forget Sid . . ."

"Oh Blake . . ." Dani cupped his face with her hands. He was warm, strong, his words so reassuring. "I don't know . . . Maybe just a minute. Coffee. We'll have coffee . . ."

Dani's hands dropped to his chest. She wanted to laugh away his tender loving care. She had never known what to make of his gentleness or how to graciously accept it. She needed to get home and start the ball rolling. It would be easier than admitting how much she needed what Blake had to offer. She needed to . . .

"No. No coffee . . ."

Giving her no time to formulate a plan, order him about, turn this act of love around to fit her purposes, Blake slid his arm around her waist, pulling her up toward him. She came easily, her lips protesting, but her body melting into his as it should, and he kissed her. Their mouths met so tenderly that, when her eyes closed, Dani thought she might be dreaming. But it was no dream because her hands, instead of pushing Blake away, curled up into his shirt until she was pulling him into her as they sank back onto the couch.

"Blake," she murmured when his lips drifted from hers, but his name was drowned in her sigh of pleasure as those same lips trailed down the side of her neck.

"Dani, just be with me. Please," Blake murmured, pulling her closer and closer until they were as close as two people can be. There was the sound of zippers, the tease of cold air against bare skin, flesh upon flesh and silk strewn in between. "Don't think, my love. This is the one thing I can do for you. Let me. Let me now . . ."

"Sid . . ." Dani tried valiantly to stand her ground, but all was lost. Her hands were as busy as Blake's and equally effective.

"Forget . . . him," Blake whispered, the words broken, hyphenated by his ragged breathing.

"Just for tonight," Dani promised before she was lost in their lovemaking as she had been lost so many

44

times before. One night of indulgence wouldn't matter. And she needed this, needed Blake. Sid had probably forgotten his threat by now so she could probably forget him . . . just for tonight.

Sid poured himself a brandy and took a long burning drink as he settled himself behind the desk in the library. His wife was long gone, sweeping off to the opera in a gown that cost more than his secretary made in six months. The huge house on the hill was quiet as a tomb and the important task was at hand. It was 7:10 P.M. when he reached for the phone. By 7:50 he had managed to reach Sam Browning, Managing Director of BBD & O, Bob Creighton, head of J. Walter Thompson, Michael Green at Chiat-Day and finally, Jim Allenby, CEO of Saatchi & Saatchi. Sid sat back, confidently speaking to this last, and most important, colleague.

"Jim, Sid Pregerson here. I just wanted to let you know that I had to let Dani Cortland go today. Yes, yes, a sad day for us. She is an extremely talented woman. But, man to man, I thought I better talk to you now just in case she shows up on one of your doorsteps. She's trouble, Jim. Yes, Dani. I know, I know, she had me fooled too. She's been actively soliciting kickbacks from printers, typesetters, everyone she could get her claws into. A terrible thing. Very disappointing."

Sid managed to sound disconcerted. Kickbacks were nothing new; still, no one liked to talk about them. Given the quality of her work, this alone wouldn't be enough to do Dani in, so he put the icing on the cake.

"What really made it worse," Sid confided, "was she

was soliciting favors from some of the representatives as well."

Sid laughed as the man on the other end of the phone expressed his desire that Dani Cortland would solicit him.

"don't we all feel that way, Jim. Unfortunately, she was asking a lot. Dani Cortland is out of control. She's overstepped the bounds. She's dangerous. I don't think any of us need the kind of scrutiny of our agencies that she would bring, Jim, if you catch my drift."

Jim Allenby knew exactly what he meant.

Sid Pregerson didn't want Dani Cortland to work.

No problem.

Dani Cortland wouldn't work anymore.

"You weren't going to say good-bye?"

Startled, Dani looked up, her sweater clutched to her chest. Blake was watching, hovering in the doorway between the hall and the living room. She hadn't meant for him to find her like this. Her way would have been better. There would have been a note, an explanation offered with a flourish, and Blake would have understood. This, though, was different. This made her feel as if she'd been caught with her hand in the cookie jar and there wasn't much she could say to change that.

Silently Blake walked toward her, touching her face, running his fingers across her cheek, down the slope of her jaw, hesitating for just a second to look at her. Dani didn't say a word. What was there to be said? The scene was set so beautifully it was the perfect reprimand for her.

Three in the morning, the odd, grey, one dimensional time of a day when the world sleeps and the

46

sleepless search for comfort. Dani, sleepless, her mind whirring on and on, chose wrong again. Instead of reaching out for Blake for consolation she had begun her run. So typical. That's what his eyes had said about her behavior. So typical, so hurtful, so lovingly accepted. It was the last that made her look at herself and wish she had made a better choice. Failing that, there was nothing to do but go on.

Slipping into her slacks, pulling on her sweater, Dani was just flipping her hair out of her collar when Blake came back.

"Coffee." He handed her a mug, handle side first. "Careful. It's microwaved. Hot cup."

Dani took it, sipping while Blake settled himself on the couch. He wanted to talk. Embarrassed, she joined him, tucking her feet under her, curling up on the opposite couch.

"I'm sorry. I didn't want to wake you."

"Nice of you to consider my feelings." There it was. The sound of Blake's hurt, the anger that was more effective as an undercurrent than anyone else's tidal wave of fury. Dani had always admired that trait. It was a hell of a creative way to let someone know where they stood.

"Blake, I'm sorry. I couldn't sleep. I just wanted to go and get some things done . . ."

"You're going to make business calls at three in the morning?"

"I wasn't going to call anyone," she rallied. "And there's no need to get sarcastic. I couldn't sleep. I needed to move around. I was going to straighten out my portfolio, make lists of people to contact. I was going to be constructive with my insomnia. Jesus, Blake, why do you always make it seem like I'm insulting you personally by being myself."

47

"Because you are, Dani."

Blake's mug was on the coffee table. He leaned forward, elbows on knees. The front of his white terry robe fell open revealing a strong expanse of chest. Dani's eyes flicked toward his nakedness then back to hold his gaze.

"I beg your pardon, Blake, but my predicament has nothing to do with you, therefore I couldn't possibly insult you by wanting to leave here to rectify it."

Her answer was cool. The words sounded good. But even she knew they were just words. She felt the truth in the pit of her stomach. No need to verbalize it, Blake would do that for her.

"You do have a short memory, Dani. If I recall it was you who walked in on my closed set and shut it down. I left a one hundred and fifty thousand dollar job because you needed me. I was happy to do it. I'll pick it up double time today. It was you who wanted to cry on my shoulder, giving me every detail of your showdown with Sid. Fine, I was happy to listen. And I didn't exactly hear you begging me to let you go when we got up here. In fact, I would say that you and I were of one mind and body a few hours ago. So, after all that, after dragging me into your problems, your wicked little scenerio of power brokering that you swear was a move made for the good of the agency, using me as your sounding board, accepting my understanding and love, you don't think getting up in the middle of the night and running is just a tad bit impolite?"

Dani looked into her cup, warmed her hands around it, feeling like a petulant child. Everything he had said was true but she didn't want to admit it, couldn't admit another bad judgement call after what happened with Sid.

"Men do it all the time, Blake."

"Not this man."

Dani shrugged, chagrined. There was no arguing the truth but Blake wasn't finished.

"This man never has, never would, doubt if I ever could, walk out on a woman after such an intimate experience. But you're not any woman, Dani. You're the woman I love, whose talent I respect but whose selfishness is wearing just a bit thin. It hurts like crazy when you do something like this."

"But Blake you know how it is in a situation like this . . ." Dani insisted, pleading with him to understand as he always did. But he was tired and he was wounded and the early hour made everything seem worse.

"Dani, I'm sick of your career being the most important part of your life. I was sick of it when we divorced and this is not exactly making for a good cure. You come to me as if you need me, then you treat me as if I'm a convenience. I can sympathize with women now. No wonder they're wary of men if this is how they're treated. I swear to God, Dani, this is about the last time I'm going to lay down and let you walk on me. I'll love you, I'll care about you, but I'm not going to do this anymore."

"Blake." Dani was off the couch, her cup joining his on the coffee table as she slipped to the floor by his feet. Her hands covered his but he made no move to take them. "Blake, I'm sorry. You know that. But I can't help the way I am either. You know that too, don't you?"

"Yes. Yes," he said and sighed.

Falling back onto the couch he drew her to her knees until she knelt between his legs, her hands folded under his on his chest. He looked at the ceiling but

Dani knew he was seeing all their days and minutes together since the moment they'd met. Perhaps he was weighing the good and the bad. The bad would outweigh the good, she knew, but the balance would be tipped by that unexplainable electricity between them. Neither would deny it was the inexplicable touch of their souls that kept them on that thin yet oh so strong tether.

"You forgive me?" She asked.

"I accept you," he answered.

"That's better than nothing, I suppose."

Dani ventured the opinion knowing he might disagree. As usual her instincts were correct. Blake smiled. It was an interesting picture. His face shadowed by the ever changing light of morning, his eyes glinting as if fired from within, shaded by lashes so dark and thick she was envious. He was so beautiful, so marvelous. If only the fire in his heart burned as hers did for the things she longed for. But if it did would they have survived as anything but enemies? Interesting idea that would never be tested. She was Blake's obsession.

"No, Dani, acceptance isn't a good thing. Acceptance isn't something you settle for and you never figured that out. Success in your personal relationships and acceptance in your business ones should be the goal. Not vice versa." He lifted his head and graced her with a soft, sadly sweet smile, then shook his head. He lifted a hand and placed it on the side of her face. "Jesus, I wish you'd get it right. Or one of these days I'm just going to have to cut myself loose. Leave you to your own devices. Then you'll self-destruct, Dani. A super Nova named Dani Cortland. What a brilliant but sad ending. How would you like that?"

"I wouldn't." She grinned tentatively. Sensing an

end to all this Dani freed her hands and tickled him through the lush fabric of his robe. He chuckled gratuitously. But his heart wasn't in it—yet. "What on earth would I do without you, Blake? You're my touchstone, you make me see things the way they should be."

"I'm not asking for miracles here. If you could see things the way they should be we'd still be married."

"We've gone over that a hundred times and I refuse to discuss it again. Especially now . . ."

Dani pushed herself away and stood up. Blake didn't move. Just sat watching her. The woman wore him out. She had no idea the wounds he carried in that heart of his. Big ones, little ones, scratches and pinches here and there. But then he remembered that her heart was in worse shape than his. Peter Cortland had hit Dani's young heart with a mortar years ago and left a crater that Blake hadn't able to fill with trust and love. He couldn't blame her for any of this. He could only stand by and keep trying. Someday, when he was too tired, when she became too wrapped up in her frantic search for the holy grail of success, maybe he would walk away. But Blake Sinclair, looking at Dani Cortland in the morning shadows, couldn't imagine that day. So he bound up his heart and stopped the little trickle of blood she had drawn by leaving him alone in his bed, and hoped the gesture would fill another corner of her devastated one.

"Okay, my love." Blake stood too. "You're off and there isn't a thing I can do about it. Come kiss me and get out of here so I can try to get some sleep."

Dani was in his arms, happily complying. A minute later she was out the door, completely wrapped up in thoughts of the next hour, the next day, the next job, never realizing she'd left Blake nursing a heavy heart.

Chapter Five

Washington, D.C.

The Senate floor was nearly deserted. In the half-moon bank of desks, third row left, the bookish Senator from New Hampshire conferred with a surprisingly voluptuous young lady, their heads close together. Her rear end waved enticingly as she quietly attempted to make her point. Another Senator sat patiently, listening intently to a colleague make an impassioned plea to save a rare and useless beetle from extinction. The speaker, no doubt, felt quite ridiculous pleading so dramatically to only a handful of people yet, for the sake of the ever-present T.V. cameras, he pulled out all the stops: brandishing his arms, raising his voice, intoning the virtues of the beetle. A woman with red hair, a senator from Missouri, had kicked off her shoes and was reading a magazine in the far right corner of the chamber. Other people peppered the great hall, zooming in and out, hurrying to complete their most urgent business before heading home for the holidays.

Almost invisible, hidden in the shadow of the gallery, was one more man. He sat forward, leaning over the wooden desk, his hands clasped as though in prayer and his chin resting atop them. His eyes, a most notable feature, were grey and quick, missing nothing while his expression remained impassive, bordering on blank.

In general appearance he was acceptable looking and close to middle age, neither flashy nor rumpled, extravagant nor cheap. Walking down the street he might pass without notice. Stop to talk with him, look directly at him, and his subtle good looks would be gradually imprinted on the mind. Get past the odd, monotonal voice and his hidden energy and sagacity would cautiously emerge.

The man was Alexander Grant, a mid-term Senator from California.

Few of his fellow Senators had bothered with him, an appointee without the clout or knowledge to make his mark. He was welcomed politely to the Senate, then kept at arm's length once it was determined that Alexander Grant was not his mother's son. Thank God.

Margaret Grant had run a tight ship, playing politics single mindedly and ruthlessly for what seemed like a hundred years. She had made more than one committee head miserable, turned more than one committee press conference into her personal stage. Thankfully she was dead and Alexander was serving out her term at the pleasure of the Governor of California. After the next election, though, he would be gone and someone with more staying power would sit in his chair. That's what almost everyone thought. A time would come when there would be many Senators who would regret neglecting Alexander Grant; many who would swear they had known all along that he was a politician to be reckoned with. But that time was far off. Now even the time of day was denied him.

"Excuse me. Senator Grant?"

Alexander let his steely eyes wander to the hand on his shoulder, travel up a well-tailored sleeve, and then latch onto the hazel gaze of his mother's aide. He chuckled, barely making a sound, as he realized his mistake. Eric was no longer his mother's aide. Eric Cochran belonged to him.

"Eric." Alexander nodded.

"It's time."

"Thanks."

Alexander Grant stood up. Looking about the impressive chamber once more, he put an arm over Eric's shoulder and said, perfunctorily: "That's one fine piece of ass down there, isn't it?"

Eric looked toward the floor and the young woman, her rear end still waving like a beacon across the sea of desks. Nodding, he grinned, liking Alexander much better than he had ever liked Margaret. The lack of spice in the late Senator Grant's office had made Eric's job unbearably mundane. Now it looked like all that was going to change.

"Certainly is," Eric agreed. Tentatively he suggested, "I could arrange . . ." a wave of his hand, " . . . something. If you like."

"That would be nice. Don't put yourself out. When you get around to it," Alexander answered, sounding as if he had already forgotten the object of his interest.

They left the chamber together, Eric having the good taste not to laugh, chortle, or carry their little conversation any further. Alexander quiet as a corpse once more. Alexander and Eric. They made a fine team.

By the time they arrived at their destination, the meeting was already well under way. Alexander slipped into his chair and returned the half-hearted acknowledgements of those nearest to him. The chairman of the subcommittee was speaking at a clipped, well informed pace.

"We have only two days left before the holiday recess. I'm assuming you've all read your reports . . ."

A chuckle filtered through the ten men seated around the table. A few winked at the chairman who winked back the way only politicians can.

"Yes. Well. Be that as it may, let me recap the basics. Gentlemen, we got stuck with an ugly problem. Seems our chemical companies have been shipping enough kerosene, sulfuric acid, and solvent to South America to bury every single country they got under the stuff. Now, eighty percent of that shit is being shipped to Columbia, barrels marked for specific and legal uses. Only problem is, those barrels of chemicals are endin' up in the jungle hideouts of those damn drug lords. Can't make cocaine without these par-ti-cu-lar chemicals, it seems."

The chairman cleared his throat. Joking aside, he could be sensitive when need be. They followed suit, adjusting attitude as necessary, crossing legs, murmuring while they tuned into the rest of the briefing.

"So, our chemical companies are making a fortune shipping stuff that turns South America's cocoa leaves into cocaine. Then they ship the junk back to us."

More murmurs. Alexander tried not to laugh. They looked so worried, as if in the next moment the stuff was going to be forcibly applied to their nasal passages. The solution to such a weighty problem certainly couldn't be wrought by men like these. Wimps all.

"President's damned upset by this whole thing. Damn upset. The youth of America's being undermined by some of the biggest businesses in this United States. The chemical companies say they aren't doing anything wrong, just shipping to their end consumers. They say whatever happens once the chemicals reach their destination isn't their problem. Any export restrictions because of a supposed link to drugs would be unconstitutional."

The chairman scratched his head, flipped a page on the report, and, once thoroughly reminded of its contents, went on.

"The South Americans insist they can't control what happens once the barrels get down there because most of the drug lords have set up right and proper companies to accept shipment. They contend there wouldn't be a problem if the drug consumers weren't on our side of the world."

Now he sighed, more from tedium than concern, and leaned back in his chair. He was a leathery man from Texas who had managed to rearrange his accent and use it only when he thought it would do some good. It wouldn't help this situation. The men who looked back at him were less than inspired. It would be like pulling teeth to get some thoughts on legislation. Checking his watch he also saw that time was passing, and he had a date with a cutie who didn't like to be kept waiting.

"So, what we got is the public in the form of special interest groups. Mr. John Q. Public couldn't care less about restrictin' the export of five chemicals to the cocaine points of origin. We got the DEA askin' for intervention powers, both here and in targeted countries. We got the chemical companies screaming bloody murder about Big Brother and how restrictions will create less profit, fewer jobs, and with fewer jobs the economy goes straighter to hell than it already

56

is." He leaned forward again and chuckled at the ridiculousness of the situation.

"Looks like the good old U.S. of A. is going down the tubes because we're shipping a few chemicals down to them Latinos. Seems nobody cares we might be going to war again or blowing ourselves up while we dismantle all those missiles we got stockpiled now that Bill's sure there ain't no threats to our great nation.

"In short, boys, we're between a rock and a hard place. This is pretty high profile. We've got to draft legislation that will keep everybody happy, get to the bottom of this mess, and come out smelling like a rose."

Heads nodded around the table. The men commented to one another. Only Alexander Grant was left out of the intimate commiseration. He sat quietly, seemingly unperturbed by his isolation. They had all but forgotten about him and most were startled when he spoke.

"What about legislation that will be effective instead of just pleasing everyone?" he asked, his voice ringing clearly in the small room, curtailing the chatter, leaving a stunned silence in its wake.

The chairman's head snapped toward Alexander, his eyes small in his fleshy face. He didn't like Grant much, but he grinned, answering with his tongue firmly in his cheek.

"Oh, hell yes! I almost forgot that," the chairman grinned. "Thanks for reminding me Senator . . . Grant isn't it?"

"That's right. Alexander Grant." Alexander inclined his head, his silver eyes shading gunmetal grey as he held the chairman's gaze, matching him minute for minute. The older man leaned forward, small lips twisted into a patronizing sneer.

"Of course," the chairman said slyly. "Knew your mother well. Intimately, you might say."

Alexander ignored the innuendo. He had known his mother far better than this old bastard. Alexander's silence made the chairman impatient. His old boy accent returned in full force.

"We always do our best, Senator. But there are considerations on both sides. I think you'll do well to just sit back and watch, see what's happening here. Most of us, we've been doin' this kind of thing for a while now. We'll let you know what the right thing to do is, won't we fellas?"

He dismissed Alexander smoothly before adjourning the committee. They wouldn't meet again until after Christmas when the subcommittee would hear witnesses. Six months to hear witnesses, a year to draft a bill, and two to pass it. A little more time and there might be a new man in the White House and a new agenda. Senators took their work seriously, but they also knew government was ever changing: creating itself in an image that had long since ceased to be controlled by the men who concocted it. The subcommittee was happy to disperse. Alexander was immaterial. Outside the chamber, Eric waited for his boss.

"How was it?"

"Informative," Alexander answered flatly. "I've a lot to learn. Got time for a drink?"

"Sure." Eric accepted immediately, always willing to take whatever anyone had to give.

As they walked to the Senate office they made small talk. It was Alexander who opened the door to his mother's—his—chambers. The outer office was silent. He passed into the inner office and waved Eric to a seat.

"What's your pleasure?"

"Jack Daniel's, if you've got it," Eric said settling back and crossing his legs, ankle over knee. He loosened his tie as he watched his new boss.

Funny guy. There was no way to put your finger on him. Sometimes he seemed smart as hell, other times it was as though he couldn't find his way to the john. Nice guy or tyrant, idiot or genius, Alexander Grant just didn't wear his badge on his sleeve. Yet Eric liked him and sensed something others did not: Alexander Grant was his mother's son no matter how much he wished he wasn't.

"Of course we've got it."

Eric blinked himself back to the here and now to find Alexander holding a glass under his nose. He mumbled his thanks as Alexander sat opposite him, opened his jacket and sipped at his brandy and soda. He looked around thoughtfully before speaking again.

"Odd isn't it, how Mother always hid her taste for the finer things in life. This office is as spartan as any clerk's yet her bar," he held up his crystal glass, "is only stocked with the finest. Napoleon brandy. Imagine that."

"I always appreciated your mother's bar," Eric chuckled as he raised his glass, "so let's drink to her memory and her taste in liquor."

"Be happy to." Alexander raised his glass and muttered, "Thank God the lady herself is just a memory." Drinking deeply he set the glass aside, fixing Eric with those amazing eyes of his.

"These last months have really been a whirlwind, haven't they Eric?" Alexander opened the conversation smoothly, throwing a line out to see where his aide would take it.

"Did you expect anything less?" Eric asked. "Having a Senator for a mother must have made your life

59

a whirlwind from day one. Taking over your mother's seat when the Governor appointed you to serve out her term had to turn your life into a gale force."

"Yeah. You're right. The old broad served almost twenty-five years in the Senate—ten in the State Congress before that. Thirty-five years in politics. I was only seven when she first ran for office. My father had been dead a year. Eventually, when I was old enough to understand, I hated her for caring about the 'people' more than me." Alexander laughed. The sound was surprisingly open and free from sarcasm. It was the first time Eric had heard Alexander's pitch change. Liking Alexander's laugh, Eric relaxed, knowing there would be more. Politicians and the populace were alike in one regard—once they started sharing secrets nothing could stop them. Alexander offered a sardonic smile. "You don't look surprised that I didn't revere the eminent Mrs. Grant."

"In my position you learn to pick up on things. I figured it out pretty fast," Eric admitted immodestly.

"Really? Tell me, what gave me away? I thought I was doing pretty good walking around here in awe of everything, keeping my mouth shut and learning the ropes. Isn't that exactly what everyone would have expected of an interim appointee?"

"Go back a few sentences," Eric instructed, taking a hefty drink. "You've been keeping your mouth shut . . . about everything. If you loved your mother, respected her, or even halfway liked her I'd expect a little history. You know, sharing your experiences with the staff to let us know that you were planning on carrying out her wishes because she was a good person or a great politician. But you?" Eric ran his hand across his jaw as if that would help him explain Alexander's behavior. "You didn't say a word when you arrived.

You just watched us all. We fed you information and you didn't even burp. She didn't have a picture of you on her desk and Debbie didn't field weekly familial phone calls while we served with her. I'd guess you and your mother were about as close as two parallel lines."

"Very smart," Alexander admitted without embarrassment.

Pleased, Eric waved away the compliment. "No. I worked for your mother for two years. I thought she was a dynamite lady." Alexander reacted, slightly and not well. Eric backtracked. "Not that I had a great commitment to her. No loyalty factor, so to speak. I just thought she did what she did very well. Of course who knows what goes on inside a family? For all I know you hated her because she beat on you when you were a kid."

"Worse," Alexander answered, satisfied Eric's loyalty was negotiable. "She ignored me until she needed me. I could always count on a great deal of affection when a campaign was underway. We stood hand in hand, the perfect picture of a loving family racked by the tragedy of my father's untimely death. She was really good, Mom was. Knew how to play the campaign like no one else. Then I was sent away. I hated her. I hated politics. When I was out on my own, working in my law practice, I realized it was a waste of energy to hate either one."

"Then why did you accept the Governor's appointment?"

"Why not? I was ready for a change. My wife and I are separated. I had just handled my five-hundredth probate. I was tired of the sun in California. I don't know. It seemed like the thing to do. Maybe I even had some deep-seated psychological need to find out why she loved this job more than she loved me."

Alexander finished speaking and decided it was time to drink again. Eric listened to the ticking of the clock and the tinkling of the ice cubes in Alexander's glass, too stunned to speak. He'd heard worse stories of neglect and hatred. That didn't phase him. Rather than content, it was Alexander's presentation that gave Eric chills. He could have been reciting his grocery list or trying to decide if the water was too cold for swimming. But there was something exciting underlying his admission of curiosity about his mother's work and Eric wanted to know what it was.

"So," Eric ventured, "have you figured it out?"

Alexander didn't hesitate.

"Yes. I know why she loved politics. It's a wonderful game. I'd like to play it myself now." He paused, then asked quietly. "Want to help?"

"Absolutely." Eric grinned even as he downed the rest of his liquor.

Chapter Six

Los Angeles

Mrs. Peterson was fifty-two and square. Her hair was teased into a tight cube atop her head, her body was a block, her face reminiscent of Alice's Queen of Hearts. She'd been married for thirty years, raised five children, and worked as a bookkeeper most of her adult life. She wasn't afraid of anything or anyone. Mrs. Peterson was, at best, predictable.

So, when she ripped open Rudy Green's door, slammed it shut and put her hands on the place where most people had hips, he was ready for her. Shuffling papers frantically around his desk, he raised his head long enough to take note of her furious expression, then waved a piece of paper in her face.

"Here's the list of checks I want you to cut immediately, Mrs. Peterson. I can't believe you forgot to remind me about them. Do you realize that some of these charges date back to the beginning of summer? How do you expect us to retain good relations with our suppliers if we don't pay on time?"

"You! You . . . slime," Mrs. Peterson sputtered, grabbing the piece of paper. "I've been telling you for months these had to be paid. Don't you dare try to blame this shit on me."

"Mrs. Peterson!" Rudy's head was up, his expression one of incredible indignation. "I will not have you talking to me that way. I'm president of this establishment. A man trying to run a busy advertising agency. I'm the one responsible for getting the clients who pay the bills which, in turn, pay your salary. Now, I suggest if you don't wish to seek employment elsewhere, you try to work out a system that will free me to do what I have to do and keep yourself on proper schedule."

The bookkeeper's eyes blazed. She needed this job in the worst way. There weren't many companies who wanted to hire someone her age. Still, it galled her that this pipsqueak had the audacity to imply she was the lesser professional.

She'd been after him for months to pay what the agency owed: typesetters, printers, magazine space. The man was as tight with a buck for his company as he was loose with it for his personal use. He'd managed to sign the checks for the lease on his Jaguar, paid company funds for a grand piano and even had her overestimate his gross income so he could buy a condo in Palm Springs. Rudy Green treated clients like they were marks and suppliers like they were dirt. It was a wonder this agency managed to stay in business. But stay in business it did, and Mrs. Peterson was in charge of the debatable cash flow. Too angry to fight, too furious to speak, she turned on her heel clutching the list of payees to her rather flat chest and stormed out of the office leaving Rudy Green, president of Green Advertising, chuckling as the door closed behind her.

He liked the old battle-ax. There weren't many who

would put up with a business run this way. Her outbursts brought color to days that were exceedingly lackluster. Rudy liked it when someone called him on a bluff. The other four employees actually took their work seriously. That amused Rudy too, but not as much as Mrs. Peterson did. She'd never figured out that this business was all sleight of hand. Bring suppliers and clients alike to the threshold of a lawsuit, then make everything okay. It was like playing chicken only safer. At least it usually was.

But Rudy was anxious lately, the games he was playing were minor league and he longed to play with the big boys. Rudy was tired of Holly's Heavenly Hash and their boring trade ads. He was sick to death of Rick's Sound Systems and their predictable radio spots. Rudy wanted a shot at the stuff CLEO awards were made of and today just might be the day he wangled his way into an account that would put Green Advertising on the map.

Punching Lora Prince's extension he waited for his one and only account executive to answer. She got it on the first ring. Obviously she didn't have enough to keep her busy.

"Ready to go?" he asked.

"Yep. Sure. Anytime you say." Good old Lora, always ready to please. Girlish despite her age, her penchant for unsporting, unprofessional behavior was her most endearing quality.

"Five minutes. My office," Rudy said, "and see what's wrong with that new receptionist. Those phones are ringing off the hook."

"Will do." Five minutes later Lora was in Rudy's office, briefcase in hand. "The receptionist quit," she informed him, coyly flashing a Post-it Notes' resignation before crumpling it.

"Damn! Well," Rudy shrugged, "not much we can do about it. Get Pauline to handle the phones while we're gone and have Mrs. Peterson call the temp agency."

"Sure."

Lora disappeared. When she returned Rudy had slipped into his jacket and was holding the huge black portfolio that housed their presentation. Holding it aloft, he grinned, patting the case like a baby.

"Let's see how we can impress Apache Shoes," he sang and off they went to convince an up and coming shoe manufacturer that without Green Advertising they were lost.

Lora Prince had been kicking around the edges of legitimate advertising almost as long as Rudy. The difference was that Rudy never had his day in the sun and really didn't care if push came to shove. He fancied his situation, for the most part. Being a big fish in an extremely little pond was most preferable to having things the other way around. Now, if he could be an extremely big fish in that little pond he would be happier still.

Lora on the other hand had managed a season with the heavy hitters only to be found sorely lacking. Termination became a way of life as she hopped from one legit agency to another. Not that she wasn't intelligent. She had more smarts than she knew what to do with. It was Lora's inability to apply that intelligence in a rational and ethical manner that left her up the creek without a paddle. Given an assignment Lora invariably came up with a brilliant idea and then proceeded to implement it with the grace of a klutz.

Then she met Rudy. Tall, handsome, charming,

scheming Rudy who could make a girl believe he was going places though he'd been running in place for ten years. He didn't seem to mind Lora's mistakes. After all, what did his mom-and-pop clients know? Certainly they had no idea what constituted a good advertising campaign. As for Lora, she was thrilled that she had a job where she was accepted, failings and all. She was paid decently and had at least one other employee to boss around.

So Rudy and Lora were on and off lovers, cohorts in covering up business blunders and friends who understood that screwing a client or supplier now and again was not only acceptable but a hell of a lot of fun. Today, though, they were getting ready to do the one thing they did best. They were going to put on a show for the owners of Apache Shoes—once the owner stopped talking.

Clad in their sincere navy blue suits, pens poised over their legal pads, Lora and Rudy had scrunched their faces into expressions of interest and concern for Apache's marketing problems.

"Ve came to dis country vith nothin'," Mr. Zelosti droned on for the third time. "Nothin'! Ve escape from Romania in nineteen hundred sixty-five. Nothing in zee pockets but smarts in zee head." He tapped the side of his skull, his little eyes glittering as though he had just told them an incredible secret. "It vas my wife who came vith zee idea to make zee shoes."

Mr. Zelosti's head swiveled. He smiled at his plump wife who was draped in every conceivable symbol of their newly found wealth from her magenta silk dress to her diamond-encrusted watch. Her hair had been teased so that one wing of crackly blond hair flew out from the left side of her head. Her make-up would have been exquisite if she was dead, but was disconcerting considering she was still breathing. At least her English was better than her husband's.

"That is true. In Romania we must walk everywhere and we made our own shoes. Work shoes," she giggled. "I made the first ones on our table at home—so . . ."

She spread her hands wide over the beautiful conference table, pretending to stitch sole to upper, outlining the cut with one well manicured finger.

"Zo," her husband cut in, "ve do vell. You can zee our factory. Ve do vell vithout advertising. Vhy do ve need to advertise?"

Angrily his little eyes bounced from Lora to Rudy and back. He loved making money, hated anyone who wanted to take it away. Lora smiled. Mrs. Zelosti thought she looked Eastern European. Only Rudy knew it wasn't Romanian blood but Russian vodka that kept a glow in Lora's cheeks and a puffiness around her eyes. But even Lora's resemblance to a Romanian soul mate wasn't enough to erase the scowl from Mr. Zelosti's face. Rudy's eyes flickered her way. A pact was made. This was a man's job.

Carefully Rudy tapped his pen on his empty yellow pad, bowed his head, moving only his eyes to look from one Apache Shoe owner to the other. Mrs. Zelosti was smiling at him, liking his pointy toed shoes, his slick-backed hair. Mr. Zelosti still looked mad. Rudy pushed back his chair, stood up, and leaned over the table.

"You, Mr. Zelosti, have just answered your own question," Rudy began softly, his voice rising like an orator's with the next breath. "You need advertising and public relations the same way you needed new machinery as your business grew from a tabletop operation to a real force in the fashion industry.

"Apache shoes have made a name for themselves because of the excellence of the product and your own fine reputation as hard working, savvy professionals. Look around you and you see Apache shoes on the feet of every young woman under the age of twenty. That is a testament to your product, Mr. Zelosti. A testament!

"However . . ." Rudy's voice dropped an octave. He shook his head, appalled at what he must say next. "Look at your distribution. You are only in specialty stores, Mr. Zelosti. Bootlegged Apaches are sold on the boardwalk at Venice Beach. You're the pedestrian's Joan & David!" He went on sadly. "You could be so much more except for one thing . . ." Rudy looked him in the eye and splayed his hand on the table. ". . . your image.

"Imagine, Mr. Zelosti, your salespeople being invited into Nordstrom's, Neiman Marcus, perhaps Harrods! Imagine feet that have never worn anything but Jordan pumps suddenly encased in Apache shoes. Isn't that what you want?"

Rudy was around the table, grabbing a less than attractive shoe from the display rack to hold it aloft like a talisman.

"Don't you want to be a force to be reckoned with, Mr. Zelosti?" The little man harumphed, nodded. Rudy moved in for the kill. "Well, the only way you're going to do that is to follow your instincts as a businessman," he nodded toward Mr. Zelosti, "and an artist." His green eyed gaze passed to an adoring Mrs. Zelosti. He paused so she could fully appreciate his reverent smile.

"Tell the consumer what will happen to her when she puts on a pair of Apache shoes. Show her how to become the woman she wants to be—do it through pictures in magazines, do it through words with radio, do it through—" Rudy's intake of breath, his fluttering of lashes indicated that this next thought was nearly orgasmic "—do it on television. Create the Apache image, the Apache woman, and the ultimate success will follow."

Exhausted Rudy returned to his chair. Evangelist-like he had given them the word and now Lora was going to pass the hat.

"What Rudy says is absolutely true," Lora began, "and it's going to be a challenge to make a mark against your competitors. We've brought a bit of information with us that you might find interesting. Competitive expenditure reports, clippings from the top magazines where they editorialize your competition, statements from store buyers—we took the liberty to poll a focus group of those buyers who are not familiar with your product and some of the results are astounding."

"You did research?" Mrs. Zelosti breathed in amazement.

Rudy inclined his head, a young man shyly offering unadulterated love.

"Because we believe in your product," he admitted. Rudy could almost see their minds working. Mrs. Zelosti was casting herself as the Apache woman; Mr. Zelosti would take credit for the idea of hiring an agency. His children would inherit not just a good business but an empire.

Rudy grinned. This was almost too easy. Now all he had to do was get them to sign on the bottom line.

"We've brought a sample contract with us, Mr. and Mrs. Zelosti, just to give you an idea of how advertising works. Perhaps you'd like your attorneys to look it over, but it's all really so simple and time is money.

Being the astute businessman you are, you'll grasp the concepts of the contract immediately as well as how beneficial the fee structure is to the client.

"You see, when we contract for space or time on your behalf the stations or magazines pay us a commission. Yes, that's right, it's built right into the cost of your ads. Sort of like a travel agency. Of course you then pay for all the production costs plus commission on that. Usually twenty-five percent of the total cost of production on commissionable items excluding art direction and copy charges that are billed at a flat rate of one hundred and twenty dollars an hour . . ."

Rudy didn't miss a beat. The smooth modulation of his voice never broke as he inflated the commission fees by a good ten percent and added creative charges that could buy the best minds for a year. He slid the papers across the huge table. Mr. Zelosti reached for them, grasping them in his hands and looking them over. He was no longer listening to Rudy, so Rudy took his que and went to work on the lady of Apache's house.

"You know," he cooed, wandering around the table then perching himself close to her, "we may want to consider something like the Georgia Holten campaign. I'm sure you know the one—Vogue, Town & Country, Architectural Digest—very classy. I was responsible for that campaign."

Bingo. Mrs. Zelosti's eyes widened.

"No," she breathed, overly impressed.

"It was tough, I'll admit. It took months to get it just right. But I think the thing that made the Georgia Holten Handbags campaign a success was the client understood the concept from its inception and were behind it one hundred percent. That takes real taste, a sophistication so few people have these days . . ."

71

While Mrs. Zelosti was leaning forward to hear more, Mr. Zelosti was furrowing his brow. They weren't going to wrap up the Romanian shoemakers that day, Rudy could see. This was a small disappointment but not unexpected. It was time to get a move on it. Rudy eased himself off the table and motioned to Lora.

"We understand this is a big decision," Rudy announced as he packed up his briefcase, "so we'll leave you to discuss our proposal. But before we go we'd like to invite you to visit us at our offices. We think Green Advertising is the right place for you. We can give you the personal service a large agency can't. We want your business. It's as simple as that. And to prove it, if you decide to go with us, we will create your first campaign free of charge. No art charges, no copy charges. That's how deeply we feel about Apache Shoes. Mr. and Mrs. Zelosti, it was a pleasure."

Surprised by this sincere speech and Rudy's intention to leave before they could ask more questions, the owners of Apache Shoes followed his lead and stood up. There were handshakes and promises to call very soon.

Lora and Rudy were in the parking lot five minutes later. Rudy slipped on his sunglasses while Lora slipped into the car. When he was beside her she swiveled, one dimpled knee pointing at him while she tucked her leg under her body.

"What's this shit about free creative?"

"Liked it, uh?" Rudy grinned, winking despite Lora's inability to see behind his dark lenses.

"I think it's stupid, Rudy. Since when do we give it away?"

"Since never," Rudy answered, chucking her under the chin. "We'll just pick it up on production. Make sure and tell Sam that I want the lowest possible cost on separations when we do the first ad."

"You're sure feeling your oats. What makes you so sure we're even going to get this account? It's a little out of our league you know."

Rudy laughed. "Nothing's out of our league. We'll get it. Mrs. Zelosti will make sure of that. We'll get it."

"I won't hold my breath."

"Oh ye of little faith," Rudy clucked happily. The Jaguar roared to life and Rudy headed back to Century City. Just before the Robertson off ramp Lora remembered something she had wanted to ask him.

"I didn't know you worked on the Georgia Holten Handbags account."

"I didn't. But what do they know? They'll never check and if they do," Rudy shrugged, "what the hell? Half the fun of this business is making people believe the promises. Right?"

Lora didn't answer. She just listened to the sound of Rudy's delighted laughter as the rented car pulled smoothly off the freeway and they headed back to Rudy Green's house of mirrors.

Chapter Seven

The hotel room was like a cocoon. No sound penetrated the triple pane windows. Not a ray of winter-bright L. A. sun shone through the heavy drapery. There wasn't a thing to disturb Dani yet still she couldn't sleep.

Turning on her side, her long satin gown tangling itself about her legs, she stared at the illuminated digitized numbers on her travel clock. The deep browns and blacks of the tortoiseshell casing enthralled her while crazy thoughts assaulted her exhausted mind. Would time cease to exist if she snapped the case shut, the numbers banished to a different dimension and she with it? Falling into the bottomless pit of the Twilight Zone had a certain appeal. It would be better than what was happening to her now. Tears stung the back of her eyes, trepidation had managed to grow tentacles that threatened to strangle all her hopes and depression pressed down on her like a lover turned mean.

Today was her anniversary, God help her. Six months of unemployment. *I used to be a vice president.* That and a quarter might get her a cup of coffee. *I used to make decisions.* Without an agency she was nothing. *I want to die.* One hundred and eighty days ago she had let her anger at Sid Pregerson override her good sense. She walked out on a vice presidency at a fine agency. Six months ago she had taken Blake's words to heart, embracing dignity and morality, walking away from success, and where had it gotten her? Certainly no job offers in New York, not a bite in Chicago. Even her own backyard, San Francisco, had closed down tighter than a drum.

Of course she had taken the usual meetings, the phone calls from friends and colleagues who commiserated, offered their help though they were powerless to make good on their offers. Hell, the jobs Dani was qualified for were their own.

Naturally there had been the initial talks with agency owners and general managers. Those first few weeks had been heady with relief as one after another interview was concluded on a high note. They'd look into the situation, promised to find a place for her, couldn't wait to get her input on their accounts.

So sure was she that all would go well, so arrogant was she, Dani had turned down the first offer that came her way. In her certainty she became magnanimous, loving, in control and she showered Blake with affection, convinced the world was hers. She had cooked for him. He had ignored his own work, and once they had even taken the ferry to Sausilito for a day of Bloody Marys and boutique hopping. They slept together, touching and loving and laughing—each reminded that the other's allure was not completely spiritual. The professional barriers wedged between them were nothing when Dani felt optimistic. All that happiness and Dani, so sure . . . so positive . . . so absolutely confident, never imagined another offer might never be made.

But days turned to weeks and weeks became months

and the confidence became dread. People smiled at her. They nodded. They promised to call back but didn't. They looked at her portfolio and there was nothing to interest them. The men in high positions became more elusive, sounding embarrassed when she finally reached them, insisting they had nothing for her before she had a chance to pitch them. Even that first offer had been filled by the time she realized what was happening and scurried back to grab it. It was as though a tidal wave had hit the job market and washed out every possible opening. Sid had made good on his promise. He was systematically destroying Dani, always one step ahead of her, beating her to the punch everywhere she tried to make contact. That was when fear became part of the equation.

Frantically Dani branched out, sending hundreds of resumes to every agency of worth. She made phone calls, forcing herself to sound like an advertising professional rather than a woman on the edge of despair. It had taken awhile but finally she had managed an interview at a small yet prestigious agency. Today was the make-it-or-break-it-day. Scared to death, Dani was about to find out if Sid's reach exceeded his grasp.

Unconsciously Dani's suede-shod foot tapped silently against the carpeted floor. A look at her watch. Another minute wasted. Forty precious minutes in all! Fifteen was reasonable, forty cooling her heels in Paul Winfield's outer office was ludicrous.

Behind a black desk a secretary gave Dani the evil eye. Fortunately, Dani hadn't taken leave of her senses completely. She didn't wilt. There was enough of the old spirit left to save face and take a bit of initiative.

She was off the leather couch and across the room in five steps, planting herself in front of the witch.

"Excuse me." Good tone. Tight. Dominant. Condescending in just the right degree. She had the woman's attention. "Would you please remind Mr. Winfield that my appointment with him was for ten?"

"I know, Miss . . ." The secretary raised her bifocals, referring to her calendar with a great show of forbearance. She could play the game as well as anyone. Maybe better. She, at least, had a job. ". . . Miss Cortland. Mr. Winfield knows you're here. I'm sure he'll get to you when he can. If you'll just take a seat. Perhaps a cup of coffee?"

Dani flushed, angered and embarrassed at such an insufferable situation. In San Francisco she had learned to expect this kind of treatment but this was Los Angeles! Could Sid possibly have called every agency on the continent? Trying not to think about the old bastard, Dani closed her eyes and briefly saw herself, strong and professional. Imaging. It couldn't hurt. Question was, could it help? She opened her eyes, speaking carefully.

"I would appreciate it," Dani said again. "If you would remind him that I've been waiting for the better part of an hour . . ."

"And as I said, I'll remind him at the first possible opportunity. Believe me, I couldn't forget you're here."

Yet forget she did, the moment a discreet buzzer sounded. The secretary of the year reached for the phone. That sleight of hand banished Dani quite effectively for the duration of the call then brought her back to the here and now with a flick of the eye and an I-told-you-so smirk.

"I'm afraid Mr. Winfield has just had a change of

schedule. He's asked me to extend his regrets for keeping you so long, Miss Cortland. Perhaps another time."

Instantly the woman's head was down, her hands busy, digging into her neat stack of papers. Dani was now expected to leave without protest. Strangely enough, she almost did, until she realized that this was the proverbial end of the rope. She'd had enough. Dani Cortland did not walk out like a whipped puppy with her tail between her legs, and no tight-lipped secretary was going to be the one to try and make her.

"Another time? *Another time?*" Dani laughed, her platinum hair swinging an animated denial.

"Yes," the secretary answered coolly, "another time. I would suggest you call for an appointment next week . . ."

"No, I don't think so. That's quite impossible." Dani heard the tremor in her voice but ignored it. This was her last chance and this witch wasn't going to suggest any such thing, much less she call in a week. "I flew down from San Francisco just for this meeting. Mr. Winfield's letter was terribly encouraging. I need to see him today. I need to show him my . . . wait."

Dani rushed back to the sofa. Grabbing her portfolio she brought it back to the desk, fumbling with the huge zipper.

". . . Look, if you could just have him look at my work. I've got so many things here that fit right in with this agency . . ."

Dani flipped one of the huge, plastic sleeves. Ashley Cosmetics' last campaign was uncovered in all its glory. The ad slick was huge and beautiful and it brought to Dani the truth of the matter: she *was* talented. She was worth more than her father, or Sid, ever thought she was. She was everything Blake told her she was . . . she was alone. The secretary's eyes were on her. Dani could feel the pity in them. She'd rather have the contempt. Pity was enough to erode the pretense, in the face of it Dani's indignation crumbled and, in the rubble, she found humility. Low and soft, just shy of begging, she spoke.

"Look, I need to work. I've got to get back to work now. You know how this business is. People forget. A few more months and my samples will be useless. I'm really good. Really. If you'd just bring this into Mr. Winfield so he could take a look . . ."

"I'm sorry," the woman replied quietly, her voice sympathetic now, her eyes cowardly. Mr. Winfield's directions to make this woman suffer were one thing, but torture wasn't in her job description. "It's impossible."

"Please?" Dani breathed, almost choking on the words. "Please. It's so important . . ."

The other woman stood up, putting out a hand, gently closing the portfolio.

"I'm truly sorry. If you'd like a glass of water before you go, I'll be happy to get it. But you must see, I can't possibly do anything to help you. I'm just his assistant. He's the boss . . ."

Dani was turned, the woman's hand under her elbow. They wanted her to go. Everyone wanted her to disappear. People were laughing. Or worse, they were afraid to associate with her. How did it come to this? Why couldn't she control this nightmare? She couldn't because she was beaten. No, she was *almost* beaten. *Down but not out, Dani.* That one thought was just enough. She eased her arm out of the secretary's hold, gripped her portfolio and was ready for action.

"I know you can't do anything, but I sure as hell can."

In a flash she pulled herself together. She was Dani Cortland, former vice-president of Pregerson Advertising, and a double door wasn't going to stand between her and the man she'd come to see.

"What? What are you doing?" The secretary was still stuttering as Dani pushed into Winfield's office. Flipping her hand backward she shoved the door closed behind her and scanned the room.

An impressive office. Large enough to host a meeting of twenty. Light. Airy. Pearl grey chairs and a large antique desk. Big, potted trees. On the wall were out-takes of shoots, favored ads, stats of exquisite logos. It was a working office. An oh-so-powerful office and being in it made Dani feel alive once more. She was home, her self-doubt squashed by a resurgence of vanity. Six months of this bullshit was enough. Behind the desk, half turned to a drawing board was the man and he was damn well going to see that he needed her. This time she wouldn't take no for an answer.

"Mr. Winfield, I'm Dani Cortland and I've been waiting to keep our appointment. Your secretary said you wanted to reschedule. Well, Mr. Winfield, I don't believe that for an instant. I think you just didn't want to see me, and believe me you should want to."

Now that she was talking, selling herself as only she could, Dani became powerful and confident. She strode toward the desk, taking mental notes. Winfield, general manager and creative genius behind his agency, took off his glasses slowly. He had no non-sense eyes and the worn face of a rich man who'd worked damn hard for every buck. His hands were beautiful, long fingered and quiet. He still held a pencil in one as he crossed them on his desk. Paul Winfield was as immobile as she was animated. Dani moved in for the kill.

"You should want to see me because I know your agency needs creative people that can match your thinking—maybe even beat it. I've been in this business a long time. I know you're aware of my work because at least two of my spec campaigns beat yours in the last three years for the Belding Award. Now, maybe you're on deadline. I can understand that under normal circumstances, but these aren't normal circumstances. I'm here. I came from San Francisco and that's not around the corner. I'll take five minutes of your time, and all I ask is that you look at my portfolio then tell me you can find anyone who will produce the way I do."

With one great sweep of her arm Dani brought the huge black case onto the desk and opened it to her best work. She stood back, her face flushed with excitement, her arm extended so she could flip the sleeves that protected her work.

"Here. A prime example. It took a lot to convince the client to go with such a subtle sell, but in the end it paid off. Only the colors of the earth, no show on the product. And we're talking cosmetics here, Mr. Winfield. Most people think a woman wants to see another woman wearing the cosmetics. Wrong, she wants to believe she'll transcend the norm. She wants to be as beautiful as nature and she sure as hell doesn't want to compare herself with a model.

"And this." Dani flipped another page when he made no move to do so. "Hard hitting trade advertising in a field that's traditionally oblivious to this sort of thing. This and received over 250,000 calls on the 800 number three days after it ran.

"And this . . ."

The pages flipped again and again and again. Dani reeled off statistics, pointed out subtleties, spoke of production difficulties. Finally she stepped completely away from the desk leaving the portfolio open to the last and most important page. She was grinning from ear to ear, invigorated by her pitch. But she wasn't stupid either. Paul Winfield hadn't had the courtesy to even look at the glossy pages that chronicled her professional life. In fact he hadn't even blinked. Instead Winfield's clear eyed gaze never left Dani's face, his lips didn't quiver with a smile, his eyes hadn't sparked with interest. Dani hadn't reached him on any level.

Minutes ticked by while he sat in judgement of her. Dani's smile faded in the silence, her self-respect was pulled away, examined, and discarded. When he finally spoke, Paul Winfield's words were less a death sentence than an eulogy. Everything had been decided, not by him, but by a man in San Francisco who wanted her to crawl back to his agency, his bed . . . him.

"You're everything I expected, Ms. Cortland, and quite a bit that I didn't."

Dani's eyes flickered; she guarded against a smile not of pleasure but of the prelude to hysteria. She understood now. Sid had talked to him, Sid had lied to him. Sid had pushed the knife into her back and this man, along with all the others, was turning it slowly. With her dying breath she tried to get him to stop.

"I am. I would be an asset to your agency."

"I wasn't referring to your work, Ms. Cortland. Rather to your style. Sid mentioned you were unpredictable, among other things."

Dani cringed at the mention of Sid's name. The theory of his vindictiveness was one thing, the corroboration of it quite another. Horrified she watched as Winfield's clear, calm eyes hardened, turning to ice then to stone.

"Whatever Sid Pregerson is saying, Mr. Winfield, is untrue . . ."

Dani took one step forward, steeling herself to present her case. The effort was wasted. Winfield closed her portfolio with calculated determination, his eyes locking with hers to underscore how little her work meant to him. The sound of the industrial zipper sealing away her work was like the final twist of the blade. When he was finished, Winfield turned back to his drawing table, dismissing Dani as he began to sketch.

She stood silently, paces away from Paul Winfield, her soul melting in the light, bright office. Soon there would be nothing left of her and everyone would have exactly what they wanted.

With her last ounce of strength Dani stepped toward the desk. The hands that retrieved the portfolio couldn't possibly be hers. They shook. They looked too pale. The handle slipped from her grasp once, sending a child-created paperweight crashing to the floor. How could a man that revered what a child made be so cruel? Hadn't she too been a child in need of attention once? But no longer a child, he could ignore her, do this to her. She tried again, clutching the heavy case to her as though it might hold her up long enough to get out of the office.

Wavering, she made her way to the door, turning to see if he was watching. But Paul Winfield hadn't moved. Once she stopped.

"I wouldn't need to be a vice president. I could do basic art direction . . . I wouldn't even mind paste-up . . ."

Her voice was so very small Dani wasn't sure it carried until she saw Paul Winfield sigh, his shoulders lift in frustration under his cardigan. Without looking at her, he answered.

"There's nothing here for you, Ms. Cortland, not even a position in the mail room. There won't be much for you in the real agencies. Look elsewhere Ms. Cortland."

He was sketching again as she left.

Chapter Eight

Thursday was the kind of day that suited Rudy Green. Thanksgiving loomed yet the sun was warm, the sky was blue, the clouds high, fluffy and perfect for contemplation.

Into this splash of radiance Rudy stepped, stopping in front of La Femme and Men just long enough to let passersby drink in his glory. A few of them actually took him up on the offer. A redhead with pert breasts and an average face gave him her best smile. It wasn't good enough. Rudy looked right through her to the blonde whose eyes flicked over him before she hurried on her way.

And why shouldn't they look? Every Thursday Rudy got the works. He was coiffed to hair-splitting accuracy. Half an inch off the back, though a bit off the top would have made him look more the executive and less an Elvis clone. His nails were done, buffed not polished. The masseuse had kneaded and patted, though anxiety seldom lighted on Rudy long enough to penetrate muscle. All this left him feeling quite choice on Thursdays.

He shot his cuffs, admired his Rudy Green trademarks—huge gold nugget cuff links—and whipped out his keys. With a flourish he released the car alarm and slid in, leaving his good mood outside the Jag. Without an audience, Rudy Green was forced to introspection. Problems abounded; his ducks were not in a row.

There was never enough money. The furniture for the condo in Palm Springs had cost an arm and a leg. Faceless landlords had raised the rent on his office space, and the gold chain and matching bracelet he had picked up on a whim on Rodeo hadn't helped the old cash flow. Of course, at the time that little purchase was made he thought he was celebrating the acquisition of a new account—Apache Shoes.

Which brought him to his second problem. The cobbler immigrants were taking their sweet time about signing the contracts that would tie them to Rudy Green for a good long while. During the last month he and Lora had made fifteen phone calls, taken the Zelostis to lunch twice and sent flowers when Apache won some innocuous shoe design award. Still Green Advertising didn't get the business and Rudy was at a loss to understand why.

Sure they were always happy to see Rudy; Mr. Zelosti asking for free advice, Mrs. Zelosti fawning over him but each time he asked them about the contracts, each time he subtly suggested he was entertaining competitive accounts, they gave him a song and dance and it was making Rudy damned nervous. Either the gruesome twosome were smarter than they looked, or they didn't have an urgent bone in their collective bodies.

Making a sharp left on La Cienega, turning the wheel a bit harder than necessary, imagining it was Mr. Zelosti's neck, Rudy tried to ignore the obvious and failed. It was no longer a matter of wanting the

Apache account; Rudy needed that damn piece of business in the worst way or he'd have to close up shop and go back to selling type. He'd rather roast in hell.

Heading toward the freeway, and his meeting with Apache Shoes, Rudy continued to mull over his options. Making a hard right onto the on ramp Rudy realized there was only one way to take a good chunk out of the monthly overhead. He'd have to fire Lora. She'd understand. Lora was used to this kind of thing. God, he'd hate to do that to her, but if he absolutely had to . . .

Rudy was in the conference room, a stunning smile plastered on his face as he was introduced to the heir apparent of Apache Shoes. Joan Zelostis was the pebble in the wheel, the fly in the ointment, the goddamn reason the Apache contract hadn't been signed. From Joan Zelosti's twenty-year-old beady eyes to her bulging thighs, she was the spitting image of her mother without any of the older woman's endearing affectations. To make matters worse, the kid was a college student. It would be hard to charm her. Cancel that. It would be impossible even if he had the guts to try.

"Hello, Mr. Green." Her voice had a definite edge to it. Fingernails on a chalkboard.

"Nice . . . nice to meet you, too." He swallowed hard trying not to notice the number of chins she sported. Rudy cleared his throat yet still his voice was an octave higher than normal. He'd never been good with surprises. "Your mother tells me you're advising them on my proposal."

"I'm just trying to help." She shrugged as if to say it was nothing. Rudy hoped that was the case. He was sorely disappointed. "My parents keep me up on

87

what's going on, but I won't officially be part of the company until I graduate."

"When will that be?" Hope springing eternal had a bitter taste.

"I'm a sophomore. Two years. I'm attending the University of Santa Barbara."

"Majoring in?" Rudy prodded, almost afraid to hear the answer.

"Marketing," she said, flatly triumphant.

"Great," Rudy muttered sullenly. Then to the little group gathered about the conference table, brightening as best he could, "It will be great to have someone who understands the advertising business."

"Mr. Green," Joan tsked, "I already told you, I won't be joining the company for another two years. Secondly, I don't know anything about the advertising business. I said marketing. I know that advertising and promotion are a necessary and expensive part of the marketing mix . . ."

Rudy cringed. Like a whale breaking the surface for a breath she spouted Marketing 101 platitudes at him. He crossed his arms and tried to stare her into submission. She would have none of it. Joan couldn't trade on her looks so she used her dour personality and marginal intellect to make her mark.

". . . Finally, your tone implies that you believe you will be working with Apache Shoes as the advertising representative of record."

"I never meant to imply that . . ."

"No . . . no . . ." Mrs. Zelosti mumbled, touching his sleeve in a show of support.

". . . I only want to show my interest in your parents' business."

"Whatever." Joan dismissed his explanation, her mouth twisting in a gesture of disdain. She ignored her mother. "Anyway, I took your proposal to a professor of mine and asked him what he thought."

"Do you think that was wise?" Rudy countered. "Professors often haven't been in the working world for a long time. Is he up on the intricacies of advertising in the nineties?"

"No. He admitted he wasn't. He called a friend of his for advice, and I passed that advice on to my parents."

Joan looked toward her parents who were nodding vigorously, more than willing to let their daughter run away with the meeting. Mrs. Zelosti smiled at him as though he was about to be told he had a terminal disease. He swung back to Joan.

"And just what was that advice, Ms. Zelosti?"

"The first part was to ask you to reconsider your fee structures. But I decided to let you think about that. Let us know what you've decided when you come back to my parents with a creative presentation."

Rudy laughed triumphantly. He had her now.

"Ms. Zelosti, spec presentations just aren't done these days." Rudy examined his cuff links, a gentleman allowing a lady the time to pull herself together after a tussle in the hay. "They're far too expensive and the process asks that an agency make a creative decision without proper knowledge of a company. I think your professor has been hitting the books too long."

His insolent black eyes darted toward her less impressive dark ones. Unfortunately, the chagrin he expected to find in them was missing. The kid had only the utmost contempt for him. Maybe she was more astute than he gave her credit for.

"I don't think that's the case, Mr. Green. He did say it was unusual to ask for spec work, but not if the budget is substantial. My parents were thinking about starting with five million. Media only. Production over and above. And my professor's friend has already committed his agency to a speculative presentation. I believe they're rather a large firm. Maybe you've heard of Dailey & Associates?"

"Vaguely, Ms. Zelosti," Rudy answered, his heart sinking lower than the sun at twilight.

Happily, Joan Zelosti laid out the ground rules. "So, Mr. Green, you may want to think twice before you decline in participating in this . . . I think the word is review?"

"Rudy, a review," Mrs. Valeska Zelosti cooed.

"Review," Mr. Zelosti reiterated, looking as though he had thought of the idea.

"A review," Rudy muttered in disbelief, his grin and his confidence lost in the more immediate emotion of despair. "Why not? Let's have a review."

Chapter Nine

"Alexander, you can't expect people to jump on your bandwagon. You just weren't visible enough when your mother was in office. Most politicians have been glad handing since the cradle and getting on the old boy's team is damned tough."

Eric lounged on a lovely sofa of pink chintz. Absentmindedly his hands slipped over the fabric as he sipped his drink and lectured Senator Alexander Grant. The tall man paced in front of the stone fireplace sliding an annoyed glance Eric's way now and again.

"Will you stop fondling that piece of furniture?" Alexander snapped.

"Sorry," Eric grumbled, wrapping both his hands around his glass to keep them still. "I just never felt comfortable around all these flowers and needlework. It's not exactly the kind of decor one would expect in a Senator's home."

"Mother's stuff. She wasn't your run of the mill senator. I've only been living here since the funeral. I'll have it recovered if it bothers you so much."

"Don't worry about me," Eric reminded him. "Worry about the people you want to impress. Money folks are going to want to see a take charge kind of guy. How you live is one way to make a statement without saying much of anything."

"Yeah. Okay. I'll take care of it." Alexander gnawed thoughtfully at his bottom lip, his eyes trained on a crewel-work chair. He seemed lost in the intricacies of the stitching so, when he suddenly strode to the sofa and planted himself next to his aide, Eric was startled. These bursts of energy from a man so often removed were startling.

"So what you've been telling me ever since we got back to California for the recess is this: when people hear the name Margaret Grant they go ga-ga; when they hear Alexander Grant they think I'm some kind of poet."

"Hardly poetic, but yes, that's the gist of it."

Eric felt suddenly tired. Alexander's peculiar zeal was a bit much for him. Nobody became a politician overnight, you had to be groomed for it, just as Eric had been trained to pull the strings behind the scenes. He hated to admit it, but throwing in with Alexander Grant might have been the worst move of his own career.

"Alexander, even if you had a voting record that appealed to every segment of the California population, who do you think would know about it? The press doesn't cover every decision you make, and last time I looked, your campaign coffer was in sorry shape. Unless your mother left you seven or eight mil somewhere, you're in big trouble."

Alexander shook his head and stood up. Towering over Eric, Alexander shoved his hands in his pockets and contemplated the oriental rug under his feet. When he spoke it was with the dreaminess of private memories, better contemplated than verbalized.

"Mother was very scrupulous. No kickbacks, no bribes. She owned the house free and clear when my father died. Not that she didn't leave something, but I can't touch the principal on her estate. It would be financial suicide. And the interest isn't going to make a dent against someone who can raise a couple of million at the snap of his fingers."

Eric sat forward and let his glass dangle between his knees. It was almost empty and he had a taste for more. Instead of asking for another drink he too pondered the rug; he spoke in that strangely detached way people do when a satisfying desire is sorely limited by reality.

"Then all I can say is raise a couple of million dollars. That's your only choice. With money we could do an immediate blitz campaign. You still have a good core group of volunteers. They don't know you well, but there is the loyalty factor toward the memory of your mother. And you're going to have to fire them up to get the bucks in from the small contributors. It's tough now with all the new regulations. Hell you can't even raise a couple hundred thousand giving speeches to the Veterans of Foreign Wars anymore."

Alexander took it all in, his lawyer's mind processing the information neatly, compartmentalizing it and generating viable solutions. But his mental gymnastics were cut short. Eric had more to say. They were due at the Arts for AIDS benefit in forty minutes and this couldn't wait.

"There's another thing, Alexander," Eric began cautiously, curious to see how Alexander handled a personal assault. "It seems that the people who are aware of you aren't all that crazy about you."

Slowly Alexander swiveled his head, those strange

grey eyes of his locking with Eric's dark brown ones. The younger man controlled a shiver.

"Really?" Alexander asked, quiet, cold, he seemed neither surprised nor bothered by this little piece of information. He waited, nervous because, in the following silence, there was the directive to continue. Eric took a deep, controlled breath and met Alexander's unreadable gaze.

"They don't trust you. You make people nervous. You lack warmth. You lack a definable personality and you're fighting a ghost who had all those things going for her. You and I understand that she wasn't exactly Mother Theresa, but she sure as hell convinced everyone else she was. You're aloof and standoffish. People don't think you'd kiss their babies."

Alexander laughed. "They're right. I wouldn't kiss their babies on a bet. I didn't even like kissing mine. Eighteen now and I like her less. Monica is a tiresome girl. Confrontational. But I can see your point. Incredible. The key to power is making people feel like you haven't got it, they have to be comfortable. That's going to be tough. Even my soon-to-be-ex doesn't feel comfortable around me and we slept together for years."

"It's a problem." Eric shrugged, feeling better.

"It is," Alexander admitted, no more offended than if Eric had mentioned a spot on his suit.

In the contemplative silence that followed the doorbell rang, reminding them that they were not the only two people left on the earth. Both men looked toward the foyer. Eric perked up. He was ready for some company.

"Guess that's her," Eric mumbled, standing up and slipping into his dinner jacket. Critically he eyed Alexander's ensemble. The man wore clothes well. He would photograph beautifully. Feeling the need to be needed, Eric tugged on his boss's lapels until Alexander looked perfect. Then the young man prayed someone would be interested enough to point a camera Alexander's way.

Alexander tried not to think of Coral. His too many-years-younger-lover. She had come to his bed soon after they met during a tour of a proposed offshore drilling site near Malibu. According to Eric, Coral was far too young and sexy to be his public escort so he arranged for the more acceptable societal companion Alexander was about to meet. Eric filled him in.

"Marni Lewis. Heads your Los Angeles volunteer effort. Good family from Hancock Park. Your age. Looks older. Widowed. Bright. Don't try and bullshit her. You need her. She would have preferred you called to invite her to this shindig, but fully understood when I told her you were immersed in learning all you could about the needs of the state, especially those of crack kids. That's her pet cause. Her only other interest is the symphony."

So briefed, Alexander went to the door. There he found a woman of respectable figure and face dressed in a blue faille gown. He felt nothing, neither disappointed nor encouraged. Indifference was one of his talents.

"Ms. Lewis." Alexander held out his hand, greeting her warmly, immediately pleasing her. Alexander traded on the last. Instead of shaking her outstretched hand, he slid his own around hers, drawing her into his home. "I apologize for the difficulty in picking you up this evening. I'm afraid I was delayed at a meeting with the administrators of St. John's Hospital. I'm trying to

95

help them set up a clinic for children born addicted to drugs. I hope you'll forgive me."

Marni Lewis beamed. Eric smiled at the oh-so-easily transformed Alexander Grant. He even looked different—softer, kinder, those grey eyes full of smoke instead of steel—as he brought Marni into the living room. "Of course, I'll be devastated if you don't let me see you home after the benefit. Have you met Eric Cochran?"

"Yes, of course. He was so much a part of your dear mother's administration, I'm delighted he'll be with you. Nice to see you again, Eric."

Marni never glanced in the younger man's direction though she said her hellos crisply and clearly. Her reaction to Alexander pleased Eric to no end. If Marni so easily succumbed when Alexander turned on the charm he could do to the same to the voting public. It looked like Eric just might have a job well past '96. Yes indeed, things were looking up. Now if they could only get some money and let people see Alexander Grant in action.

"Coral?"

"Hi." Her voice was low and silky, inviting though he could barely hear her over the din. "So how is it? Tons of celebrities? Politically incorrect women draped in the skins of dead animals?"

Alexander leaned back against the wall. He chuckled and put his hand over his free ear, watching the action in the huge ballroom of the Century Plaza Hotel from the relative privacy of the telephone enclave.

As Eric promised, the affair was one not to be missed. Every big name in film, every politician in a two-hundred-mile radius flitted in and out of the crush of people looking for cameras, anyone with a microphone to turn their way. But the press preferred the politically active movie stars to elected officials. Alexander often thought the U.S. would save a lot of time and money by just letting Hollywood take over the country. While he was just one of the crowd, Marni, at least, was on a decent footing with the press so he let her do her thing and turned away from the throng.

"You've hit the nail on the head, my darling. Fools and idiots at every turn, all looking quite lovely."

"Sounds like fun," Coral's comment was a tad wistful. Despite her high, and unusually educated political conscience, she was basically a hell of a good looking woman who liked to show off her considerable assets. He'd be damned if he'd keep her in the background for long. Once his divorce was final, the election won, Alexander fully intended to indulge himself.

"Coral, listen, I'm about ready to wrap up here. Thought I might come by. I've got to drop Ms. Lewis off first, so it could be around midnight before I rolled in . . ."

"I suppose that would be all right . . ." Coral began, only to be cut off. A man, his voice muffled, interrupted her. Interesting, Alexander thought. The phone was in the bedroom and a man was close enough to Coral to come across the line. He heard Coral mumble something back to her companion.

"Who was that?" Alexander asked more quickly than he intended, surprised by the instant and insane shot of jealousy that ran from his groin to his throat.

Coral chuckled. "Your middle age machismo is showing, darling. Don't worry, it's only a guy from my karate class. I had a couple of them up for drinks tonight and things just got going. He wanted more

97

tequila. He's okay if you like hair that looks like a helmet and a ton of gold wrapped around various body parts. I prefer silver-templed politicians . . . for the time being."

Alexander listened to her self-satisfied sigh, imagined her couched against the countless pillows on her huge bed, the phone dragged from the small glass table to rest on her flat stomach. She would have flipped her long, wavy, red-gold hair over the shoulder that wasn't cradling the receiver. Her sharp brown depthless eyes would be trained on the mirror opposite the bed. She would watch herself, see the way her lips moved, enjoy her own beauty. Alexander smiled. Her self-absorption was challenging and exciting.

"Don't you know any women?" he murmured. "I thought females liked to do their nails when the man of the house was out for the night."

Again came the guttural chuckle, a sound that said she was thoroughly delighted by his jealous comment and not at all concerned. "Jesus, Alexander, you've got a lot to learn and one of the first lessons is not to overstep your bounds. Come if you want. No work tomorrow so we can play as late as you like."

"See you as soon as I can."

Alexander hung up the phone. He had turned into the little plastic alcove while he spoke to Coral, not so much worried about his privacy as for quiet so he could hear every word. He couldn't imagine what he had been doing all his life married to Polly, homemaker extraordinaire. His newly discovered sensual side was proving quite exciting to explore.

Turned away from the party as he was, Alexander hadn't immediately noticed the short man who stood patiently behind him. When he turned, he was startled as much by the man's hideous brocade dinner jacket as he was to hear a voice so close. Despite the intimacy of their stance, the man's voice was low and tentative.

"Senator Grant?"

"Yes?" Alexander's eyes narrowed. He composed himself in the few moments it took to hang up the phone and present his politician's smile. "Excuse me. I didn't mean to tie up the line. It's all yours."

Alexander began to move away. The little man in the brocade dinner jacket put his hand out, not toward the phone, but toward Alexander, his fingers lightly touching the Senator's arm. There was no mistaking what he wanted.

"I didn't want to use the phone, Senator. Thank you though. I was hoping that you might have a moment. To talk."

"Certainly," Alexander said heartily, remembering Eric's warning that attitude was all important. Unfortunately, his attempt at cordiality proved poor. His voice was tinny, his hand on the man's shoulder felt heavy and a sixth sense warned him to be wary. Alexander removed his hand. His face fell into its mask-like expression.

"Actually, I was hoping that you might have a few private moments to speak with myself and my boss. My name is John Meaker. The gentleman who is waiting for you in room three-twenty-one is Paul Luellen."

Alexander's eyes darted over the other man searching for something that would clue him in to the importance of this invitation. The name Luellen rang a bell, but he couldn't put a handle on it and the little round man was no help. He stood quietly waiting for Alexander's answer, a Mexican standoff, black tie style. Beyond them, in the ballroom, the band played, people laughed. The little man in the horrid jacket, the party, the speeches, all seemed so tiresome at that moment. The only thing Alexander Grant really wanted was to be in bed with Coral, her long legs wrapped about him, her hands doing the things her hands did so well. He smiled and took his first step away from Mr. Meaker.

"I'm so sorry," Alexander began, "but I was just on my way out. A private meeting isn't possible at the moment. Perhaps, if you would call my office . . ."

Mr. Meaker's hand was now firmly on Alexander's arm, effectively curtailing Alexander's excuse and escape. The Senator stopped short, turning his tall body toward the annoying man. His grey eyes were flat and menacing. He was about to put Mr. Meaker in his place when the little man belied his name.

"Senator," he began, his voice stronger now, a bit foreboding. "Mr. Luellen is waiting for you on the third floor of this hotel. He is very anxious to meet with you. He feels that you, indeed, are the kind of man we would like to see in the Senate for many years to come. Mr. Luellen has heard that you are going to make a bid to keep your late mother's seat in the next election. He would like to personally offer his support. He would very much like to meet with you to discuss the—endless—possibilities."

Alexander nodded, his eyes sparkling with an interest he masterfully controlled. He almost smiled. The real game was beginning and it had nothing to do with all those one man, one vote idiots dancing around on the floor. It had to do with men like Paul Luellen who beckoned him with veiled promises, and unattractive messengers. Paul Luellen was becoming more interesting by the moment.

"I think I would enjoy having a drink this evening with Mr. Luellen. Let me just tell my lady friend I'll be gone for a while. Perhaps I should invite my aide to join us?"

Alexander raised an eyebrow, uncertain of the protocol in such a situation, knowing only witnesses were necessary for many circumstances these days.

"That would be acceptable to Mr. Luellen. Shall we expect you in," Mr. Meaker looked at his watch, "ten minutes, Senator?"

"I'll look forward to it."

John Meaker melted into the crowd as easily as he had materialized from it. Alexander buttoned his jacket, stepped back into the ballroom, scanned it and located Marni in the far corner talking with a tall blond man. Then he saw Eric dancing with a short redhead in front of the bandstand.

It was Marni he whispered to first. Her smile was understanding and proprietorial, much the way Polly's used to be. It set Alexander's teeth on edge but he grinned back, squeezed her shoulder with promise, then went on to Eric. A touch on his shoulder, a look from him, was all it took for Eric to make his apologies to the redhead he danced with and follow his boss.

They were silent until the doors of the elevator closed.

"What's up?" Eric asked as though he could not have cared less. In truth his heart was racing. This was the first time Alexander had initiated the game of follow the leader.

"We're going to a surprise party." Alexander answered as the elevator doors opened and they walked toward room three-twenty-one, "I'm just not sure who is supposed to be surprised."

Chapter Ten

John Meaker opened the door of room three-twenty-one. He smiled courteously and stepped back allowing Alexander and Eric to enter. His brocade dinner jacket had been removed and was neatly folded on one of the double beds. The room itself was like many other rooms in many other fine hotels: immaculate, uncluttered, a hundred square feet more room than Travelodge accommodations and appointed in colors that whispered a gentle good night instead of screaming lights out.

In the corner of the room, over the requisite octagonal table, hung a cloud of white smoke. In the center of that cloud sat a man who, in polite circles, would have been described as portly. In real terms he was obese. To say he was dressed casually was to imply he wore some type of structured suiting. Rather he was swathed in yards of fabric: green jersey on the top resembling a polo shirt of sorts, flimsy enough to outline each full roll of skin that started from his chest and ended overlapping his groin. His legs were the size of chemical drums and were covered in denim but could hardly be defined as jeans. Alexander had only a moment to wonder if he was going to see the gentleman attempt to balance himself on what appeared to be tiny feet before he spoke.

"Senator Grant," came the greeting, a voice quieted by the burn of smoke and the effort of breathing. "I'm Paul Luellen. Does that name mean anything to you?"

Alexander moved forward keeping time with the cadence of the big man's words. He stopped in front of Luellen, just at the perimeter of the mushroom cloud of cigarette smoke. Eric remained behind near the door, near Mr. Meaker.

"I'm afraid it does not," Alexander conceded politely.

"No reason that it should. Just wanted to see if I was dealing with a bullshitter. Know what I mean? Never could stand a man who'd fall all over himself just to look like he knew everything." Luellen nodded toward a chair. "Want to sit?"

"Thank you."

Alexander pulled out a chair, opened his jacket, and made himself comfortable. For a few moments Paul Luellen's eyes locked with Grant's. The fat man allowed himself a look at Alexander's well-tended body, his handsome features. Alexander saw no envy in those eyes. Neither man smiled. Nothing had been said or done to please either. Paul Luellen, a man of few words and little time to waste, decided to test the waters by jumping in with both feet.

"I own Radison Chemical, Senator. The main plant is in San Pedro, California. Smaller facilities are scattered from Northern California south to Mexicali. I keep a low profile for reasons that are easy for a smart man to figure out. Mostly nobody knows I'm one hell of a rich man 'cause nobody gives a shit about chemicals unless they react bad to 'em. Chemicals are like air to the general public; they want 'em there to do what they should, and they sure as hell don't want to find out what they'd do without 'em. Know what I mean?"

Alexander nodded aware of what was happening behind him: Eric moving casually toward the table, coming to rest shoulder to the wall, just behind Alexander, John Meaker remained stationary.

"Good." Paul Luellen lit a cigarette from his last butt, inhaled, then continued. "So. Now you know what I own. Let me tell you what I've been doin'."

Luellen tried to lean forward but didn't get very far. A wisp of smoke toyed around his lips. He breathed in as though he could suck it all back.

"I don't care for politics very much, Senator. Never really minded who was in office or who wasn't 'cause I figured one pansy was just about like another."

Alexander raised his brow slightly, but the huge man didn't exempt present company. Alexander found this rather endearing. Must be nice not to have to care what other people think.

"So." Another breath, more smoke, more background. "My company didn't get involved in politics and neither did I until about ten years ago. The EPA was getting crazy about pollution and such. Even then I had minimal contact with the whole deal. Mostly Radison made contributions to certain environmental groups, a couple of politicians, and kept our noses clean when it came to waste. We did okay."

Puff. Puff. In and out, a breath away from death. "Now I'll tell you what I know about you. Then I'll get down to it."

He cleared his throat. Alexander had just a moment to ponder the chemical reactions in this man's body before his attention was arrested again.

"I hear you're testing the waters to make a run for the Senate seat your mama left. Appointment is great, ain't it? You've got the memory of your dear mother to rely on and you're smart enough to know that by the time the election rolls around her memory ain't gonna buy you much. Two years is long enough to forget your favorite whore much less your favorite Senator." Paul Luellen took a final drag on his cigarette, snuffed it and, with one hand, shook out another. This time Meaker moved in and held a light under Luellen's cigarette before moving back to his place again. Alexander took the opportunity to rearrange his imaginary marbles. He still wasn't in the game but he would be by the time it was his turn to shoot.

"Mr. Luellen, what you're telling me is hardly new or impressive. Now, I do have plans for this evening and, if you wish to contact my office to discuss any problem Radison Chemical might be facing that I could possibly help with, then please do so. But I must say, this is all a bit too theatrical for my blood. I'll say good night now if there's nothing else."

Alexander rose, motioning to Eric simultaneously. Paul Luellen didn't let him get very far before lowering the boom.

"Senator, I like your style, and I want your help. I want you to make sure there is no new legislation going through that subcommittee of yours restricting export of kerosene, solvent, or sulfuric acid. I want you to make sure that any bill is deader than a doornail before it gets to full committee."

Alexander turned slowly back to Paul Luellen, his eyes flinty. Little had been said, much asked for, and even more implied. Without looking to Eric for support, Alexander tried his wings, delighted to find himself soaring for the first time since he took his mother's Senate seat.

"I have office hours, Mr. Luellen. That is where I see lobbyists. To date, the PAC for the chemical industry hasn't seen fit to drop in for a visit. I assume the chemical industry's Political Action Committee has determined that I will vote as the subcommittee chairman directs given that he is a member of my own party. So, Mr. Luellen. Mr. Meaker," Alexander turned his body toward the shorter man but kept his eyes on Luellen nestling inside his cloud of smoke, "you could have saved yourselves a great deal of trouble. When I'm approached through the proper channels I'll be happy to discuss my thoughts on the possible legislation that will result from the subcommittee hearings."

Alexander fell silent engaging in a moment of predatory eyeballing with his host. The hired hands watched to see whose boss would blink first. Neither did. Paul Luellen laughed. It wasn't a hearty sound, nor a particularly mirthful one, yet it broke the spell.

"Senator, if you meant what you said you would have been through that door by now. I think you're damned curious about the kind of 'help' I'm willing to give someone who sees eye-to-eye on this thing with me. And you should be curious. Word has it your people've been running around this great state of ours testing the waters, trying to find out if you're electable. Further word is, you're not. You're a nobody, and all you got is the fading coattails of your mama to hang on to.

"But being with you these few moments, I don't think you're a man to bow out. You've just got a heap of work to do in the next twenty-four months, and you'll need all the help you can get. Help like in-kind contributions, hard cash, bodies to get out the vote . . ."

106

Paul Luellen raised an eyebrow and squashed the tip of his cigarette into the ashtray. It took a few moments for the smoke, and Alexander's thoughts, to clear.

"You could be setting me up," he suggested.

"I could," Luellen admitted. "But I ain't. You ever see one of them stings on television? You ever hear about one from your colleagues?" Paul laughed gently, again Alexander was struck by the smallness of his voice. "Those idiots in the FBI make everything so complicated. If I was setting you up, we would've had a hundred meetings by now, and I would've waited for you to tell me how much it took to buy your vote. I would have watched the greed in your eyes and made you turn toward the camera. Hell, all I've done is tell you, as a concerned citizen, that I don't want to see our economy hurt by restricting the export of certain chemicals."

"You did a little more than that, Mr. Luellen. You laid out your shopping list."

"What ain't clear yet is your price. What can I, as a concerned citizen, do for you Mr. Senator? What do you need more than anything in the world right now?" Paul Luellen picked up the pack of cigarettes. In a show of incredible self-denial he tossed it back on the table without taking one. "What do you want, Senator Grant?"

"I want to retain my seat in the Senate," Alexander said without hesitation, "I want to become a member of some standing in the eyes of my constituents, and, ultimately, the national arena. That's what I want. That will take money and power. Which have you got, Mr. Luellen? Money or power?"

Luellen laughed, shifted his incredible bulk to the other side of the chair, pulled a cigar out of nowhere, and lit a match. Turning to watch the flame, he stuck the cigar in his mouth, brought the fire close, then slid his eyes back to Alexander before lighting the tobacco.

"I got both, Senator. I got enough of both to keep you in the Senate till the day you die. You just promise to remember me as a good friend all the days of your life, and what I have is yours, Senator, just as long as you can remain discreet. How you get my help into your camp, though, is your problem."

"I think I can work within those parameters, Mr. Luellen. Indeed I can."

They smiled at each other then. It had all been said. Only the details remained unconfirmed. The match had burned low. Paul Luellen shook it out. He hadn't lit his cigar. Pity, that. Thankfully, everything else was just as it should be.

"It's going to be tough, Alexander. You're acting like all Luellen has to do is hand you a check then you raise your hand and vote no. Things don't work that way."

"A reprimand is neither called for nor appreciated, Eric."

Alexander swung the car left then made a sharp right, straightened the steering wheel and cruised a mile or so in silence. Surprised by the scolding, Eric pushed himself upright and glanced warily in Alexander's direction.

The last few months had been heaven for Eric. Alexander Grant hanging on his every word, looking to him, Eric Cochran, for guidance, gossip, and instruction on the formalities of Senate proceedings. So maybe Eric had become a little high handed, maybe he was feeling indispensable. He had a right. Now the man was acting like he knew it all and that just pissed

Eric off. But Eric knew where his bread was buttered. He smoothed his hair and rearranged his tie waiting for Alexander to indicate he was still in good graces.

"Eric, you are not my creator, my mother, nor my babysitter. Certainly I needed, and still need you, but I am not stupid. I have watched and learned during the last few months. I haven't wasted my time or my energy, and I am almost ready to make a mark. Until this evening I wasn't quite sure what kind of mark it would be—team player or maverick. It appears maverick is more appropriate."

Alexander paused thoughtfully, drumming his fingers on the steering wheel.

"I don't just want to retain this seat, I want to stand out in a crowd of rather ridiculous, overly frightened men who are far from effective legislators. It shouldn't be too difficult given the help Mr. Luellen has offered. You've obviously found fault in my acceptance of his proposal. Why don't you elaborate on your concerns, but make sure you don't lecture me, Eric. I don't want to be lectured any more. I am Senator Grant. You are my aide. Remember that."

Chagrined, Eric cleared his throat.

"Senator Grant," he began. Alexander smiled just as an oncoming headlight illuminated his face. Eric looked away, unable to come to grips so quickly with the change in Alexander. "There are a number of ethics bills in various forms passing through the House and Senate. One has even reached the President's desk and is waiting for his signature. These bills deal with curbing campaign financing. Soft money, bundling, even in-kind contributions will more than likely be outlawed. Even Political Action Committees may bite the dust. Honorariums are being called into question."

"Not all these restrictions are law now, are they?" Alexander asked.

"No," Eric admitted, drawing the word out slowly. "In fact most of these restrictions will probably never become law. But all these techniques for skirting campaign contribution laws aren't enough to handle the kind of cash flow Luellen is talking about."

Eric was in his element. He understood what was involved in the transfer of money, and in his excitement he turned toward Alexander, pleading with him to understand what he was getting into.

"We're in a highly charged moral mode today and it won't let up. People have no trust in politicians. Political renumeration is such a high profile subject that any show of ostentation will put your butt in a sling. Not only would you lose an election, you'd probably be brought up on ethics charges if anyone found out you were taking directly from Radison Chemical instead of individual contributions or through PACs. It may be kosher if it was within the limit, but it wouldn't look right."

"Any gift within legal limits wouldn't do me any good, Eric." Alexander's foot pressed against the accelerator and they went faster than Eric thought was safe. "You were the one to point that out."

Eric nodded. There was no need to confirm the statement. In the next moment Alexander swerved and stopped his car next to Eric's. He spoke slowly without looking at his companion.

"We've learned something tonight, Eric. There is a way for everyone to get what they want without risk. We just need to find it. No, *I* am going to find it." Alexander hadn't moved. His hands still gripped the wheel and he stared straight ahead. In the midnight darkness Eric felt small and insignificant next to Alex-

110

ander Grant's determination. "In or out, Eric. Which will it be?"

Which indeed. He had little to offer Alexander Grant now. Not money, or power or even knowledge. The man was a quick study. But one thing remained Eric's alone and that was his ability to protect.

He would be Alexander's guide. He would watch for the mine fields and the bombs and the single sniper bullets that might cross Alexander's way. He would walk him through the misery of the Hill, taking Alexander as high as he could go. And, when Alexander reached the top, Eric would be right there with him. It was enough. And, if Alexander Grant went as far as Eric thought he could, Eric's second place would be awfully good.

"I'm in, Alexander."

Slowly, confidently, Alexander smiled. "I knew I could count on you, Eric." Alexander reached out and touched Eric's shoulder lightly. A gesture of thanks or impatience that he should be gone, Eric wasn't sure. So he grinned back as he left the car and let Alexander Grant go on his way. Eric was quickly forgotten.

Twenty minutes later Alexander was loosening his tie as he walked across the street to Coral's Brentwood apartment. Nonchalantly he strolled through the front door as someone else was leaving, and waited in the well-lighted lobby for the elevator to collect him.

Someday there might be a need to worry about who saw his comings and goings. Tonight, though, he could do what he pleased. He could stay the night with a woman half his age and the only one who might care would be Polly. He sincerely hoped, though, his soon to be ex-wife had lost all that ill-placed faith that he would return home. So, damn Polly and full steam ahead with Coral. Tonight he would take his pleasure and, perhaps, very soon the people of the United States would care enough about him to watch his every move.

The elevator doors finally opened. Alexander entered the car and saw himself reflected a thousand times in the beveled mirror tile. He pushed the third button, leaned back against the mirror, and watched his passage in space recorded by digital green numbers. When the doors opened again Coral's voice was the first thing he heard. He saw her a moment later, struggling with a man who either had great difficulty standing or was attacking her from a rather odd and ineffectual position.

"Unfaithful already, Coral?" Alexander asked as he approached the awkward couple.

"Alexander," Coral wailed with relief, "come help me. Rudy passed out. I've been trying to get him off my sofa for the last hour."

The man in Coral's arms managed to turn his head and squint in Alexander's direction before his head lolled to the side once more and his weak smile turned sickly.

Alexander pulled the man upright, turning his own head away from the smell of tequila and pizza that oozed from every pore. Although Coral's friend looked ridiculous in his karate pajamas, Alexander could tell he was a handsome man. A little peacockish by Alexander's standards, but handsome nonetheless.

"You going to manage all right, buddy?" Alexander had him propped up against the wall.

"Sure, no problem. Just needed to get my sea legs, know what I mean?" The words weren't terribly clear, but slurred in a most charming manner. Alexander wanted nothing more than to believe in his near sobriety.

112

"Great. So, if you're all right, you better head on home. Can you drive?"

" 'Course I can drive. Been doin' it since I was six-teen. Drivin' and every other important thing in life." He winked as suggestively as he could Coral's way, pushed himself off the wall, and stumbled down the hall toward the elevator.

"Good night, Rudy," Coral called, exhausted. His hand moved to wave, instead ineffectually flopping by his side. Coral giggled. Leaning into Alexander she wondered, "Think he'll make it home? Maybe we should have called him a cab?"

"He'll be fine. That kind always is. What is he, used car salesman?"

"No. He owns a small advertising agency."

"Looks it," Alexander muttered, then said, "I think you're going to have to get a better class of friends."

"I already have," Coral murmured, giving her full attention to the man at her side. Her long fingers caught the ends of his bow tie. She pulled and Alexander grinned, happily allowing himself to be led inside. They were naked five minutes later. Ten minutes after that, having worked up a respectable sweat, Coral and Alexander lay side by side, delightfully satisfied.

"I ought to send you out with middle-aged matrons more often," Coral breathed, absentmindedly running her fingers the length of his body and back. Alexander rearranged himself to take full advantage of her ministrations.

"It wasn't Marni Lewis who got the adrenaline flowing," Alexander said sleepily.

"Oh?" Coral was on her elbow, her heavy breasts pressing into his ribs, her arm flung over his shoulders. "Do I have competition from one of the younger, politically aware types?"

113

"No competition anywhere, babe," Alexander laughed, his hands spanning her waist so that he could keep her just where he wanted her. "Tonight I found out that politics and power can be a rather potent aphrodisiac. It's true what they say—when you can feel success within your grasp everything in life is better."

"I'll attest to that," she muttered, lowering her lips to kiss his chest, nibbling her way across his skin until her teeth managed to find his nipple. He moved under her, pulling her toward him.

"Tell me, Coral, in the real estate business, what do you do when you have a poor listing you want to move quickly?"

"I fix it up," she whispered, running her tongue up the side of his neck.

"Anything else?"

"I make sure I know where all the flaws are so I can hide them." This bit of information was accompanied by a rather aggressive open-mouthed kiss against his ear. Alexander held her back, looking at her. Beautiful face. Big hair. Big bust. Slender hips. Long legs. She wouldn't age well and that was sad. The nice thing was Alexander really liked her. She exhibited a decent amount of intelligence and carried out her business with a certain style. Coral thought he was waiting for more. She gave it to him.

"And I advertise, Alexander. It's like putting on spandex, you know. Advertise fast and hard. Move it before anybody looks too close. That's the way I get rid of a bad listing." A smile teased the corners of her full mouth. It was too late to be serious. "Now, my darling, I've told you what you want to know. So shut up and show me how you ram a bill through the Senate."

Chapter Eleven

"At the sound of the tone, leave a coherent message. I don't have time to try and figure out what you want. Running as usual. Talk with you soon. Ciao."

If she could have, Dani would have reached over and annihilated the stupid machine before it spewed forth such sickeningly cheery, flippant nonsense. Unfortunately, Dani's body was no more. It had turned into a lump of lead; its molecules had been reordered, metomorphosizing into a slug swathed in a terrycloth bathrobe. The notion that her physical being might be too busy to answer the phone, the mere idea that another human being would want to talk with her, was as bizarre as Sid Pregerson sending her roses and an apology. Even the mundane aspects of living had been ignored in the past few weeks. Eating, dressing, moving beyond the distance between her bed and couch, were beyond Dani's energy or desire. She had been stricken with a kind of virulent virus. The disease was despair, the cure beyond her now fragile ego. Returning home Dani's systems began shutting down until neither mind, soul, or body had the power to regroup.

The one thing in the world she could do brilliantly she would never be allowed to do again. The one person who could give her comfort was to be avoided at all costs. Blake who had never failed to come to her aid would only offer pity and that would be worse than any other humiliation. Hadn't Papa always said you were finished when someone you respected pitied you? Oh hell, what pessimistic thing hadn't Papa said? Now the world was proving him right. Dani groaned and buried her face in the sofa pillow, pulling her robe tightly around her, trying to block out the message that had already begun recording.

"Dani? It's Jenny. Checking in for the hundredth time. What are you doing for Thanksgiving? I know it's still a few weeks away . . ." Jenny's hesitation was underscored by a mechanical beep. The tape needed to be changed. Dani would do it in her next life. "Please call me before Saturday. I'm really getting worried. Bye, honey. Hope all is well and . . ."

The message cut off before Jenny finished. Just like her to talk too long. Opening one eye Dani looked over the edge of the pillow. She peeked through the crack in the plantation shutters. Outside was grey and ugly, the fog as thick as whipped cream. A perfect, depressing day. San Francisco at its best.

Peevishly Dani hugged her pillow tighter and flipped over, closing her eyes tight as if that would make the world go away. Surprisingly it did. The annoying invitation played through Dani's head until the words became nothing more than a string of monotonous sounds and she fell asleep. Hours later, she was awake again, groggy and vaguely aware that the banging inside her head wasn't a dream but a real commotion outside her door.

"Dani! Dani! I know you're in there. The lady next door saw you three days ago. Come on Dani, open up. Now!"

Bang. Bang. An insistent fist on the door again, coming through the door. Oh Lord! Blake's voice. Blake's banging.

"Dani, honey, please. We just want to make sure you're okay . . ."

A gentler, more earnest rapping. Sweet, pleading voice. Jenny was there too. Oh, Christ! Oh damn! Dani rolled onto her back and pulled the pillow over her face. She squeezed her eyes so tight tears pushed through but the banging kept up, the calling continued and there was that little edge creeping into Blake's voice that was a sure fire indication he'd had enough.

Well so had she. How dare they violate her right to depression! How dare they try and rescue her when she preferred the tragic death of a marketing martyr. The situation was terminal and she was damn well going to enjoy it! Driven by righteous despair, Dani shot off the couch. Indignation blazing, she yanked her robe around her, shook her limp hair out of her eyes and, without a thought for her sleep swollen eyes, threw open the door and glared at Jenny and Blake as regally as if they had disturbed her beauty regime.

"All right? See? I'm fine. Go away," she snapped. At least she thought that's what she said. But her voice was a croak, her imperious tone nothing more than a faint whisper. God, how humiliating. There was only one thing she could do.

"Arghhh!"

With that more eloquent and satisfying cry Dani pushed the door shut, but Blake was faster, his reflexes fresher. Both his palms hit the door at the same time, and he shoved hard. Competitive as always, Dani tried to fight back, but she hadn't eaten too recently and her days had been filled with sleep and mind-numbing stints with the television. Her arms weakened and

117

Dani fell back, defeated. They were inside like a shot, Jenny on one side, Blake on the other, lifting her up. She shook them off wearily as if she still had her pride. Unfortunately, even that was going fast.

"There's a law against this, you know," Dani complained, half turning, not wanting to look in their eyes. "I'm not sick, and you have no right bursting in here. Either of you." Her eyes narrowed, sharp little points of sky blue. Her lips puffed out, a pout worthy of a three year old. "I just haven't felt like seeing anyone."

"No wonder you don't want to see anybody," Blake said as he leaned close and kissed her cheek, "you look like hell."

Dani crossed her arms. Forceful body language, that made her feel invincible. Jenny shot Blake a look of caution. She'd heard the concern in his voice but doubted Dani had. There was another approach. Jenny stepped up to the plate praying for a homerun.

"Come on, sweetie, you just need a shower. Let's get you cleaned up. Then Blake and I are going to take you out for a huge steak. What do you say?"

"I don't want to go anywhere. I don't know why you didn't just wait for me to call you back. I mean, you hardly gave me any time to call you back, Jenny. I just got your message then you show up at my door and barge into my house . . ."

"What message?" Looks careened between Blake and Jenny. Confused, concerned glances were exchanged with incredible rapidity.

"The message you left this morning," Dani insisted angrily.

"Dani, I didn't leave a message this morning. The last one I left was the day before yesterday. I've called so often, and haven't heard a word from you, I just had to do something. That's why I called Blake and had him come with me."

"That's not true . . ." Dani's head was up, her eyes frantic as they jumped from one person to the other. ". . . I heard you . . . just an hour ago. You're trying to make me think I'm crazy. It was just this morning . . ."

"Christ . . ." Blake breathed.

"Blake . . ." Jenny warned.

"Both of you . . ." Dani sputtered, hot tears stinging the back of her eyes. Maybe she was crazy. Maybe this was how the world ended, not with a bang but a god-damn whimper. Her whimper! There was only one thing left to do—get Blake and Jenny out of her hair. "Both of you just . . . leave . . . me . . . alone . . ."

The last word was elongated into in a rounded cry of astonishment as Dani was lifted heavenward, slung over Blake's broad shoulder. She raised her fists, ready to emulate Scarlett O'Hara to Blake's Rhett Butler. But Blake wasn't as smooth as Rhett, and, when it was clear the trip would be bumpy, she hung on for dear life, sputtering as he strode over the deep white carpet-ing in the living room, up the three steps to the raised dining area and onward to his destination.

"What are you doing? Blake, put me down."

"I will not. I vowed to take care of you in sickness and in health, Dani . . ."

"Christ, you fool," she cried, "we're not married anymore. We're divorced with a capital D. I've got the papers to prove it."

"Tough," Blake shot back, turning the corner and heading down the hall. "When I make a solemn prom-ise it takes precedence over any goddamn piece of paper. Now . . ." without breaking stride he kicked open the bathroom door, ". . . you're going to get

119

yourself together or I'm going to put you together. Enough of this ridiculous behavior."

Still holding her, Dani still struggling, Blake leaned over the free-standing, claw-footed tub, twisted the chrome faucets, flipped the shower extension on and whipped Dani off his shoulder. Masterfully, he peeled the robe off her body, grabbed her shoulders and kissed her until neither was sure if the steam filling the room emanated from them or the water pouring out of the shower head. Just as Dani moved into Blake, just as she realized how very sensual her nakedness was against the cut of his clothes, he had her up again, his hands clasped her under her arms. She was lifted into the tub and kissed briefly yet thoroughly once more. Just before he pulled the shower curtain around the tub and left her alone, he ordered, ". . . Have a good cry, Dani, then let it be. You've got too much going for you to throw it away. Worse, you're letting Sid win. I swear Dani, someday you're going to lose something you really care about if you don't start thinking. First you jump in the deep end, then you throw in the towel."

The door was slammed, Dani was wet and Blake felt a whole lot better.

"So?" Jenny jumped from the couch the minute Blake was back.

"So?" Blake raised an eyebrow.

"Is she going to be okay?"

"Absolutely," he answered.

"How do you know?"

"Because I love her and I'm not going to let her give up," he answered, the twinkle in his eye disappearing the moment his back was turned to Jenny. He hoped loving her would be enough this time.

Jenny rose, leaving the couch and going to Blake.

She hadn't been fooled by his show of optimism. She adored Dani, respected the hell out of her, but it had to be miserable loving her the way Blake did. Damn lucky woman, Dani, and if she didn't watch it Blake Sinclair might just take off one of these days. Tiptoeing, her hand on Blake's arm, Jenny kissed him on the cheek.

"Hang in there."

With a half-hearted chuckle Blake patted her hand and nodded his thanks for the encouragement. Jenny was out the door, knowing that Blake Sinclair needed time to be alone—with himself and with Dani.

Restless, Blake wandered the living room, picking up one of Dani's beautiful things now and again: a glass sphere, cold and perfect, sitting in the lap of a tri-cornered pedestal made of golden daggers, the jade carving they'd brought back from Japan when they were there shooting that car spot, a book of poetry, unopened, unread, the binding exquisite. If nothing else Dani had a great eye for . . .

"So is anyone going to get me something to wear or am I going to have to run through the house naked in front of my guests!"

Blake laughed and put the book back on the side table. Things were looking up if she was in a demanding mood. Far be it from Dani Cortland to let her defenses down longer than a minute. Shaking his head Blake headed for the bedroom.

It had been a while since he'd been in that particular room. From the looks of it Dani hadn't used it much either. The couch was obviously the perfect place for her depressive antics. The bedroom, white and peach and pristine was meant for much more complex emotions.

Going to the dresser he pulled open the top drawer

and lingered over the choice of lingerie. Finally he held up a tiny piece of silk, navy and naughty looking. Thinking them quite fetching Blake tossed the panties into the air, caught them behind his back and opened the next drawer. Rummaging he managed to find a T-shirt. Almost new, he could hardly imagine Dani buying such a thing until he unfolded it and found it emblazoned with the name of a printer. A freebie, naturally. Finally her immaculate closet was penetrated and Blake pulled a pair of pencil slim jeans off a hanger as . . .

"A girl could freeze to death before you managed to bring her a few clothes, Blake Sinclair."

Dani stood in the doorway wrapped in a towel, her hair wet, slicked back from her high forehead. Pink tinged her cheeks and the tops of her shoulders. The shower had been hot and her skin blushed and pulsated. But no amount of heat or water could wash away the red rims around her eyes, the swelling of her delicate skin where the tears had fallen fast and furious down her cheeks.

She tried that Cortland cocky smile, the one that said no-matter-what-I'll-never-admit-I'm-scared-and-hurt.

Blake grinned back, the one that said, I-won't-mention-the-fact-that-you-look-like-your-heart-is-breaking-and-I-wish-I-could-mend-it.

He held up the clothes. Dani came to him, reaching for the denim, afraid to touch his hand and be lost again, embarrassed to be weak in front of him.

"Not terribly attractive."

"You'd look great in anything," Blake said. A whisper, nothing more. There was something in his throat, a painful something that made it so hard to talk. He ached for her.

122

Dani tipped her head. The smile was gone, a wry twist of her mouth in its place. Blake thought he saw her tremble so he too turned to stare at the pile of clothes in his hands.

"You know you don't need to stay with me, Blake. I'm really okay. I was just being silly. Really childish, you know?"

Dani ventured a glance, her blue eyes meeting his. She found the truth right there in his dark ones. He understood that she didn't want to be believed. She wanted what he had to give. She wanted him to take charge. She wanted Blake to make Sid and all this misery go away.

"I don't think it was childish, Dani. You've had a hell of a time lately. Everybody needs to rest. Even you."

Dani nodded. This time her shoulders shook and the eyes that looked away so quickly were frantic, brimming with tears again. The panic was coming, the loneliness, the aloneness and Dani didn't know how to stop it any more than she knew how to share it.

Instantly the clothes were dropped to the floor between them and Blake had his arms wrapped around her. Hands up, palms flat against his chest, Dani dug her fingers into his sweater and hung on like a kitten clasping anything within reach afraid to fall. Her body shook.

"I don't want to . . ." she whispered but her voice caught.

"I know, darling," Blake answered, his own heart breaking for her.

"I don't want to cry," she said with one last courageous effort. "I'm a big girl . . ." a sob punctuated her protest. "I . . . can . . . take care of . . . myself . . ."

"Shhh," Blake soothed and the kisses started. He

held her tighter, his lips traveling gently over her forehead, his fingers moving tenderly over her bare arms. The towel was damp between them, her hair wet but he didn't care. Her whole being was giving into her misery, the puzzle of her predicament.

"I was so good, Blake . . ."

Her voice was failing as surely as her confidence and he couldn't bear to see that happen. He wouldn't listen, couldn't listen to what may actually be the truth. Perhaps he'd believe she was finished someday, but not now. A beaten Dani wasn't one he had ever known. To believe that she might give up was to believe that someday they would truly go their separate ways and that was a possibility he wouldn't accept.

Slowly he swayed with her, holding tight to keep her safe from her self-doubt and sorrow. Somehow they slow danced across the room, Dani enfolded in Blake's loving embrace. Her sobs were small and insecure, private little things that Dani would deny uttering a week from now. But it wasn't a week from now and she needed so much from him, intimate things that no one else had ever given her. Dani needed Blake to simply let her be Dani. It was his first and always gift to her.

Without letting go, Blake pulled back the thick quilt from the bed before peeling the thick towel away from her body. Gently, carefully he sat her on the edge of the bed marveling at how beautiful she was. Then, with the utmost regard, he helped her into her bed and covered her to the chin. The bedclothes shuddered with her sobs, her whimpers, her sadness. Quietly Blake rounded the bed and stepped out of his shoes. Without a second thought, he moved in beside her, clothes and all, and she was in his arms once again.

They lay for hours like that until finally Dani's tears

stopped and she slept more deeply than she had in weeks. In Blake's arms there was safety, beside him the world was held at bay, in him she trusted. No one would ever know that Dani Cortland was afraid. They would never hear it from Blake's lips and Blake would never remind her of it again.

So when she breathed softly and deeply, naked beside him in the huge bed, Blake lay awake watching. Through the night until the next morning he watched the woman he loved.

Chatter drifted in to her from the other room. Conversations so relevant, so hip, so well thought out they could only be important to those with more money than brains. It was the kind of idiocy that intrigued Dani when she was the center of attention but, hidden away in the kitchen, the subdued and introspective timbre of the collective voice made her want to scream. Only Jenny's straight-forward laughter, blasphemous in such pseudo-erudite company, and a male voice belonging to the genius behind the new automated outdoor boards, could be distinguished from the general hum.

Leaning against the beautiful black marble counter top Dani tried to block out the noise. It interfered with her concentration on the thunderous black cloud above her head, the one that had been there threatening a torrential rain of discontent for the last two weeks—ever since she'd let Blake talk her into moving into his place—only until she felt better, of course. That cloud had almost doubled in size since this Thanksgiving soiree began. She had been in the kitchen for a very long time and was all but forgotten. Blake was in the other room hosting this orphan's

125

Thanksgiving, being kind even to the outdoor board genius who had invited himself.

The cloud grew bigger as she realized even Blake hadn't bothered to check on her. He was out there moving smoothly through the ten people in his living room, lowering himself onto the arm of a chair for a slightly more intimate conversation with a special guest, thrilling some lucky woman with his touch as he offered to refill her wine. Dani grabbed an olive off the crudite tray and popped it in her mouth. Another followed. Eating helped . . . a little. Damn Blake. How dare he be having so much fun when things weren't going well at all. Not . . . at . . . all. Another olive, the satisfying crunch of a carrot and Dani had managed to shrink the black cloud, but she couldn't shake her dissatisfaction with Blake. The fact that Dani was in his home didn't mean she was there to stay and that was something he just didn't understand. He was acting like a newlywed.

Not that Dani really had anything to complain about. She felt better and looked better than she had in the last month. Being with Blake again, having him care for her, willing away the days reading or shopping had done more for her state of mind than a week in the Caribbean. He had convinced her, finally, that what she had lost—thrown away, she reminded him—was less than nothing. A job, no more and no less. What she had gained was the chance to rearrange her life. She had friends, time, and a man who loved her. Fate was kind, he said, and Dani believed Blake. He could be so very persuasive. In fact, when he argued his case between the sheets, the lasting glow kept Dani content for days on end.

Now, alone, waiting for the food to cook, Dani realized she wanted more than just this. She'd had it with the joys of homemaking, lovemaking, and merrymaking. It was time for something real to happen. Strength was returning, recovery from her professional malaise was almost complete. She missed having a pencil in her hand, missed strategy sessions for products that would someday be immortalized on film or in print. She missed fighting with account executives, sitting in meetings and eating the same kind of sandwich three days in a row. She missed presenting her ideas to a client and screaming at suppliers who didn't make their deadlines. She missed high heels, her working clothes and her briefcase. Jeans were great for a weekend, but Dani was beginning to feel a contempt for the casual—clothes and life—and things were going to change. Dani Cortland was going to take charge again—starting now.

With a flick of her wrist the oven door was open. Her mitted hands grasped the huge turkey and whipped it out onto counter top. Onto the platter the ill-fated bird went and out to the dining room. A burst of laughter from the living room fueled Dani. The table was ready in moments. The curtain was up and the show was about to hit the road.

Pushing through the swinging doors Dani surveyed the group of guests and announced, "Dinner's served, folks." With a grin she held up a huge knife. "And I'm carving."

Dani Cortland was back and in control.

They worked in silence, Blake clearing the table, Dani washing and rinsing. He moved carefully between the dining room and the kitchen, aware that Dani's mood had swung from confidently happy to morose by the time the last of their guests had left. It wasn't until he walked through the kitchen with his arms full of linen that Dani spoke.

"I don't remember us having so many beautiful things when we were married. When did you get this set?"

Dani held an exquisite wineglass up over her shoulder for him to see. Even through the suds the crystal was so delicate it looked as though the Dionysian design had been etched out in thin air. Blake came toward her, slipped the glass out of her hand then wrapped his arms around her waist so he could pull her into him. She began her washing chore again, dreamily, as though her body was on automatic pilot.

"We had nice things when we were married," he murmured, drifting a bit as she was. "I have a few nicer things now. But what good are they if it's just me around to enjoy them?"

Dani snorted a small laugh. "You and whatever lady friend you happen to have in for the weekend."

"Dani," Blake chuckled, twirling her around so that he could look at her, "I never told you I was going to be celibate waiting for you. I only said that I loved you more than anyone in this world, and I hoped you'd come back to me. But I wasn't about to put my life on hold and mope around while you made up your mind which rainbow you wanted to find the end of." Blake laughed gently, burying his lips in her silken hair. She swayed against him for a moment, reveling in the feel of their molded bodies but somehow peeved that Blake should know her so well.

"I never expected you to do that," Dani complained softly, tight-lipped as she pulled away. It was late and her good humor had lessened with each passing hour.

"Of course you did," he teased, pulling her back, twirling her toward him. Face to face now she looked

128

away while he dipped his head, insisting she meet his eyes. But Dani was feeling frustrated, needing to be helped, not understood and loved, faults and all. Blake was playful. He laced his hands behind her back and pulled tight, forcing her damp and soapy hands to clutch at him. "That's what I really love about you— that deep, black little hole somewhere in the center of your heart that swallows everything in its path. It's like a minute flaw in a diamond; that flaw makes the stone all that more precious. I know the only thing that would make you truly happy in this world is for you to be just a tad more successful than I. Or for me to be less content with my life. Dani, you've always wanted to get the best of me. What you don't understand is that you have always been better than me because you have the drive. Now maybe you'll see that if we simply take each other as we are we can be successful and happy too. What do you think? Like to take a stab at it again?"

Contrite, Dani tugged at his shirt. Her fingers were pink and tender from the hot water, small and delicate against the exquisite tea dye of his cotton shirt and she lowered her cheek, resting it half against her hands, half against him while he stroked her hair.

"Why can't I be satisfied?" she asked more of herself than of him, her voice small and sad. "Why? I was so sure tonight that I could get back into the swing of things. I had a minute there when I felt strong again. But listening to everyone talk, I realized I didn't have anything. It's been too long and Sid did his job too well. I know I've had it so why can't I just accept it? Why can't I be happy with you?"

Blake sighed. How often he had asked himself that same question and not come up with an answer.

"I don't know, babe. That's just the way you are.

Other people are like that too, wanting so much and stopping at nothing to get it. What has always been a mystery to me is why I'm your competition. Why can't you pit yourself against a stranger?"

He laughed a little and was rewarded when Dani chuckled too. He hugged her tighter, knowing there were no words to convince her that she was worthwhile in and of herself. Pulling the towel from her waist he turned her toward the living room and flipped out the kitchen light.

"Let's leave the rest for tomorrow. I say we get to bed so I can show you exactly how thankful Thanksgiving can be."

Dani balled her fist and hit him lightly, snuggling into him all the while, wanting to please him because she loved him too, "I suppose I have one or two things I can think of that might make me realize I'm not doomed yet."

"Hey! Optimism!" He kissed the top of her head, squeezed her tight then let her go. "I'll lock up."

Dani nodded, waiting by the hall door while Blake dimmed the lights and lowered the blinds. His shoes made hollow sounds on his bleached peg-and-groove floor, his shadow loomed large on the pristine white walls. Casually she watched, absentmindedly unbuttoning her blouse, until he was back reaching for her again.

"What's this?" Blake covered her fingers. "I was hoping you'd let me do that."

"Blake." Dani pushed his hand away gently, annoyed that he was trying to make the evening so special and sorry for her peevishness at the same time. "It's not like this is the first time."

"It could be," he teased. Dani's eyes rolled. Practical he was not. She turned on her heel and headed

130

down the hall, Blake following happily. She had to tell him in no uncertain terms that she simply couldn't carry on like this much longer. Luckily, the phone rang, saving her from trying to explain the unexplainable.

"Damn," Blake muttered.

Dani's head swiveled, her platinum hair swinging, her hand clutching her blouse shut as if the front door had just opened. For an instant they stood still, eyeing one another in the half light until finally Dani clucked, "Oh, go get it." She waved her free hand. "You know you're dying to. If it was for me, I would."

"But it's Thanksgiving . . ." Blake protested without much enthusiasm. Dani almost grinned. Blake who swore that pleasure always came before business was a liar. He was as committed as she.

"And the Pope is Catholic, but clients still worry. Go!"

With a smile, a flash of white teeth and a hand through his hair, Blake went back to the living room and caught the phone on the third ring.

Dani leaned against the hallway wall, a half smile on her lips. She could hear his voice drifting toward her. The client was holding up a hoop and Blake was jumping right through it. *Hello. Howareya. No problem. Happy Thanksgiving.* She was almost ready to tune out, almost ready to save herself the heartache of wishing the call had been for her when he called to her.

"Dani? Honey, do me a favor? My portfolio's in the den. Bring me the Apache Shoe layout. The one with the woman on the Eiffel Tower."

"Okay."

Blake went back to his conversation while Dani rummaged through his portfolio. She flipped past mechanicals, photocopies, two or three storyboards, fascinated by what she saw. These things were very, very good. Blake at his best, his eye capturing some interesting perspectives on the boards. Too bad he wouldn't see the same thing on film. An excellent job all around though it wasn't the approach Dani would have taken. She would have . . .

She would have nothing! Hell, she didn't even have a job. Grabbing the board she shoved it under her arm and gave it to Blake. He smiled his thanks. She curled up on the sofa, arm propped on the back, her head nestled in her hand as she listened, jealously watching him work.

"Yeah, Wally, I've got it right here. No, no you weren't wrong. I do want to shoot this stuff on location, and I want to make sure that whoever you're going to get to model is a top pro. We're going to have her hanging from a girder on the Eiffel Tower. Be sure to put in extra bucks for special permits, insurance, that kind of thing."

Blake paced as he listened. Obviously whoever was on the other end wasn't too sure about the scope of the shoot.

"Okay, I understand," Blake quietly reassured him. "I know that this is a spec presentation, but I really believe we've got to hit them with both barrels. They're talking five to ten million in media money. A first time advertiser willing to drop those kinds of dollars is no slouch. They'll want the best, right? Don't worry about it. The campaign is a winner. What else is there to worry about? It's only Tomkins & Jawarski and that other really small agency, what's its name?"

Blake paused to listen, his expression never changing while he nodded.

"Yeah, Green Advertising. L.A., isn't it? Jesus, how did they ever get in the running for a chunk of business

132

like this? The agency's a joke. Apache is in the bag so estimate it high. Give us room to maneuver. Okay. Yeah. Fine. I know. I'll be ready. Right. The week before Christmas. We're the first ones up. Bye . . . Wally, don't worry. I'll be ready. Best to the family. Bye."

Blake hung up, looked at Dani, then grinned mischievously. She laughed right back, her humor fueled by her eavesdropping.

"Account people never change do they?" She ran her hand through her hair, letting it filter through her fingers.

Blake was beside her. "You'd think we had all the big guns in the industry after this account. But we've got it in the bag."

"Who're you working with?"

"Dailey and Associates."

"Not much of a line-up for a hunk of change like that," Dani murmured, images of Blake's presentation running through her mind only to be pushed out by dreams of her own revisions. He shook his head, agreeing even as his fingers caressed the nape of her neck. Casually Dani picked up the portfolio for one last, close look.

"Like it?" Blake murmured, his lips following his fingers to that soft spot just below her ears.

"Yes, I do," she answered thoughtfully, warming to his caresses while focusing on his work. "I really do, but . . ."

"I was hoping you'd say that," Blake sighed slipping his hand inside her blouse, his fingertips closing over her erect nipple before floating across her full breast. He wasn't talking about the campaign at all! Christ. Embarrassed, Dani pushed him gently away.

"Blake, wait . . . don't . . . ." She put the storyboard

133

on the coffee table even as Blake reached for her again.

"Wait, what?" he laughed, pulling her closer.

"Wait a minute," Dani laughed back without feeling, her elbows locking as she kept him at bay. She pleaded then. "I want to talk about the campaign. It's important, Blake."

"What's there to talk about? We're due for presentation soon. Everything's done . . ."

"But I can help," she insisted. Dani could see that he didn't understand yet how important this was to her. She begged now, not caring about her dignity. "Blake, please, let me help." Dani was on her knees, balancing on the soft couch as she pulled her blouse together so Blake wouldn't be distracted. "I think I know a way to make it even more effective than it already is. Blake, listen, we could really set that account on its ear if we worked together. I could just . . ."

"Dani." Softly, sadly he admonished her. He stopped her mid-sentence with a quick, understanding kiss. "No, Dani. I'm sorry. I don't even want to hear your ideas. Everything is done. Complete. Fini. Dani, there isn't a place for you on this pitch. Let's just make love and put all that creative energy of yours into the one thing we do so well together."

"Blake, be serious," Dani whispered, pleading. Pulling her hands away from him, she hid her hurt—a hurt beyond anything she could have imagined.

"I am being serious, honey. I know this is hard on you—the inactivity, the boredom, the cold shoulder you've been getting from every agency. But I can't be the one to offer the solution with this presentation. Dailey hired me, not me and my team. I have a contract which I cannot, and will not, change even for you. Dani?" Blake tipped up her chin seeing that tears were winning ground over defiance. "I know you understand that."

She nodded. "I was just hoping. I need it so badly, Blake. I need just one break."

"I can't, love. You know that," Blake whispered as he took her in his arms once again.

"I know, darling. I know," Dani responded, her words lost as their lips met. She and Blake melted into one shadowy form in the darkened living room. Desperate to share what good things she could with Blake, Dani's hands began to explore his marvelous body as her mind fought to banish the idea that was forming in the back of her mind.

But the plan was so intense it took on a life of its own and, try as she might, Dani couldn't separate herself from it. Like an addict, her need was too great, her desire for what she thought to be perfection so tangible, she couldn't ignore the scheme that presented itself. Not for Blake, not for anyone.

Trying once again, hoping to exorcise thoughts she knew to be unprincipled, Dani fired her passion to a point well above boiling. Her hands traced the lines of Blake's muscles, mapping out the amazing mystery that he was while she fed her physical desire with her mental gymnastics. Her body moved and snaked beneath his while her heart pounded with excitement over what might be in her future. And, when he entered her, when Blake lay atop her lost in his final pleasure, Dani came too, crying out in ecstacy and shame because she knew she could no longer deny what she would do, even at the expense of the man she loved.

Finally, they collapsed, their bodies slick from exertion. Blake cuddled close to Dani who cradled him

135

with one arm around his shoulders. Her other hand slowly toyed with the his strong fingers.

"Happy?" he asked.

"Ummm," she answered, closing her eyes and biting back the need to tell him what she was planning. Happiness was more than a matter of the heart.

Dani turned her head away from him, fighting as she had never fought in her life to find that clear path toward what was right. Beside her, naked and warm and inviting, Blake lay content with his life and his love. Dani turned her head back and, even before she could truly come to grips with what she was doing, asked the question.

"Tell me, Blake, when are you set up to present this stuff to the shoe client? Will you be in Los Angeles long?"

And, even as the last note of her voice faded into the night, as her hands caressed him lovingly, Dani Cortland grieved, knowing she had just sold her soul to the devil, and Blake was her barter.

Okay, so maybe it wasn't the most ethical thing to do. Maybe it was underhanded. Maybe she should have talked this over with someone before just going ahead and doing it. But there was no one to trust and, once begun, Dani knew she couldn't go back. Life was too short and Blake would forgive her if there was ever an occasion for him to find out. All those maybes were moot now anyway. She was standing in front of the door of Green Advertising in a Century City highrise in Los Angeles.

Dani had left Blake with a kiss and an embrace she thought would last forever. Every moment they were together she expected him to caution her against mentioning his work to anyone. She expected something that would indicate he knew what she was up to. But Blake had only hugged her and accepted her explanation that it was time she got on with her life. Yes, she would call, she told him. And she had. She had called him after she packed and told him she was going to L.A. to check out a few leads. There was a bit of truth there. Of course she'd check in. No, maybe not dinner for the next week or so because she had a zillion things to do since she'd been goofing off for the last few weeks. Of course she'd see him for Christmas or at least they'd be in touch, his schedule being so tight and all. Love you. You too. Bye. Kiss. Kiss. Bye. She'd said all this, promised all this, thankfully without having to look Blake in the eye.

She had played her part well and it made her uneasy. But that didn't stop her from closing her suitcase, putting her portfolio in order, and leaving without even a call to let Mr. Rudy Green know it was her intention to see him that first week after Thanksgiving. The lack of notice wouldn't matter though. What she possessed ensured he would ask her to stay—if he didn't throw her out on her ear before giving him her information.

Taking a deep breath, knowing her next move would be grounds for throwing her out of any decent agency, Dani opened the door to Green Advertising and walked in.

The place was quiet and small. A young bespeckled girl sat in the receptionist's chair sorting invoices. She looked up and gave Dani a shy smile before lowering her eyes bashfully. Dani's eyes flicked to the nameplate. Serina was the girl's name.

"May I help you?" she asked, laying aside the invoices.

"I'm here to see Rudy Green," Dani announced without breaking stride. "That's his office there, isn't it?"

"No. That's it." The receptionist pointed to the office next to the one Dani had guessed belonged to the boss.

"Thanks, no need to let him know I'm here. He's expecting me . . ."

Dani moved on, quickly, the element of surprise a necessity. Thankfully the girl at the front desk was so flustered she didn't come after Dani, simply made ineffectual noises about Mr. Green being busy as Dani strode confidently past her, going directly into Rudy Green's office. Dani was already talking when she threw open the door to the office and shut it just as quickly.

"Mr. Green, my name is Dani Cortland and I am an incredible art director. I realize this introduction is unorthodox, and I usually don't do this to people. However, I have information I think you might want to hear regarding Apache Shoes. I also have the wherewithal to create a campaign that will beat out your competition during this review and land you this account. Mr. Green, you won't regret this. Just give me five minutes to convince you."

The man at the desk, phone cradled on his shoulder, looked at Dani and smiled a very small smile entrancing Dani with his beautiful eyes.

"That's a very interesting way of conducting a job interview, Miss Cortland. But I'm afraid your speech has been wasted. That," the man pointed toward the opening door, "is Rudy Green."

Dani looked over her shoulder in time to see a dark haired man push through, his brown eyes flashing angrily.

"And that," fumed Rudy, "is a gentleman who was thinking of hiring Green Advertising. I'll have to assure him that people do not barge into our offices as a matter of course. Now, I would suggest you leave before I call security and have you thrown out."

Dani's head snapped back to the man at the desk. Her face colored under the scrutiny of his silver grey eyes. He shrugged his shoulders, smiled wider and introduced himself.

"Senator Grant, Miss Cortland," he said smoothly, "and I certainly hope Mr. Green doesn't throw you out before he hears your proposal. I have a feeling it's exactly the kind of thing Rudy would be very interested in indeed."

Chapter Twelve

"Rudy, I don't think this is the best time for our chat."
Alexander smiled at Dani, Dani grinned back, and
Rudy wanted to cry. Torn between strangling the
blonde and throwing himself at Alexander's feet.
Rudy knew there was only one thing to do: beg. Mur-
der should be a private matter.

"Senator Grant," Rudy spread his arms wide, a grin
both charming and nervous plastered on his face,
"come on, we just started. You haven't even seen the
agency! Green Advertising is . . ."

Alexander stopped him with a proffered hand. "I
know what Green Advertising is, and I'm not disappointed." Grant eyed Dani who eyed him right back.
Alexander chuckled appreciatively, his eyes back on
Rudy. "Yours must be an exceptional firm if you have
beautiful women beating down your door to work
here. So, given the choice, I'd defer to Ms. Cortland if
I were you." Alexander gave Rudy's hand a com-
manding shake. "Perhaps we could continue this evening? Eight. My place. I'll leave the address with your
receptionist. We'll have drinks and discuss . . ." One
last look at Dani, long enough to undress her with

those grey eyes of his and put her back together. ". . . the future."

"That sounds great, Senator. Sure," Rudy enthused, wiping away the beads of sweat on his upper lip. He followed Alexander to the outer office, flattering him shamelessly. "I'll bring Ms. Prince. She might be able to answer any questions about . . ."

Alexander turned slowly; still, Rudy was brought up short. He stepped back, quieted easily by a look from the Senator. "That won't be necessary, Rudy. There are certain things we should discuss man to man. We must be sure you and I are well suited before committing campaign funds to your agency."

"Hey! Senator, no problem! Man to man. Right." Rudy danced from one foot to the other, stuffing his hands into the pockets of his trousers, grinning like a fool. Grant's smile was much smaller, almost bemused.

"Coral said you were an interesting man. It wouldn't surprise me if we were actually doing business soon."

With a nod of his head he wished Rudy good-bye. Rudy grinned appropriately until the door was shut. Falling against it, he banged his head gently once, twice, three times on the wood, counting the minutes until Grant would be out of earshot. When it was safe he pushed off, his anger barely under control.

"Serina, open the door. I'm going to toss that broad out of here feet first."

"Oh, Mr. Green," Serina moaned.

But it was no use. Rudy had already slammed the door to his office with such force Serina's desk shuddered. At the reception desk she covered her face with her hands, quietly waiting for the sounds of violence she was sure would ensue. She knew the signs. For

141

eighteen years she'd had enough of her parents' anger to last a lifetime.

Rudy leaned against the door, his body tense, his stomach knotted against the murderous thoughts careening through his head.

Dani was neither perturbed by his anger nor embarrassed by her ill-timed entrance. Instead she looked him over, then checked out the office before finding the key to opening a meaningful dialogue. It came in the form of a framed advertisement. She plucked it off the wall and flicked one nail against the glass.

"Nice work. Too bad your agency didn't do it," she said flatly. "This is a very big no-no. Leading people to believe this is your stuff. Shame on you, Mr. Green."

Rudy was on her in two long strides, grabbing the frame, cradling it possessively. "I don't know who you are, but I'm going to call the police and have you arrested for trespassing. Then I'm gonna call my attorney and slap a suit on you so fast your head will spin."

"Really? And just what are you going to sue me for? Walking into your office?" Dani laughed, admiring his attitude, knowing she had the upper hand.

"How about harassment? Loss of business? I'll sue you for . . ." Rudy sputtered, unable to think of anything more vile.

"And I'll sue you, Mr. Green, for fraud. You are misrepresenting your agency to potential clients. That," she pointed to the frame in his hand, "was created by me eight years ago when I was a fledgling art director. It certainly has class, doesn't it, Mr. Green? I can't believe you try to convince people this two-bit agency can create that kind of advertising.

142

Wouldn't it be interesting to walk around this office and figure out what you actually created and what you stole, Mr. Green?"

Dani grinned, baiting him with her sarcasm, deflating him with the truth, feeling powerful before remembering how much she needed Rudy Green. Moving toward him she took the frame and put it gently back on the wall while she backtracked.

"Look, I don't want to sue you. We've all done things like this. When I first started out I used to put every ad I even looked at in my portfolio. It was my agency, right? But I never claimed work from outside my agency. Too dangerous. Heads have rolled for that kind of behavior. For less, in fact."

Dani paused, thinking of Sid and her own predicament. Her head had rolled for much less as far as she was concerned. Stepping back she viewed the picture, straightened it, then walked over and sat on Rudy's couch while he circled around to the desk. Dani flicked a nonexistent speck of dust off her linen skirt and made herself comfortable. Spreading her arms over the back of the sofa she grinned.

"A lecture on ethics I don't need, Miss . . ."

"Oh dear, I forgot. I haven't properly introduced myself. It's Cortland. Dani Cortland. I recently worked at Pregerson Advertising."

Dani leaned forward, offering her hand. To his credit Rudy simply raised one dark eyebrow rather than falling off his chair. He also didn't take her hand; Dani could accept that.

"I've heard of you," was all he said.

"I'm flattered."

"Don't be," Rudy drawled. Dani ignored him.

"You probably didn't hear I'm the forgiving type though." Dani chuckled and cocked her head toward the wall and the pirated ad, covering her anxiety. This guy was small potatoes, but if he threw her out it was all over. Dani sighed and shook back her hair. She could feel Rudy Green relaxing. The imminent danger was past. Now there was only the electrical charge of wary curiosity.

"Actually, I don't mind if you display my work, because I intend to be creating more of it. And I intend to be creating it here."

"Bull," Rudy barked, hardly able to believe what he was hearing. "You run a potential client out of this office, catch me in a slight breach of professional etiquette, and you expect me to give you a job? That's rich, lady. But since this has been a really interesting conversation, and you're not bad to look at, I won't throw you out right away. I'll give you a couple of more reasons why I can't hire you.

"First, I haven't got enough to pay for your cab fare back to the airport. This agency is sitting on bills, praying to collect on outstanding invoices, and the only ray of hope on the horizon is the man you just sent packing."

Rudy held up two fingers as if she was a slow child. Dani smiled and battered her lashes, unphased by his indignation. Rudy rolled his eyes.

"Second, I don't need a creative director. This is a small shop. I got an art director. He may not be the swiftest, but I pay him reasonable dollars and he doubles as a production artist. He makes changes when I ask him to, he doesn't fight with the clients." Rudy leaned forward. "Lady, what more could I want?"

Dani matched his posture, her blue eyes twinkling triumphantly. She clasped her hands around her knees, looking like a gorgeous little girl with a very big secret.

144

"You could ask for award-winning ads on your walls to replace those hijacked ones. You could ask for respect from an industry that doesn't even know you exist. You could ask for accounts that have budgets in the millions not the thousands. You could *be* someone, not just pretend to be."

Rudy licked his lips, torn between reacting to her insults or her promises. He chose the promises.

"What if I want those things? You got a magic wand you're going to wave and the world falls at my feet?"

"Hire me and I'll make sure you get them."

"How?"

A tremor coursed up Dani's spine. She fought back the hope, buried the desperation. Blake's image flashed in her mind and the tremor traveled to her heart, resting deep in her chest, warning her that what she was about to do was wrong. She almost stopped. For an instant her eyes closed. When they opened again the sparkle had dimmed, her decision had been made and there was a tiny tear in her heart.

"I know what Dailey's going to show to Apache Shoes. I can do better for half the budget. I can land the Apache Shoe account for you."

Rudy watched Dani in silence, his eyes locking with hers. Then came a shaky cackle of disbelief. He slapped the top of his desk.

"And I'm Cary Grant."

He shook his head, still chuckling. He glanced away and then slid his eyes back again. He eyed her, searching for her halo or the hidden camera.

"What's in it for you?"

Dani felt faint. He was biting. She talked fast as much to inform him as to keep herself from kissing him for giving her a chance.

"I want you to foot the bill for the presentation. I'll

145

work here without salary. You'll have to find a place for me to stay. I haven't got any cash to spare. Things have been tough the last couple of months. Suffice it to say I intend to regain my momentum with this one, and I'll take you with me if you're willing to risk a little cash and a lot of elbow grease."

Dani breathed deeply, pacing herself, terrified to speak of failure now that a small success was on the horizon. Steeling herself for a lightening bolt from on high, she took the plunge and presented the worst case scenario.

"If we don't land the account, I'm out of here sticking you with bills you would have been stuck with anyway. If Green Advertising is awarded the account then I'm made a full partner. No cash contribution, but I lay a five million dollar account at your feet. What do you say, Mr. Green? Do we have a deal?"

Do we have a deal? How in the hell was he supposed to know. Rudy crumpled in his chair. Its back was loose and tipped a little too far. He put his foot out to steady himself, fussing just long enough to really give this thing some quality thought. This was almost too good to be true. Either way he came out smelling like a rose. There was only one thing he wanted.

"I'll agree on one condition. You sign the partnership papers before we actually present to Apache Shoes. I can have them here first thing in the morning."

"I'll want to see the books," Dani countered.

"No problem," Rudy grinned, "look all you want. They won't get any better. We're in deep shit. You sign the partnership agreement now. That way if we lose you're responsible for half the debt. If we win you still have what you want."

"Why would I do such a stupid thing?"

146

"Because you're that desperate . . . and so am I," Rudy shot back. He'd been in her situation enough times to read the signs. She wasn't as cool as she thought and he wasn't as stupid.

Dani's smile faded, her shoulders sagging slightly. The light at the end of the tunnel was pinched out, but only for an instant. Energy surged back and she was ready to sell her soul for a chance to get what she so desperately needed—she wanted her life back and Rudy Green could give that to her. She'd already sold Blake out, now payment was due in the form of Rudy Green's proposal. Why not? She would use her frustration, her humiliation and her talent to get what she needed to survive and she'd worry about everything else later. Dani was up, holding out her hand, looking Rudy in the eye until his hand was in hers.

"You've got a deal—partner."

"Rudy. Nice to see you. May I introduce Eric Cochran, my aide."

Eric nodded. Rudy did the same. Alexander shut the door, but it was Eric who herded Rudy into the living room.

"Drink?" Eric motioned to the bar in the newly refurbished room. Gone were the chintzes, replaced by nubby raw silk in muted colors suited to a man of Alexander's station.

"Sure thing. Scotch, bourbon, whatever as long as it's straight up." He gave a little laugh and looked around as he slowly made himself comfortable taking time to size up the Senator's digs.

The house was big, and on plenty of land—worth a pretty penny in L.A. The furniture was newly covered, a few antiques scattered about. Good taste. Nothing

147

outlandish. Easy on the eye. Comfortable. The senator, though, was another matter. Enigmatic? Eccentric? Bored? Rudy didn't have a clue.

Scotch in hand, Rudy took a sip and wished he was home trying to figure out what in the hell he'd gotten himself into with Ms. Dani Cortland instead of having a boys night out with a politician. What had seemed manna from heaven had quickly turned into a fireball from hell.

Lora had blown a gasket when she'd found out about Dani. Rudy had expected congratulations, or at least relief that there was hope for the Apache account. Instead good old Lora acted like he just dug her grave and was helping her in. Ranting and raving the minute she got him alone, Lora made it clear she should have been made partner after giving him the best years of her life, the best of her thinking. He was an ungrateful wretch, a miserable excuse for a man, a wimp swayed not by clear headed thinking but by tits and ass. That was when Rudy decided the time wasn't right to ask Lora to take Dani in. So he'd silently taken all she'd dished out, slinking out of the office only after he'd heard her leave.

"Rudy?"

Rudy shuddered, startled by Alexander's voice and touch.

"Yes? I'm sorry, I just drifted off for a minute."

"Understandable," Alexander chuckled, "after the day you had. I was just asking you what happened to that woman who barged into your office. I've told Eric what an extraordinary experience that was."

"Advertising is an industry of drama, all right," Rudy said. He brightened, thanking God he had something good to report about that most embarrassing situation. "Yes, Dani Cortland. She's an incredible

148

talent who will be a full partner in Green Advertising."

"Isn't that just a tad unusual, even for advertising?"

Rudy's scoff was immediately drowned in his scotch. Everything was peculiar right now.

"Green Advertising *is* a tad unusual," he said, realizing he didn't care about impressing the Senator. Compared to Apache Shoes, Senator Alexander Grant's re-election budget was probably small potatoes. Yesterday producing glow-in-the-dark posters and cheap television spots would have sent Rudy into the throes of ecstacy. Tonight it was just more grunt work.

"I see." Alexander glanced Eric's way and Rudy could have sworn it was a look of triumph. "That sounds a bit disreputable."

"You could call it a lot of things," Rudy answered cautiously, feeling the wind shift.

"If it were, would you tell us?" Eric jumped in, prying at the opening Alexander had chipped away. It was then Rudy's antenna went up, his feelers out. These guys didn't just want to talk about Day-Glo signs. So Rudy put his vest on and decided to play his hand close.

"You show me yours, I'll show you mine," Rudy answered, before indulging in a drink and a direct look into the grey eyes of Alexander Grant. Rudy had issued the invitation, he was ready to hear more.

"Interesting. A careful man. I like that." Eric looked down and swirled the ice cubes in his drink then speared Rudy with a sharp look. His mouth was moving and all the nice things were coming out of it, but there was a tone, an ominous pitch that intrigued Rudy. This guy was good.

"Rudy—you don't mind if I call you Rudy?—Senator Grant has to be very careful about who he confides in also. You're very much alike in that way. We respect that. There are many people who would treat a Senatorial confidence, shall we say, lightly. Considering how you feel about your business, we assume you'd be circumspect about your clients."

Rudy nodded, trying to understand exactly what the kid was telling him. "I'm pretty tight lipped if that's what you mean."

"Exactly. That's exactly what I mean." Eric beamed, but Alexander warned him to composure with a glance. Eric came at Rudy again, speaking slowly, choosing his words carefully.

"Rudy, we're looking for more than someone to advise us on advertising. We want a teammate. Someone we can trust to do a job efficiently, quietly, and without question. Someone who can roll with the punches and still give us one heck of an advertising campaign. The kind of campaign that can reelect Senator Grant to a full term."

Here it comes, Rudy thought, the pitch for free advertising. A tax deductible contribution. He was ready to make a graceful exit when Alexander, who had stood wordlessly in a darkened corner of the room, walked forward and stood right in front of him.

"Rudy. I need the works: advertising, public relations, image consulting. I need it fast and I need the best. Unfortunately the best isn't available to me because of certain restrictions that I must impose upon myself due to the high profile of my contributors. So, Rudy, I have to rely on an agency, a man if you will, with street smarts," he deferred to Rudy. "I need someone who can get the job done in a way that perhaps more reputable firms would not understand."

Rudy was half out of his chair, fist clenched by his sides. His agency might not be one of the big five, but

150

it sure wasn't a shady little hole in the wall. He didn't care if this dude was President of the United States. He didn't need to sit here and take this shit. Almost eye level with Alexander, almost ready to tell him what he thought, Rudy reigned himself in as he heard the rest of Alexander's little speech. Slowly he sank back on to the sofa, all ears.

"In return for such help, I can promise you that you will be well taken care of, Rudy. Very well taken care of, indeed."

There was something in those grey eyes that said the guy wasn't kidding. Two offers he couldn't refuse in the same day. Rudy Green's luck was changing. It scared the shit out of him, but you only lived once. Rudy didn't smile, he held himself at the ready. After one long drink he swiped at his lips with the back of his hands.

"What exactly is it you have in mind, Senator Grant?" Rudy asked, holding his now empty glass toward Eric who rose to refill it immediately.

Alexander flipped out the lights in the hall, the living room, and kitchen before he turned on the security system and made his way wearily to the bedroom. There he walked directly to the huge bed that had been his mother's, sat down heavily, and turned on the low bedside lamp.

Behind him Coral turned under the sheets. Her hands were on his back, her nails raking lightly over his shirt as she pulled herself out of sleep.

"Did he go for it?" she mumbled in a voice husky and heavy with slumber.

"Was there any doubt?" Alexander's laugh was listless.

"Guess not." Coral wrapped her arms around his waist and snuggled closer. As always her nakedness was exciting, but tonight his body betrayed him. He was exhausted, too tired even for Coral. He slipped out of his shoes while she murmured on. "Had him pegged the first day he walked into the karate school. Fast talker looking for a fast buck. Shallow, shallow, shallow . . ." She yawned and he unzipped his pants. She fingered his skin as he bared it, sleep waning, energy growing. She sighed. "Still, if he can help I'm glad. Did you tell him you wanted him to hire some new creative types to help out on your stuff?"

"Yeah. He didn't like the idea. He thinks I'm hiring him for his expertise despite the fact that I was actually honest with him. He swears this new woman is the only creative mind we'll need."

"The one you saw today?"

"Um-hmm," Alexander unbuttoned his shirt and slipped it off.

"Just make sure her mind is all you use . . ." Coral's nails dug into Alexander's back. He flipped around and grabbed her wrist so suddenly it frightened her. That surprised Alexander but no more than his delight at having caused that spark of fear deep in her eyes. He hated being tied down. He'd had enough of that with Polly.

"Don't tell me you're jealous, Coral. That's an absurd emotion."

"Of course not." She twirled her wrist out of his grasp, her eyes defiant now. "Just protective."

"Only when I'm here with you, Coral, remember that."

"I think you're mistaken, Alexander," Coral cooed. "I think you're mine wherever you are. I just haven't done my best to convince you of that yet."

152

"Maybe you should work a little harder then."

"Maybe I should," she answered as her arm wound around the back of his neck and she pulled his face down toward her.

Alexander, fueled by the memory of the feisty platinum-haired woman who had stormed into Rudy Green's office, closed his eyes as his mouth closed hungrily over Coral's, exhaustion banished. He imagined her body was slimmer, her hair shorter, her face more chiseled. He imagined she was that woman and the fever in him grew.

Roughly he pushed away the covers and found Coral naked and wet, ready for him. In another moment he lay atop her, taking her roughly and happily, knowing that it would never be he who needed her the most. Soon, he promised himself, he wouldn't need anyone or anything at all.

Chapter Thirteen

"Jesus Dani, don't you ever sleep?"

Rudy stood in the hallway, scratching his shoulder and twisting away the night kinks in his neck. His boxer shorts were pale blue, the most conservative morning attire Dani had been privileged to see. In the early days of their very platonic co-habitation, he insisted on showing himself off in the briefest of briefs colored fire engine red or passionate pink. One pair even had a see through quality that actually captured Dani's attention for a split second. Who was she, after all, to ignore a reasonably attractive male? Especially one who seemed to be destined to head a pretty hot advertising shop.

In the two weeks since Dani's arrival, Rudy had signed not only Senator Grant but the industrial division of Radison Chemical too. Things were rolling right along. Now all they needed was Apache Shoes to round things out. After all, the Senator would disappear after the election and Radison Chemical was only good for a brochure or two.

"Rudy, why can't you get dressed before you start walking around in the morning?" Dani asked, adding another stroke of the marking pen to the third frame of the Apache storyboard.

"Just because I have a house guest who's a prude doesn't mean I have to change my ways," he complained, his voice sleepy and cranky like that of a big kid. "This is only temporary may I remind you. I must have been crazy to let this happen in the first place."

"Part of the deal, remember?" Dani said, ignoring his petulance. "Lora would have burned in hell rather than take me in, and Serina, sweet thing that she was to offer, only has a studio. So it was your place or you pop for a hotel. Tell me, was there ever any question as to where I'd end up?" Dani glanced his way, grinning, thoroughly amused.

"Yeah, yeah." Rudy ambled past her to the kitchen. Stoneware clanged against tile, a pot was lifted and replaced. Seconds later he was back in the living room, his eyes a bit brighter. He collapsed into a barrel chair, trying to focus on Dani's work.

"Thanks for offering," Dani drawled.

"Uh?" Rudy looked at his steaming mug. "Sorry." They sat in silence for a few minutes before Rudy was fully in control of his senses. "So?"

"So why doesn't this television spot look right, Rudy?"

Rudy gave a sleepy eyed look at the storyboard and mumbled, "She's wearing the fucking shoes. Nobody, and I mean not even a babe like that, could look good in those things."

"Rudy! Rudy, Rudy, Rudy," Dani breathed. "I think you're right!" Dani was up on her knees holding her fingertips over the feet of the woman in the illustration. She sat back and closed one eye, seeing a vision. Her face flushed with excitement and the ideas started rolling again.

"You know something else, it's not upscale enough. Take off the Indian maiden's shoes, put them beside the stream, here," she poked at the storyboard, "then we've got the Indian maiden slipping out of a long fur coat, something wild and dangerous looking, just before she steps naked into the river and . . ."

"Broads don't wear fur anymore. Haven't you heard? Nobody's supposed to kill animals." Rudy yawned and rubbed his eyes. "You're not supposed to eat 'em, test 'em or wear 'em."

"Okay, okay. I forgot about political correctness," Dani pulled a face. "How about this: the fabulous looking babe holds a pair of shoes up to the sun—really graceful, long fingers, great chest—the sun's setting . . . no, no the sun is rising . . . she's illuminated, she lowers them, and lays them on the ground in front of her. The ground is an indistinguishable color in the bright sunlight, we only know the woman is outside because there are plants around. A slow-motion pan and we see that she's really lounging in this incredible bed, and the plants we thought were forest are indoor trees around the bed. The woman turns onto her stomach, she cradles her chin in her upturned palm and looks through the open French doors. We see the Eiffel Tower . . ."

Dani bit her tongue. The Zelostis would have just seen the Eiffel Tower, a suggestion made by one of the country's leading photographers, Blake Sinclair. Why couldn't she keep him out of her mind until this was finished? Quickly she changed the rhetoric.

"Make that the pyramids. We bring the music up, then back down again and the voice over says: Apache Shoes. Created in America for worldly women. Oh my God, it's marvelous."

Dani's laughter trilled as she sat back on her heels,

156

elated by her story. She saw the finished spot—and triumph—in her mind as clearly as she saw the room around her. Rudy had to hand it to the lady. She was a visionary and even more underhanded than he in some ways. What she called using an advantage, Rudy called selling out her ex. Of course he hadn't told her that when she ran through the Thanksgiving scenario with the photographer to convince him her information was solid. Rudy had just nodded and listened and thanked God she wasn't his type. That way he'd never be the schmuck in her life. Love and lust weren't on the agenda where Dani Cortland was concerned, but Apache was.

"I thought you said the key to beating Dailey was to make our spot cheaper than theirs. Now we're doing the same thing they are. We can't send a crew to Egypt any cheaper than Dailey."

"Don't be absurd," Dani chided, peeved she would even have to explain this to him, "we're not going anywhere. This is a studio shot. All we need is a decent photographer and a really good set designer. It will look as good as Dailey's shot. The entire production can be brought in for under twenty thousand. Blake charges that for shooting the kind of location campaign they're presenting."

"Sounds like a guy you should have held onto."

"Rudy," Dani pushed herself off the floor gathering the storyboards. The last thing she wanted to talk about was Blake. "Is money the only thing you think about?"

"No. I think about the things money can buy and sex. Two things that never seem to be on your mind."

Dani twirled toward him, her silk dressing gown fluttering open, revealing a long, long expanse of leg then closing before Rudy had a chance to fully appreciate the view.

"I'm as healthy as they come in both respects. I just have a lot on my mind right now and so should you. In a few weeks Green Advertising is going to be hotter than a barbeque on the Fourth of July."

"Looks that way," Rudy agreed, a tone of fearful hope tinting his confidence. Dani ignored this. One moment of indecision and they were lost.

"Apache will just be the icing on the cake. In fact, a press release on Radison and Senator Grant should go out before we present to Apache. That will give us marvelous credibility."

Rudy buried his nose in his coffee cup and mumbled, "Senator Grant doesn't want a release to go out on the assignment."

"Don't be ridiculous," Dani said, knowing what was good for the agency was good for their client. "He hired us to get his name in print. Telling the world we'll be handling his advertising means his name will be in print."

"No, Dani." Rudy stood up abruptly, a bit of coffee sloshing out of his cup as he came fully awake and nasty. "I don't want to screw around with this. He knows what he wants. He isn't some fluffy headed guy selling shaving cream to blue collar workers. I'm new in this area, and so are you. We do what he wants. Period."

"And I have an opinion," Dani maintained. "Or have you forgotten that I'm a partner?"

"It would be hard to forget since you seem to have taken over just about everything in the agency, not to mention my home. But you're a forty-nine percent partner so my word is still final. Or didn't you read the fine print on the contract you signed?"

"I read it," she snapped before retreating, still not secure enough to push the envelope. "I just thought you'd like to take advantage of my experience with Pregerson and use it to your benefit."

Dani tilted her head, magnanimous in her righteousness, assuming her partner would be cowed. But Rudy surprised her. He came closer, the scent of night still lingering on his near-naked body. He put his face close to hers, smiled and demolished her.

"But you ain't playing at Pregerson now, are you Ms. Cortland? The only reason you're my partner is because no other shop would have you. So what makes you think you're any better than me? This is my pond. I know how to swim in it. You want to drown? Fine. Go talk to Grant and see us lose his business. I'm going to shower."

With that Rudy walked out, leaving Dani feeling defeated. The door to his bathroom slammed and the excitement of the Apache campaign quickly died. Rudy had merely underscored the obvious. But he couldn't have wounded her more effectively if he had taken out a knife and buried it in her gut.

Dani hiked the storyboards tighter into her arms and escaped to her bedroom. An hour later she was dressed, revived, and ready to go. What happened between her and Rudy was a spat between new friends, fledgling business associates. She'd apologize. They'd both feel better.

Yet, when she knocked on Rudy's door there was no answer. He was gone and she was alone in a place that didn't belong to her, in a city she didn't know, with friends far away and ignorant of her mission. For an instant Dani was afraid, envisioning her life always like this—alone and lonely. It was then that Dani made her New Year's resolutions. She would apologize to Rudy and keep her mouth shut the next time she saw Senator Grant. She would wrap up the spec work on the Apache presentation and be back in San Francisco by Christmas Eve where she would make this a Christmas to remember for Blake. And, when it was all over, when Apache was in the bag, Dani swore to herself that she would think before she spoke, before she acted, before she ever hurt anyone again. After all, she wasn't cruel or ruthless. She only did what she had to do. Unfortunately, Rudy—and Blake—just hadn't figured that out yet.

Lora Prince was mad, no doubt about it. Dani Cortland's sudden appearance and rise to savior status pissed her off royally. Rudy didn't even have the time of day for her now that the Apache Shoe review was coming up and two new clients had signed on. But what did Dani have to do with any of that? She, Lora, had done the grunt work on Apache. Radison Chemicals was a loser if she ever saw one and the Senator wasn't good for a large or consistent budget. So big deal. Dani dressed good, had a bit of class, drew a fine storyboard. Well, two could play at that game too and Lora had taken her best shot at two out of three. New hair, new clothes. When Dani Cortland got bored and took her marbles home, Rudy would see a brand new Lora.

With a final swipe of her too-orange lipstick Lora patted her newly streaked, newly straightened hair, and opened the door to the office.

"Morning, Serina," she greeted, stopping at the front desk to check for nonexistent messages before calling up Serina's pity by pointing out the obvious. "No messages?"

Serina sighed. Lora would find a hundred things to do until some mention was made of the tremendous change that had been wrought. Hoping for re-enforcements and knowing none were on the horizon, Serina swiveled away from her typewriter, pushed her glasses up her nose, then fingered the naked rubber band that pulled her long hair severely away from her face.

"Your hair looks real nice, Lora," Serina said quietly, with as much sincerity as she could. She even managed to keep her eyes on Lora's and put a small smile on her lips.

"I thought it might be time for something new," Lora laughed, relieved that Serina noticed and trying desperately not to let on how much this meant to her. She tugged at the skirt of her almost-designer suit. "Feels great, you know, to do something different. You ought to try something like this, Serina. You're really a pretty girl, but you should wear make-up and stuff. It would really help and, in this business looks count, believe me."

Just as Lora was flipping her new, straight hair behind her ears Dani opened the door and breezed into the office.

"Morning ladies. Rudy here yet?"

Dani stopped at the desk too and flipped through the message center, plucking a pink slip out. She looked up expectantly, unaware the silence was heavier than usual. Serina cleared her throat.

"He's in his office."

"Good," Dani said. Then, smiling at Lora, "You really went all out, didn't you? Looks good."

"Just a few changes," Lora sniffed, painfully aware that for all her work she was no more than a caricature of Dani Cortland. Even more painfully aware that Dani was being gracious. Turning abruptly away, her

161

voice tight against resentment and embarrassment, Lora left them.

"I'll be in my office. When the gift baskets come in from Nordstroms give me a call, Serina."

"Sure thing, Lora," Serina muttered, keeping her head lowered so Lora wouldn't see how sorry for her she was.

Dani leaned close and winked at the girl. "Trying is half the battle, Serina. Nothing else really matters in this world than that you do the best with what you have. If you ever stop trying, you might as well pay for your plot."

"Sure thing, Dani," Serina said softly, just before her boss disappeared into her office calling to Sam as she went.

Yet Serina continued to watch the door through which Dani had vanished; she strained to hear her voice coming through the thin walls. But Dani Cortland was working, lost in creating advertising and Serina, though forgotten, could not forget Dani. For the first time in her life Serina wanted to be more than she was. Vowing that someday, she would be someone, mean something in the world, Serina went back to her work feeling better than she had about herself in a very long while.

"Is that the last of them?"

Dani leaned back in her chair, exhausted.

"I think so," Sam replied, gathering up the storyboards and tucking the huge pieces of cardboard under his arm. "They look good, Dani. I'm really proud of this work. Never thought I'd say that about anything we did in this agency. Even if we don't get the

Apache account, it's been neat knowing we can pull something like this together."

Dani smiled. Tired though she was, the young production manager's comment meant a lot. If this kept up, Papa would be put in his place once and for all. Not to mention Sid Pregerson, the old lech.

"Thanks Sam. That means more than I can tell you."

He nodded, not having the foggiest idea where he should go from there. Deciding not to press his luck, he took off to put the last touches on one of the boards. He was going to make this look even more perfect than Dani could imagine.

Putting her head on her desk, Dani closed her eyes and rested, her thoughts rambling. Had Serina managed to chart the objectives and strategy section of the presentation booklet correctly? Were her San Francisco plants still alive? Had Blake revised his presentation? Did Blake miss her the way she missed him? Feeling the tingling and temptation of sleep, Dani forced herself up, tossed back her hair, and went to fetch another cup of coffee. She was yawning, rotating her sore neck when she walked through the door of the coffee room unaware at first that the room wasn't empty.

Rudy and Senator Grant were sitting at the room's small table, their heads together, their talk quiet. Two pairs of eyes shot up and glared at her as soon as she walked through the door. Dani's sensors were quickly up. She'd seen looks like that before. This was private.

"Excuse me," she muttered, nodding their way. "I didn't know you were here. I'll be out of your way in a second."

"No problem," Rudy muttered petulantly. Alexander recovered nicely, inclining his head as though it were an invitation into the public place.

Dani scurried past them. Curious as hell, she lingered with the pot, hoping they might strike up their conversation again. But it wasn't to each other they spoke, it was to her.

"Ms. Cortland?" Alexander Grant waited for her to look at him before continuing. "Rudy's been telling me that all I need to win is a blanket television campaign. I was wondering if you would agree with that? A voter's opinion if you like."

Dani sipped her coffee slowly, resting against the little counter. If *that's* what they were discussing, then she, indeed, was no better than an average voter. But she'd play along.

"Well, Senator, television's nice, but as a voter I'd wonder why nobody else was tooting your horn—say free media space, public relations that kind of thing. As a marketing professional I'd say you were crazy to blow a small budget on a scheme like that. But, then again, I'm assuming your budget is small. Rudy's keeping that information rather private." Dani endured Rudy's killer looks calmly before saving his face. "But I'm sure he was explaining it simply, and would have gotten to the intricacies if you hadn't been interrupted."

Dani flicked another look Rudy's way. Why would he suggest such a thing on the Senator's meager budget? Rudy squirmed. She dismissed him, warming to her subject. "As a woman I'd want to know more about you than what I saw on a flag waving commercial. But then, advertising is a very subjective thing."

"What would you suggest?" Alexander prodded.

"I don't know." She shrugged, trying to keep her distance from the account Rudy guarded so jealously.

"I suppose I would suggest you create an image close to what the majority of voters 'think' they want to see."

Alexander chuckled, "Become a common denominator so to speak."

"Exactly. You know, putting your research results together with what we know to be fairly standard preconceived political attitudes, should point out a path that doesn't include shooting your wad on television to get a higher profile."

Alexander laughed heartily now, "You do have a colorful way of looking at things, Dani."

She smiled at him over the tip of her cup. He was a damned good-looking man once you took the time to really study him. And those eyes were something else. Shot correctly they could be mesmerizing, even in print.

"I've been told that before," she responded.

"Top of the head suggestions?"

"Easy enough," Dani said, her tone clipped and professional once more. "I'd say use Alex instead of Alexander if you're not discussing policy. Align yourself with a celebrity backer who is known for creating warm-fuzzy feelings." Dani snapped her fingers in Rudy's direction. "What's the name of that guy who plays on that family sitcom? He's a doctor and his wife is an artist and they have ten adopted kids on that show. You know, the comedian who always gets the credit for bringing us back to old fashioned values."

Rudy thought, delighted when he came up with the answer. "Oh, yeah, Daniel Sweeny."

"That's him. Align yourself with his causes. Be seen with him if you can. You can't afford him as a spokesperson but use him anyway you can. Set yourself up with one of the powerful members of your party who's willing to speak up for you. Finally, and I don't think your going to like this . . ."

"Try me. I can take anything."

"Okay." She heaved a sigh, gave her head a little shake, and laid it out. "Reconcile with your wife. There's nothing the voting public likes more than a stable, married politician."

"Really?" Alexander raised an eyebrow. What an amusing thought. Polly would faint dead away if he asked her to take him back. Coral, on the other hand, would erupt if such a thing could be arranged.

"Really." Dani scrutinized him, surprised he would take her suggestion to heart so quickly.

"I like it. Yes, all of those are very interesting recommendations. I'd like to discuss them further. Are you available for dinner?"

"Are you asking me for a date, Senator?" Dani laughed.

"Why not? I'm still free until you send me back to my wife."

Now he was chuckling too. Dani, bright eyed, glanced toward Rudy who didn't look the least bit amused. If she had known just how much he hated the idea of Alexander Grant and her being within shouting distance of each other she would have been amazed. But Dani put his morose attitude down to juvenile jealousy and ignored him, making a date with Alexander Grant.

Later she would realize that there were many questions she should have asked: of Rudy, of Alexander, and of herself.

166

Chapter Fourteen

"That's it. The last straw, goddammit! Taking over my account!" Alexander was gone and Rudy raged, dogging Dani as she headed back to her office. "I'm getting just a little sick of this, lady. You storm in here, demand a job, promise me the moon. So far all I've seen is you strutting around here like a peacock. You spend a fortune on a spec campaign. For Christ sake, you moved into my place rent free and now you take over my fucking account after I told you hands off! Just who in the hell do you think you are?"

The pained look on Serina's face as they passed registered in Rudy's mind, but he was powerless to curtail his outrage. His voice rose, reaching an amazing octave as the office fell silent. Phones were quietly hung up and ears pricked to catch the drift of Rudy's tirade.

Lora Prince pushed aside her work and sat back, straining to catch every word. Thank God. Finally there was trouble in paradise. Maybe now Rudy would throw the bitch out on her ear and things could get back to normal. On her feet, ear pressed to the wall of her office, Lora tried to eavesdrop. Unfortunately, the acoustics stunk. Rudy's voice was still raised but muffled and Dani's was nothing more than an infuriatingly controlled murmur. Lora sat back down hoping she could at least open her door in time to see Dani leave Green Advertising for good.

"Rudy, calm down," Dani muttered, tired and disgusted with his childish behavior. "This is the silliest thing I've ever heard. Senator Grant is not your personal toy. You have to share if he says so. Alexander wants some input from me. It's that simple. Weren't you giving me lectures this morning on doing exactly what the Senator wants?"

Dani put her coffee cup on her desk and swung around it landing gracefully in her chair. Crossing her legs she took a deep breath and toyed with a pencil.

"Yeah, I remember. But what I saw going on in there didn't exactly look like business. The way you looked at him, lounging around like that, smiling that way. What is it, Dani? Thinking of offering account advice to our esteemed client on your back? That's not exactly good for business."

Dani rallied, cold and quick.

"That kind of talk isn't exactly good for our partnership, Rudy. I sleep with whom I wish and whom I wish to sleep with is none of your business. I don't use sex for business purposes—to keep it or enhance it. Period. Get your mind out of the gutter, Rudy, and get real."

"Look," he rallied, frustrated and fearful, "I know about women like you. You're only turned on by two things: power and money. Well I happen to know Alexander Grant doesn't have big bucks so it must be his power. Is that it? Is that why your going to jeopardize an account?"

"Rudy? Rudy!" Dani laughed in amazement, shaking her head and bouncing gently in her chair. "Will you listen to yourself? How am I going to jeopardize anything? I'm going to give him some solid ideas that you don't seem to be able to come up with. You're going to run the guy into the ground if you blow the budget on TV. Somebody needs to talk to him straight. If it's done over dinner, so what?"

Rudy swung away, stuffing his hands in his pocket as he checked out the view. Dani's eyes were on him and he felt her curiosity. She wasn't dumb and he was acting like an idiot. Soon she was going to start asking questions and that kind of concern he couldn't afford. Before she could poke her nose in where, as a partner, it did belong, Rudy heaved a mighty sigh and salvaged what he could of a bad situation.

"Okay." He was tight-lipped, controlled, and able to face her again. "Okay. I overreacted. I was out of line. You threw me with the wife stuff, know what I mean? His girl—the woman who steered this account our way?—well she's a friend of mine. A good friend. I don't want to see her get hurt, and I don't want her mad enough that she's going to start putting ideas in Grant's head like we're not the right agency for him."

Rudy embellished the truth easily, almost convincing himself Coral was his only concern. Dani bought it.

"Hey, Rudy, I'm sorry," Dani said, looking properly contrite. "That is a sticky situation. I didn't know there was a personal relationship involved here. Christ, for a minute there I was beginning to wonder if I should be looking over my shoulder. You made it sound like the world would end if I even talked to Alexander. I should have known better. And . . ." she paused, finding it tough to admit she was wrong, but

169

admit it she did in the name of partner relations "
. . . and I sometimes forget how hard you've worked
to build Green Advertising. I guess these last few
weeks have seemed out of control. Good for business,
bad for friendship, huh?"

Dani shrugged, endearingly chastened. Rudy's
world was changing and he was lashing out trying to
keep it the same. Hell, she'd reacted a whole lot worse
when Sid worked his black magic on her.

"Look, Rudy, I promise to stay on the edge of this
thing. But the Senator obviously enjoys dealing with
women." Dani stood up and moved around her desk,
shoving some papers aside so she could perch on the
edge. Her fingers tangled in his sleeve. He tried to
shake her off, still pouting, still worried. She hung on,
gently tugging him toward her so they could make up.
"You've got to admit I'm right? His budget can't hold
a heavy, exclusive television schedule."

"Yeah, I suppose." If the floor had been dirt Rudy
would have stubbed up a little cloud of dust. He hated
to abandon his anger. It had been rolling around the
perimeter of his mind ever since Dani showed up. Like
a cave man, he wanted to bash her over the head and
let her know who was boss. Unfortunately she was
smarter than he, so forsake his fury he must. Not sure
he could survive without Dani, he met her half way.
"You're that sure these ideas of yours are going to
help him?"

"No doubt about it," Dani answered. "But look, if
this other woman is a good friend of yours, then
maybe I'll just cool the wife thing and let him take his
chances."

Rudy shook his head and stuffed his hands into his
pocket. "Naw, that's okay. It makes sense. Just do me
a favor . . ."

"Anything," Dani said and crossed her heart.

"Just stick to the creative and leave the business stuff to me. I'll feel better. He doesn't want budget information to leak out. Politics and all. Doesn't want the competition to know what he's got . . ."

Dani held up her hands, "No problem. I won't have time to worry about his budget once Apache comes in anyway. I probably won't even be able to give Alexander the time of day." She was silent for a second, then gave the sleeve of Rudy's jacket one last tug. "Friends again?"

Rudy grinned, but it was a weak effort and he couldn't look at her until the lump in the pit of his stomach had settled. What ifs were pinging around his skull like pinballs. What if Alexander thought Dani was in on their arrangement? What if he slipped up and Dani figured it out? What if she got curious and started checking the. . . . There were lots of those nasty little questions and all he could do was hope Alexander Grant was as circumspect as Rudy was expected to be.

"Sure. Friends. Why not? Sorry. I was a little out of line. Guess I'm not use to sharing."

"Who is?" Dani responded.

"Coral's going to have to get used to it if Grant goes back to his wife."

Dani couldn't argue with that one. Smiling now at a calmer Rudy, Dani squeezed his hand and pushed herself off her desk.

"I've got work, Rudy. I'm leaving for San Francisco tomorrow so you'll have your home to yourself for Christmas. Then, January third, we walk into Apache Shoes and walk out with Mr. and Mrs. Zelosti's signatures on the bottom of a contract. Believe me, this is

171

going to be the most fabulous New Year either of us ever had. I promise."

Rudy managed a smile too. "Sure. Whatever. I've got work to do too. Just remember what I said. Creative is okay with Grant, but that's it. It's my account."

Dani inclined her head. "No problem."

"Just remember," Rudy warned again, and this time Dani thought she might have heard him growl.

"I will," she answered. Curiouser and curiouser she thought, before settling back behind her desk and forgetting Rudy the minute the door closed.

Head down, thoughts dark, Rudy headed toward his own office only to find Lora waiting for him. She picked up his pace quick as a flash, scurrying after him.

"What's going on?" she asked, pushing at her hair as though hoping she could nudge it back to its curliness. "Sounded like World War Three in there."

"Nothing's going on Lora. It's taken care of." Rudy walked on, oblivious to the new hairstyle, the new clothes, and the hopeful look in Lora's eye. Peeved, Lora followed, ignoring the slight, and anxious to hear the latest.

"Could have fooled me." Lora laughed, but Rudy didn't bite. He wasn't himself and this wasn't old times. She hated things running smoothly, hated meetings behind closed doors. There weren't any more almost-missed deadlines, no more giggling over crazy schemes, no more cutting corners. All of a sudden Green Advertising was legit, and Lora blamed Dani for taking away all the sparkle—even in Rudy.

"It was nothing, Lora." Rudy stopped suddenly.

172

Lora veered into the wall and almost bounced off it. Rudy hardly blinked. "Lora, did you need me for something?" he confronted her wearily, anticipation over Apache warring with his fear that Alexander Grant was playing with fire. There was Radison Chemical to consider, too. And on top of it all Rudy was lonely. It was all too much for a hustler like him, this feeling like he was the one being taken for a ride.

"No, Rudy. I didn't need anything. I never need anything. I just take the bones that're thrown my way and I'm damned grateful for all your scraps. Maybe we can actually have a chat sometime, go to dinner, you know, stuff we used to do before Dani Cortland made Green Advertising her personal playground."

That was when Rudy snapped. His mask of weary gloom was ripped away, revealing the beast within. Lora had hit him where he lived, it hurt like hell and he might never forgive her for it.

"Don't ever say that Lora." He leaned close and she could smell his aftershave, a more subtle scent than she remembered him using. She blinked, strangely unnerved by this Rudy who talked low and mean. A ruthless guy headed for the big time, not someone out to make a fast buck. "This is my business, Lora. It always has been and always will be. Don't ever say something like that. Don't even think it. Because if you do, you're out. Got it?" Lora stared. Her mouth opened but there was nothing she could say. He didn't mean what he said, couldn't mean it. Not after all they'd been to each other. But he got in her face and proved her wrong. "Do you get what I'm saying, Lora? Don't ever push me like that again or you are history."

Rudy turned on his heel leaving Lora openmouthed by the copy machine. Good lord this was serious. Dani had done this. She was responsible, not Rudy. Rudy loved her, Lora was sure. Maybe not in the forever-after way, but in a way that was special to them. The old Rudy would never have canned her. He wouldn't even have threatened it. Damn Dani Cortland! Damn this whole stinking place! It was as alien to her as Mars and it was beginning to scare Lora Prince half to death. After all, if she didn't have Rudy and Green Advertising, what did she have?

Twirling away from Rudy's office Lora stormed back to her own. There she brooded about the changes that had been wrought in both the agency and Rudy Green. There she listened for sounds of Dani packing, for tears, for apologizes but there was only silence. And, when Dani finally left, it was at her normal six o'clock hour. Rudy hadn't thrown her out. The queen bee was still in the hive. Serina finished typing at six-thirty. At six-thirty-five Lora Prince poured her first glass of bourbon from a bottle she intended to finish before she left the office—if she could leave the office.

"Fucking ten o'clock. Ten fucking o'clock. Ten o'-clock. Fuck this . . ."

Lora Prince was in her cups, staring at her digital clock while she swigged from her bottle. She had abandoned the glass about nine. She had abandoned any idea of working earlier than that.

"Yaa, ten fucking o'clock and one minute."

Lora half fell over her desk, a very unattractive drunk. Her color didn't heighten prettily, it flared like a pimple on prom night. Her eyes didn't glitter pleasingly, they watered, smearing her already ill-kept make-up. And, at times like this—alone, smashed and feeling sorry for herself—Lora forgot to square her

174

shoulders and hold in her stomach. She rounded off to the nearest, widest inch of chubbiness.

It was in this state that Lora abandoned her chair, desk, and digital clock to stroll through the deserted office. The only thing she hadn't forsaken was her bottle. That dangled from her fingers and was brought up with an expert swing when she wanted to wet her lips. Even Rudy, good old Rudy, didn't know that she, Lora Prince, could sock away a fifth and still be in control of her senses. Hah! At least that was something she could beat Miz Dani Cortland at. So what if there were times she couldn't quite remember those blessed hours of intoxication? She always came out of it and always managed to be at work right on time. Lora giggled, imagining what people would say if they knew about her little problem.

Unfortunately imagining took up no time at all. Lora knew exactly what people would say: 'Oh yeah?' That was about all she was worth. Not, 'Oh no, not Lora Prince? That wonderful woman?' or 'I don't believe it! How can she manage her affairs so well if she hits the bottle?'

No, nobody would ever say that about her. Swing. Swig. Sigh. She put her hand out against a doorjamb. It was Dani's office. Lora lifted the bottle. Now with Dani, it was a different story. People would be shocked if the big D had one too many. People wouldn't believe it. People would try to help the comely Ms. Cortland—bitch that she was. Well, Lora just bet that broad wasn't as perfect as she pretended to be. She bet there were all kinds of shitty things Miz Cortland was hiding. Stuff that would hurt Rudy if he knew.

Unable to think, hate, and stand at the same time, Lora stumbled against the door. It swung back and hit the wall. Frightened by the noise she pulled herself up and back as she held a hand out to steady the door and herself, finding her hate still intact. She would tell Rudy about that woman. Dani Cortland was a witch. She had seduced Rudy, her Rudy, and it was up to her, Lora, to save him . . .

Just then, as she blurily envisioned herself Joan of Arc, she heard the turn of a key. Alerted, Lora sniffled and swiped at her eyes and nose, trying to dry either or both as she desperately attempted to pull herself together.

"Rudy?" she called hopefully, hoarsely, stumbling toward the darkened outer office. There was a sloppy hiccough in her voice that couldn't be banished in favor of a bright and welcoming sound.

Heavy footsteps. It was him. Oh, my God, he came back for her! He remembered her. Good old Rudy wouldn't leave her like this. He knew she was feeling left out, and he'd come all the way back to get her. What a guy. It took so little to make her happy. All anyone had to do was notice she was . . . alive.

"Rudy?" Lora stepped forward, swiping at her still-moist nose, her burning eyes.

He'd stopped. Damn, she'd have to go to him. Maybe he couldn't find her. But he wasn't even trying. She took more steps, unsteady but moving her forward. He should be hearing her now, he should be coming to her. Instead Lora could hear him at Serina's desk. What on earth would he want there if he had come back for her? Stumbling, righting herself, Lora managed to get to the doorway. Holding on for dear life she peeked around the corner.

There, bent between the desk and the chair was a man, but it wasn't Rudy. This guy was old and gangly. When he straightened, he blinked at Lora, neither surprised by her presence nor terribly interested in it. In his hand was a wastepaper basket; in front of him was the huge bin into which he put every piece of discarded crap from every office on every floor in the stupid building. Lora's chin quivered, her eyes watered. Not tears of course, just a reaction to the surprise of seeing this guy. Hell, never tears.

"Well, sure. You're not Rudy." Lora felt herself compacting again, shrinking back to the messy little drunk she was. No matter how hard she fought it, the old janitor's eyes made it impossible to keep her shoulders square and her chin high. Those old eyes of his had seen worse than Lora, she imagined, but she knew not by much.

"Trash?" She laughed a sad and ugly laugh. "That's what you're here for? Trash?"

"Yes, ma'am," he said, eyeing Lora warily as though he should be afraid of her. She snorted.

"Well, looks like you've found the trash in this office." Lora rolled around so her back was to the door. Slowly she rubbed against it, scratching an itch that wouldn't be calmed. Her eyes closed, she talked to the janitor. He was kind enough to listen. He had, after all, all night. "Yeah, guess I'm just about as trashy as you can get around here. Bet you didn't know we had all kinds of weird things in this office. Hell, it's like a garden 'round here." Lora's eyes flew open and she waved her bottle toward Serina's desk. "There. Right there sits the prettiest little wallflower you ever saw. Doesn't say a word, doesn't even try, and she's gorgeous. Doesn't know it of course. Can't figure her out." Lora raised the bottle as if toasting the absent receptionist. "Nice kid though. Nice."

She thought about this for a moment, shook her head as if trying to shake loose another nice thought about Serina. The effort was too much so she continued on with her story.

"Back there?" Her head lolled toward Rudy's dark office. "Why that's the oak in the forest. Tall and strong and spreading his mighty branches over all of us, protecting us, letting us work for him. Yeah, a big, strong oak. That's Rudy all right."

"And there . . ." Her head jerked toward Dani's office, her lips curling into a sneer of disdain, ". . . That's the queen bee's hive. She's something that one. Can-do-no wrong, Dani.

"And me? Hell, I'm the compost heap. Yep. Trash is trash my good man. Lucky I was here when you came. Wouldn't want you to get in trouble for not doing your job now, would we?"

"No ma'am," the old man replied.

"No, ma'am," Lora repeated. "Ma'am. Thank you. I thank you for that. I toast you, my good sir." The bottle was up. It was two-thirds down. Lora thought of sharing but she didn't think there was enough. Never enough. Still, she wished she had something to give him. He was nice enough to listen. There had to be something . . .

Lora smiled. Then she grinned. There was something.

"You . . . You wait right there, my good man. Wait for me." Lora stumbled away, calling over her shoulder, arms flailing in her excitement. She had just what he wanted. In the lobby the old man heard a thump and thought about going to help. But she was staggering back before he could move his bin.

"Here! Here!" she called gleefully, dragging with her huge pieces of cardboard. "Look at this. Trash. More trash than you've ever seen. It's good trash. Look

". . ." Lora held up the big pieces and the janitor peered at them, letting his eyes slide suspiciously to Lora.

"You sure you want them tossed, Miss? They look pretty nice. Good pictures. Nice stuff."

"You think so?" Lora peered around the storyboards, cocking her head one way, then the other. "Naw. I think you need glasses. This is trash if I've ever seen trash. Toss it out and it's forgotten. If I get rid of this . . ." With a grunt Lora heaved the storyboards up and over and into the bin. The effort set her back a few steps. She recovered rather nicely if she did say so herself. She whispered, knowing the old man would keep this secret. "If I get rid of those things, I get rid of her. It's simple. Should have thought of it long . . . long . . . time ago. So there you got it. Trash. All the trash we have here." Lora twirled, the bottle knocking against the side of Serina's desk. "Now I'll be a flower again and she'll be shit. Know what I mean? Know what I mean about being walked on? The flowers and the forest and everything . . . the shit . . . everything . . . ?

"Yes, ma'am," the old man murmured sadly.

"Thought so," Lora whispered, her back already to him, her shoulders sagging. Her mind already blocking out the things she'd said, the things she'd done. Blessed blackness was coming on as it did more often than not these days. Muttering she wandered back to her office.

"That's all. No more trash here. That's all. Now maybe things can get back to normal. Rudy will want things back the way they were . . ."

When he was sure she was not coming back, the old man made the rounds, emptying every wastebasket in the Green Advertising Agency except the one in the office at the end of the hall. He'd peeked in and saw

Lora passed out on her desk. He didn't want to disturb her. A good sleep was just what the poor woman needed.

It was almost eleven and Serina knew she was being silly. How could she have spent so much money on all this junk? Spread out in front of her on the daybed was a stand up mirror, jars and pots of cosmetics, and a magazine that promised she'd be gorgeous in five minutes if she followed the directions on page twenty-four.

Leaning toward the mirror Serina tried to close her eyes and look at her lids at the same time. She had put the shadow on right but still didn't look like the woman in the magazine. Try as she might she just couldn't get it right.

Finally, knowing the next day was a working one, she packed all her treasured boxes and brushes and combs back into the plastic case she had purchased especially to keep her cosmetics, washed her face, and climbed into bed.

When the lights were out she marveled at the difference one person could make. Since Dani had come to the Green Agency everybody was different. Things worked the way they were supposed to, Mrs. Peterson didn't yell as much, Lora Prince stayed in her office and didn't make Serina do all her work anymore, and Rudy Green was kind of—she searched for a way to describe what had happened to Mr. Green. He stood taller, he didn't swagger. Rudy Green said hello so nicely in the morning, like he was looking at her for the first time.

And Serina knew that she had changed, too. Watching Dani every morning made Serina want to be beautiful. So the pots of potions and colors had been purchased and carried home. Life was changing and running fast in front of her. She would follow for a while and see where it took her.

Dani left Alexander Grant's home a little after eleven. They had dined well, conversed as though old friends and planned a campaign that would reshape the Senator's image. When he had balked, Dani wooed. When he began to cut a tangent to the road Dani was building she guided him back. When he held her hand a bit too long as she was leaving, she laughed and he did too. They were attractive people, too smart and too busy to get into anything personal. They both knew it, but it didn't stop Alexander from trying and Dani from appreciating his effort. But Blake was waiting and it was with him she wanted to celebrate the season and her own rebirth.

So, secure that Alexander Grant was on the right track, positive that the Apache account would be hers in a few short weeks, certain after such a coup she and Blake could meet on common and solid ground, Dani Cortland packed her clothes and headed out. In a few hours she would be with the man who loved her and now she could love him back. She was almost where she always wanted to be. Even Papa would have been proud.

Chapter Fifteen

"It was fabulous, Dani. A top drawer presentation. You would have loved it. Everybody was cooking. Apache Shoes is in the bag for Dailey, and yours truly will be shooting the award-winning campaign."

Blake picked up an olive, sucked the pimento out then positioned the olive between Dani's breasts. Adjusting for the break at her rib cage he narrowed his eyes and let it go. The chilly green oval bounced merrily down her naked body straight as an arrow until it hit the dip in her stomach. It veered off and rolled onto the rumpled sheets.

"Damn."

"Blake, this is juvenile," Dani complained, not knowing which she objected to more, his silly game or his constant chatter about his triumphant presentation to Apache Shoes. Christ, she should play fair. She should tell him what she was up to, but then what . . . ?

"Shush. You're absolutely no fun," Blake muttered, fishing for another olive.

"Blake, it is impossible to bowl olives into my navel. The olive isn't perfectly round and my body isn't perfectly straight. I think there's a law of physics or something." Dani lifted her head lazily, raising her martini glass for a sip before snuggling back on the pillows as another olive careened off her body.

"It's the challenge of the thing Dani. Don't breathe, that might help. No, no, tighten your stomach muscles. That's the problem. You're far too soft for my olive to stay its course. Come on, honey, for me?"

Dani giggled and sucked in her already washboard tight muscles. She closed her eyes, loving the way Blake's laugh sounded as the olive finally came to rest in her bellybutton. When she felt his lips nibbling at the olive, Dani grinned and turned onto her stomach just as the prize disappeared into his mouth.

"You're nuts," she sighed.

"And you're being incredibly mysterious." Blake rolled over and crawled under the covers, his head close to hers on the pillow, the fingers of one hand wound in her silky platinum hair.

"That's a silly thing to say," Dani murmured, setting her drink aside, turning so they were nose to nose, a hair's breadth from one another, a kiss away from the truth. She knew what was coming and wasn't sure she had the courage to lie to him face to face. It was time for diversion.

"Ever since I got here I would say I've laid myself bare in the most basic ways," she purred.

With a grin she took his hand and laid it on her hip. He ran it the length of her thigh and back again, beaming at her as he spanned the dip of her waist. His black eyes darkened, clouding with desire until Dani was sure he would be begging for mercy in the next few minutes. She would love away his questions, convince herself that Los Angeles was another life that had nothing to do with the man in bed beside her. But

Blake was persistent, and when he wanted something even Dani couldn't stop him from going for it.

His hold tightened and he pulled her close, her breasts pressing hard against his chest, her lips almost on his, her eyes cautious as those lips formed words that chilled instead of thrilled her.

"Just an observation, love, but I would say things are going very well for you. I just want to know what it is . . ." he kissed her lightly, ". . . that makes your eyes light up. I'd love to think it was my prowess, but I have a feeling there's more to it. What is it . . ." he pecked her beautiful lips again, ". . . that put the bounce in your step again, makes you shake back your hair like a horse anxious to be out the starting gate . . ." Another kiss that trailed down her neck to her breasts, then his hands were on the back of her head and she was forced to look him in the eye as he asked her to share the truth. In answer she spoke near lies.

"Shh," she whispered, her hungry mouth on his. She would tell him what he wanted to hear: she wanted him, she needed him. Dani would make him forget the questions so she could forget that the answers would hurt him. But Blake stayed her, pulling back gently on her hair until she looked at him full in the face.

"I won't shh, Dani. I know you too well and this is just too intriguing. What's going on in L.A. Is it some revenge thing on Sid? Another man?" Blake wiggled his eyebrows, joking, she knew, but still tentative in a part of his heart. "I know! You've figured a way to rig the lottery. No. Forget it. That would be too easy for Dani Cortland. You've found a leprechaun and you're holding him hostage for his pot of gold. Which one is it, Dani? Tell me about it. Tell me now . . ."

So. Here it was. Christmas Day and Blake was asking for a special present. He wanted honesty and intimacy far beyond that of the physical, and she hadn't the wealth of spirit to give it to him. It would be so right—and in a way so easy—to tell him about her adventures in L.A. And what was there to the story, really? She had overheard his conversation about Rudy Green, seen his storyboards, taken a chance. It wasn't as though she'd undermined his presentation. He wouldn't have changed a thing if he'd known of her involvement with Rudy . . . or would he?

"None of the above, darling," Dani answered idly, pulling away from him to lay on her stomach and rest her head in the crook of her arm. She closed her eyes, words of admission on her lips. Unfortunately, it was easier to sidestep then walk head on. "I'm doing speculative work. If something comes of it, good things will happen. If it doesn't then no harm done and I'm back to square one. But at least I'm working."

"My how things have changed," Blake teased, his finger running up her spine before his hands stretched over her shoulders and he began to knead. "It used to take a client with a couple of million and the promise of more to make you glow like this."

"Well now it doesn't, okay? All right? Some people have changed, Blake. Some people's lives aren't just full of triumphs, one right after the other."

Quickly she rolled off the bed, angered more at herself for not doing what she should than at Blake's insistent questions. Blake's arm shot out and grabbed her.

"Dani?! Hey . . ." Blake laughed, confused as he flipped his dark hair away from his eyes. Dani tried to shake him off but he tightened his grip. "Honey, what's the matter . . . Hey, I'm sorry. What did I say?

"Blake, cut it out. You didn't say anything. I just don't feel like talking about what I'm working on. You know how it is. Superstition. I don't want to jinx anything," she answered testily, wishing she could put a stop to the feelings of guilt as easily as she could stop Blake's questioning. "Besides, I'm hungry. We haven't eaten all day."

"Somehow I don't think this is about food. Come on, sweetheart, talk to me! You're acting like I've just told you your best friend thinks you're the lowest form of life. Whatever it is you're working on can't be that bad. I mean work is work. Do you honestly think I'd laugh at you if you told me?"

"I . . . Blake, I . . ." Dani reached down and grabbed his shirt, discarded hours ago in the heat of passion. She slipped into it, fingering the buttons, trying to make some sense out of the whirlwind inside her head. She'd never questioned her actions before. Dirty tricks and pirated information were part of the business. Everyone appreciated that. Yet now she felt different. Playing these games on someone she loved made Dani uncomfortable. Worse than that, she felt as if she had betrayed Blake in the most intimate sense of the word—not by what she'd done but by her silence.

Suddenly she felt so alone. Papa would have thought her silly for even considering a tip of her hand to Blake. But Papa was dead and all his conniving had brought him money, never love. If she told Blake about the last few weeks now, what would he think? Well that wasn't a tough one to answer. He would think she was trying to hurt him. Maybe if she'd told him her plan Thanksgiving night he might have encouraged her to go to Los Angeles. Now there was a history of silence and half-truths and Dani knew it was that silence that would hurt him more than anything else. This was uncharted territory and it scared her to death. God wasn't there someone to help her? Jenny?

Of course, Jenny, dear friend. Only she understood how hard it was for Dani to be Dani. Yes, only another woman could understand the need to achieve something without the help of the man she loved. Jenny . . .

Jenny nothing. Angrily Dani tried the buttons again but they just wouldn't do what she wanted. God, she was just too old for this intrigue and too smart not to realize the danger in omission. There was only one thing to do. Come clean and take her licks now. A week from now it might be worse.

"Blake, I have to tell you . . ."

"Dani, don't say another word." Blake scooted over the bed, the sheets draped artistically over him at the hip. Opening his arms, he offered her a safe haven, no questions asked. "I'm sorry. It's my fault. I had no right to pry. What you do is up to you just as what you tell me is your choice. I'm curious because it's been so long since I've seen you so happy. It does my heart good, Dani. It gives me hope. I swear, whatever you're doing, keep it up. I love having you back. I love it . . ."

His fingers wiggled invitingly, his head cocked; his eyes sparkling with the deepest love, the utmost sincerity and Dani softened, her blue eyes misting. Wasn't she incredibly lucky to have a man love her like Blake did: without question, without demands. Someday she, Dani Cortland, would love him back properly. Someday, she vowed, she would give more than she had ever received. In that moment Dani realized something she'd never been able to come to terms with. Love was amazingly generous and she had been miserly with it. The minute Apache was decided—in her favor or not—she would tell Blake what had been happening. Apologies would be the order of the day.

Now, though, Dani chose to believe that he didn't really want to know what was going on. In the quiet she saw Blake's smile falter, his brow furrow with worry, and she wanted to kiss every line away with gratitude. His arms dropped. Blake was defeated.

"How about a break, Dani? We'll just forget business, I promise. It's Christmas Day and I haven't seen you in weeks. The only thing that really matters is that you keep coming back here when you can. Now come on, come back to bed. I won't ask anymore, just show me how much you missed me these long, long weeks."

Grinning again he raised the sheet. An invitation almost impossible to refuse. Dani sauntered toward the bed, one hand clutching Blake's shirt around her middle, baring her legs and the length of her neck. The other hand plucked at the sheet. She elevated it higher and raised an eyebrow.

"My last Christmas present?"

Blake inclined his head. "Don't ever say you never get anything you can use for Christmas."

Blake's shirt dropped in a crumple of cotton to the floor seconds before she slid back between the sheets. "Never, ever will I say anything like that again," Dani murmured, her hands winding themselves around his ever growing tribute to her desirability. Blake moaned, his arms encircling her as he pulled her close. She felt so safe, as if this wiped out her deceit and made an honest woman of her. One last time that evil gremlin of guilt reared it's horrid little head and poked at her heart, pushing her conscience until she thought she would confess. Overwhelmed by Blake's love, by her own surprising need for honesty, Dani moved closer, her arms now wrapped tightly about his neck. A drowning woman clinging to life.

Dani whispered urgently, her breath hot and staccato on his ear. "Blake, I should tell you about what I've been doing. The job I'm after is . . . Well, it's actually not what . . ." Jesus, the words were hard to say.

"Dani . . . ?" Blake muttered, his hands exploring the body he knew so well. His hand cupped her behind and she was lifted atop him.

"What?" she breathed, settling in for a leisurely ride.

"Shut up," he whispered.

"Blake . . ."

But his lips were on hers and she couldn't speak. And he didn't want to hear it. Blake really didn't care what she was doing in the L.A. outback. He wanted her no matter what. Good or bad, Blake loved Dani and Dani just then was very, very good at convincing herself he always would.

Rudy Green stood in front of his Christmas tree with the pen a type company had given him. With the tip he flicked the glass ornaments on his sparsely decorated tree, trying to recreate "The Little Drummer Boy." He'd been at it for close to an hour and the challenge was waning.

Sighing, he stuffed his hands deep into the pockets of the new Ralph Lauren robe he had bought and wrapped for himself. Opening it a few hours ago he'd managed an exclamation of surprise and delight in a desperate attempt to fill the dreadful silence of Christmas Day. The older he got the more the holiday silence freaked Rudy. Clearing his throat he pulled the burgundy velour robe close to his body and flipped the hood over his head. Covered from head to toe he marched slowly around the room humming. On the third pass around the tree he figured he'd lost his mind. Rudy Green playing kids' games was not a Rudy Green he liked. Tossing the hood back he headed to the shower and ran a stream of hot, hot water over his body.

Finished, refreshed, Rudy hummed as he dressed and tried to envision all the wonderful things the New Year was going to bring, not the least of which was the respectability that would be his once Apache Shoes was on board. There would be money, awards, money, prestige, other accounts, and money, money, money. Patting his hair in place, spritzing it with hair spray, Rudy imagined the accolades he would receive, the cars he would drive, the office complex the agency would move into once they were really on their feet—no, the building he would build to house the agency. He grinned into the mirror. Everything would be his. He would make the world spin, dance to his tune, pay court. . . . But his euphoria deflated as easily as it had been pumped up. All could be lost, too, if Alexander Grant . . .

Oh hell! Dejected, Rudy tossed his brush into the sink and went back to the living room where he carefully arranged the pitiful cache of gifts under the tree: a sample sausage and cheese pack from a printer, Cooks champagne, Aramis aftershave, and a calendar of naked women from his staff. The last he put far under the tree.

Pushing himself off the floor, Rudy plumped a pillow on the couch and grabbed his car keys. What he needed was food. A good thick steak, a salad and—though he didn't want to admit it—company even if it was that of total strangers in a restaurant.

* * *

Rudy put a hand to his cheek and found it was freezing. He'd been standing in the frozen food section too long. Tossing a piece of plastic covered beef in his cart, Rudy sadly pushed on to warmer aisles.

Four restaurants he'd tried and four had been closed. McDonald's was open but Rudy drew the line at a Big Mac for Christmas dinner and the fellowship of a pimply faced teenager. So he hit the grocery store. With Christmas Muzak assaulting him he pushed a wobbly-wheeled cart up and down the deserted aisles of a local grocery that was miles from his own neighborhood.

Just as he turned down the sundry aisle, just as he felt so low he thought he might die, just when he was ready to scream, he stopped short and stared at the woman—girl, really—who was comparing the labels on two bottles of aspirin. His first instinct was to turn and run. A second later the cart was redirected, pointing right at her. Rudy Green wanted to hear a little chatter and hers would be as good as any.

"Serina?"

He was beside her now, that old Rudy Green smile plastered across his face. Startled, she turned at the sound of his voice, her hair loose, flowing over her shoulders, free of that awful rubber band. Her eyes, without her glasses, were clear and beautiful. Her body was lean and fluid as if the tension of her workday never existed. Serina looked . . . beautiful . . . and that realization softened Rudy's expression, erased the almost naugahyde shine of his tanning bed complexion.

"Mr. Green?"

Serina blinked, then scrunched up her eyes, bringing Rudy into focus. Assured that it was, indeed, her boss grinning at her in a grocery store on Christmas Day,

Serina began to wither. Her head dipped, embarrassed to be seen in torn jeans and a shrunken old sweater that clung to her full breasts and bared her tiny waist. God, if only she could fall through the floor. If only she hadn't had her Christmas headache. If only she had remembered to buy aspirin before the holidays. If only she could think of something to say!

"Yeah, it's me, Mr. Green." Rudy grinned, pushing back his jacket. He laughed slightly, shaking his head to keep himself from sounding like a fool. Either he was losing his mind or Serina lead a double life. She looked as yummy as pumpkin pie.

"Yeah." Shyly her head rolled to her other shoulder, her long hair swinging like a curtain over her cheek. In her hands the aspirin bottles were held between nervous fingers. She laughed too. "It's me. I'm really surprised to see you. Merry Christmas."

"Yeah, well, you know. I like to kind of keep a low profile on the holidays. Most people make too much of them."

"They do," Serina agreed. "Spending all that money then it's all over until the next year."

Rudy nodded heartily, knowingly, bosslike. "You got it. Everybody makes too much of Christmas."

Serina nodded. Rudy nodded. They were silent for no more than a minute but those sixty seconds were painful to them both.

"So, I don't want to keep you. I mean you've probably got stuff to do . . ." Serina said.

"Sure, I . . ." Rudy began. Before he could finish, the heavens opened above him and the spirit of Christmas fell right out of the sky and Rudy Green did something he seldom did voluntarily: he told the truth. "No. Actually, I was just picking up a steak. Thought

I'd throw it on the old hibachi and have myself a Christmas barbecue for one."

He shrugged, waiting for her to laugh, to ridicule him. But Serina smiled as if she understood, even liked him.

"That sounds good," Serina said shyly. "I love the smell of a barbecue and I never could figure out why people thought you could only do it in the summer. This is California, after all." Her smile became big and beautiful, reaching every corner of her gorgeous face as she glanced over her shoulder as though inviting him to check out the yuletime sunshine.

Rudy laughed, trying to be cool but increasingly aware of the butterflies batting around in his stomach. Damned if he was going to let a kid get the best of him. He tried to regain his footing. "Only problem is it's hard finding briquettes anymore. Bad marketing. If it were me I'd stock 'em year-round in L.A. I'd . . ."

Rudy paused, his dissertation on the marketing of briquettes seeming to hold Serina enthralled. Her eyes were wide and bright and on him with an intensity that made him shiver. When she realized he'd stopped talking she blinked, stood up straighter as though she just discovered she'd done something wrong and was hoping no one had noticed.

"Well, I guess you're right," Serina agreed shyly.

Rudy laughed. "Yeah. That and ten bucks will get you a fruit cake. Guess it doesn't matter what I think about briquettes, does it? They don't have them here. Well!" He sighed, giving her a chance to say something that would stave off the inevitable. When she didn't, he had to move on. "Anyway. I suppose I better let you go. You probably have people waiting for you."

"It was nice seeing you," Serina offered as she put

back one aspirin bottle and started down the aisle with the other.

"Merry Christmas," Rudy called.

She looked behind her, wistfully he thought. "You too."

Sadly Rudy pushed his cart the other way wondering who it was that his receptionist was going home to. A boyfriend? Mom and Dad? He imagined a fire in a fireplace, voices chattering back and forth, silly family jokes being exchanged, maybe even a carol or two sung for good measure.

To ease his loneliness Rudy grabbed a package of Ding-Dongs and tossed them in the cart, made a sharp right, and pulled up short. Serina was standing halfway down the aisle. Rudy rolled right up to her.

"I don't actually have anyone waiting for me," she said.

"My broiler can handle two steaks," Rudy answered.

Serina fell in step next to Rudy's cart. He glanced at her, thinking it strange that it felt as though she had always been there beside him.

"Yo! Rudy!" Lora brandished half a bottle of brandy Rudy's way and fell toward him the minute he stepped off the elevator. Her arms encircled his neck, the bottle clunked against the back of his head. She smelled like a distillery and felt like a two-ton albatross. The bag of groceries was smashed between them. "Merry Christmas, boss."

Stunned, disappointed, but not yet angry, all Rudy could say was, "Same to you, Lora."

He pushed her back as gently as he could, gave the bag a fluff and a hike and looked at her. Even the warmth of the brandy wasn't going to be enough to keep the chill away for Lora. Before either could say another word Serina stepped out of the elevator. Lora's jaw lost all elasticity and hung open as she stared.

Serina the receptionist? Only now the girl looked gorgeous and she was standing next to Rudy like it was her place. Lora blinked, stumbled, and put her arms out to set herself right. The brandy sloshed and Serina reached for her.

"Hi, Miss Prince," she said gently, cupping her hand under Lora's elbow the way she'd done so often for her own mother. Lora straightened and tried to focus on Serina's face, trying to remember how to say thank you. But all she saw was pretty—skin, hair, smile—and she felt worse than before. She looked to Rudy. He would understand why she didn't want this girl touching her, being here. But all she saw was the look of embarrassment and disappointment in his eyes. She wasn't wanted or needed. After all these years working with Rudy, sleeping with him when he needed her, he couldn't even pretend he was happy to see her on Christmas Day? Betrayed! That's what she was. First with Dani Cortland and now with Serina-the-goddamn-receptionist. Well, Mr. Rudy Green could just go to hell. Lora dug in her heels. She was there for the duration.

Alexander screwed Coral two days before Christmas to the strains of Eric Clapton's Crossroads album. They began their frantic grappling during "Wanna Make Love to You" and ended half way through "Midnight," enjoying a cool-down during "Cocaine." It was a sort of farewell performance. Coral was headed to the Carribean and Alexander was going back to his wife, Polly.

Polly. They had had a twenty-five year history before Alexander realized Polly's unconditional love was only a substitute for his mother's lack of it. When he finally understood that, Margaret was dead and Alexander had taken a connubial powder. His pretty wife, his please-don't-muss-me wife who adored him from afar just wasn't cutting it anymore. His priorities had changed and the picture of perfection was nothing compared to the realities of physical satisfaction. So he began to fool around. It felt great and pretty Polly was put out to pasture.

Yet, when Alexander broadsided her with his intention to separate, Polly had actually become hysterical. Real distress, authentic passion, had made her beautiful and Alexander had almost changed his mind. But the moment came and went so quickly, he stayed the course and was happier for it. Now all that was about to change. Here he was, Polly's Christmas Glug in hand, ready to beg her to return to him. It was proving harder than he imagined.

"The tree looks wonderful, Polly." Alexander nodded toward the overtinsled monstrosity. He got up, went to it. He had to look at something other than her pathetically expectant face. "I honestly don't know how you do it year after year. This may be the most beautiful tree you've ever done."

"Well, I don't have a job to keep me busy like so many women. And I don't have . . ."

Polly bit her tongue, just in time. She'd almost told him exactly what she was thinking; that she had no husband or daughter to cook or clean for any longer. But her therapist had said Alexander was not the type of man to respond to pleading. She agreed. So Polly smiled widely rather than brightly, before her brow furrowed. Lowering her eyes, abandoning her smile, she looked deep into her cup, searching for the future in the lay of the steeped cloves. Finally, Polly looked directly at Alexander, something she'd seldom done while they were married.

"Alexander, let's not play ridiculous games. You know I would have turned the world upside down if you'd wanted it. I've never made any pretense the other way. I don't hate you, I love you. I always have and always will. Now, tell me why you're here."

Alexander lowered his lashes, guarding against the sparkle of cynical amusement he felt. Poor, poor Polly. If only she knew what games he was playing. Polly would never understand the logic of his strategy nor could she perform properly if she thought this was anything other than a complete and full reconciliation. When he looked at her again it was with clear eyes, devoid of every emotion save devotion. That, at least, Polly could understand.

"All right, Polly. I won't insult you by dragging out the purpose of my visit." He stuffed his hands in his pocket and was in front of her with three calculated steps. "I came here tonight because I don't think I want this divorce. I know I wasn't kind when I left. I know that you felt you were somehow at fault. But you never were. You didn't deserve the treatment I gave you."

Alexander turned his head as though ashamed of the pain he had caused. The truth was he had never thought of her much at all after their fifth anniversary. He moved to the fireplace and fingered the stockings hung there with such care. This was a nice touch. Worthy of a politician.

"It had to do with age, with wondering if my life

197

would have been different if I had spread my wings, done things on my own rather than having a helpmate standing beside me."

He moved back to the tree, seeming to search for his way home in the bright gold bulbs. Instead, he checked the sincerity of his expression. It was perfect. He sighed. This was too easy.

"I think every man must wonder about that at times."

Alexander shook his head and laughed sadly. From the corner of his eye he saw Polly hang her head. He moved in for the kill, lowering his voice, whispering the words she so much wanted to hear.

"I know that was no excuse to hurt you. If I had only stopped for a moment—realized this might be a passing fancy." He too hung his head, a proud man brought down. "I'm so sorry, Polly. So very, very sorry."

Then they were silent. On the stereo a string quartet massacred "Jingle Bells" until the needle slid off the record. Polly rose and went to the hi-fi, a piece of machinery as sorely out-of-date as the mistress of the house. Gently she switched off the machine and went to her husband. Standing behind him she rested her hands on his back.

Facing him would have been a mistake. Her triumph would be his downfall. Goodness always won out. Goodness and patience. He had so much to be ashamed of, but she wouldn't make him pay. Polly Grant was better than that, a bigger person than he, and Alexander needed her. She would take upon herself the guilt and the pain and the blame. Her heart swelled as she thought of carrying so many important things inside her for the sake of Alexander's peace of mind. Polly lived for her husband. She would suffer for him too.

"Don't do this to yourself, Alexander," she said quietly, controlling the fluttering in her throat, the beating of her heart. "You're home now. You'll never have to go away again . . ."

Alexander twirled toward her, taking her hand in his, and burying his face in their joined fingers. Hardly a suave effort, but effective nonetheless. Polly felt a shiver pass through Alexander's body and into hers. She raised her chin even higher, proud that she could have such an effect on him.

". . . Come home," she urged softly. "Come home now. We'll forget everything."

"But so much has changed. I'm a Senator now. I'll be away so often. You have no idea the rigors . . . how lonely . . ."

"Alexander." Polly watched her husband closely, on guard against insincerity as she asked, "Do you want to come home because you miss what we had, or is there some other reason?"

Inside, deep in his gut, Alexander Grant let out a sigh of relief. He crushed her hands to his chest, leaving his conscience behind as he looked deeply into her eyes and answered. "I swear, Polly, I want to come home because I need you. You have no idea how much I need you . . ."

"Keep the motor running, be back in a minute."

"Well hurry up, Sam. We're due at my mother's in ten minutes and I don't want to be late." The young woman leaned back, flipping the gear into neutral, humming along with the music while Sam dashed across the parkway and up to the glass doors of 1800

Century Park East. Inside he saw a guard, half asleep, at the lobby desk. Making an apologetic face, Sam waited while the fat man pushed himself away from the desk and waddled toward the door.

"Sorry to bother you," Sam said quickly, "but I forgot a present at my desk. I'm just going to run up and get it real fast, okay?"

"Which office?" the guard asked, suspicious of anybody who'd want to get into their office on Christmas Day.

"Green Advertising. Fourteenth floor. Come on, be a pal."

"Got a key? 'Cause if you don't I'm not going to go up there with you. I gotta stay here and guard the lobby."

"I have a key. Won't be a minute," Sam assured him, already easing past to the desk where he signed his name before rushing to the elevator.

"Only the one on the right workin' today," the guard hollered.

Sam pushed the button and tapped his foot as if that might bring the elevator sooner. His girlfriend was ticked off as it was. She hated to be late by even a minute, but he knew all would be forgiven when she saw the gold chain he had for her. He could have kicked himself for forgetting it the day before.

Dashing into the elevator he pushed the button and stood back. Five minutes later he was in the darkened office and had his hands on the small silver box. Then, unable to resist, he went into Dani's office for one more look at the Apache presentation. Damn, wouldn't he love to be in on the meeting! Seconds later, though, Sam wasn't wishing himself at Apache or admiring the work he'd done. Sam was reaching for the phone, forgetting his girlfriend who was sitting in the car getting more pissed off by the minute.

Dani had thrown on one of Blake's shirts but neglected to button it. She was as close to being dressed as she had been all day. Despite the fog and the chill outside, she felt warm, glowing from the day of lovemaking and the heat of the kitchen. Knowing she should wait for Blake to get out of the shower but unable to deprive herself of the pleasure of being the first to taste their Christmas dinner, Dani dipped her fingers into the compote then filched a handful of celery. Taking the stuffed chicken breasts out of the fridge she was just about to finish off the seasoning when the phone rang. Ignoring it, Dani turned on the oven and hummed a little tune while she sprinkled the paprika then tied the chicken into little parchment packages. The machine picked up after the fourth ring.

"You've reached Blake Sinclair . . ." the recording began.

". . . . lover extraordinaire, fabulous in the sack, a man among men . . ." Dani adlibbed over the rest of the message, utterly delighted with herself. A minute later her smile disappeared and she was rushing for the phone, praying Blake would languish in the shower a few minutes longer. She could hear the answering machine and it wasn't good.

"Dani, it's Rudy. We've got trouble with the Apache presentation . . ." Diving for the phone she grabbed the receiver, silently cursing Rudy with every ounce of energy she had.

"Rudy, what? My God. How did you get this number? Don't you know better than to leave a message on this machine?"

201

"Shit, Dani, don't give me orders. At least not before you say hello. Blake's listed so I called. This is serious. Three of the presentation pieces are missing."

"Don't be ridiculous," Dani scoffed under her breath. "I put them in a portfolio in my office the day I left."

"Well they ain't there now and that is a fact unless Sam's suddenly gone blind. We're missing the television board, the industry growth chart, and the competitive share chart."

"This is absurd, Rudy. Those things don't just get up and walk away . . . they don't . . ." Dani paused, a horrid thought pricking at the back of her mind. "Rudy? What about Lora. Do you think she'd sabotage the presentation?"

"Dani, give me a break. What possible reason could she have for doing that?"

"I don't know but it's the kind of thing she'd do . . ."

"Cut it out." Rudy was pissed but what the heck. Something happened to that presentation and Lora was the only one who hadn't wanted a thing to do with it. She'd been causing more trouble than she was worth. What was more important: his sensibilities when it came to Lora or finding out what happened to the presentation? "Jesus. There isn't a reason in the world for her doing anything with them so drop it."

"Damn." Dani bit her lip, her eyes darting to the doorway, her mind imagining that the extension had been picked up in the bedroom. She spoke quickly, her thoughts racing. "Okay. Okay. I'm sorry. Still, those things don't just get up and walk away. I want to know how they disappeared and when I get back I'm going to find out."

"Fine," Rudy snapped back, "but in the meantime what do you suggest we do, Sherlock?"

"Not panic. That's number one. We don't panic. We can be royally ticked, but no hysteria. First, turn the office upside down and see if you can locate them . . ." Dani whispered angrily.

But Rudy was quick. "Sam already did that and he lost his girlfriend in the process . . ."

"Okay." Dani's finger found its way to her mouth. She bit down on her nail, thinking hard, finding miracles elusive. "Look, there's duplicate stats on all that stuff. Sam knows how to paste it up since he did it the first time. If anything's missing Serina has the original typed copies."

"The storyboard . . ."

"I know. That's tougher. Look, all the type houses are closed. I have an idea. I think I can get to a computer and reset type. Just make sure all the illustration stats are ready for me when I get back. Christ! I can't believe this is happening."

"You're not the only one," Rudy grumbled.

"I know," Dani answered back, her voice a hoarse whisper. She pulled Blake's shirt tight around her body as she sank into a chair near the table. Miserably she wondered if anything would ever go smoothly in her life again. Ever since her run in with Sid a black cloud had followed her. Just when she thought she'd ducked it, back it came. Dani puckered her lips and blew out a cleansing breath. "Look, I've gotta go before Blake comes out of the shower. If you can get those charts done I'll reconstruct the storyboard somehow. I've got six days. I'm going to need you to fax me the copy. I'll call you tomorrow with a safe number."

"Okay. Get on it right away. We can't go into that

203

presentation without the storyboard. We'd look like idiots," Rudy muttered.

"Don't you think I know that?" Dani railed, her stomach churning with, of all things, fear. All this work, the intrigue, for nothing. She was so close to winning and now. . . . What? What had happened to those pieces? Maybe this was divine retribution for all the arrogant thoughts she had ever had, all the deceptions she had ever executed, all the self-centered little things she could have forgone in the face of Blake's love. Whatever was happening Dani didn't like it and, if there was a God, he'd get her through this. If he did, she swore she would be different. She would be more careful, more forthright . . .

"Rudy, please, don't pay any attention to me. We'll make it and everything will look great. I've been in tighter spots. We'll do fine. Just hang in there, and call if you run into a snag. But call my place this time. I'll check my machine. I might even be there. Okay?"

"Yeah, okay." Rudy hesitated, embarrassment rife in the silence. "Dani, this means a lot more to me than I thought it did. It's not just about money anymore."

"It never was, Rudy."

"Right. See you when you get back, Dani."

Replacing the receiver Dani sat quietly for a moment, her mind racing. When she had come to what she considered a reasonable conclusion she pushed herself off the chair and walked thoughtfully into the bathroom. Blake, towel wrapped securely around his waist, was leaning into the mirror as he shaved. Dani wrapped her arms around him, cupping her body against him.

"Who was on the phone?"

Dani let her nails slide over his bare chest, kissed the hard, straight line of his backbone, lay her cheek against the broad, muscled expanse of him before she answered. The truth would be best.

"My client in Los Angeles."

"Ah, the mystery deepens . . ." Blake snapped his wrist. Dani heard the plop of shaving cream, imagined his satisfied smile as he waited for her to say more. She didn't. He wiggled his rear end, prodding her on. Then he laughed. "Are we finally going to get some specifics out of you?"

Dani chuckled half-heartedly. "I've got a presentation coming up. Whether I land the job permanently depends on it . . ." Dani hesitated, waiting for a question, just one that would make her tell him what she was doing. But all she heard was another plop of shaving cream, a satisfied sigh as he inspected his handiwork. She tightened her grip on him. He'd had his chance. She'd be honest, just not specific. "Anyway, it seems there was a little problem with a storyboard. I'm going to have to reconstruct it."

"Oh, baby, that's a shame. When is it due?" Blake bent, splashed his face, toweled it, then pivoted so that Dani was leaning against his chest. Wrapping his arms around her he smiled. "Want to see if I did a good job?" He grinned and raised his eyebrows. Dani shook her head, preoccupied with the problem at hand, pained he should want her even though she deceived him.

"The third. That's when they're due." Her wry smile was reflected in Blake's disappointed eyes.

"No way. You can't possibly get it together by then. All the typesetters are closed until after the holidays."

"I'll manage. I just won't be able to spend a lot of time with you during the next few days. I'll do some work at my place, hand letter if I have to. Forgive me?" Dani tiptoed up and kissed him lightly on the chin, wrapping her fingers through his long, damp hair.

"No. But then that never stopped you before did it?" Blake asked sadly. But the depth of his hurt was lost on her. She wasn't with him any longer.

"Maybe it should have," she whispered. For a long moment they looked at one another. Blake sensing something was wrong but unable to put his finger on it; Dani terrified she would try to set things right and screw them up even worse. She grinned and gave him a pinch and the confusion in his eyes disappeared. "No, you never stopped me from doing anything, and that's why I love you. And that's why we're sporadic roommates instead of happily married yuppies."

"That could easily be changed." Though she didn't think it was possible, he held her ever closer. His lips nuzzled into the soft spot on the side of her neck.

"Someday," Dani agreed, whispering as his lips trailed further down her body, his tongue flicking her warm skin just under the collar of her borrowed shirt. Her mind swelled with thoughts of what she should do at that moment then burst through to a plane beyond rational thinking as Blake's lips followed the swell of her breast and tracked the exquisite circumference until he had explored her like uncharted territory.

"Maybe now . . ." he breathed lifting her up, her long legs twining around him, securing her to him like a delicate vine to a mighty tree. They were together, so tight Blake no longer had the luxury of the taste of her body, her lips were all that was offered and he captured them hungrily. Dani squirmed, closer and tighter until she could feel that he wanted her as much as she desired him. In their heat he lowered her down, teasing her to passion and pulling her up again while his tongue explored the hot, sweet depths of her mouth. She pushed into him, tiny noises of discontent, a child's anger at not getting what she wanted, escaping her throat. Blake pulled back, kissing her gently, laughing at the happiness she brought him. Peeved that their love play should be interrupted, Dani lifted her hips and ground into Blake, nudging his towel until she felt it give, then fall away.

His laughter was silenced as the strength of his love took on a life of its own. In its place came the determined quiet of need and want. They both stopped playing; they both began giving. Lowering herself so that Blake could enter her, Dani realized this was a moment never to be forgotten. The moment when Dani Cortland and Blake Sinclair made the rest of the world simply disappear and all she wanted was him.

Chapter Sixteen

Dani picked up the phone before it completed its first ring. She'd been waiting for this call for days. Now it was New Year's Eve and time was running out.

"Jenny?"

"It's me," came the answer. "I think everybody's gone except James in the mail room, and he's making noises like he's out of here in about two seconds."

"Great. Nothing like the holidays to clear out an office. I kind of expected you to call earlier," Dani said hoping this sounded like a good natured protest, instead of cold panic. The last thing she needed was to have her gift horse bolt.

"Hey, what do you want from me? I'm sticking my neck out as it is," came the petulant reply.

"Jenny, I know that. I can't tell you how I appreciate it. If I could have found anyone to set this type for me I would have. But Pregerson is the only agency I know that has in-house facilities. Listen, when this agency I'm with is three times as big as Pregerson I'll bring you on board as a vice president."

Jenny laughed, the tension easing. "No thanks, Just give me solid employment—preferably in San Francisco—and I'm happy. I don't like risks."

"God you're so simple."

"You got it, and I'm going to be simply furious if you don't get down here immediately. While I may not be Bridget Fonda, there are certain guys who appreciate my charms and I'm seeing one of them tonight. So can we get this over and done with?"

"I'm on my way. Wait in the lobby and sign me in."

"You got it."

The two women rang off. Jenny made one more quick sweep of the agency to make sure no one of note was left to see Dani Cortland arrive, then went to the lobby to wait for her. Fifteen minutes later Jenny's cheek was dutifully kissed and Dani managed to chatter her thanks until the elevator deposited them in front of the agency's offices where Dani promptly froze.

Her hand gripping the briefcase seemed to lose all feeling, her knees became weak and Jenny, looking over her shoulder as she unlocked the door, saw the fear on Dani's face.

"You all right?" Jenny asked quietly, coming back and putting her arm around Dani.

Dani laughed, her voice shaking, her smile was faltering. "Sure. This is just really, really strange. I think . . . I thought this was all over . . . the jitters . . . you know?"

Jenny nodded and gave Dani a squeeze. "Yeah, I know."

Dani hiked her briefcase higher.

"Jesus I loved this place. I felt important here. Now I'm worried if I walk in there I'll find Pregerson has part of my soul."

"Dani," Jenny laughed gently, "will you listen to yourself? You sound like a gypsy talking about curses. You're giving me the creeps."

"Sorry. Can't help it."

"I'm beginning to feel a little weird myself. Let's get in and get that type set then go have a drink. I want to celebrate the New Year not Halloween, and any minute now I'm going to start seeing ghouls."

Jenny pushed open the door. Dani slid in after her, feeling no better now that they were inside. Like every other uninhabited work place, the Pregerson offices had an abandoned feeling made even more unsettling by the signs of recent life: tiny lights flashing on the receptionist's console, papers piled up waiting for attention, the smell of a cigarette snuffed not too long ago, air conditioning too cold with no bodies to absorb the chill. Dimmed lights melted into natural illumination that was diffused by the fog outside so that Jenny and Dani stood softly outlined by a silvery luminescence.

"This way," Jenny whispered, her voice urgent in the stillness. Without a word, Dani followed though she knew the way perfectly well.

In the typesetter's glass office both women settled in quietly. Dani pulled up the swivel chair in front of the impressive bank of computers, copy at the ready. Jenny flipped on the machine and the printer then stood back.

"Going to do any fancy stuff?"

"No," Dani answered, pulling out her paper and setting it to the right of the computer, "I want to get in and out as fast as I can."

"Want me to stay and help?"

With a furtive glance, Dani shook her head. Better Jenny didn't see what she was working on. No sense putting her in an awkward position. She was, after all, Blake's friend too.

"Don't be ridiculous. Go on and get your office

cleaned up so you'll be ready to go. I'd hate to see Mr. Wonderful wait one minute more than he has to tonight because you've exhausted yourself setting type."

"If you're sure."

"I am. So shoo. I'm sort of getting into the déjà vu aspect of this in a weird sort of way."

Jenny obliged. "See you in thirty minutes."

Twenty-five minutes later Dani took the last sheet of type from the printer, re-read it and slipped it into her briefcase. She would finish the paste-up the minute she got back to Los Angeles. Tonight, she and Blake could have one more lovely evening to themselves.

Smiling, thinking of the night ahead, Dani snapped her briefcase shut only to realize she wasn't alone. Still smiling she looked up assuming Jenny had come to fetch her, but it wasn't Jenny at all. A familiar shadow darkened the doorway. Instinctively Dani pulled the attaché to her chest as though to protect the precious type inside while her blue eyes locked with ones she had hoped never to see again. Sid Pregerson stood, straight, tall, and expressionless, watching her from the other side of her glass cage.

They stared at one another as they had months ago, yet this time not a word was exchanged. Moments became eternities. Dani and Sid seemingly locked in their optical embrace for infinity. It was Sid who suddenly broke the connection, moving off, turning from her as though she had been nothing more than a forgotten thing: an office light left on, a typewriter still purring, a phone that stopped ringing the minute he reached for it; Dani was no more to him than that.

Realizing this, angered by this, preferring Sid's fury or disgust to his apathy, a hot flush raced through Dani's body and flamed her cheeks. She grasped the back of the chair, crushing the upholstery with her

211

nails as though to physically restrain herself from going after him. There was nothing to be gained by confrontation, no satisfaction to be had since she couldn't hold up the Apache account as proof of life after Pregerson. She still had nothing and he had everything. And there was Jenny to consider . . . Jesus! Jenny!

Alarmed, Dani forgot her fear, abandoned her anger as she tore down the hall, opposite the way Sid had gone. Praying she would reach Jenny before Sid made his rounds, Dani hurried along, easily remembering the layout of the interconnecting corridors.

Forcing herself to slow down, she walked down the last hallway, cautiously poking her head around the corner before making the turn. Throwing herself back against the wall, Dani closed her eyes in defeat. Sid was standing in the doorway of Jenny's office, the drone of his voice evident but the words incomprehensible. When Dani looked again he was gone and she moved into Jenny's office. There she lowered herself into a chair, defeated as she watched her friend methodically pass a pen through her fingers. Jenny looked at Dani with a smile that was a curious blend of irony and despair.

"How did you miss him?" Dani asked when she final found her voice.

Jenny shrugged. "I don't know. Maybe he was in the bathroom. Maybe he was just wandering the wrong corridor at the right time." She tossed the pen on the desk. "Thought I'd checked everywhere."

"What did he say?"

"He asked me if I'd brought you into the office."

"And you told him?" Dani urged.

"What could I say?" Jenny answered, tossing the pen onto her desk. "I told him I'd asked you to meet me here because we were going to dinner in the city."

"Good thinking . . ."

"Then he asked me why you were using our highly sophisticated, very expensive equipment when you no longer worked here."

"Damn," Dani breathed.

"I told him you were working on your resume. You'd been having a tough time, and I felt sorry for you. I wanted to help you save a few bucks."

"And he said?"

"Sid?" Jenny rolled her eyes. "He nodded, drawled something about how commendable my sympathy was, but charity had its limits. Then he wished me a happy New Year and he left."

"Just like that?"

"That was a pretty mild reprimand, don't you think?" Jenny asked with a dry little laugh, a self-pitying smirk.

"Maybe the holiday spirit got him. I think you're in the clear."

Jenny's pretty brown eyes fastened on Dani. She tapped her bottom lip with her finger then leaned forward and crossed her arms on the desk.

"Do you really believe that?" she asked quietly.

Dani shook her head sadly. "No."

"Neither do I, Dani. Neither do I."

Dani paid the cab driver and slid out of the car as best she could. The red dress she'd bought for New Year's Eve was a stunner: just short enough, tight enough, and bare enough to guarantee Blake's admiration. But it wasn't meant for getting out of cars—just meant for getting out of. Hopefully Blake would oblige because after the day she'd had, Dani needed some cheering up.

God she felt miserable even though Jenny told her not to worry. But Dani couldn't shake the feeling that she was screwing up royally at every turn. First with Blake and Apache, now Jenny and Apache not to mention the missing exhibits. It had all seemed so simple, been so much fun, in the beginning. Now her pursuit of Apache might cost her Blake and her best friend's job.

Giving her dress one more tug, flipping her white-blonde hair behind her ears to show off her shoulder length earrings, Dani draped her calf-length fox over her shoulders and buzzed. Blake buzzed back immediately. Dani chuckled. They were off to a great start if he was that anxious to see her.

Heels clicking, Dani climbed the stairs toward the living room, knowing that's where he'd be waiting. Halfway to her destination, Dani stopped and leaned against the banister, her ears pricked. Funny. She didn't hear anything. No mood setting music, no movement, not one sound of habitation. The air had an empty feel. Each picture, each stair, each room grew less familiar in the odd atmosphere of desertion. Shaking her head, banishing such ridiculous thoughts, Dani cleared her throat and called out, "Ready or not, here I come. I'm going to make this a New Year's celebration you'll never forget, Blake Sinclair." Two more steps. She paused. Three. Two more to go. "Blake? Come on, this is spooky. Answer me."

She was on the landing and the door was open, the room was dark. January brought night quickly and Blake hadn't turned on a light, hadn't bothered with a romantic candle or two. Uneasy now, Dani hovered at the threshold and scanned the room. There were no

214

glasses on the table. No telltale bottle of champagne. No caviar on ice. No Blake.

"Honey? Blake?"

Blake Sinclair was a man of extreme faith. He believed in himself, in those he cared about, and in life. He didn't worry about what would happen to him on any given day. He set goals and achieved them. Simple as that. Then he moved on to the next thing. He left no enemies in his wake, no bodies laying about, he hid no skeletons in his closet. He didn't lust after money or power or women. Instead he appreciated money, adored women, and never thought about power because he had always had it by virtue of being himself.

Men wanted to hate him but couldn't because his word and handshake were as good as gold. He offered both to people he instinctively trusted and gracefully withheld them from those he didn't.

Women wanted to possess him and failed. It was impossible to own a man like Blake Sinclair because he admired women, seeing them equal to himself in every sense of the word. That wasn't to say he didn't enjoy the obvious differences. It seemed to Blake that equality was far more pleasurable than the constant worries and resentment of a disparate relationship.

So it seemed to just about everyone that Blake Sinclair was perfect. He wasn't jealous of those wealthier than he, he admired those more creative than he (though there weren't many who qualified), he laughed at the vanities of his business while thrilling at the endless surprises seen through the eye of the camera. Even he hadn't known that his life was lacking until he met Dani Cortland.

God, how she had come into his world. Like a burst

of light on a black country night she turned her smile on him and, though he went about his business, showing her his reel, talking shop, Blake knew he had been nothing until the moment he saw her.

His artist's eye had defined her. He longed to see her in any light: sunrise and sunset and every moment in between. She was constructed of the most elegant angles that cut intricate patterns out of the space in which she moved.

Dani spoke and her voice brought depth to the everyday sounds around him. Hers was the voice that made him snap to attention, turn and watch for her, wait for her, cherish and be amazed by her. From day one until the present Blake couldn't explain it. He found it impossible to define his adoration so he never questioned it in the same way he never questioned the luck of his talent and his success.

And when they had finally touched—not the touch of colleagues or friends but the touch of lovers—Blake had known he had found the piece of him that was missing. He had found his passion. What he had accomplished before Dani was beautiful, what he created after they came together was extraordinary. And, like everything else of import in his life, Blake pulled Dani to him and became part of her, believing she was part of him too. Oh, how he believed in her. They moved as one, felt as one. They married and lived together and Blake helped her fight those driving forces that at times dragged her away from him. Blake learned to hate the memory of Peter Cortland but never the creature Peter Cortland created. He could never hate Dani no matter how frantically she felt the need for success, no matter how frightened she was of loving him deeply and without question. Blake lived content in the knowledge that he had given Dani as much as she had given him. For her gift of passion, he offered reassurance of her worth. And even when the day came that they couldn't live together any longer because her demons became too insistent, the old lessons impossible to leave by the wayside, Blake loved her still.

How could he not? Dani was his fate, she was part of his soul. They wouldn't be apart forever because Blake had endless love and loyalty to give. He wanted her. He loved her. Had there ever been a time when he hadn't gotten exactly what he wanted?

Then she'd come back. Giving herself to him. Making him smile. Loving him, living with him the past weeks as if they'd never been apart. It seemed she'd left behind the sadness. It appeared she was finally confident in herself, ready to compete with the world and not with him. God how complete he had felt.

Dani was his again . . .

Dani was happy again . . .

Tonight Blake had thought to propose once more . . .

But tonight . . . she had . . . again . . .

Blake tried to raise a hand to rub his tired eyes but found it impossible. Instead he sat and listened. She was coming. She was calling and the sound of her voice shattered what was left of his heart . . . again.

Dani took a step forward, flipping the switch nearest her. A light went on in the hallway. Hardly bright, but enough to send a golden glow halfway through the living room. A heartbeat later, before she could call again, the huge chair near the bay window moved. Slowly and deliberately it swiveled. Openmouthed, her

217

heart nearly stopping, Dani watched until she was face to face with . . .

"Blake!" she breathed, one hand over her heart. "You scared me to death. I didn't . . . Blake . . ." Dani moved closer, peering through the shadows, ". . . you're not dressed . . ."

Dani went no closer. Every nerve stood on end as a sense of dread invaded her mind and heart. Stunned by her reception, Dani couldn't begin to think of what was wrong. Words pounded in her head. Sick . . . ? Sad . . . ? Angry . . . ? Frightened . . . ? But these were mere words, none of which could describe Blake. His expression was stony, unreadable and unwelcoming. He could have been thinking anything, feeling anything, and all Dani could do was stand and watch this person she didn't know. This man who never failed to reach out to her with open arms, failed her now.

Without a word, Blake reached out and touched the table beside him. Confused, a half-smile playing on her lips, Dani waited. A surprise . . . that was it . . . Blake had planned a surprise. Then she heard it. A click. A small sound, followed by the whir of . . . a tape. Blake's answering machine came to life.

"Dani, this is Rudy. We've got trouble with the Apache presentation . . ." came an all too familiar voice.

"Rudy, What? My God. How did you get this number . . ." Dani answered.

Rudy's message! She'd never erased it, leaving it for Blake to find and Blake to ponder over and Blake to understand. Now she quaked in her high heels and her too-tight dress. She felt faint but couldn't reach for anything to steady herself because her arms were clutched about her waist as though to hold herself together. Blake had her in his sights, his eyes cold, his

218

expression blank, his home no longer hers to share. Dani's lips trembled trying to find words that would make this all right.

Click. Blake turned off the offending message.

Click. The machine rewound.

Click. The voice came again.

"Dani, it's Rudy. We've got trouble with the Apache presentation . . ."

"Rudy, What? My God . . ."

Dani's lips came together, forming the first letter of the name she wanted to cry out. Her eyes closed, her body swayed, teetering and then staying linear by sheer force of will.

Click. Click. Click.

"Dani, it's Rudy. We've got trouble . . ."

Click. Click. Click.

"Dani, it's Rudy . . ."

Turning slowly, desperate to be away from Blake, his hurt, his mute condemnation, Dani walked out of his home and out of his life without a word. There was nothing she could say to defend herself now, no words to make him understand her betrayal had only been business. For the first time she understood that there were some lines that couldn't be crossed. Papa had been wrong. So very wrong to tell her that everyone understood the drive to succeed. And now that she knew he'd been lying, where was she to go? Who was she to turn to for sympathy? Who, on this earth, would let her cry in their arms? Blake was gone as surely as if she had slammed the door in his face and sent him on his way.

The last thing she heard was the click and whir of the answering machine as Blake continued to torture himself.

"Come on, Rudy, it's just about to start. Come on."

Lora sat cross-legged on the couch, her body draped in a sweat suit of the palest pink, her hair tousled and already returning to its natural curly state. She had discarded her shoes by ten. Her face was flushed with a raspberry red streak that ran from one cheek across her nose to the other side of her face. Right on the tip of her nose a zillion little blood vessels were ready to burst. She had thoroughly enjoyed New Year's Eve, celebrating by sampling every bottle in Rudy's liquor cabinet.

"Come on, Rudy! This movie isn't going to wait for you."

"Shut up, Lora. The whole world can hear you."

Rudy stalked into the living room, resplendent in black velour. The hair atop his head was perfectly combed. He had applied aftershave. He had thought he and Lora would have a good time tonight. He might even be able to forget Serina with a good roll in the hay. She was just a kid after all. Just a nice, sweet, loving kid. Not for Rudy. Women like Lora Prince were Rudy's type.

But the minute he saw Lora, Rudy knew his heart wasn't in it. He didn't have the energy to screw Lora Prince. Actually, being alone on New Year's Eve would have been preferable than Lora soused and an adult flick he had no desire to see. They had worked like dogs recreating the presentation, Lora disavowing any knowledge of the missing boards, Sam in a tizzy, and Serina near tears when she found out what had happened. But they had put them all back together, finishing on New Year's Eve and only Sam with a date. Serina slipped out of the office before Rudy could say a word, leaving ample opportunity for Lora to latch on. So here they were, munching on pizza, Lora wanting one thing and Rudy quite another.

"Come on, Rudy," Lora commanded, slurring his name a bit. Rudy shook his head and sank down beside her, splaying his long legs in front of him.

"That's better," Lora cooed, running her hand up his velour-encased thigh. "Nice fabric."

"Yeah, I guess."

Lora bit her lip, angry that Rudy hadn't responded to her advances. She took another gulp of her drink, watched the ice cubes fall back into the glass, and tried to figure out how she would cheer Rudy up. Taking the remote control in her free hand she turned up the volume. The tape was just starting, the title ripping across the screen: *Nurses of the Night*.

"This ought to be good." Lora nuzzled against him. Without thinking he put his arm around her. Lora grinned. She knew him as well as she knew herself. He couldn't resist her when she insisted on his attention.

"I don't know, I'm not much in the mood . . ." Rudy began. Then he fell silent. He was watching a hospital room, a handsome man lay in a pristine bed, his body half-covered by a sheet. Through the door came a woman dressed as a nurse. Her uniform was short and tight but Rudy didn't notice, he was focusing on her angelic face. Such a beautiful face. The woman crossed the room and, when she bent over the man in the bed, Rudy realized that he seemed to know the woman. She had that gentle, delicate look he had so admired in . . . who? In a flash it came to him. She was almost as beautiful as Serina. Serina . . .

Rudy's arm tightened on Lora's shoulder. Surprised, she leaned closer and put her hand over his most private part, feeling it grow and grow as she

221

began to gently knead him. Then, just as quickly as his excitement came it was gone. The woman on the screen had opened her uniform, exposing her huge breasts and offering them to the man on the bed. Rudy turned away. There was no way that woman could have reminded him of Serina. Serina would never do a thing like that. Serina wouldn't. . . . Or would she? If she were loved, and cared for, and wanted.

Beside him Lora moaned. Rudy glanced down at her. His hand was inside her top, his fingers pulling gently at her breasts as he daydreamed about the girl who was only the receptionist. Surprised by his thoughts, embarrassed by the gentleness he had felt, Rudy turned on Lora who was already wriggling out of her clothes and grappling with his. He was Rudy Green, after all. He was a man about town, not one of those idiots who fell for sensitive types. Naw. Rudy Green was made of stronger stuff and he was going to show Lora Prince exactly what that stuff was. After all, she was the only one around to show. And, for one moment, just before he entered her, just before he heard her cry out his name, Rudy Green was ashamed of himself. He wondered what Serina would say if she knew . . .

"Excuse me, Senator Grant. There's a phone call for you. I'm afraid we don't have an extension for the table."

The apologetic maitre 'd hovered at Alexander's elbow trying not to look at the ridiculous green metallic hat atop the Senator's head.

"Thank you. Where can I pick it up?"

"Just past the front entrance to your right."

Alexander nodded. The man disappeared. Alexander slid the silly paper hat off his head and covered Polly's hand with his own.

"I'm sorry, darling. Even in Fresno, on New Year's Eve, there's no escape."

"I understand completely," she answered, watching her husband with a look of adoration that reminded him why he had wanted a divorce. He forced a smile then pushed his chair back. Glancing around the dining room he caught the lay of the land. The Governor was still seated at a table for six. His party was having a good time and Alexander nodded as he passed only to be rewarded with one of those I-should-know-you smiles. Picking up the phone he sat on a leather-like chair which was this outback's idea of class and spoke.

"This is Senator Grant."

"And this is Senator Grant's aide," came the flippant salutation.

"Eric? What are you doing? It's New Year's Eve."

"And I am dedicated to you above and beyond the call of duty. I have just made intimate contact with the secretary to our esteemed head of the subcommittee on which you sit."

"How nice for you. But I'm not interested. Any reminder that there is a world outside of Fresno, California and the company of my reconciled wife makes me green with envy."

"No, Senator, no, no, no." Eric breathed the way inebriated people do when they think they're sober. "I called to tell you something important. Your friend Basset's going to stack the deck so the recommendation will go his way—a vote for legislation against exportation. He's been doing a little back-room politicking. Undecideds are being wooed like crazy. It's going through."

"But I'm undecided," Alexander broke in.

"Basset figures you mean diddly-squat," Eric laughed, finding the adjective quite amusing. "Far as he's concerned you're his party and you're his vote according to my companion. So there's going to be a ban on the export of certain chemicals to South America. A complete ban. Wouldn't be too great for Radison, would it?"

"No, not good at all," Alexander muttered. "Well, Eric, you've done a fine job. Hopefully the lady who supplied you with this information isn't too objectionable a companion."

"Nah," Eric snorted. "Besides, even if she was, my eyesight's failing by the minute. I'll still get it up, though, don't you worry."

"I'm sure you will. Just remember to keep your mouth shut while you're doing your payback."

"The lips are zipped, Senator," Eric chuckled. Then he asked. "So, you're going to fight the committee on this?"

"We'll see, Eric, we'll see."

"But Radison . . ."

"I'm fully aware of my obligations all around, Eric. I'll be in Los Angeles for a few days to consult with the agency and see Coral. I'll be back in Washington by the fifteenth ready to attend the subcommittee hearings. I presume your hangover will be history by then?"

"Yes sir, boss," Eric answered, his assurance all but drowned out by a sudden roar of merriment.

"Good. Now, Happy New Year and the best to your lady. Buy her a drink on me."

Alexander's expression was grim as he hung up. Things were moving along much as he expected. He was in the middle of the tightrope and his balance was

224

good, and Radison's money was only one part of the reelection equation.

Instincts in play, Alexander moved toward the Governor, stopping just long enough to take Polly's arm and escort her quickly toward his table. Once there Alexander reached a hand toward the surprised Governor.

"Governor Hadley. Alexander Grant."

"Of course . . ." Governor Hadley half-rose and took Alexander's hand before he had figured out who Alexander Grant was. When the old man finally filled in the blank he did so with great satisfaction. ". . . Senator Grant, of course. Nice to see you."

"My wife, Polly. We just wanted to come over and wish you and your wife a very happy New Year."

"Well, thank you. I certainly appreciate the thought, Senator. In fact, yes, I believe it is the New Year. Well, fancy that."

His right hand still in Alexander's grasp, the Governor raised his silly gold hat in a mock salute and leaned into Polly Grant who offered her cheek for a kiss. At that moment a photographer pointed his camera toward the little party. Alexander squared his shoulders, put his hand on Polly's waist and smiled most charmingly. The photographer clicked, capturing for posterity the Governor and Polly obscured by Alexander Grant looking, fit, fabulous and finally electable.

Coral put out her tongue and tasted. The honey was warm and gooey but not as warm as the skin it coated. Her fingers dug into the man's thigh, she positioned herself atop his leg and began the sweet journey upwards, thoroughly licking him clean inch by inch. As

225

her head came within reach, the man wound his fingers through her tousled blond hair and guided her efforts. He made no sounds of pleasure but Coral knew by the muscular tremors and the rising of his glory above her that she hadn't lost her touch.

His name was Raoul. He was bronzed and beautiful, his black hair slicked back from an almost perfect face. He had caught her eye on the beach that morning, they had traded names only minutes ago. There hadn't seemed to be much time in between for talk.

Having completed her culinary task, Coral slid between his legs and continued her ministrations though she heard him light a cigarette. The pungent odor of the smoke heightened her excitement yet she fought to control it. She was in the Caribbean. Everything was cool. No one got too excited about anything except maybe a knife in the back. "So what do you do in the United States. Are you kept?"

Coral took a breather, her fingers absentmindedly taking over for her lips.

"I sell real estate. I try to save the environment. I sleep with an important man."

He chuckled and took a drag of his cigarette. "You were my woman I would tie you to the bed. There would be no real estate." He drew out the "e" in "real" until it had an edge on it. Coral laughed. He was a caricature of a gigolo and she loved it.

"I don't think my man would want to do that," Coral sighed.

"He is stupid."

"No, he is smart."

"So you will marry him?"

"No. I'm smart too."

Coral smiled, scooted up beside the man, took the cigarette from his hand and dropped it in the half-empty glass beside the bed thinking that what she said was true. Any woman would have to be a little crazy to set her cap for Alexander Grant permanently, and there wasn't a crazy bone in her body, nor thought in her head. Coral knew exactly what she was doing. The thing with Alexander was never meant to be until death did they part.

Dani sniffled. She hiccoughed. She didn't want to cry again but she knew it was inevitable, just as it was inevitable that Blake would eventually understand how sorry she was. Once she had a chance to explain, everything would be all right. But, dammit, she needed a chance. Another unwanted sob and Dani punched the buttons on her phone again. Sitting back, her fox coat thrown over her like a blanket as she listened to Blake's phone ring, Dani threw her arm over her eyes, her heart breaking as his machine came on again.

Dutifully exhausted, she listened to him invite her to leave a message. Below her condo the city caroused in high good humor as the clock struck midnight. This wasn't working out at all. Slowly, the beep sounding, Dani began to replace the receiver. But another burst of happiness from the nameless throngs on the street changed her mind. This wasn't a life and death thing and Blake better darn well understand that. The receiver was back on her ear, her free hand swiped at her tears, and she sat up, careless of her dress, her coat, and her words.

"Okay, Blake. I'll talk to this stupid machine." She sniffled. "You're probably there. I just want you to know that someday you're going to find out what this is like. You're going to want something so bad you'll do anything to get it . . ." Dani hiccoughed again, more tears were on the way, a torrent of them, so she hurried on. ". . . you're going to find out what it is to need something even at the expense of someone you care about. I swear to you, that's when you'll feel bad about tonight. You're going to be miserable then. Think about it. You've never had to compromise, you've never had to beg, you've never had to . . ."

The machine clicked off. Dani slammed the receiver back on its cradle and fell back on the sofa, the promised tears pouring down her cheeks.

In his townhouse Blake still sat in the dark, his finger on the button that had curtailed Dani's message. Quietly, with no one but himself to hear he said, "I already know, Dani. I know what it is to hope and beg and I'm not going to do it—not anymore. There's nothing I want that badly."

Chapter Seventeen

"Rudy, I don't like that woman and I won't work with her. She thinks I jinxed this presentation. She thinks I had something to do with those missing boards . . ." Rudy raised a brow in question, ". . . Oh, for God sake, not you too."

Lora rolled her eyes. She tsked, she made all the right indignant noises, she crossed her arms. The only thing she didn't do was admit she couldn't remember the night in question. She'd been drinking, Lora knew that much for sure, but everything else was a blank. She could have done it—probably should have done it—maybe did do it. But it didn't matter now. The presentation was back in order and everything was fine—except for the fact that Dani Cortland was still hanging around giving orders. Lora was back up again, leaning over the table.

"We've been together a hell of a long time, and we've shared a shitload of misery, and I just don't think it's fair that you let her call the shots. That's all there is to it. You've got to get rid of her."

Lora was at it again, gripping the edge of the table as though her life depended on it. In front of her a burger and fries cooled, a salad wilted, her Coke lost its fizz, and Rudy Green tried not to blow up.

She had been at it for an hour, her tirade beginning in the car with one comment that grew to a novel of grief. Lora didn't want Dani at the presentation, arguing that it was their contact, their legwork that had gotten them into the review. Lora had a point, but as long as they had Dani, Rudy was going to use her. By the time they found a place to eat, sat down, and their food was brought, Lora couldn't talk about anything except Dani. If she kept it up she was not only going to blow a gasket she was going to blow the presentation. Rudy was having a hard time deciding what to do. Why couldn't Lora be like other women? Like Dani—all business; like Serina—nice and sweet and beautiful.

Rudy forced himself to look at her, his last fry dangling between his fingers dripping ketchup. Carefully he chewed, knowing that he needed her for a while yet and knowing that no matter how much he wanted to get rid of her he probably never would. There was a code of honor that Rudy lived by when he had to. But Rudy was changing. Green Advertising was changing. Why couldn't Lora do the same?

"Look, sweetie, Dani doesn't think you did anything with the storyboards, she just wanted to know if you knew anything about them. As for leaving her at the agency, that would look pretty strange since she's the creative director and this is a creative presentation. She knows how important you are, she's not going to upstage you." *Lie. It was impossible not to.* "You just took it the wrong way when she said she'd present first."

"But that's the point, Rudy. Why does she have anything to say about who presents and who doesn't?

230

It's our account not hers," Lora wailed. "We contacted them, we did the ground work . . ."

". . . And they weren't going to give us their business because we were two such nifty people. If we get it, it's because of Dani's work. Come on Lora," Rudy cajoled, "you've got to admit that. Because of her, we may land this business. Don't you want to say I work for Green Advertising and be proud of it?"

"I'm already proud of it," Lora pouted, knowing it wasn't pride, but safety she treasured.

"Jesus." Rudy threw his napkin on the table, catching a glimpse of his hand as he did so. He wore only one rather plain ring and it shocked him to see his hand looking so naked. He supposed showy jewelry wasn't right for the office like Dani said, but he still felt weird—half dressed.

"So, what are you going to do about her?" Lora mumbled, taking Rudy's attention back as if it belonged to her.

"About Dani?"

"Yeah, about Dani."

"Nothing," Rudy admitted, surprised that she would even ask. "Why should I?"

"Because she's just not good for us." Rudy cringed. Jesus, Lora had them linked at the hip. A minute later he breathed easier when she qualified that statement. "She's not good for the agency."

"I think she is, and right now I don't want to talk about Dani or anything other than the job at hand. We'll meet Dani at Apache, we'll present our stuff like professionals, and after they make their decision we'll talk again. But, if we get it, I'll bet my bottom dollar you'll feel differently about Dani."

"And I bet I won't," Lora snapped. "I'll always disagree that Dani was a good thing to happen to this

231

agency, but I'll go along and do what I'm supposed to. I'm not going to screw it up and give her the satisfaction of gloating."

"She's not doing that, Lora . . ."

But she ignored him. Nose tipped in the air she said, "We're going to get that account Rudy and we're going to get it because of me."

Triumphantly, delusionally, Lora pushed herself out of the booth and headed for the parking lot. Rudy followed with a prayer on his lips and the hope that Lora Prince would soon tire of working for the Green Agency, and him.

"Dani?"

Serina hung shyly on the doorframe, doing her best not to irritate her boss, but vexing her nonetheless. Dani looked up, a smile on her lips but still that awful pained look in her eyes. Whatever happened over the Christmas holiday obviously hadn't been good.

"Yes, Serina?"

"I think you better come." She inclined her head toward the coffee room.

"What's wrong?" Dani was up. Serina wasn't the type to disregard not-to-be-disturbed orders unless it was really important.

"Rudy and Lora are back," Serina said as she stepped back to let Dani pass then fell in step as Dani hurried down the hall. "I think Lora's not feeling too well."

Dani picked up the pace, hitting the coffee room at top speed. Instantly the situation was apparent and her heart stopped palpitating. Neither Rudy nor Lora was in as bad a shape as Serina thought. Of course Serina had probably never had one too many, so Dani excused her anxiety. Dani smiled, the first real smile she'd given any of them since her return from San Francisco. Hands on hips she surveyed the scene. This was her family now, these were her friends. She would treat them better than she had treated her love.

"You two decide to stop and pick apart the Apache presentation over a few beers?"

"What's it to you if we did?" Lora groused, on the defensive as usual. Rudy had probably had a few too but looked more disheartened than drunk.

"Just asking. Thought you might have invited me along."

"Fat chance," Lora grunted.

"Lora," Rudy warned. To Dani he said, "Did it seem as awful to you as it did to us? Jesus, they hardly said a word, Dani. Just thanks and bam, that was it. I don't know. It wasn't what I expected. Our stuff was good. It really was."

"Of course it was, and I don't believe for an instant we bombed. They were quiet, sure, but we were the last on the list. They've already sat through two dog and pony shows. They were just tired."

"Bullshit . . ." Lora muttered.

"Maybe . . ." Rudy said, but there was little hope in his voice.

"Of course . . ." Dani began, but Serina was motioning to her again, the phone in the corner of the conference room clutched to her chest. Dani nodded, acknowledging her briefly. ". . . Rudy, why don't you get a cup of coffee? You'll feel better. Believe me, you're just not used to this . . ."

Dani skirted the conference table and took the phone. Serina whispered in her ear.

"They wanted Rudy. It's Mr. Zelosti. I thought maybe you better take it, considering . . ." She inclined her head and wiggled her eyebrows. Dani grinned, actually feeling like her old self.

"I'll take it in my office."

Serina nodded and put Mr. Zelosti on hold. Dani was with him a second later. Their conversation was short and she had to compose herself before returning to the conference room, picking up Sam on the way. They might as well all hear this at once.

"Rudy. Lora. That was Mr. Zelosti. They've made a decision."

Sam slid against the wall and stood beside Serina. All eyes were on Dani. Rudy's suddenly bright and alert, Lora's dark and transparently hopeful that failure was in the air. Serina's breath was held, her hands clasped in front of her as if in prayer, her eyes not on Dani, but Rudy.

"He awarded the Apache Shoe account to . . ." Dani held out her arms, her face transformed as she hollered, ". . . Green Advertising! He said they were left speechless by the way we had captured the spirit of their company."

Dani was still jabbering, trying to reiterate everything Mr. Zelosti had said, but her words were drowned out by the whooping and hollering from the little group. Rudy had Dani in his arms, twirling her around, passing her on to Sam who jumped up and down while Rudy kissed Serina once, then twice then moved away from her, amazed at how marvelous she felt in his arms. Then Dani was at him again and Sam had Serina by the hand, mouths were moving, rebel yells and giggles abounded, kisses and hugs all around. A champagne cork popped and no one noticed that Lora, inadvertently left out of the hugs and kisses, had disappeared, going to her office alone. It would seem that Dani would be around forever now and it made Lora sick to her stomach.

Suddenly the door of her office opened and Rudy, Serina on his arm, poked his head into her office. Lora grinned. He had come for her, good old Rudy.

"Lora, come on," Rudy said, his eyes softening in the face of such a forlorn expression. "Champagne. We all deserve it. Especially you."

"Thanks, Rudy," she whispered, all the good feelings for him returning full force. "I'll be there in a minute."

"Well hurry it up. We're leaving in fifteen minutes for a night of celebration. Dinner and drinks on the Green Agency. Right, partner?"

Lora's grin widened by a mile, her heart nearly bursting. Partner. How long had she waited for this. Finally, Rudy had seen the light. Partner. It was too good to be true, and a moment later Lora realized that it wasn't.

Rudy's head turned, his eyes looking elsewhere. Instinctively Lora's gaze followed and she saw Dani poke her head through the doorway, her hand laid possessively on Rudy's shoulder.

"Absolutely right, partner," she said. "But don't forget, you own fifty-one percent. That means you pick up fifty-one percent of the bill. I want to keep this partnership on the up and up."

The trio laughed. Dani disappeared, her white hair flipping behind her as she turned away. Rudy kissed Serina on top of her head without a second thought, shooed her off then winked at Lora.

"Hurry up, Lora. We'll have a special toast just for you. I'll never forget you deserve a lot of the credit for this."

Then he was gone too. Lora, openmouthed, stared

at the now empty doorway. Partners. Not she and Rudy. Dani and Rudy. Lora wanted to kill. Lora Prince wanted Dani Cortland to pay for taking what was hers. Somehow she would. Someday Dani Cortland would be sorry she ever saw the Green Agency.

"Of course I miss you, Polly. I know we didn't have enough time to ourselves with the holidays. Unfortunately that's the way things are going to be from now on. There's an election coming up and I'm counting on you being my eyes and ears in Northern California. I'll cover Southern California as best I can. Then when I think we have all our ducks in a row, a campaign manager we can trust, I'll find us a house in Washington. Um-hm. Yes. Oh, hold on Polly, I think I hear someone knocking."

Alexander put the receiver on the table, wrapped his terry robe tighter and went to the door. On the other side, much to his delight, was Coral, looking beautifully bronzed.

"Hello, Senator," she purred when he opened to her, but Alexander put his finger to her lips. She closed the door quietly behind her.

"Nothing, dear, just the paper boy," Alexander explained, almost laughing when Coral opened her blouse to show off her tanned breasts. "A skinny little guy. I don't know how he manages to hit the mark every time."

Coral set her purse on a chair and sauntered to the bar. There she poured herself a drink, looked around the room, then made her way back to Alexander seemingly oblivious to his conversation. Nestling in behind him she let her fingers slip beneath his robe then down his ribs until she reached a portion of his anatomy with

236

a bit more topical interest. Alexander stayed her hand, saying an incredibly controlled good-bye to his wife.

The receiver replaced, Alexander let go of Coral's hand and leaned back into her, turning his head so that his cheek lay against her fall of velvety hair.

"How was St. Thomas?" he asked.

"Fine," she said, her voice husky. "I gather your wife's back in the picture?"

"A public relations coup," Alexander drawled.

"Congratulations."

"There will have to be some changes, naturally."

"Certainly." Coral gripped him tighter so that he wasn't quite sure if he was in the throes of pain or ecstasy. "I suppose we'll be spending more time indoors."

"I imagine that will be the case, Coral."

"No problem, Senator. No problem at all."

It was five-thirty and dark outside and the news of Apache's account assignment to the unknown firm of Green Advertising lay as heavily on Blake Sinclair as the fog over the city.

Dani would be celebrating right about now, playing around with her friend Rudy Green. Correction. Her partner, Rudy Green. Funny what you could find out once you started looking. Actually the association didn't surprise Blake. He had known she was desperate. He just hadn't realized she was also reckless. The only question he had was why. Any other account, any other agency, but this! God, it stuck in his craw. All the years he had loved her, forgiven her little mean-spirited trespasses because he honestly believed she couldn't help herself. Papa and his success-at-all-costs philosophy was just too ingrained. But he had never thought, never considered, that Dani would honestly use him. Yet used he'd been and he wondered just how much she had taken from him.

"Blake?"

He looked up, taking a minute to focus. In the two years they had worked together, Blake was still unnerved by the sight of Regina at night. With that chalk white make-up, the rings through her ears and nose, the half-shaved head, she looked like a voodoo spirit. When he realized it was only his assistant, he almost laughed—almost.

"Regina. It's late. I thought you'd gone."

She shrugged, coming toward him on those spindly legs of hers.

"Yo, Blake. Just wanted to tell you I'm sorry about Apache. I know it meant a lot."

"Thanks," he answered, "at least you understood."

"Hey," she responded and Blake took that to mean she understood more than he thought she did. "Anyway, I've been out there reading the newspaper, you know? Anyway, I couldn't decide about this all day and now maybe things are even worse, but yo, what can I say?"

With that bit of eloquence Regina stepped all the way forward and put the personals in front of Blake. She pointed, he looked.

"Thanks, Regina. I think I'll pass."

"Hey, no problem." She backed off, hands in the air, obviously unable to carry the paper back the way it had come. "Just thought you should be aware. Just aware. I'll take off then. Sorry about everything."

She disappeared into the shadows, her white, white face hanging in the dark like a disembodied mime until it too disappeared. Now Blake did chuckle. She was a piece of work and he appreciated her concern but he didn't need to see that little bit of news. In fact, Regina had overstepped her bounds just a bit on this one. She had planted just a little seed of anger but he could feel it growing to a full fury. Rather than lose his temper, rather than let *her* do that to him again, Blake scooped up the newspaper, rolled it into a tube, swiped at his desk while he pushed back his chair and reached for the trash can. But curiosity got the better of him. He hadn't read the entire thing. Wishing he had more self-control, knowing he didn't, Blake opened to the page Regina had shown him. There was a message for everyone to see, their friends to look at and understand. It wouldn't take much to read between these lines. A simple message that spoke volumes of betrayal and pain.

"Blake, I *am* sorry. Dani."

And who in this little world of theirs, this tight-knit family of advertising people, wouldn't have heard that he was working for Dailey, wouldn't know that she was working for Green. Who wouldn't put two and two together and figure that once again Dani Cortland had screwed Blake Sinclair.

"Not this time, Dani. I've learned my lesson. You're history."

The paper was in the trash and Blake Sinclair was out of the office. He'd left her behind for good. He only wondered when his heart would get the message and kick in.

Chapter Eighteen

"I can't believe it," she breathed.

Rudy couldn't have been more pleased. Dani Cortland was almost speechless, her pretty mouth opened in awe and—dare he say—respect. Finally he had done something she was impressed by.

"Believe it. Daniel Sweeney will be the official spokesperson for Alexander's campaign. He is signed, sealed, and delivered and will be appearing in our television spots, the radio voice-over, even show up at a couple of speeches."

"And . . ." Dani prodded.

"And . . . ?" Rudy responded.

"And what is this going to cost the Senator's poor little budget?"

"Don't worry about it. Sweeney thinks Grant is the right person for the job." Rudy shrugged, his eyes darting away for a second. "What can I say, even television stars have political leanings."

"Rudy," Dani laughed, "I've got to hand it to you. You really pulled this one off, and I didn't think it was possible. I hope Alexander understands just how important you are to him."

Now it was Rudy's turn to laugh, but it was a rueful sound. "I think he knows."

"Great. So when are you shooting?"

"We'll shoot his cameos this week then in the next couple of weeks we'll do Alexander and his wife."

"How's that working out?" Dani asked, honestly concerned, entertaining second thoughts about her advice. She wasn't exactly batting a thousand when it came to personal relationships.

"I guess it's okay. He's not the kind of guy to open up, if you know what I mean."

"True. Well, maybe the guy's got a chance in this election. You did an incredible job. Daniel Sweeny! I can't believe it! I hope you're at least going to get some PR mileage out of this."

"I think Alexander's ready to pull out all the stops," Rudy agreed. They were all feeling more comfortable now and it was time to loosen up on a lot of things.

"Okay, so we've got Grant settled, let's get down to the rest of business."

"I suppose," Rudy sighed, wishing there was time during regular working hours to take care of business. He hated working late, especially when Serina was waiting for him. "Can we try to wrap this up fast, Dani? I've got plans tonight."

"Serina again?" She raised a brow and chuckled. It was nice to see someone happy in a relationship. "Nice going, Rudy."

"Yeah. She's something special. So, since we're on the topic, how about making Serina next order of business. She wants to move off reception. I thought she could help Sam. She'd be great in production."

Dani shrugged. "Sounds good to me. I always thought she had more on the ball than we gave her credit for."

"Done," Rudy said, beaming. But his delight was short-lived. Dani had another topic on the agenda that wasn't quite as easily taken care of.

"Good." She sighed, shuffled some papers, hemmed and hawed for a minute or two, then got down to it. "Rudy, we've got to talk about Lora. There's no getting around it."

"Dani, I don't want to . . ."

"Listen to me," Dani insisted. "This isn't the Green Agency of old. We can't afford the kind of mistakes she's making now. We had to eat the cost of printing Radison's brochure because she didn't proofread it properly. She's been promising the magazines that we're going to purchase far more space than we intend to. Rudy, Lora is . . ."

". . . is right here so watch what you say."

Lora ambled into the conference room, her blouse pulled half out of her skirt. She'd been drinking, a usual occurrence now after five, and she was in a mean mood.

"I've got a bottle of wine in my office. Want some?" Rudy shook his head and looked away. Dani scrutinized Lora silently and the woman's bleary, angry eyes looked right back.

"No thanks, Lora," Dani said quietly.

"Why not?" she demanded, her voice far too loud for the small room, her hands flailing out as if she were addressing a crowd instead of two embarrassed colleagues. "The way we've been celebrating around here lately, gettin' one new account after another, poppin' the cork to toast the latest acquisition, I thought we all had kinda got into the habit. Come on, just one little drink? I'll share mine."

"No, Lora, thanks," Rudy said quietly. "Listen, we're sort of busy and all of us want to get out of here at a decent hour. I know you've had a long day too, so why don't you head on home? Have a hot bath. Get yourself something to eat. You'll feel better."

Rudy surprised himself with his little speech. Nine months ago he and Lora would have finished her bottle and another then ended up on top of his desk, naked save for his gold chains. It was a sad picture and he pitied them their history, he still pitied her and that was even sadder.

"I know," Lora said as she wobbled to a chair, "you have to discuss me. You have to settle me. Well, I won't stop you. I'd like to hear what you have to say. I'd like to hear exactly how you think I've screwed up."

Dani and Rudy exchanged a look. Rudy uncomfortable with Lora's directness; Dani annoyed that she would make a scene.

"Okay, Lora, if that's the way you want it . . ."

"Dani," Rudy objected but she quieted him with a look that said she would be kind though it would kill her.

"Lora, it's no secret you're having some trouble adjusting to what's happening to this agency. It's not all your fault. We understand that. I think we're all amazed at how our lives have changed. I certainly never expected to be living in Los Angeles. I don't think Rudy expected to be running a multimillion dollar agency. But we've adjusted, Lora. We're even having a good time working our tails off. Everyone except you, and I think it's time that changed."

Dani filled her lungs. She spoke quietly as she got to the bottom line. Lora had to be put on notice.

"The games are over. I know you resent my coming here and what you consider my interference. But screwing with agency business, stumbling around here drunk half the time, isn't the way to let us know that you're not happy. We haven't come this far just so you can put the Green Agency back where it was. Even if it kills me, the reps for the magazines and broadcast stations, our suppliers, and our clients are going to respect the way we do business.

"So, Lora," Dani finished, her voice coming hard and fast, surprising everyone with its intensity, "Rudy and I are not going to pay for your fits of anger. We're not going to cover your ass because you're pouting when you should be thrilled that you are a part of this. We want you to be a part of the team. Let us know if you want to be. If you can't play by the rules then . . ."

Dani shrugged, resigned and standing tough. Green Advertising meant more to her than she had even realized. Now that Blake was gone what else was there but dedicating herself to the love she chose over a living, breathing man. Her game playing had cost her Blake for the second time in her life. She had ruined their marriage because she wanted to outdo him; she had ruined their friendship because of competition. Someday she might be able to fix things with Blake. Until that day came she would protect this agency and its clients from everything and anything that threatened it. Even if the thing that threatened it was Lora Prince.

"You feel this way, Rudy?"

Lora's head flopped heavily toward him, her face flushed red with anger and the effects of booze. She was fighting to keep her eyes open.

"Lora, I . . ." Rudy began helplessly.

"Well do you!" Lora's sudden scream unnerved the partners. Dani was half out of her chair, Rudy reached toward Lora but she knocked her chair to the ground trying to get away from him. Her fury added inches to her height and sobriety to her comportment. Her voice softened with obvious effort. "Well, do you? After all these years you're going to let this clothes hanger order you around? Jesus, Rudy, this is your agency, and I was your friend. Doesn't that mean anything?"

Lora hiccoughed, but it was only a sound to cover the catch in her throat. She blinked to cover the welling of tears. She caught her bottom lip in her teeth to stop the quivering, biting hard to remind herself that she should be royally pissed.

"We used to have fun, Rudy. We could out-talk anybody. We could make 'em believe anything. Now we're going to be choir boys? Rudy. Aw, Rudy, tell her to go to hell. Tell her we don't need her. We were doing okay before she came. Go ahead, Rudy. Tell her and I promise I'll be good if we can just get it back the way it was. Just you and me, Rudy. Tell her."

Lora had leaned over the table so that she and Rudy were almost nose to nose. Dani watched, mesmerized by Lora, curious about the deep desire this woman had to keep things as they had been, trapped by the mundane, destined to forever grovel at the wrong end of the rainbow. Rudy shuddered, a slight but painful tremor. He reached for Lora, covered her hands with his. In disgust she drew back and looked down on him. Her eyes never left his but she spoke to Dani in a voice so filled with hate that Dani turned away from it.

"Don't think you're home free yet, bitch."

Walking as best she could Lora went through the door and down the hall without another word. When her door at the end of the hall slammed, Rudy whispered, "Don't ever do that again, Dani. I'm the senior partner. This is my agency. Lora has been with me when things were really bad. Don't you ever make her feel so small again." With a fast and fitful shove, Rudy pushed his chair away from the conference table. Then Rudy, too, was gone.

Dani stayed in the conference room listening to Rudy help Serina into her jacket before they left for the evening. She stayed there until she heard Lora stumble out the front door. She stayed until the ringing of the phone almost drove her mad. Feeling sorry for herself, feeling alone and miserable, Dani picked up the receiver deciding it would be better to talk to anyone rather than sit alone in the darkened room.

"Green Advertising," Dani answered.

"Dani?"

"Jenny?"

"Yep."

"Oh, Jenny. Just what I need. A friendly voice."

"Don't hear from many since your little trick with Apache, huh?"

"I don't want to talk about it."

"Good, because I have something to tell you. Sid fired me."

"Oh my God. New Year's Eve. The bastard . . ." Dani breathed, the weight of the world pressing down harder on her shoulders.

"I saw it coming," she said with a verbal shrug that sparkled a minute later. "I landed a job before the ax fell."

"Something you like?" Dani asked, needing a good answer to assuage her guilt.

"Better than that. Something I can use to my advantage. How soon can you be in San Francisco? I think you and I have to talk about exacting a pound of flesh from Sid Pregerson."

"Give me a few hours. Dinner."

"Great."

"Jenny?" Dani said just before she hung up. "Your timing couldn't have been better. Thanks."

Alexander followed Lewis Basset up the stairs of his posh Washington townhouse into an extremely comfortable room on the second floor. The little woman had taken Alexander's hand without shaking it, welcomed him without looking him in the eye, then handed him over to Lewis who offered a drink in this, his private study, the place where all his important talks were held.

Large, Alexander could see the room would be bright in daylight hours. Expensive shutters covered the huge windows, walnut paneled the walls. The furniture was oxblood leather, tufted and worn just as it should be for a man of Lewis's age and stature. A huge desk stood in one corner. Books lined the walls from floor to ceiling. Though Lewis Basset didn't smoke, the room was heavy with the smell of tobacco, a not altogether unpleasant scent here. The leather, the smoke, the old books all came together to create an atmosphere of power and Alexander loved it.

He chose to sit on the huge couch. He chose scotch to drink and it was given to him in a heavy glass. He also chose to make Lewis responsible for the meeting. Alexander may have been summoned, but he was not going to be a courtier anxiously awaiting the king's pleasure. Lewis caught on quick. This talent was a prerequisite for a politician and he decided to let the little man from California have it his way for now. He sat comfortably in an armchair, his feet on an ottoman. He smiled at Alexander.

"So, young fella. How are you finding all of us? Everything your mama said we were?"

"My mother never said much about her colleagues one way or the other," Alexander answered politely, completely at ease. "Personally, however, I would say you've all lived up to my expectations."

Lewis chuckled. All you had to do was ask him a direct question to get what you wanted. Now he could relax.

"We are a pretty impressive group, ain't we," Lewis said, his accent thickening. "Well we try, Alexander, my boy. Sure we do. And we also try to do just the right thing, know what I mean?"

Alexander raised an eyebrow. Lewis didn't bother to interpret that little reaction. As long as the boy knew his place that's all he cared about.

"Naturally, I was gettin' kind of worried there when we weren't gettin' a rise out of you during those hearings on this chemical problem. You been sittin' there for months listenin', askin' a question every now and again. You just never told us what you think of the whole thing. See, we're pretty casual around here when the cameras aren't turnin'. We need to know what one another is thinkin' so we can all sort of work toward the same goal—'specially those of us in the same party, if you know what I mean?"

"I think I do."

"Wouldn't do to have any embarrassing miscommunications. So I thought maybe you'd be more comfortable if you and me just had this little chat. You know, in case you have any questions you were too nervous to ask, bein' new and all."

Lewis kept his lips together and waited. He'd shown his cards, and all his kindness. Now Grant had to give a little. If he didn't, it was time to play hardball.

"That's kind of you, Senator Basset."

"No, no, call me Lewis," said the older man magnanimously.

"Lewis," Alexander reiterated slowly as though trying to decide whether the name felt right on his tongue. Without making a decision, nor taking his eyes off his colleague, he murmured, "Very kind of you. I'm afraid I'm still not up to speed on protocol. My aide is helping me greatly, but there is no substitute for lessons heard at the patriarch's knee."

Lewis beamed. Smart ass youngster, he thought, but it was thought with a grudging admiration. Margaret's boy knew how to use his words and his brain together. He knew what side his bread was buttered on.

"Hope you're not calling me old, Alexander," Lewis laughed.

"Never. I admire the longevity of your leadership. You know when to deal and when not to. That seems to be a lesson not many learn properly here in Washington."

"Well said," Lewis commented, suddenly serious. All pretense of courtesy now gone. He didn't mind sharing a little bit of what he knew, if that's what it took to find out where Grant stood on the chemical bill.

"I'm glad you understand that. The art of the deal, as it has been termed, can be exceedingly exciting and rewarding. A Senator doesn't make much in the way of money. You gotta make it before you get here, then make it work for you while you're here. But the power—that's exciting. Makes your soul rich. Keeps your mind tight, remembering what went down and where and with who. That's the real thrill. But you gotta recognize where to throw your weight. I think you're a smart boy. I think you've already figured it out. But you tell me yourself. What do you think of all these hearings? How do you see the workings of this old government?"

Lewis leaned forward as he spoke, his gnarled fingers laced. The glitter in his eyes matched that in Alexander's as they faced off.

"I've found the process quite interesting," Alexander said as he put the drink on the coffee table in front of him and rested his arms on his knees. "It also seems to be a waste of time and taxpayer money." Alexander paused, lowered his eyes then locked stares with his host. "But it's a damn good show, and now what we have to figure out is what do we recommend so that we all come out smelling like roses."

Lewis Basset raised his hands and clapped slowly. "You're a quick study, boy. And all this in such a very short time. So what do you say? What would you recommend we do? My private poll says that the three Republican brethren on our little subcommittee don't want to offer any concessions. They want to drop the whole matter without so much as a nod toward legislation that will pacify the special interest groups. They vote big business every time.

"But we're Democrats, Alexander. You, me and two other of our colleagues who sit on this damned subcommittee. We're for the people, and they expect us to show them that we are. But we can't alienate all those powerful chemical people either. So what would you do, Alexander? What would our newest Senator suggest?"

They sat in silence and considered one another, each believing they could read the other's mind. Lewis thought Alexander was trying not to show how intimidated he was by the senior Senator's challenge. He was wrong. Alexander wasn't intimidated in the least. He was thinking ahead.

The subcommittee would take another few months to wrap up its hearings. The full committee would take a few months more. The primaries were coming up and Lewis Basset's endorsement during the primaries might mean the difference between success and failure. And the answer Alexander gave now would mean the difference between Lewis Basset's seal of approval or active opposition.

"Senator Basset, I have the greatest respect for you. I wouldn't presume, after only a few months on the Hill, to know the wisest course of action. I thought I might follow your lead for a while, if that is acceptable to you."

"That, Alexander, was a wise answer. I will guide this subcommittee to a good and proper conclusion. You can count on that." Lewis grinned, his mouth open, his teeth not quite straight. "Now, boy, is there anything I can do for you? Anything at all?"

Now it was Alexander's turn to smile. There was, indeed, something Lewis Basset could do for him. And, when it was done, it would be Alexander who would be calling the shots.

Chapter Nineteen

"Pregerson lost the TransTam account about a week ago. Somehow Sid convinced them to hold off announcing for another month or so because he's afraid there's going to be a run on the agency. TransTam was a big chunk of business. Not enough to kill the agency but certainly enough to cripple it."

"Jesus, that must have really wounded the old bull." Dani shook her head. Much as she hated Sid, there was a part of her that sympathized. Dani saw his predicament in a new light since she'd become an agency owner herself. Luckily, this was only a small part of her, the rest of her rejoiced.

"It's hard to tell with Sid, but I'd guess he was upset. Anyway, he used that as an excuse to can me. Of course he let the entire account group go and just tacked me on for good measure. Heck, I never worked on that account in my life." Jenny scoffed. "Doesn't matter. I was already out of there. I'd been looking ever since New Year's Eve."

Jenny picked at her salad, too excited to eat, too anxious to get to the bottom line. She abandoned her fork, crossed her arms, and leaned forward.

"To make a long story short, I'm employed. Guess

where I ended up?" Dani shook her head, awfully curious and clueless. When Jenny was assured of Dani's complete attention, she dropped her bomb triumphantly. "You are now looking at the Advertising Manager of Ashley Cosmetics. Pregerson Advertising's second largest account after the now defunct TransTam."

Jenny beamed. Dani choked.

"And I think it's about time Ashley Cosmetics changed agencies. Think Green Advertising would be interested?"

Dani coughed louder, choking as she laughed, nodded, and gleefully accepted the assignment.

When the cab stopped in front of the restored Victorian Dani handed the driver a twenty to cover a ten dollar fare. She hopped out of the hack before he could dig for change and sent him on his way with a wave of her hand. She wouldn't change her mind—not about anything. Christ she felt good. Strike that. She felt great. Not only had Jenny handed her Sid on a platter, she had given her something much more important. Jenny Jensen had shown Dani the road to salvation, and she was going to take it.

Now she was taking the first step. Her plan was perfect. By the end of the night, Blake would be in her arms again and this time, she was damn well going to make sure he stayed there. There was only one problem. Blake hadn't returned her phone calls, hadn't responded to her ad, so how on earth was she going to make him listen?

Snuggling into her coat, as much for courage as comfort, Dani rang the bell and waited. Nothing. She rang again. Impatiently she stepped back and looked up. Blake's not-at-home lights were on. Damn. He could be on assignment in Timbuktu, romancing a new model at his favorite hole-in-the-wall around the corner, or poised on the edge of the Golden Gate ready to plunge for want of her for all she knew. Well, at least she could count the last out. Not Blake's style.

Hitching her coat about her she listened to the forlorn sound of a fog horn and shivered in the night chill. Dani paced. She hated to be uncomfortable. Fog should be enjoyed from inside a warm home. Those who thought walking in it was romantic were missing a few marbles. Pacing, straining against the bone-chilling cold, Dani did mental gymnastics trying to remember all the mundane little things Blake used to insist she know when they lived together: how to shut off the gas in case of earthquake, ditto for the water, how to disconnect the electric garage door, where the extra key was kept.

Clear as day, Dani could envision the gas shut off, the water shut off, the grinding mechanism of the electric garage door, but as the damp air permeated her coat, melted through her almost nonexistent silk blouse to attack her skin and bones, Dani couldn't remember where Blake hid his damned key.

Settling down on the stoop, Dani nestled her hand in her chin and watched the traffic go by. When a cab appeared at the end of the block she sat up straighter, primping, sure it was him. But it drove on. When one slowed as it approached she was on her feet, expecting Blake to emerge, pay the driver, then turn a forgiving face her way. Each time she was disappointed. Finally, her hair plastered to her face from the heavy fog, teeth chattering, she was just about ready to give up when a light went off in her head. The key was in the mail box. Well, not exactly in it . . .

Rushing to it, Dani flipped the ornate wrought iron cover and eased her hand through the narrow opening. Gingerly she moved her fingers, conscious of the sharp corners as she searched, then found, what she was looking for. Looping her finger around the thin, plastic line she pulled with a gentle, even motion until three feet of opaque fishing line attached, blessedly, to a key lay in her hand.

Untying the key, Dani stuffed the filament back into the box and with stiff, near blue fingers let herself into Blake's very warm home.

"Cortland, you are a genius," she muttered as she clattered up the three flights of stairs to the master bathroom where she promptly raided Blake's stash of European bath salts and settled herself into a steaming tub. It was ten thirty.

"God I feel like a herd of elephants ran over me."

Eva Talbot rubbed the back of her neck with her long, ebony fingers. She was six feet tall in her stocking feet; with heels she towered over Blake by three inches.

The first time he shot her had been five years ago. Blake had been impressed, but Eva was still a girl whose youth could not be disguised with make-up and furs. In five years she had absorbed the best of New York and Europe and every point in between. She was a beauty with a quick mind. He liked her a lot. The feeling, it seemed, was mutual.

By seven, without so much as sneaking off to a secluded corner of the set, they knew they would be having dinner together. Halfway through the linguine it was understood they would be spending a few more hours, if not the next few days, in each other's company before Eva jetted off to her next ten-thousand-dollar-a-day-assignment. He pushed open the door and let her pass, flashing on the many times he'd held this same door for Dani, loving her, desiring her. His heart clutched and in his mind's eye flashed the brightness of her hair, her eyes . . .

"Aren't you coming?"

Startled, Blake looked up and blinked. For a moment he was confused. He'd been dreaming blonde and he was looking at dark. A chocolate-colored woman with raven hair, cheek bones that threatened to slice the film that shot them, not a sunlight woman with silken hair. No, she wasn't Dani, but then he should be glad of that. Eva had enough sense to treat those she liked with respect. Thank God she wasn't Dani.

"After you," Blake said, shutting the door as he stepped into the foyer. He brightened, grinning with the hope that Eva wouldn't see that he still hurt for Dani. "Up the stairs for food. Up the next flight for a place to kick off your shoes and rest that elephant-trampled body."

"You mean I have a choice?" Eva was quite genuinely amazed. Most men preferred to get right down to it. How lovely to find that Blake was truly a gentleman.

"Absolutely," Blake answered graciously as he took her coat and calculated the easiest way to remove the unitard she wore so beautifully.

"Can I have both?" Her almond-shaped eyes twinkled and she turned on the stairs.

"Naturally," Blake murmured, approaching her, sliding his hands around her very trim waist, his eyes traveling up her body. Breasts were eye level, perfectly formed and unencumbered under the matte stretch of fabric, long neck encased in more jersey freeing only her face. Such an exquisite package.

Eva placed her hands lightly on his shoulder and her lips, more certainly over his. They kissed for a long, long time before Eva made her decision.

"I think we should gather up a midnight picnic in the kitchen and high-tail it up to the third floor where we can get comfortable. We'll munch before deciding what else we should do with the evening."

"Will a picnic at eleven o'clock have the same magic as it would at midnight?" Blake asked.

"Baby," Eva cooed, "you are lookin' at a witch, one who can make magic at any hour of any day."

"Why don't I doubt that, Eva?"

"Because you are one smart man, Blake Sinclair," she whispered, kissing him gently before sashaying up the stairs like she owned the place.

Dani heard Blake's voice just as she reached to pop the drain on the tub. Abandoning her clean-up, she toweled herself at top speed and ran a brush through her hair. Damn! She'd wanted to be gorgeous before he got home. She looked like a drowned rat, make-upless, wet hair, goosebumped. Leaning over the marble vanity Dani closely inspected her skin, pinched her cheeks and . . . froze.

Mid-pinch Dani was paralyzed. Something wasn't right. Blake was talking. My God he'd gone over the edge. He was talking to himself. Then her stomach lurched. He wasn't talking to himself, there was a contralto to match his bass. He wasn't alone and, though Dani couldn't hear the words, she recognized the mating lingo. Well, she would see about this. She'd confront Blake and his date! She'd . . .

x

257

Do nothing of the sort. This was a moment for maturity, level-headedness. After all, Blake hated her right now. He'd probably toss her out on her ear if she did that. She'd rather just wait it out. Yes, a much more mature option. Besides, Blake needed to be in the best possible frame of mind when he saw her and, hopefully, the lady in the next room would put him there.

Knowing it might be a long night, Dani blessed Blake for insisting that a magazine rack be a standard accessory in the bathroom. She took his robe off the hook on the door and, ever so quietly, gathered her clothes. With only the toilette for company, she settled in for the long haul.

". . . Soda crackers are lower in calories than Ritz crackers. Pickles have only fifteen calories for each medium-size dill. A stalk of celery only has seven. Then, when I've got the menu planned for the entire week I go to the store and purchase everything on my list and follow it to the letter when I'm hungry," Eva lectured. "If I didn't can you imagine what the camera would see? I mean you would be lookin' through your lens, Blake, and see nothing but blubber."

"Then how do you explain the fact," Blake asked lazily, "that you are now lying naked in my bed eating everything in sight. I have a feeling smoked oysters are not exactly the most calorie conscious food . . ." He held one above her lips, they opened and the oyster disappeared past her very straight white teeth. She chuckled as she chewed.

"Not to worry. I'd say I worked off every calorie a few minutes ago, wouldn't you?"

"I'd say you're absolutely right," Blake agreed,

leaning down to kiss first her lips then each naked breast before reaching across her for his glass of wine. So taken was he with the dark tips of her breasts he hit the glass sending chilled wine spilling over her naked body.

With a yelp and a laugh, Eva jumped, wiping her bare skin frantically and, in the process, toppled the bed-tray. Wine, oysters, cheese and crackers flew everywhere.

"Sorry . . . sorry . . . oh, God, sorry . . ." Blake mumbled, trying to right everything.

"No, my fault . . ." Eva said simultaneously, grabbing at food, glasses, and plates.

"Hold on, this is getting us nowhere," Blake laughed, "I'll get a towel. Maybe it would have been better if you were fat and ugly. Then I would have just given you a beer in the kitchen and sent you on your way."

"No you wouldn't," she called as he headed to the bathroom. "You wouldn't have brought me home in the first place."

"Right you are," Blake retorted and pushed open the bathroom door.

Still chuckling he grabbed the towels, took a look at himself in the mirror just to make sure he wasn't covered with cracker crumbs and was already rushing back to the bedroom when he stopped. The towels in his hands were heavy and wet and that was very, very wrong. His eye like a camera lens pulled in for a close-up, scoped the room slowly, carefully, half hearing Eva's banter from the other room. Vaguely he was aware that he was making answering sounds, his mind was definitely elsewhere.

Wet towels grasped in his fist he saw that his robe was missing, no longer hanging on the back of the

259

door. There were droplets of water on the vanity tile. He sniffed. The scent of bath salts lingered in the air. Slowly, carefully, he moved toward the separate toilette room. The final bit of evidence that his home had been invaded—the door was closed and he never, ever closed that door.

"Blake, hurry or your mattress will be soaked," Eva called, still laughing.

Palming the door, Blake opened his mouth to answer but then they would know he was near. . . . His hand shook as he considered who *they* might be. Sweat beaded his hairline and he told himself no self-respecting killer would use his bath salts before an attack.

"Be a man, Blake," he murmured and increased the pressure on the door. It wasn't tightly shut. Dragging in a breath, frightened for the first time in his life, Blake prepared to do battle for his home. Determined not to let his courage wane, he pushed the door open, fixing himself in front of the opening, eyes wide, fear rampant, and fists primed.

There was movement, scurrying in the little room. He found *them.* He was face to face with *them.*

"Ah!"

"Ah!" a voice whispered in terrified reply. Blake's ferocity melted to surprise until it was obliterated in an expression of utter shock. Dani, huddled in the corner near the toilette, snuggled into his robe clutching the latest issue of *Photography Today* to her breast.

Dani's fright turned to shock then surprise then absolute delight as she looked up at Blake. He'd never looked more desirable. Biting her lip, trying not to laugh, fully aware they were not alone in the house, Dani let her eyes travel up his naked body, not bothering to hide her approval as she whispered.

"I love the show, Blake, but your entrance left a lot to be desired."

Blake backed out of the little room slowly, mutely. He had almost done battle, stark naked no less, with his ex-wife while one of the world's hottest models picked smoked oysters from the folds of his bedsheets. He shook his head. He turned toward the sink and splashed his face with cold water. When he looked in the mirror he saw Dani was still there, no mirage. She was real and having the time of her life. The last thing he saw as she closed the door was her fingers meeting her lips as she blew him a kiss knowing she wouldn't have to wait much longer to have Blake to herself.

"Dani!" Blake bellowed then took the stairs two at a time. "Dani, get your butt out here right this minute!"

He was ready to drag her out if he had to, but by the time he arrived, breathless from his sprint, Dani was already sitting on the messed bed looking quite the sprite. She cringed, more from distaste than fear, when he ground to a halt in front of her, fists clenched, his face bright with fury.

"Blake, I've never seen this side of you. It's strange, but . . ." Dani batted her eyes, clamming up the moment he growled.

"How did you get in here?"

Obviously this was not the time for cute, fun and games or any other little ploys Dani had at her fingertips. Truth was the order and she obliged, wanting to get the third degree over with as soon as possible so she could get on with her agenda.

"The key in the mailbox."

"How long have you been here?"

"Long enough."

"I had a woman in here, Dani. A very nice woman. I have just sent her back to her hotel with a very lame excuse as to why she couldn't spend the night with me. She was hurt and she was ashamed that we had made love and I didn't have the courtesy to allow her to sleep here or, at the very least, see her back to her room."

Blake's voice quavered as if his fury was physical and it was cutting off his air. His voice fell an octave, he spoke through his teeth. Dani lowered her lashes. Finally she was ashamed. She didn't give a damn about the model, but Blake's honor meant a great deal to him. She couldn't hold his gaze. Once again she'd hurt him and she was sorry. Why couldn't he see that? Blake's breath was coming easier now, his chest was rising and falling at a rate that was considered border-line for a heart attack. He half turned from her, running his hand through his hair, his other hand resting on his slim hips now covered with a pair of cut-off shorts. He sounded so plaintive when next he spoke, she wanted to take him in her arms. Dani stayed still knowing he wouldn't find comfort there—yet.

"However, Dani, I think the lady would have been even more embarrassed had I told her that the reason she had to leave was because my ex-wife and ex-friend was sitting in my bathroom for God-knows-what-reason and had listened to what should have been an extremely intimate, private exchange."

"I wasn't listening," Dani protested, her head shooting up defiantly only for her to wither under his black gaze.

"I don't care if you were deaf, dumb, and blind for the last few hours, the fact is you're here. You've been here when you knew you shouldn't have been and you didn't announce yourself when you should have!"

"Blake please!" Dani said, deciding the time was right for a bit of righteous indignation. He had never spoken to her this way and she wouldn't have it now. She hadn't murdered anyone for goodness sake. "I do not care for you screaming at me."

"You don't . . ." Blake stuttered, incredulous at her audacity. Even for Dani this was too much!

"No I don't," she complained and pulled his robe tighter about her, flipping her now dry hair away from her face, her blue eyes flashing with righteousness. "And I'll tell you something else, Blake Sinclair. How on earth was I supposed to announce myself? I was in the tub having a warm soak because I'd been outside waiting for you in that damned fog for hours and I was so cold. I could have gotten pneumonia if I didn't get warm. So when I finally managed to get the door open I took a bath."

Dani shook her head as though clean hair proved that right was on her side. Blake stood taller, trying to turn his head away. It was useless, the smell of soap and shampoo drifted toward him. He wanted to kill her, he wanted to love her. He didn't want to listen to her, but it seemed he had no choice. She was on a roll.

"I didn't know you were going to have anyone with you. In fact, I think I was rather discreet. I believe I handled the situation much better than you did. When faced with the depressing option of announcing myself or staying put I took the one that led to my discomfort not yours and certainly not that bimbo you had with you."

"That was not a bimbo. That was a woman of beauty and honesty—which is more than I can say for the present company—and I will have to buy out a florist to make this up to her. Even then, I'm still not sure she's going to forgive me. Dani . . . Dani . . ." Blake's finger was wagging at her but his thoughts were speeding like a locomotive and for a moment he lost track of words. Throwing his hands into the air he raised his eyes in the general vicinity of heaven. "Dani, save me from you. You love me so much you can't live with me. You screw me around on the job. You sit in my bathroom while I'm making love to another woman. You compete with me at every turn. You leave me just when I need you the most and then you're indignant that I'm upset with you. Dani, please explain this to me."

Blake's shoulders sagged helplessly. This was beyond him. He was like a little boy ready for bed, dressed only in his favorite shorts. His feet looked small, his chest had lost some of its definition. Blake was a broken man and it was the wide-eyed blonde on the bed that had piled on the straws that broke the camel's back. Slowly he shuffled toward the bed and sat down heavily. Dani, sensing victory, scooted up behind him, took his shoulders in her hands, and leaned her chin in the crook of his neck. Instinctively he nuzzled into her seeking any comfort he could.

"I came to apologize to you for Apache," she whispered, punctuating the sentence with a kiss behind his ear. "I didn't know you cared so much about it." Blake pulled away; Dani tugged back. "Okay. Okay. Honesty. I did know it meant a lot and I knew it was wrong not to tell you what I was doing. But it was such a small thing at first, a little pinch of conscience. Blake, you always accepted me as I was, you never seemed to mind my games before. Admit it, sometimes they even amused you."

"But you never played against *me,* Dani. You never screwed me."

"I know that now," she admitted quietly, apologizing with more little kisses up his neck. "I'm sorry. I should have realized it would make a difference. I did know it actually. But by the time I knew how wrong all this was it was too late, too important. I couldn't let go." Dani hated admitting the wrong. It felt awful, all this groveling so she launched into the good part, the icing on the horrendous cake she'd baked. "But it's all going to work out now. I've changed. I'm the woman you wanted to spend your life with. I can see now that I don't need to best you or anyone else. God, it's been awful Blake. My eyes are open now, and I can see this is all my fault. I sabotaged my own career and I did the same thing to us. I'm the one that's kept us apart so many years, and for nothing. Blake, I need to be with you, work with you. That's how we can be happy again."

"I don't know, Dani. I don't think I can take this roller coaster any more," Blake sighed. His head listed. She stroked his beautiful hair away from his neck and dug her fingers in. His muscles were corded to breaking, poor thing.

"Sure you can," she murmured, trying not to let him hear her apprehension. He had to listen to her, she wanted to make amends. "Think about it, Blake. Together again, living, loving—working. We haven't done that since we were kids and obviously I've been doing a lot of it wrong. But I could learn, Blake. You could teach me. It could be so wonderful. Darling? Please? I'm so very sorry for everything I've done. I can prove it. I've brought a present."

Dani snuggled in closer, pressing her body against his, letting the robe fall open so that flesh was pressing against flesh. She felt Blake stir and held her breath. She didn't want his desire alone; Dani wanted Blake to see that she was trying to rectify all the mistakes they—she—had ever made.

"You want to hear about it?" she asked, digging her fingers deeper into the muscles in his shoulders, praying he would give her a few more minutes to convince him of her sincerity.

Blake answered, his voice flat and beaten. "Then will you leave?"

"If you want me to." Dani closed her eyes, thanking God for this one last chance.

"Okay. What is it?"

"I've brought you an exclusive, my love. I've brought you Ashley Cosmetics to do with what you will."

Chapter Twenty

"It must be very difficult for you, Mrs. Grant, having your life turned upside down like this just when you were exerting your independence as a single woman."

"On the contrary. I feel rejuvenated reconciling with my husband. I am committed to Alexander Grant, not only as a man, but as the best candidate to serve our country and our state in the Senate. He's a sincere man who puts honesty above all else. One need only look into his face, into his eyes, to see the level of his commitment to his task. We need men who think before they speak, men who calculate the benefits and the drawbacks of decisions they make. Men like Alexander Grant . . ."

"I can certainly see that you're committed Mrs. Grant and I'm afraid we're out of time . . . This is . . ."

The interviewer turned full-face to the camera as the half hour talk show ended, music coming up effectively cutting off Polly's impassioned speech about her husband instead of her lamentable loss of freedom. With the flip of a switch Polly Grant was left alone to consider how she'd done.

Picking up her teacup she headed toward the

267

kitchen thinking the part about a man of vision was a nice touch. Alexander would love it when he saw it, if he saw it. She now had twelve tapes, twelve interviews completed on her own while he worked in Washington.

Polly washed her teacup thoughtfully, not feeling quite as wonderful as she thought she should. Much of that was her daughter's fault. Oh the vile things Monica had said about Alexander not really wanting them to be a family again, just wanting to have a house to stay at in Fresno, a place that made it look like he had a home. But Polly had put a stop to that talk immediately. Eighteen though their daughter might be, she was still their child, and children should respect their parents.

The teacup now put away, the towel folded meticulously, Polly was headed back to the living room to read the promotional material Alexander had sent to her when it struck her that, perhaps, in a way Monica was right—they weren't like a real family. Families talked to one another, heard about one another's day, were interested in one another's activities. It was lonely having no one to talk to about this great adventure she and Alexander had embarked on. Since Monica didn't want to be her confidante, Polly would just have to take matters into her own hands. Yes, spreading her wings, making her own decisions, sounded quite the rational thing to do.

Back on the couch she picked up a pad of paper and began to make notes. After all, she was a Senator's wife. She didn't need to be told what to do . . . did she? Wasn't she someone worthwhile? Wasn't she needed? Alexander said she was.

* * *

Eric moved swiftly down the long corridors of the Senate building. The sun had already set, lights were on in some offices, but most were dark. He had been at work since six. Lunch had kept him going until four, he began fading about five and thought that he would be forced to take a nap on Alexander's couch if the subcommittee didn't break soon. Then it happened and his adrenaline started pumping and his feet started moving and now he was there pushing through the chamber doors as unobtrusively as possible and leaning down toward Alexander's ear he whispered frantically. Alexander shuddered only to control himself instantly.

"I'll be there as soon as I can. I want you to call Senator Gibson. Tell him I won't be at his little . . . cocktail party tonight. Also call Allison and cancel. We're voting at the end of this session. I think the outcome is pretty set."

"I should say," Eric whispered, fully aware that Alexander was going to have to vote with the Republicans if he was going to honor the deal with Radison.

Alexander smiled knowingly, "Just go do what I told you. Come back if you'd like. You might catch the tail end of the vote. And Eric? Don't worry."

"Right. See you in a few minutes."

Eric walked sedately out of the hearing room and flew down the corridor retracing his steps. He was back, still shaken by the turn of events, fifteen minutes later.

Breathing a little easier he slipped into one of the chairs and looked at the tired committee members who had just begun to vote. The three Republicans cast theirs against limiting export and any further powers for Drug Enforcement. Most of the Senators looked bored. Senator Basset, looking sure of himself and content, cast a vote to pass on a recommendation to the full committee that further legislation supporting curbs be enacted. Democratic Senators Smithson and Carlton cast their vote with Basset. All eyes turned to the junior Senator, Alexander Grant. Eric smirked. Old Basset was going to fall on his face when he heard Alexander's vote.

Alexander's eyes flickered to Eric, a smile tipped his strong, narrow lips upwards.

"Gentlemen, I shall have to vote with my esteemed colleagues. I would like to see a recommendation go to the full committee for eventual consideration as a bill on the floor."

Eric felt his stomach heave. He wasn't sure his legs would hold him as he rose and waited for Alexander to come to him. What had Alexander Grant done? Damnation was waiting for him in his office right that minute and with the vote he just cast, hell, Radison Chemical style, wasn't far away.

"Darling, what a surprise."

Eric stood back while Alexander rushed into the anteroom of his office and gathered his wife in his arms. It was an amazing sight. Alexander Grant didn't flinch. Eric, if he hadn't known better, would have sworn the guy was actually happy to see this woman.

"Oh, Alexander," Polly whispered, embarrassed by Eric's presence, "I'm so happy you're not angry."

"Angry? Never. I'm just surprised. I've been cooped up in those subcommittee meetings for so many months I'd almost forgotten what a beautiful wife I have. You've met Eric?"

Polly peeked around her husband, "Yes, he was kind enough to get me some coffee."

270

"Coffee? He should have brought you something more substantial. I'll bet you haven't had a thing to eat. I know a marvelous little restaurant. We'll have the best meal in Washington to celebrate before I take you back and show you my poor little apartment."

"Oh, but I'm not really very hungry . . ." Polly began, relieved that Alexander wasn't angry; relieved that he was where he always said he was—working.

"I insist," Alexander said smoothly. "Nothing but a celebration will do tonight. Now, the bathroom is just down the hall. You'll want to freshen up. I'll just check my messages and we'll be on our way."

Doing as she was told, Polly left the two men and went to powder her nose, triumphant now that she had proved Monica wrong. He did want her. Alexander had been thrilled to see her. He had just been so busy he'd forgotten to ask her to join him; he was too embarrassed by his poor accommodations. He was a kind and gentle and loving man. Now she knew it beyond a shadow of a doubt.

Eric and Alexander watched Polly disappear, their smiles fading the moment she was out of sight. Immediately Alexander took Eric's arm, his eyes flattening to gunmetal grey as he lowered his voice.

"Do you still have your key to my apartment?"

Eric nodded.

"Good. Get over there now. Allison left a robe behind the door in the bathroom and a couple of things in the third drawer of the dresser in the bedroom. Get rid of the pink shampoo and the extra razor and tooth-brush. Do it by ten. That's when I'll have Polly back there."

"You got it." Eric grabbed his raincoat and was almost halfway to the elevators when he remembered to ask the big question of the night. "Alexander?"

"Yes."

"You voted for a recommendation to curb chemical exports."

"So I did." Alexander admitted, looking quite pleased with himself.

"Radison won't be happy," Eric warned, feeling the sweat pop out on his forehead. Guilt by association was not one of his favorite things.

"I don't remember telling you to worry about Radison, Eric."

They watched one another for a long moment before Eric backed off and went on his way fit to be tied. Alexander was going to have to learn that this was not the way to make friends and influence people—not by a long shot. Angrily Eric pushed through the door and stepped into a night that promised a beautiful morning. Alexander Grant had an extremely short memory. Someday he'd be sorry he discarded Eric so easily. Someday he'd come begging for his help, then Eric would show him. He'd help, of course, but not without a healthy dose of I-told-you-so.

"Why Alexander, this is absolutely lovely. Quite charming," Polly enthused as she walked through the two bedroom flat Alexander called home in Washington.

"Glad you like it. But it is a bit small. Not at all what we're used to at home."

"But Alexander, home is wherever we're together. That's what this reconciliation is all about," Polly reminded him.

Alexander had his coat half off when Polly took over, easing it from him before he could object.

"I can do that Polly," Alexander snapped.

Slipping out of it he tossed it on the rented sofa and went into a kitchen ill equipped for a family, but perfect for a man who entertained a lady with a penchant for nibbling and sipping. He could actually feel Polly shrinking behind him. Her distress over his harsh words was palpable, yet he knew she wouldn't reprimand him though it would have been preferable to her martyr routine.

"You're sorry I came. You're angry I'm here." Her voice was so forlorn it couldn't even be considered a wail. This was simply a whisper of pain and loneliness as she heaped real and imagined guilt upon herself. Exasperated, Alexander went to her and took her in his arms.

"I'm not angry," he said softening his expression as best he could. "I'm not, Polly. It's been a long day and I've never been good at surprises in the long run. Remember how I hate being surprised on Christmas?"

"I do, and I could never understand it," Polly answered, perplexed.

"Oh, I suppose that's a bit untrue, an extreme example. It's just that I'm a very methodical person. I like to be prepared so I don't disappoint anyone."

Alexander lied easily. He had never told Polly that he didn't like surprises because he was so often disappointed. Better no present than one that fell below the mark. Twirling herself into his arms, she put her arms around his neck and smiled, satisfied with his answer.

"As if you could ever disappoint anyone."

Alexander held her away, amazed by the woman's ability to deceive herself. Hadn't he coldly, ruthlessly cut himself off from her when he wanted out of their marriage? Now she stood cuddled into him, expressing her belief in his goodness like a new bride. Was it any wonder he had tired of her?

"I try not to, Polly. Now, sit down and I'm going to get us both something to drink. It's been a long, long day and I, for one, need to unwind."

"That sounds wonderful. I'll just put my suitcase in the bedroom. Be back in a jiffy."

Alexander threw a kiss her way. She pretended to catch it and put it on her lips. A coquette at her age. Frightening. Shaking his head as he reached for the wineglasses, Alexander realized he was oddly thankful Polly had come. He was tired and found the idea of a good night's sleep welcoming. Allison, his Washington diversion, was a randy little thing and demanded a good deal of attention unlike Polly. Loosening his tie, he settled himself on the sofa, tilting back his head and listening to the sounds of Polly settling in. Far be it from her to ever feel comfortable if her toothbrush wasn't hanging just so. Polly, so predictable she'd probably bore herself to death one day.

Polly put her night cream and cosmetics into the medicine chest after she'd taken a wash cloth and dusted the shelves. She wiped the sides of Alexander's shave cream while she was at it, hating the look of dried foam on the can. She hung her toothbrush on the little hook provided before carefully rinsing the tubular traveling case.

That done Polly went to the bedroom, shook out her clothes and hung them up. This took some time since she had brought so many things for their trip to Los Angeles in a few days. Finally, adjusting the bookmark in her paperback, she opened the drawer on what would have been her side of the bed had they been home in Fresno. As she pulled, a beige plastic case slid forward, knocking against the front of the drawer. A flat case with no markings but of a size and shape immediately recognizable.

Polly stood motionless for a moment, looked at the thing before twirling her paperback into her chest, holding it there as though it were an amulet worn to protect her from things like this. Her jaw tightened, her lips pulled into a thin line that lay uncomfortably against her teeth like a taut rope. Her eyes felt as though they were bulging against her lower lids. In her heart was a pain so severe she could neither fight it nor succumb to it, only stand rigidly while it tore through that vital organ.

Slowly Polly placed the book in the drawer. Her fingers hovered than swooped down until she held the thing in both hands, covering it protectively as one would a small, newborn animal. A great vibration coursed through her. She snapped the lid, hesitated, then opened it. Slowly, delaying the inevitable until finally, there it was—a dome shaped diaphragm, flesh colored and repugnant, malleable, so dirty looking despite its cleanness, every piece of information she needed to know on the lid: the name of the woman to whom this thing belonged, the doctor, who prescribed it, the woman's address. Polly barely saw it all; she couldn't focus. There was, after all, no need to know the particulars, her mind could conjure them up so easily. Alexander naked, sweating, pushing and poking at another woman. A woman young enough to need protection from pregnancy.

"Polly, are you all right?"

Alexander's voice crept up to her, surrounding her until she felt as though she had to cast it off or become as soiled as he. She waited, controlling herself, reminding herself that he was all she had and was all she had ever wanted. She couldn't make herself undesirable, not now. And there must be an explanation. The apartment was furnished, wasn't it? The furniture was rented. Certainly, that was the case. This had been left by mistake. Polly had known there was a logical explanation.

Covering the case again she turned only her head and spoke over her shoulder, making sure her voice had a smile in it.

"Of course. I'm fine. Just finishing up. I'll be in in a minute."

"Good. I didn't realize how late it was. I'd like to get to bed soon."

"So would I, Alexander," Polly said quietly as he left the room.

Carefully Polly put the diaphragm back into the drawer and left the room, willing herself to forget her discovery. She had simply erased those few moments from her memory and, as she sat down, she smiled at her husband believing herself to be filled with love for him just as he was for her—only her.

Chapter Twenty-one

"Dani?"

The receptionist's tentative salutation floated through the darkened room but Dani clicked the slide projector remote twice before acknowledging her. It took Dani that long to remember the lady's name. Betsy. Now why was that so difficult? She had interviewed the poor woman, she had been just as thrilled as Rudy to find someone over twenty who was willing to work a front desk since Serina's promotion to production. The least she could do was give her the courtesy of remembering her name.

"Yes, Betsy, what is it?"

"Mr. Green is on the phone from the Senator's shoot and he'd like to talk with you. I told him you and Mr. Sinclair had been locked away all morning and didn't want to be disturbed, but he insisted."

"That's all right. No problem. Can you put it through to my office?"

"Sure, right away."

Dani slid her shoeless feet off the chair she had been using for a footstool and pushed herself upright. Silently she passed the remote control to Blake. Rising, she kissed his lips before leaving him to sift through the test photos for Ashley Cosmetics. Dani padded to her office, sans shoes, ignoring the raised eyebrows as she passed. For the first time since her odyssey began Dani didn't care what anyone thought of her. Exhaustion was actually something she would welcome; it would beat being one of the living dead. They were growing too fast and making too many personal commitments to their important clients.

Dani smirked at the thought. All their clients were important. Ninety percent of them were accounts worth over ten million dollars. For an agency the size of Green Advertising that alone was amazing. And to have two was unbelievable. She and Rudy were going to either have to start forking over big bucks for superior talent or they would both be dead before the next new year.

"Rudy?" Dani greeted him wearily as she picked up the phone.

"Hey, sweetheart, how are you doing?"

"Not bad. Blake and I still haven't found the face we're looking for." She sunk into the chair behind her desk attempting to swivel out some of the tension in her body. "We shot twenty-five models over the last month. We've used a total of one hundred and fifty roles of thirty-five millimeter and twenty cartridges of Polaroid and we still don't have the look we want."

"From what I saw of the creative I' not sure the face matters all that much. We can retouch. It's really the ocean colors that are going to pull this together, right?"

"Oh, Rudy, please," Dani wailed. "This is *Ashley Cosmetics,* not a door-to-door operation. The face has to be perfect, the neck, the shoulders. We even need the body to be excellent just in case we decide to go full on this thing."

"Okay, you're the creative genius, Blake's the incredible man behind the camera. Just don't get so wrapped up in the right look for Ashley that you miss the Apache deadline. And, if we're going to make the fall sweeps the Ashley stuff has to be shot like tomorrow."

"I know that," Dani sighed. "I wish to God I hadn't promised Jenny that Blake and I would be exclusive on this Ashley stuff. If I had a solid senior art director it would sure loosen up my time. By the way did I tell you we've had inquiries by that chain that makes Buffalo wings? One of us should be following up on this stuff."

"Don't remind me," Rudy wailed, then changed the subject. "Listen, what if Blake took over on Ashley?"

"Blake's a great guy behind the camera, a wonderful director, but this is our agency Rudy. We hired him. I don't want to give him more control than he should have."

"Now that's a trusting, loving relationship," Rudy laughed, but there was a sarcastic note to it.

"Hey, it works for us. We've never been happier. We're exactly where we want to be."

"Sorry, guess it was none of my business."

"You guessed right." Dani was sorry the minute the words were out of her mouth. The strain was getting to all of them.

"Listen, I didn't call to shoot the breeze. I've got a few problems down here, and I think we really need a woman's touch to straighten things out."

"I thought Lora was taking up the slack on Alexander's shoot."

"She's part of the problem," Rudy answered.

"Oh no, not again," Dani sighed.

"Not in the way you think. You see . . ."

"Don't tell me she came on to Daniel Sweeny? That's all we need is Lora chasing away our free, and normally very high priced, talent. Jesus."

"Lighten up, Dani," Rudy warned. "The problem isn't with Sweeny. He did his clips and he's been gone for hours. The problem is Mrs. Grant has taken an unusual liking to Lora and vice versa. They're feeding off each other and going in all the wrong directions."

"What exactly is the problem Rudy?" Dani asked impatiently.

"I don't really know except we're not getting through to this woman. It's the way she's dressed. She won't wear the stuff we brought along. Her attitude; she's acting like she's a teenager, trying to be kind of . . . I don't know . . . controlling. It's just not like the first time we shot her. She was okay then. Jesus, Dani, couldn't you just come down for an hour?"

Dani lowered her head into her right hand and rubbed her eyes. Throwing her head back, trying to figure out if she felt refreshed, Dani looked up at the ceiling and realized she didn't. She would give anything to go back to her place with Blake for a back rub. Then she remembered. There would be no back rub tonight or for a week at least. Blake was due back in San Francisco for the weekend to shoot an automobile spot and she was going to spend the weekend finishing up the Ashley presentation. Some reconciliation!

"I'll be there. You're at Parker's doing the stills?"

"Yep and we'll have to cancel the shot at the school if we don't wrap this up by three. Hurry, Dani."

"You got it."

Listlessly Dani went back to the conference room. Blake still sat where she had left him. The only sounds in the room were the methodical clicking of the remote, the whir of the motor in the carousel. Dani watched dust motes dance in the light radiating from the projector and noticed how it illuminated half of Blake. He looked incredibly desirable and ultimately untouchable. A marble statue, one side brightened to perfection, the other side imaginary in the darkness. From where she stood Dani couldn't even detect movement in his critical eyes as he assessed the gorgeous women on the screen. What was he looking for? She had seen at least three models that would satisfy her and Ashley Cosmetics. Yet something was under Blake's skin and he couldn't let go of it.

Quietly she went to him, draping her arms over his shoulders, laying her cheek alongside his.

"Time for a break, mister," she whispered, resisting the urge to kiss him because cheek-to-cheek was so lovely.

"In a minute," Blake murmured.

"I know that tone of voice. That means you'll think about going to the bathroom and getting another cup of coffee three hours from now."

Blake laughed without moving his eyes from the screen. Another face, another pair of seductive lips and limpid eyes filled the white space. Another beautiful face that dissatisfied her man.

"Blake, I think I liked it better before we were happy. At least then I thought you had something I wanted. Now I realize the only difference between us is you're a fanatic and I'm just plain crazy about work."

Blake laughed again, this time relinquishing the remote in favor of her hands.

"Not true. I simply have an incredible amount of dedication and concentration. Now, what were you trying to tell me?"

281

He snuggled back into her, his shoulders pressing against the swell of her breasts. He breathed in her scent.

Closing his eyes Blake tried to imagine how they had come to this. How on earth, after years of trying, had they simply fallen into step with one another? Had their differences been so old and stale that they had fallen away like autumn leaves? Or was this what Dani had been trying to show him for years. That the only way they could truly love and care for one another was if they really shared their work equally, two powers with the same objective. The only problem with that theory was what happened when one of them fell off the merry-go-round? What happened to them when the job failed one or both? Certainly they wouldn't fail the job. That thought was completely absurd. He patted her hands not really caring what the answer was, enjoying only the fact that they were happy and productive and that there was no end in sight.

"I was trying to tell you that I have to go out for a bit. Rudy is shooting Grant's stills for the general election spots and he's having trouble with the wife. Can you keep on going here?"

"Naturally," Blake sighed. "It's dirty work but someone has to do it."

Dani slapped his head playfully, "Since when is staring at a bunch of Venuses dirty work?"

"Since I'm fully aware of what most of them look like without their make-up and the proper lighting. Jesus, I don't understand why I can't get what I want. It's as though I'm seeing the right woman and not recognizing her. I've never had anything like this happen before."

"Don't worry, it will come. I just hope it comes before you have to leave and go up north. I'd really

282

like a decision so I can start on the presentation materials."

"I'll try, babe. If you're not back by the time I have to go to the airport I'll leave a selection on your desk with my preference. Then you can make the final decision."

"Okay. I'll try to make it back though. I want to see you off," Dani said slipping into her shoes, feeling them pinch across the instep. Blake stopped clicking. He was grinning at her.

"What?"

"That was such a nice thing to say. I feel like a commuter being brought to the train station."

"Don't push your luck, sweetie. I'm too tired for jokes like that," Dani warned good-naturedly.

"Well perk yourself up before you tackle the Senator and his wife. Just remember, they aren't professionals. Walk them through their paces gently."

Dani smiled. "Am I ever anything but the soul of discretion?"

One more kiss atop Blake's head and she left him to his photos and his laughter. Grabbing her purse she headed out to the studio where she would meet Mrs. Alexander Grant for the first time.

"Hi, Parker," Dani said as she strolled past the director who was lounging in a chair, a look of resigned disgust on his face.

"Hi Dani. You here to fix things?"

"I guess. Are they in there?"

Dani nodded toward a large back room where models changed.

"Yep. I don't think that woman understands what we're trying to do here. The way she keeps jumping

283

around the set you'd think this was an ad for sneakers."

"Well, I'll see what I can do."

"Please," he drawled. "I would really like to go home sometime today."

Dani shot him a thumbs up and went in. Rudy and Alexander sat on one side of the room silently. Lora stood, hovering near a high-backed make-up chair in which sat Polly Grant. She didn't look half bad and Dani wasn't sorry she had insisted on their reconciliation until she saw Polly's eyes. Behind Polly's curiosity about Dani there was a darkness, a blankness that seemed more natural than the smile that was just beginning to take shape. The mean and nasty expression magically disappeared as she turned in the chair. Dani went directly to her.

"Mrs. Grant, I'm Dani Cortland, the creative director on your husband's account. I'm also Rudy's partner. I'm sorry I wasn't at the first shoot to meet you."

"I'ts very nice to meet you, Miss Cortland." Polly put out her hand as she had been instructed to do when she met someone new, but she shivered when Dani took it and withdrew hers quickly. "I've read the scripts for Alexander's commercials and I think they are very nice. I guess that is what you mean by being creative director—you thought them up?"

"Yes, in a way, that's exactly right," Dani answered with a reassuring smile. She heard Alexander rise. Looking over her shoulder she grinned encouragement. "Nice to see you, Alexander." Behind her she felt Polly stiffen and immediately rearranged her agenda. "You're looking well, Senator."

"And you Dani."

"Thank you. Rudy. Lora." Dani greeted them too before getting on with business. No sense in making

Polly Grant nervous by playing advertising maven. "How are things going here?"

"Well, I think we've sort of reached an impasse," Rudy began, leaning forward and nestling his clasped hands in his lap, "Mrs. Grant brought some of her own things to wear because she thought she would feel more comfortable in them. But I think we should stick with the items the stylist picked out. So we've been trying to figure this little problem out for a while and, since you're here, maybe you could give us your opinion . . ."

Rudy's voice trailed off. Dani smiled affectionately. A year ago Rudy would never have been so tactful. A year ago she would not have been so short-tempered. If Rudy could contain himself, she certainly could do the same.

"I'd be delighted," Dani answered. "Let's take a look. What have you got, Mrs. Grant?"

"Polly, please," came the gracious response and the blank look. She reached for the hangers beside her. "I've brought two of my favorite outfits that I think make me look so wonderful. This red and black print fits well and then this sky blue suit. I usually wear it with these pearls. I think I'll come across as peppier if I wear one of these. Lora agrees. In fact, we discussed this at length."

Dani glanced at Lora, who glared back defiantly. Dani ignored her. Polly was holding the outfits in front of her, looking down at them as though to decide which one would look best. Dani cringed. The woman needed wardrobe help.

"You know, Lora is right in many ways. When you do a commercial with real people, as we say, it is often better to make them comfortable by asking them to wear their own clothes . . ." Aware of Lora's astonishment, Dani ignored her. The compliment was nothing but fluff. She'd deal with Lora later. ". . . But that thinking is usually reserved for testimonial commercials. Things of that nature." Dani lowered the dresses, put the hangers together and quietly slid them onto the rack beside the dressing table. "This shoot is different. We're trying to create an image for your husband and, like it or not, you're part of that image. People want to believe that you support him one hundred percent . . ."

"But I do, and I think my appearing in his commercial or by his side will prove that, no matter what I wear. Don't you agree darling?"

Polly looked around Dani, demanding her husband's attention. Alexander gave it curiously, as though trying to figure out why she was being so belligerent.

"I believe whatever the experts tell us, and Miss Cortland is an expert," he answered quietly.

"Is she really?" Polly said wryly.

Dani took a half step backward, knowing now that the dynamics were not what she had initially assumed. This woman wasn't nervous about appearing in a commercial, and she wasn't simply anxious to look her best. Polly Grant was deliberately trying to put herself in the spotlight; she was actually trying to sabotage this shoot. Time for the big guns.

"I am the expert, Mrs. Grant, and if you doubt that perhaps you and I should discuss my qualifications." That might put her mind at ease. "In fact," Dani added calmly "Lora could fix us some coffee while Rudy and the Senator go find Parker." Dani shot Rudy a warning look. He started to shake his head but she was insistent. "You could shoot a few stills for the

286

PR kits while Polly and I talk. It won't be long. I promise."

Dani Cortland and Polly Grant watched one another while the others filed out, then Dani sat down. Polly did the same, crossing her legs demurely and contemptuously at the ankle. Suspicion and dislike for Dani vibrated from the woman like heat waves on hot asphalt. "Mrs. Grant," Dani began but Polly held up her hand in protest so Dani revised her opening. "Polly. I don't think either one of us wants to pussyfoot around here. For some reason you've chosen this day and time to take a stand on something that is not readily apparent to me or the rest of the staff. Your husband may know what's going on, but that isn't any of our business.

"Our business is to make a good commercial with the least amount of difficulty and within budget to help your husband win an election. The longer we play games about wardrobe the more money it's costing your husband and the less effective the final spot will be. Do you understand what I'm saying, Polly? Are we agreed that what is important here is your husband's victory, and not whether you wear red or blue?"

Dani felt it coming, the escalation of her annoyance that this stupid woman would risk blowing her husband's career because she wanted attention. But she held her tongue while Polly leaned forward, her hands resting comfortably on her knees, her face a mask of concern. It seemed as though she were considering everything Dani had told her, as though she couldn't find the words to explain how contrite she was. Yet, instead of an apology, Polly Grant asked a question.

"Are you sleeping with my husband?"

Dani, her body and soul tired from months of overwork, felt herself give away. Exhaustion bowed her shoulders, astonishment made her shake her head. Polly Grant was an absurd woman and Dani had no energy to give her. What little reserve there was she wanted to give to Blake. Straightening, Dani stood, walked over to where she left her purse, picked it up, then looked back at Polly Grant.

"Your husband needs you," she said wearily. "I would suggest you put on the beige suit, and do something constructive. I have someone who needs me much more than you do."

"Messages."

Betsy held out a stack of little pink message slips as Dani walked by. Dani scooped them out of her hand.

"Blake still here?" Dani asked without breaking stride.

"Yep. Haven't heard a peep out of him. Everything all right at the shoot?"

"It's a matter of interpretation, but, yes, things were fine when I left."

"I'm glad to hear that," Betsy pronounced as though she had known it would be okay all along.

"Me too," Dani mumbled, flipping through her messages as she headed toward the conference room. Slipping into the darkened room she announced, "I'm back."

But Blake didn't move so Dani did. If he was asleep she'd never let him forget it. Sliding her hand over his shoulder she bent down to kiss him awake. But Blake wasn't sleeping. He was staring at the screen, his fingers tented beneath his chin, deep in thought. Dani slipped into the chair next to him and lay her hand on his thigh as she settled back.

"You think this is the one?" she asked, hardly able

288

to get excited since she had rejected this model ages ago.

"This is the woman I've been looking for," Blake confirmed quietly.

"I don't know, Blake." Cautiously Dani voiced her objections. "She just doesn't seem to have much depth. She's not your usual choice. She's flat, no character. I'm not sure I could really recommend her to Jenny and Ashley Cosmetics."

"Look closer, Dani," Blake whispered, "look very close. Look past the model in the forefront and zero in on the background. What do you see?"

"I see cables being moved." Dani squinting to see what it was Blake saw.

"Do you see who's moving the cables? Look closer Dani. Get up and walk toward the screen."

Mesmerized by Blake's voice, pushed forward by the conviction she heard in it, Dani did as she was told. She passed in front of the projector, darkening the screen for an instant before moving to the side so she could look closer at the small background figure moving the cables.

Then, only a foot from the screen, Dani saw her. That head turned in the opposite direction of the body, the lips partially opened, full and enticing. The woman's hair whipped behind her in a cloud of color, her neck swanlike, curving slightly at the throat. The collar of her work shirt was open so that one had a glimpse of the rise of her breast. Her hands gripped a cable, strong and capable. But it was the woman's eyes that the film captured so exquisitely. They were haunting when you focused on them, clear, hazel, and transparent as though you could look through them into her soul. Film had shown Dani what everyday contact could not. Film had captured an essence in the woman that might have gone undiscovered had it not been frozen as it was on the screen. Dani's breath caught and she realized that she had been staring at the screen for a very, very long time.

"You see it too, don't you, Dani?" Blake asked quietly, triumphantly.

"She's beautiful." Dani sighed, slowly rotating from the screen to face him. "I just can't believe I didn't see it before."

"Call Rudy, Dani. Tell him we're on our way over. San Francisco can wait." Blake looked back at the slide. "She's the one I want. Serina."

Chapter Twenty-two

"Well if it isn't the gruesome twosome. I thought you would be on your way to San Francisco, Blake." Rudy grinned at Blake and Dani, surprised by their sudden appearance.

"Plans changed," Blake answered, "Can we come in?"

Rudy shrugged, then motioned them in. "Sure."

Dani avoided eye contact with Rudy as she marched after Blake. Far be it from her to spoil his surprise.

"Serina and I already ate dinner," Rudy said, shutting the door, trying to figure out what brought the inseparable couple to his door and not the airport. "How about a beer?"

"It should be champagne," Blake said, looking at every corner of the room as if he expected Serina to suddenly materialize. Rudy pulled a face.

"Beer's all we've got tonight, Blake."

"I think that was just an expression, Rudy." Dani flipped her purse on the table and collapsed on the sofa.

"Don't tell me you two are going to tie the knot again?" Rudy grinned, glad he had finally caught on that this was an occasion here.

"No. This news is good," she said, actually blushing, "but not that good."

"This news is definitely better," Blake agreed, much to Dani's chagrin. "Where's Serina?"

"She's just getting out of the shower. Be here in a minute."

"Great. That's great. So, while we wait for her let's get to it. Here."

Blake dug into his pocket, withdrew the slide and put it in a portable viewer. He handed it to Rudy who took it tentatively and put it to his eye. Dani raised a brow. Blake's excitement was understandable, but the intensity of it struck her as odd. Was this, she wondered, how she had been all these years? Single-minded to the point of abruptness? She watched as Blake moved up behind Rudy, listened while he whispered passionately.

"The new Ashley woman. That's her."

"Nice for a blonde . . ." Rudy began before his voice trailed off to a low whistle. He blinked, lowered the viewer then brought it back up quickly. His body tensed, his attention was riveted. Gotcha!

"You saw her didn't you?" Now Blake's whispering was urgent. He had a convert. "There, in the background."

"She's perfect, Rudy." Dani had moved around her partner and stood beside his other shoulder unable to watch from the sidelines.

"We couldn't believe it either." Blake muttered quietly. He reached for the viewer but Rudy didn't want to share. Only when Serina called from the hall did the three people in the living room turn, abandoning film as they waited for the object of their admiration to join the party.

"Hi, Dani. Hi, Blake." Serina smiled brightly but

the expression froze as she stopped short, fully aware that the three silent people in the room were looking at her strangely. "Are you guys okay?"

"Better than ever," Blake murmured, walking toward her, taking her by the hand and leading her to the dining room table as Dani and Rudy converged on them. There was a lot to talk about.

"I'm not going to tell you again. I think you're crazy." Serina crossed her arms defiantly. Pretty as she was, Dani was almost inclined to agree. But she'd seen the film, she'd seen the transformation. They had proof that Serina was wrong. First, though, they'd hear her out. "I don't even look like myself in that picture you showed me. It must be a trick of the light. I'm not a model, and I'm certainly not the Ashley woman. You need someone well-known. Somebody who knows what they're doing. Rudy, tell them."

"No," Blake said quickly. "Rudy can't tell me anything I don't already know. That wasn't a trick of the light. That picture is proof of your untapped ability. You take on another persona through the camera's eye. Serina, that's a talent you can't waste. Ashley Cosmetics will be delighted with you because they know beauty and that's exactly what you personify."

Serina opened her mouth to protest, but what was there to say? They were fighting about opinions, and it was impossible to win, but she could be worn down. Frustrated she looked to Dani for support.

Dani shrugged. "You can't deny what you see in that picture. You're gorgeous. You're a natural."

"But that's just it. I'm not. I was working, not posing. I think I'd die if you stood me in front of a camera and told me to look one way or the other. And all those people poking at you, stylists and hair people, people looking at you on the street. I just don't know if I could do that. I'd mess everything up if you made me stand all by myself and took pictures of me. I couldn't do that."

"Of course you could. Blake and I would work with you . . ." Dani outlined a plan of attack that would bring Serina the confidence she so needed, but the young woman wasn't listening. Instead she watched Rudy standing by the French doors contemplating the view.

Since the first night they had made love so many months ago, Serina knew there was no other man for her except Rudy Green. A week ago she had happily moved in with him. All this time Serina waited for him to talk about their future. She wanted to hear him say that they would be married, they would have children, that they would be happy together forever. But Rudy hadn't and now Serina wondered if it was because he was still holding out for something better. There was no doubt he loved her, but for Rudy appearances counted for so much. Maybe he didn't want her for forever because she was just Serina, plain and simple. Perhaps he'd love her more if she were the Ashley woman.

Pushing away from the table, ignoring Blake and Dani who were making plans for her future despite her objections, Serina went and put her arms around Rudy's waist. Snuggling into him she flipped his arm around her shoulder.

"So," she asked quietly, "what do you think about all this?"

Rudy eye's flickered her way. He smiled into her wide, hazel ones then kissed the top of her head.

"I think it's really an opportunity," Rudy answered.

"Does that mean you think I ought to do it?"

Rudy shrugged. He sighed. Which answer should he give her? The old Rudy would have pushed Serina; the new one wasn't sure he wanted to share her.

"It means it's an opportunity. You have to decide what to do with your own life. I can't decide for you."

"But if I asked you to decide for me," Serina insisted.

Rudy smiled sadly and pulled her in front of him, wrapping his arms around her protectively. Serina leaned her head against his chest, listening to the comfortable sound of his heart beating, knowing she would do whatever he wanted. If he wanted her to be a model she would try her best; if he wanted her to say no, she would say so gladly. A picture was just a picture, after all. Love was everything.

"I don't know, babe," Rudy sighed. "You could make a lot of money. It would be better than lugging cables. I don't know." He buried his lips in her hair, smelling the faint scent of oranges, feeling the silkiness. "I only want what's best for you."

"What about us?" Serina asked, pulling away so she could look into his eyes and see the truth when he spoke.

"I want what's best for us," Rudy said simply, without hesitation. They held one another's gaze for an eternity and Rudy, his eyes misting, looked as if he had just seen a vision. Carefully he brought his hands up and placed them on either side of her face, his thumbs trailing reverently across her cheeks. "You are so beautiful, Serina. So, so beautiful. Whatever you do, I'm with you. Wherever you want to be, that's where you should be."

"But you . . ."

"No, *you*. I've taken my risks, and landed on my

feet. When Dani came to me I could have thrown her out. Instead I took a chance and got everything I always wanted. Now Blake's offering you the same thing. Everybody ought to have a chance. Everybody."

Serina considered the man she loved, confused by answers that weren't definitive. Thinking back over their courtship, knowing so much about him now, Serina made her decision. Standing on tiptoes, Serina kissed him lightly on the cheek. Squeezing him tighter she peeked around him and called to Dani and Blake.

"Okay. I guess you've got a model," she said quietly. "What do we do first?"

Dani and Blake yelled with delight and Serina grinned, pleased that she should have made them so happy. But when she looked back to Rudy, Serina wasn't at all sure she had made the right decision. Rudy looked almost lonely. Then, before she could say anything, he smiled at her and kissed her on the lips. In his arms, his mouth on hers, everything was all right.

"I love you, honey," he whispered. Contentedly Serina lay her head on his chest. She had done the right thing. Soon she would be everything he wanted.

"I'm sorry. I've said it a hundred times, Alexander. I was only trying to, well, be more of a presence if you know what I mean."

Alexander looked askance at his wife as he pulled the car into the drive. For the first time since this charade had begun he was sorry. Until today Polly had been perfect, acquiescing as she should to all his directions. Today she had reverted and all those horrific quirks of hers he had hated during their years of marriage had surfaced again. During their marriage if they were at a party and Alexander commented on another woman's beauty or wit, Polly would assume the trait within moments. Unfortunately her interpretation of the characteristic was more often than not a caricature of the real thing and he was left immensely embarrassed. If he mentioned a particularly astute client, Polly would talk endlessly of current events. God, ever since her surprise visit to D.C. she'd become unbearably cloying.

"I know what you mean, Polly. But you are not an expert in film and I would have assumed that once that fact was pointed out to you, you would simply follow directions."

"But Alexander, I want to be more of a part of everything. I just can't imagine why I can't have some input. I know what looks good on me and a beige suit simply doesn't."

"Polly, for God's sake you looked beautiful in that suit. It was exactly right. Even I could see that."

Alexander flipped the handle and opened the car door. He was halfway out of the car when Polly reached for him, her hand possessively on his arm, forcing him to look back.

"Did you really think I looked beautiful?"

In the darkness he could see her large eyes glittering with something more than wifely hope, but he put the sinister spark down to a trick of the light and sighed. Just like Polly. Latch onto the word and let the point go sailing by. Alexander's shoulders sagged.

"Yes, Polly," he said deliberately. "You looked beautiful in that suit. You did a fabulous job on the spot. You will be the toast of this campaign and I am positive we'll win the primaries because of you. Are you satisfied?"

297

"Well, yes," Polly answered, her hand sliding away from his arm, her shoulders squaring with a false dignity. She was hurt, perhaps angered and Alexander didn't care. Politics had asked a lot from him. Tonight it might be asking too much. Polly was talking again. With a Herculean effort Alexander calmed himself. "I was only asking if you liked me in the suit. There is absolutely no need to be sarcastic. Alexander, we've been doing so well, I don't understand why you're so angry with me tonight."

"I don't either Polly," he acquiesced. "I'm sorry. I suppose I'm just tired. It's been a long day and the primaries are only a week away. There is still so much to be done. I just hope we didn't spend all that money producing that commercial today for nothing. If I don't win the primaries, then that piece of film is useless. I'll just be another lawyer in practice."

"Never that, darling. You'll always be very special to me. In fact, you'll always be the only person in my life that I can actually say I adore."

Alexander looked at her exceedingly expectant face. She was so tiring, every word out of her mouth knotted his muscles tighter until he thought they would never untangle. God what he wouldn't give to see Coral now that they were back in L.A.

"Polly," he sighed, "I believe you."

"That's good, darling, because I intend to be here, beside you, through thick and thin."

Alexander nodded and pulled himself out of the car. He heard the other door slam and Polly's heels clicking as she followed him up the walk and into the house.

"I'll make coffee," Polly called, heading to the kitchen as Alexander climbed the stairs to the bedroom.

She busied herself, removing her jacket while she waited for the water to boil. Checking the larder she satisfied herself that she hadn't missed anything while shopping that day. Twice she poked her head out the door and checked the living room but Alexander was still upstairs.

Tapping her foot, checking the water, Polly felt a bout of nerves coming on and it disgusted her. There was no reason she should feel so concerned. Everything was perfect. It was only that the coffee was taking far too long. That infuriated her. Hoping to ease the anxiety she was feeling, Polly went to the wall phone and lifted the receiver. Talking to Monica would be better than standing in this kitchen panicking.

Monica's comfort was unnecessary, though. The nerves ceased the minute Polly held the receiver to her ear. Everything stopped: her breathing, her heart, time, even space seemed to disappear. Polly Grant was absolutely stilled by the sound of her husband's weary voice and stunned when she heard a woman's murmuring response.

"Can't take it . . ." Alexander was saying.

" . . . you're a big boy . . ." A woman responded.

"So many things to consider . . . " He was saying.

Bright spots of light exploded behind Polly's eyes, pops and whirs kept her from hearing each word. Slowly, an eternity later, after she heard the upstairs phone being replaced, Polly did the same.

By the time Alexander walked into the kitchen Polly was stirring milk into two cups of steaming coffee, the lights and pops and whirs banished to the hinterlands of her mind. She looked up and pulled her lips away from her teeth, smiling at her husband. Alexander stood beside the door looking like a relay runner eager to get the baton.

"I have coffee ready." Polly held up the cups. *Show and tell, Alexander. Soon it's your turn to show me.*

"I'm sorry, Polly, I won't have time. I just checked in with Eric and there are a few things I need to go over at headquarters."

Alexander lied so smoothly, so easily, Polly felt quite proud. Alexander did everything so well.

"I see." She lowered the cups and her eyes at the same time. "What a shame. I was hoping we could order in for a pizza. Perhaps eat it in bed . . ."

The last words caught in Polly's throat, her voice lowering in a vain attempt to imitate the woman on the phone. She would work on it if that was the kind of voice Alexander preferred.

"I'll take a rain check."

"All right, Alexander." That was much better she thought. Lower, calmer. "Perhaps, since it's still early, I'll pop over and visit Monica."

"That's a marvelous idea. I hate to imagine you here all alone. I know you never cared for this house."

"Not at all. I don't mind waiting in the least. Here, I have my purse now. I'll walk out with you."

"Sure. I'll call and check on you about ten. Think you'll be home by then?"

"I'm sure I will. Do you think you'll be out that late?" Polly asked politely.

"I might be," Alexander answered carelessly, already feeling free as he handed his wife out the door and into the garage. "Do you have the keys to my mother's car?"

"I took them off the board."

"Good. I'm glad I didn't sell it. I'll get around to it one of these days."

"Yes. We don't need two cars in Los Angeles, do we?"

"I suppose not, Polly," Alexander answered absent-mindedly.

He closed the car door quickly, standing back too anxiously. Methodically Polly turned the key, punched on the lights, and fastened her seat belt. Extending her neck, lifting her chin, she looked in the rear view mirror, seeing her husband as he really was. He wanted to be away. He wanted her gone, out of his sight and probably out of his life. When he took a little step forward Polly moved her foot to the gas pedal and let it rest there. It would be so easy to press and give him his wish. Dead, Alexander wouldn't have to look at her any longer. She wondered what it would feel like, pushing that tank of a car into his body. She would, no doubt, have a moment of satisfaction before the remorse. But she couldn't hurt Alexander. She loved him.

Gently Polly pressed the accelerator and the car moved out of the garage. Her foot tapped the brake when she came alongside her husband. Polly leaned out the window, looked into Alexander's eyes and said, "I love you, Alexander. Take care this evening."

"I will, Polly. Give Monica my love."

Polly backed into the street, shifted gears, and drove to the end of the block where she made a right, a quick U-turn, then parked, her lights off. Alexander sped away a few moments later, Polly following at a respectable distance.

Fifteen minutes later he pulled into a parking space in front of an apartment building. In the lobby he pressed a buzzer. The door remained shut. Finally, the elevator opened and out stepped a redhead, tall and willowy and young. A tremor ran through Polly when the young woman opened the security door with a smile and then kissed Alexander. The woman drew Alexander into the elevator his coat off already half off. A stab of pain shot through Polly's jaw. Quickly she opened her mouth as though proving the lower part of her skull had not been fused with the upper.

There was another woman in Alexander's life. What a pity. This was certainly beneath him. This was an appalling and base situation.

Polly sat back and closed her eyes, considering what was happening. The diaphragm in Washington was one thing—easily explained away. Polly would accept that it belonged to whomever owned the furniture previously. But this woman! There was no excuse for this.

Filling her lungs, pushing hard on the steering wheel with both hands, Polly looked back toward the building and the now empty entrance.

"I will forgive you this time, Alexander, but no other. Never, ever again. The payment will be dear, Alexander, if I ever catch you doing this again . . ."

Polly talked to herself all the way home, discussing Alexander's transgressions and punishment as she washed and donned a nightgown. She refined her little speech in the dark as she sat upright in bed. It was only when she heard the front door open and Alexander begin to climb the stairs that she shut her mouth, lay down and closed her eyes. When he sat down on the bed and swung himself gently in, Polly rolled over and put her arm around his waist, feeling him stiffen. She moved righteously closer and lay awake long after he was asleep, drinking in all the miserable smells of the red-haired woman that Alexander had allowed to linger on.

Chapter Twenty-three

"Okay, Serina, come on out. Let's see what you can do."

Blake paced the studio nervously. Now and again he'd pause, bounce on the balls of his feet, hands pushed deep into the pockets of his trousers and eye the dressing room door.

"I don't think you're going to hurry them any. Dani made it pretty clear they wouldn't be out until Serina was perfect," Rudy reminded him.

Blake shrugged, and glanced in Rudy's direction, amazed the man could lounge idly when they were about to put the advertising world on its ear.

"Rudy, why is it that you were born without nerves?" Blake muttered, crossing the studio to readjust a reflector, stopping long enough to pop a strobe.

"Lucky I guess." Rudy rolled a wad of paper and shot it through the air, missing the trash can by a mile. "Why get hyped when you don't have any control? I've never had any control over women so, where they're concerned, I'm as cool as a cucumber."

"I can identify with the no control bit," Blake laughed, thinking of his own woman and his futile attempts to hold her to a middle ground. At least now he understood Dani a bit better. Obsession had a life of its own. Thankfully he was rational enough to understand that and control it. He shivered, thinking of what he could do to Serina with a camera. She would be a goddess; Venus rising from the sea. She would . . .

"Dani! Serina!" Erupting again, beyond impatience, Blake stormed to the closed door and banged on it. He wanted to begin before his body wearied of the tension and before he lost his creative edge. Fist raised once more, he never had the satisfaction of hitting the wood. The door jerked open and the stylist emerged looking peeved and superior.

"What are you doing to her in there?" Blake wailed, holding out his hands as though she might place Serina in them just because he asked. "She looked fine forty minutes ago."

"Fine isn't what you pay me for. Perfection takes time," the woman sniffed, unimpressed by Blake's performance.

"Well I'm going to give you about two seconds to get Serina out here and . . ."

"We won't even need one of your seconds, Mr. Sinclair. She's ready."

The woman stood back and pulled the door open slowly, steadily, drawing out the drama. Behind Blake, Rudy sat up, planting both his feet on the ground, craning his neck to catch the first glimpse of the woman he loved. Watching that door Rudy felt so many things: anticipation, excitement, but most of all, fear.

He knew what could happen to a woman in Serina's position. The new world would be so much better than the old one, Serina might float into it without a thought for people left behind. The idea made Rudy sick at heart. The minute she looked at him, Rudy knew he would see it in her eyes. The minute she came out of that room he would know if she was already leaving him.

Dani came out first dressed in skin-tight jeans, a work shirt, and pink cowboy boots tipped with silver toes. She looked stunning. But behind her Serina glided into the studio, eyes down as though making sure the floor wasn't going to open and swallow her. Slowly she raised her head and every heart in the room skipped a beat. Serina was beyond beautiful and she was looking right at Rudy Green for approval. In the sereneness of her gaze he realized he had never truly loved before this moment.

She walked toward him, yards of blue-green chiffon floating in the whisper of air she stirred. Her legs were naked and bared high up on her right, her left shoulder nude too. Her skin shone as though she had lain in a beach of pearl dust. Her face was a dramatic wash of sea colors: sand, foam, aquamarine and emerald. The application of the make-up made her eyes unnaturally beautiful. The colors deepened them, made her mouth full and inviting, her cheekbones prominent. And around her face her long hair was a halo of curls that reached to incredible heights before falling with amazing grace around her shoulders. Rudy reached a hand out to her. She took his. They came together.

"I feel silly, Rudy," she whispered. "Amber pinned cardboard to the back of my head. See?"

She turned her head slightly so Rudy could see it. It was an old trick to make Serina appear as though she had three heads of luxurious hair.

"And they taped my breasts so they stick up like this. Rudy, I feel really dumb."

"Don't," Rudy breathed, not daring to kiss her lips

but raising her fingertips instead. "You are so stunning nothing else matters. Serina, you are beyond description."

Rudy's eyes glistened with adoration and Serina saw herself in them, her expression just a bit disappointed. How she wished she was helping Blake with the lighting or Dani with the paperwork. But, if this was what Rudy truly wanted, she would do her best. It was so little to ask in return for the happiness he had given her.

"Well," she whispered, "as long as you like it . . ."

But there was no time for Rudy to reassure her. Blake was there with his hand out. She took it and he led her to her mark on the set looking to him for encouragement, hating the feel of everyone's eyes on her.

"Serina, this is going to be spectacular," Blake murmured, holding her hands tight and feeling the cold in them. "I want you to listen to me. I'll go slowly at first until you get into the rhythm. I'll tell you what I want you to do. If you feel like doing something on your own do it, okay?"

Serina gave him a perfunctory nod, wondering if he could hear her heart pounding. Her eyes darted around the room as she looked for any sign of her friends. But they weren't there, everyone had changed. Dani seemed bigger than life leaning against the wall. The stylist's eyes took her apart piece by piece. Rudy stood behind Blake and his eyes had become unreadably dark. And Blake, his attention was so intense it seemed to magnify everyone else's. As best she could, Serina fought down her panic. She stared into the innocuous eye of the camera, desperately trying to concentrate only on that, attempting to ignore them all but terrified that she would disappoint them. The people that meant the most to her would think less of her if she couldn't pull this off.

"Serina, watch me," Blake commanded. Her eyes snapped toward him and they began when he spoke again. "Just relax. Relax and listen to what I'm going to tell you. Relax . . . relax . . ."

Serina nodded. The lights were hot. She was already thirsty and her head hurt where the stylist had put the pins in her hair too tightly. But she wouldn't complain. They were counting on her. Blake's voice wrapped around her. He held the bulb in his right hand. Dani moved behind him, acting as assistant.

"Pretend now, Serina. Pretend you're floating in water. That's it."

Click.

"Those arms are light as can be. You don't have to do a thing to hold them up. Your head too. You're just floating in a pool under a really hot sun . . ."

Click. Whir.

"Your hands are floating up . . . you're caressing your cheeks . . ."

Click. Whir.

"You are so beautiful . . . so very beautiful . . ."

But Blake's words were lost, as was the click and whir of the camera. Behind him Blake heard Rudy breathe "My God," and Dani murmur, "Gorgeous." Everyone saw Serina move, her body taking over, the moment spiriting her away from all of them.

And, as much as the three admired her, it was Blake who finally had to stop the shoot. He was perspiring, not with the effort of his work, but with the sense that greater things were to come and the odd feeling that he would kill anyone who dared to take the ultimate picture of Serina. That, he vowed, was a privilege reserved for him.

* * *

"Workin' a little late, aren't you Senator?"

Lewis Basset hailed Alexander from the middle of a group of less important people who surrounded him. A circle of shoulders swiveled, faces looked Alexander's way, and, when they recognized him as Basset's unquestioned ally, they parted for the senior Senator.

"Just on my way back home, Senator," Alexander said, waiting for Basset to come to him. The older man did, making allowances for the young pup's attitude, as long as Grant voted the right way. As their hands met, Alexander continued, "I had a few things to discuss with one of my more important constituents, but I think we've got our little misunderstanding cleared up now."

"Didn't give away the store did you, boy?" Basset laughed short and hard. Alexander grinned.

"Not yet, Senator," he said wryly, thinking of Luellen's horror when Alexander didn't vote properly in the subcommittee. "I thought I'd wait until no one was expecting it."

"That's the mark of a good politician, Alexander," Basset chuckled. "Yes it is. Gotta know when to take a stand and when to cut your losses. I admire that. You learn fast."

"I've had a good teacher," Alexander said, throwing Lewis the crumbs he seemed to accept as reassurances. "By the way, I wanted to thank you for that very kind message you sent endorsing me. Polls show the primary is almost a foregone conclusion."

"Certainly, Alexander. Wouldn't have let you out there without my nod. After all, you've been with us for almost a year now. Know the ropes, the boys, no sense in me trying to elect the other guy and break him in all over again." With one more stone cold laugh and a slap on the back, Lewis left Alexander with a last thought. "Don't forget we're meetin' end of the week to make the final vote on that Chemical Restrictions bill. Thursday. Ten A.M."

"I haven't forgotten. I only hope we're on time. I've booked a flight home at noon to vote, then another flight to Los Angeles for the long haul on Friday."

"Won't seem like nothin', son. You'll win by a landslide. Just make sure you smile and graciously accept the nomination. Don't forget to say some good things about that wimp the old guard sent to take you on."

"I won't," Alexander answered, though the old man had gone back to where he felt most comfortable: to the center of a group of people he didn't know and didn't like.

"It will all be over soon, old man," Alexander whispered to the retreating group. "And once it is, I think I'll give you a run for your money."

Straight backed, Alexander headed home satisfied. He had listened, played all the games, planned his strategy.

There was nothing that could stop him now. Nothing and no one.

Chapter Twenty-four

"Dani, have you seen Rudy?"

Pauline jogged down the hall intercepting her boss before Dani went into the conference room.

"I think he went across the street to get an ice cream. He should be back in a few minutes. We're trying to iron out our schedule. It was too much for him so he needed a snack. Did Lora tell you that Ashley was so excited by the stuff we showed them they want to move the entire schedule up?"

"Yeah, she did," Pauline said without enthusiasm, distracted by the problem at hand.

Though Lora had been the soul of propriety over the last few months everyone agreed it had been better when she was screwing up. Now she did her work flawlessly and left the agency without fail at exactly five. There were no extra hours, no attempts to be friendly with anyone, including Rudy, no more drinking in the office, and no more attempts to beautify herself. It was almost as though Lora had given up on life—or was patiently waiting for something to happen. Dani shook her head. It didn't make sense but Dani didn't have time to worry about Lora's agenda.

"Well then you know we have our work cut out for

us. We're going to be shooting in Cabo San Lucas in a week. The rough cut will be ready two weeks later and the final with voice-overs a week after that."

Dani was walking again but Pauline was after her waving a sheaf of papers.

"Dani, wait, this is important. I know you want me to get started on the Ashley stuff, but I think we've got a major headache with Senator Grant's media buy. I don't know if Lora's been screwing around with the stations or what, but they're billing us for ten times what we ordered. At this level, every man, woman and child has seen his spot seven times in these last two weeks."

Dani stopped and grabbed the read-outs. Scanning the green-and-white striped sheets, flipping from page to unwieldy page she checked out each station's billing record.

"But this can't be right. No way could Grant's budget afford half these spots . . ."

"What spots?"

Rudy ambled down the hall toward them, an ice cream cone just beginning to drip in one hand, a lottery ticket in the other.

"Grant's spots. Rudy, I think Lora's really gone off the deep end this time. She must have been ordering time from every station. Pauline didn't do it. Do you think Lora could have been crazy enough to triple each order? Jesus, we could be in deep shit on this, Rudy. We're liable for all this time if one of our people confirmed!"

Dani blanched at the thought. Just when things were going so well, just when the cash flow was actually living up to its description, this had to happen.

Rudy took the read-outs from Dani and glanced at

them, his face falling into an expression of—fright? Then she realized he must be angry.

"I'll take care of it."

"Maybe I should talk to Lora?" Dani offered.

"I said I would take care of it." The two women stepped back. In the shocked silence, Dani flushed and Rudy rethought his response. "I said I'd take care of it. I think I know what happened. It isn't Lora's fault. She had nothing to do with this. It will take me fifteen minutes to clear this up. Go ahead and start working on the schedule. I'll be there as soon as this is done."

Leaving Dani and Pauline standing in the hall, Rudy turned on his heel, went into his office, and slammed the door. Sitting at his desk, he tossed the ice cream before dialing the three network and two independent stations. Once connected the message was the same.

"This is Rudy Green calling about the buy I made a few months ago. The confirmation for that special order has gone to my media people for approval. I made it very clear that all correspondence including the spot check on that buy was to come directly to me and no one else. I trusted you to make that clear to your traffic and billing people. If you can't manage that, then I don't see any need to spend even a dollar more with your station in the coming year and that means for this client or any other. Is that clear?"

The phone was slammed down. The reps were terrified. Their commissions would be cut in half without a buy from the maverick Green Agency. By the time he was finished everyone knew the mistake wouldn't be repeated. He walked into the conference room and grinned at Dani.

"No problem. A computer error."

"On whose part?" Dani asked. "Every station had the same problem?"

"Does it matter. It's taken care of," Rudy answered in a voice surprisingly calm. Though he meant to pull out his chair he jerked it and it fell over. Laughing anxiously he tried to hide his nervousness. "Let's just get on with all this. I don't know how we're all going to survive the next three weeks. We've got to be in a million places at once."

"You're right," Dani sighed, the media billing already seeming a mere trifle when pitted against their shoot schedule. "I'm planning on leaving for the Ashley shoot right after Alexander's acceptance speech. What do you think?"

Rudy shook his head. "Sounds all right, but I hate to shoot so quickly. I really wish Serina had another week or two with Blake before we headed for the big one."

"She'll do fine," Dani assured him absentmindedly, shuffling the scheduling papers.

"You're right. Yes, I think she will," Rudy said, thoughtfully. "We're riding high, Dani, and after Alexander wins the primary, after the Ashley campaign hits, the sky's the limit."

"It's been a hell of a scary ride. I'm glad it's over. Now we can just do business. Right?"

"Sure," Rudy agreed then said a little prayer that she was right. He would give anything to be bored out of his skull. Unfortunately he was more afraid now than ever before. Suddenly cold, a shiver ran up his spine. He almost felt like crossing himself. But the moment passed. Blissfully ignorant that the dark side was coming for him, Rudy smiled at Dani and walked headlong into the future, planning the end of his world with a laugh and a smile as he and the woman with platinum hair sat at an oak conference table.

Chapter Twenty-five

Alexander Grant sat next to Lewis Basset as the full committee on Drug Abuse and Prevention prepared to vote to pass the Limitation of Foreign Chemical Export Bill to the Senate for a full floor vote.

While the title of the bill, and the document itself, was lengthy, the content was rather simple: the United States would severely restrict the exportation of kerosene, sulfuric acid, and solvent to South America. The United States Department of Justice would be empowered to demand certain explicit record keeping from every company that manufactured, or utilized, said solvents and chemicals.

The bill continued in far more complicated langauge, but most of the Senatorial aides had culled the information down to those two basic ideas. Despite the one vote margin, there seemed to be no doubt that the bill would be passed by the full committee. It was fairly certain that, once the bill reached the floor of the Senate, it would pass easily also. This was a black day for the chemical industry in the United States and for Eric Cochran who knew that Alexander's broken promise to Radison Chemicals was the death knoll for his career. Watching from the wings, Eric sat in his

314

chair ready for his job to fly right out the window with Alexander's vote. Playing the party ticket was not going to get him re-elected. Only money would do that and Radison money would dry up posthaste after this. He cradled his chin in his upturned palm as he watched Alexander and Lewis Basset chatting away. To Eric's right and behind him a few members of the press lounged, watching the proceeding as though it were a rerun of Star Trek: interesting, but they'd seen it all before. From the floor came the predictable response to the majority leader's call for unanimous consent.

"Aye."

"Aye."

"Aye."

The bill would pass through the full committee without a problem. Alexander would be on record with a vote of "aye." Yet, when it came time for Alexander Grant to simply raise his eyes and open his lips far enough for that simple word to pass through, he hesitated.

Eric's heart skipped a beat then began to pound. He sat up; one or two of the reporters followed suit. Alexander smiled patiently as if waiting for everyone's attention. Finally Lewis Basset swung his heavy old head Alexander's way.

"What you waitin' for, boy?"

Lewis nudged Alexander's knee under the long table. Alexander's eyes slid toward the older man, cold and hard, his dislike easily read and noted. The senior senator jerked visibly. Alexander might have struck him. His face flooded with color as he hunched over the table. He came close to his young counterpart, his expression as menacing as he could make it, his voice a warning growl.

"If this is a joke, Alexander, it ain't funny. We're ready for your vote now, and we'd all like very much to call it a day. I'd imagine you'd be wantin' to get on that plane and head on home to vote for yourself tomorrow. So get on, boy. The time has come."

"Yes," Alexander answered with a small, disdainful smile, "I suppose it has." Pointedly ignoring Lewis, Alexander cast his vote.

"Gentlemen, as much as I would like to follow the lead of my esteemed colleagues who have so much more experience than I, I am afraid that conscience keeps me from voting with the majority. I have extreme doubts about the cost of affecting this program, the economic impact of the sanctions, and, especially, the wide latitude it offers the Department of Justice. Therefore, I object on a time agreement. I request that this bill be put on hold and no further action taken at this time until my staff and I have had sufficient time to look into the matter further."

In the stunned silence that followed, Alexander rose gracefully from his seat, lay his hand on Lewis Basset's shoulder and patted it before leaving the chamber and its pandemonium behind.

"We have an objection on a time agreement . . ." the chairman intoned.

Members of the press were already scrambling from their seats and headed out in hot pursuit of the brash junior senator from California.

Eric slipped out a side door and dashed toward his office where he was sure he would find Alexander.

Lewis Basset was the last to leave the room, and then only when his anger was tightly reined. He fought his way through the small crowd of reporters who were tossing questions at Eric Cochran like confetti. Cochran was fielding them like a pro, but wasn't occupied enough to let Lewis enter the inner sanctum unchallenged.

"Senator," Eric called, extricating himself long enough to lower his voice and his head as he spoke to Basset. "Senator Grant is trying to catch a plane. He doesn't want to be disturbed."

Basset glared at him. In those old eyes Eric saw the man's outrage and understood everything. Lewis Basset was irate because he saw what Alexander was taking from him and it wasn't just the chance to pass the bill. The Senator from California was young and handsome, as Lewis Basset had once been, and he was slick. No old boy games for Grant. Basset just hadn't figured out the rules had changed. He pushed Eric Cochran aside without a word and walked through the door where Alexander sat waiting for him.

"Think you're smart, boy?" Lewis asked quietly. The office was dim and seemed bigger than it had when Margaret was alive. But it was only a trick, a figment of his imagination, because the man behind the desk was bigger than the woman—larger than life now that he was puffed up with confidence.

Alexander chuckled. Lewis went toward the desk, almost stumbling, stopping only when his hands were gripping the edge of the wood. He never could abide having anyone laugh at him.

"I asked you a question, boy," he growled.

"I am not your boy, Senator, and I never have been. But I'm the only one who knew that. It never ceases to amaze me how easy it was to ingratiate myself with you. All I had to do was sit quietly at your feet and smile every time you threw out one of your homey little platitudes." Alexander pushed himself away from the desk, readying his briefcase while he spoke. "Stupid little things you thought I should know. But

317

I listened and I walked by your side because you still had something I needed. When you retire, or die, you will be thought of as a strong man of the Senate. But that's only an illusion, isn't it, Lewis? There are others like me now. Others are willing to challenge your hold because the hold is weak. That's the way it always has been in history. It's the way it will happen to me when I'm too old to do anything about it."

"You're a fool, Grant." Lewis was tired and he hated the way his voice shook. He knew he should take a minute to compose himself. Instead he ran on. "I don't know who you're paying off with that stupid trick you pulled, but it's got to be somebody big. You know a time agreement means that bill will never see the light of day on the floor. You've killed it for good. For what, Grant? For who?"

"Of course it's not a payoff," Alexander scoffed, raising his hand mockingly to his breast, "and I'm shocked you would even suggest such a thing without evidence."

"My ass you're shocked. You know I don't even care who it is 'cause that bill didn't mean a thing to me and mine. It would have looked real good on my record, but I'm already down as pullin' for it all the way. You're the one who's gonna suffer, boy," the old man said gleefully, knowing the act wasn't holding up. "You didn't count on a couple of things. You didn't count on people gettin' mighty angry that you're against fighting drugs, and you didn't count on me comin' out against you in the general election." Lewis tittered with a gleeful little laugh as though the thought had just occurred to him. "Yeah. That's exactly what I'm gonna do. You're dead in the water, boy. You won't be comin' back here. That's what I do to them that betrays me."

Alexander held the top of his briefcase, amused as he listened. The old man was so excited he had slipped into his hillbilly accent. So wild was he with his threats, his feet had begun to move until he was dancing like the maniacal Rumplestiltskin. Alexander shook his head and latched his briefcase. Picking it up he rounded the desk and stood face to face with Lewis Basset.

"Senator, the vote on this bill is going to be buried in every major newspaper in this country. It's not news. News is sex scandals. News is higher gas prices. News is drive-by shootings. News is not the death of another war-on-drugs bill. And those voters who are aware of this bill, well, they won't make a difference. They're the fringe—the kind of constituents who actually think lawmakers are here to watch out for the good of the land and the people. What a sad lot. They haven't figured out yet we're here for the power, the free ride, the backroom games.

"As to your threat to hurt me in the general election? Lewis, that is pitiful. That is laughable." Alexander leaned closer. "You couldn't possibly hurt me without hurting yourself. Or have you forgotten the kind endorsement you put on film for me? The beautiful little cameo that runs on all of my commercials? No, Lewis, you won't say a word because you would look like a dottering old fool. Endorse me one minute, deny me the next? That's not good politics. Especially since you'd have to explain why you're so angry with me. Not really because of this poor little bill, but because I dared to say no to you."

Alexander leaned away from Lewis Basset and tightened his grip on his briefcase. The elder Senator seemed to have shrunk in the last few moments, the fire had gone out of his eyes. For the first time Alexander really saw him. His suit was rumpled and ill fitting, his hair was thin and brittle, his skin mottled with age. Here was not a statesman, but a game player who was getting too slow to make the right moves. Alexander walked to the door and lay his hand on the knob.

"I have to leave now, Lewis. I have an election to win. All the polls are showing me way ahead in the primaries. Nothing can stop me. You can't and you were the only one who had a chance. Go home Lewis. Have a drink with your put-upon wife. You might actually have something in common now."

Alexander opened the door and walked into the outer office. Lewis Basset heard the cry of the reporters and glimpsed Eric moving deferentially aside. Alexander Grant stopped long enough to create a sound bite before moving on, his coterie of the curious following him down the hall. Lewis Basset waited until all was quiet before he too moved on, alone, without anyone following or listening to him, or wondering what thoughts were.

Chapter Twenty-six

"All packed? There won't be any time to do it tonight when we get home."

Serina stopped her folding and watched Rudy flip his tie, maneuvering it into a perfect knot before admiring himself. Strange though others might find such arrogance, to Serina it was endearing, as much a part of Rudy as his kindness and generosity. So she let him look at himself, indulging herself at the same time. Prosperity sat well on him. It was obviously contagious because she, too, was beginning to wear affluence more comfortably. The Ashley contract had brought her more money than she had ever dreamed of.

Serina patted the clothes she had packed, amazed that these were her things. Silks and cottons in shapes she never would have imagined for herself. But Dani had insisted that Serina seriously shop before this trip.

"If you're going to be a top model, look like one," Dani insisted blithely, before whisking her off on a shopping spree.

Dutifully Serina tagged along, pulling clothes on and off at Dani's command. When all was said and done Serina did, indeed, have her long ago wish. She looked as glamorous as Dani Cortland. And, as she eyed herself in the mirror, she wondered why her smile wasn't brighter or her shoulders straighter. Why did she seem to lose something more of herself with each wonderful thing that happened?

"Honey?" Rudy's hands lay on her shoulders. He slid them down her bare arms, pulling her gently back against his chest. "Did you hear me?"

"I heard you," she murmured, laying back contentedly. Clothes, hair, make-up, fame and fortune—none of it mattered to her. This—Rudy and his love—did. Everything else could disappear tomorrow and Serina wouldn't blink an eye. But if Rudy were to leave her there would be no reason to live. "I've finished my packing."

Rudy turned her to him and held her lightly, "You sound so far away."

"I am."

"Thinking about being in Mexico tomorrow?"

Serina shook her head, her brow furrowing, "No. No, I'm not."

"Serina?" Rudy tipped her chin up and looked carefully at her. "Are you angry about something?"

"No, not at all," Serina insisted.

"Did Blake or Dani do anything you don't like? Because if they did we can change it."

"Could we, Rudy?" Serina tried not to sound too anxious, but that was exactly what she hoped would happen. The more she was in front of a camera the more she hated it. Blake and Dani and Rudy all thought she was a natural. She felt ridiculous.

"Just tell me what the problem is," he said softly, kissing her nose. "For you, anything. Want a bigger motor home for your dressing room? It's yours. Don't like the green bathing suit? We'll change it to pink.

322

Anything to make my gorgeous star shine as bright as she can." Rudy sighed, his eyes softening as he looked at her, his arms tightening to hold her ever more closely. "Serina, I am so proud that you care for me. I hope . . ." He hesitated, ashamed to say what he was thinking. It had been difficult to admit his love, fear was harder. ". . . I hope you won't leave me when the whole world knows about you. You are so, so beautiful. Sometimes I'm sort of afraid you'll just kind of fade away from me."

His cheek was next to hers, his breath warm on her neck as he spoke. His pride and fear overwhelmed Serina. He was proud of her, he loved her, he wanted the world to want her and hope melted under the radiance of Rudy's admiration. Devastated, Serina threw her arms about his neck and pressed against him as though she could turn back time if she tried very, very hard. They clung together; Rudy fearing Serina's beauty would lead her away, Serina fearing her beauty would consume her so that she no longer existed.

"Hey. Hey." Rudy pushed her away gently. "You're going to get your new dress all wrinkled before we get to the hotel."

"I know. I just . . ."

"What? What is it you want? We can tell Dani and Blake whatever it is tonight, and they'll fix it by the time we get to Cabo. Just like magic." He snapped his fingers and laughed. "Anything for my princess."

Serina shook her head, fighting to create a smile he would believe. "It was nothing. Nothing." Turning away from Rudy, Serina closed her suitcase. Taking a deep breath she shot brightness into her voice. "Have you been listening to the news? Have you heard about the returns? I really hope Senator Grant gets the nomination."

"I've been listening." Rudy was already back to his toilette, brushing off his dark blue suit, checking out the shine on his shoes. "Looks like he's in. Let's go wish him well so we can get back here and have a personal celebration before the hard work begins tomorrow."

Serina clutched her purse, faced him and tried once more, "We could always just lock ourselves away and celebrate for the next few weeks. Forget about Senator Grant and Ashley Cosmetics. We could just go back to being plain old Rudy and Serina. What do you say?"

"I say, that's a great idea," Rudy laughed, taking her cold hands in his own, "but not until all this is over. We have a Senator to elect, a cosmetic campaign to launch and a gorgeous new face to introduce to the world. When that's done, I promise we'll go away. Just the two of us. Lock ourselves in here or jet off to Paris. When it's all over, Serina, we'll pretend we're the only two people left on this earth."

"I think it's about time to go down, don't you darling?"

Polly Grant poked her head around the door. Her smile was brittle, her body tense and the effect was completely lost on Alexander. His eyes were glued to the television screen as he absentmindedly buttoned his shirt.

It was ten o'clock and his opponent was just about ready to concede the battle. Alexander Grant would be the next Democratic candidate for Senator from California. Good-bye Margaret, Mother dear. Alexander had made his stand and survived the slings and arrows.

Easing his tie under his collar he looked back to the

324

mirror, the television reflected there so he wouldn't miss a thing. The newscaster was announcing a commercial break. The news faded and a familiar spot pulled up.

Alexander laughed, half turning so he could enjoy the full impact of his own commercial as it raged on the small screen. Flags waved, appropriate music blared. He saw Polly leaning down to talk to school children, he touched the hands of the elderly. Then, what pleased him most, Lewis Basset's endorsement. Alexander was laughing outright as he finished with his tie.

Then Polly was beside him, touching him with fingers and hands that had become more and more possessive over the last few weeks. Every time he looked at her he saw her pinched and worried face. God how he hated this charade and the election was still six months away. How on earth were they going to coexist under this kind of pressure? Then he realized he was the only one that felt the strain. Polly hadn't changed. Only Alexander's ability to abide her had.

"Let me do that, darling." Polly pulled at the already perfect knot in his tie. He jerked away then caught himself, controlling his voice and his actions.

"It's fine, Polly. It's done. I thought you were seeing to our guests."

"I was, but they seem able to pour our liquor all by themselves. We're paying the hotel a fortune for that food and drink out there," she complained.

"Polly," Alexander sighed, "the campaign fund is paying for it. It's not coming out of your food budget so don't worry."

"No need to be short with me, Alexander," she said petulantly, a surprising hint of defiance rather than hurt in her voice. Alexander slid his eyes toward her as he pulled on his jacket. "And I'm not complaining about how much they drink; it's just everyone's attitudes. The only decent person out there is your secretary. That Eric is a rude young man, and Miss Cortland seems to think we all ought to bend down and kiss the ground she walks on. I suppose that's understandable, though," she sniffed. "Mr. Sinclair seems to make a habit of it. Such showy people. I don't know how you can stand to have them around."

"Polly," Alexander laughed cruelly, "I think you've actually crossed the line. Those are perfectly nice people, all of whom have helped me get through this campaign. I would suggest if you would like to be the wife of a Senator, you learn how to get along with many types of people. You've never been able to get along with anyone, Polly, and that attitude is not going to get us very far now. So if you're done complaining, put a nice smile on your face if you can, and let's go pretend you're happy to be a part of all this."

"I am happy . . ." Polly insisted. But her husband was already out the door and, when Polly went into the living room of the hotel suite, the first thing she saw was Dani in Alexander's arms.

The ecstatic group of well-wishers left the room and headed down to the ballroom. It was there Alexander would accept his victory and Polly would hold his hand while she waved to the crowd of people who had worked so hard for this success. But Alexander and his friends had forgotten to turn off the television and they had forgotten Polly. Alone she turned off the TV, pushed down her growing resentment, and went to join the happy people waiting at the elevator.

* * *

326

". . . It is about caring not only for our state's resources, but caring for the people in our great state of California. Each and every one of you is important to me, as you were important to my mother when she served you in Washington.

"Thank you, from my heart, for all your hard work. Thank you for your support. Thank you for believing in me."

Alexander stepped back from the podium, took Polly's hand and raised it high in a sign of success, as a symbol of unity, as a promise of conquest six months down the road.

Alexander's smile was bright and his flinty eyes glistened under the lights. He looked fabulous and beside him Polly was a necessary prop. Then they both disappeared as they were engulfed in red, white, and blue balloons. A roar of approval greeted the end of Alexander's speech and didn't let up.

On the floor, in the midst of revelers, Dani was swept up in the excitement. Her beautiful lips parted as she whooped and hollered her approval along with the rest of them. Beside her Blake grinned, taking up the call until she tugged on his sleeve, putting her arms around his neck when he bent down to hear what she was saying.

"I think I see Serina and Rudy. I'm going to say hi," she hollered.

"Fine," he yelled back over the din. "Bring them over. I'll get in line at the bar. I'll have a few glasses ready by the time you get back here."

Dani nodded, dived into the crowd, and was swallowed up. She struggled past the first few rows of people in front of the podium before finding breathing space. The crowd was dispersing slowly, finding tables in anticipation of the band, the food, the drinks. It was

327

going to be a long, wonderful night and Green Advertising had more than a little to do with it. Through a hole in the crowd Dani saw Serina and Rudy leaning toward one another, each pointing a different way as if they couldn't decide where to go. Dani smiled. Looked like they needed a tie breaker. She moved to the left around a woman in pink tights and a purple dress only to run right into a tall man with the most glorious head of silver hair.

"Mr. Sweeny," Dani breathed, happy to finally have a chance to talk with Alexander's generous spokesman. "So sorry."

"No problem, my dear," Daniel Sweeny grasped Dani's arm steadying her. Then his hand moved and ran the length of her back in a gesture that had nothing to do with balance. No fool, Dani moved back a step.

"I'm Dani Cortland, one of the owners of the Green Advertising Agency."

"Of course, nice to meet you," he said, his attention already wandering since Dani wasn't going to fall into his arms. So much for the sensitive father figure image Dani thought. Well, she'd do her thing then be off.

"I'm sorry I missed you when you were filming. I wanted to thank you personally. You have been so generous with your time and your endorsement. You must think very highly of Alexander to appear in his advertising gratis. It's almost unheard of, and if there is ever anything we can do for you, I hope you'll let us know."

The actor stopped his roaming eyes and locked onto Dani's. They considered one another for a very long time, both aware that the people moving around them were watching, waiting for something to happen. Daniel Sweeny was always an object of curiosity. When he laughed and leaned close to Dani, the crowds moved on. But Dani was devastated as he whispered, "Lady, the Green Agency has done everything I want them to do for me. I pocketed one hundred and fifty thousand for the Senator's spots. There isn't a politician in the world I'd give my voice to for free. So, madam, I thank the Green Agency and leave you with this thought: pay a little more attention to business and less to your nails."

The actor kissed her cheek and, still laughing, walked away leaving Dani feeling cold in the warm room, alone in the crowd. People moved around her, parting like water around a rock. They jostled her, muttered their displeasure, but still she couldn't move. Her mouth, her mind, her legs—they were all paralyzed. Sound tuned down then out.

"Dani, are you all right?"

Someone's hand was on her shoulder, a familiar voice was speaking to her. Dani shook her head. Though it was painful she managed to look at her companion. Lora Prince was there beside her. Asking . . . what? Offering . . . what?

"I'm fine. Just fine," Dani mumbled, cautious now that the enemy might be at hand. Did Lora know? Was she aware of what had gone on with Alexander's campaign? All this time had it been Rudy and Lora using Dani? No, it couldn't be. Rudy's secretiveness made sense, but Lora's animosity, her ineptitude? Still . . .

"You don't look fine," Lora said again, the grumble still in her voice.

Dani nodded. At least that hadn't changed. "Lora do me a favor. Find Blake. Tell him I'll meet him at home."

Dani didn't bother with niceties, she was headed toward the door without so much as a good-bye. But

Lora was stubborn, she dogged Dani's steps. "I'm not your maid, you know." Dani shot her a glance that shut her up. Lora stood her ground, grabbing Dani's arm to stop her. "He'll want to know why."

"Just tell him . . ." Dani hesitated. Tell him what? That she'd failed again. That all her hard work was for nothing because Rudy Green had screwed around behind her back and their partnership was a joke? Dani lifted her chin, she would face Blake when it was absolutely necessary. Now, all she needed was some time to figure out what was going on. "Just tell him I forgot something at the office."

Dani was gone. At the main entrance Rudy and Serina still stood deep in conversation. Dani thought to confront him, but for once in her life she was going to do things right. All her tracks would be covered, then she'd have a word with Mr. Rudy Green.

Half the office was illuminated, lights left on by the cleaning crews and Dani blessed their forgetfulness. At least she wasn't walking into total darkness.

Not sure what she was looking for, Dani headed first toward Rudy's office, then the media department, then gave up on either destination and went into Mrs. Peterson's den. Digging in her purse for her key she unlocked the files, withdrew the ledgers, flipped on the desk light then stopped, trying to find the strength to open it. Forcing herself, she sat down and opened the book to accounts receivable. Alexander Grant.

Ten minutes later Dani had gone over the figures twice. She held her emotions in check, looking at the figures with an objective eye. Finished, she sat back, her eyes closed, her body heavy with relief. Everything was in order. There was even a payment to Daniel

Sweeny. Not as much as Sweeny said, but he'd been drinking. He was an actor. To him everything was larger than life.

Bouncing gently in Mrs. Peterson's chair, her hands covering her mouth, Dani considered the payment and hoped that the tapping of her fingers against her lips would still the uneasy feeling in the pit of her stomach. Finally she locked Mrs. Peterson's books away and headed to Rudy's office. Standing in the dark, she steeled herself then flipped on the lights. Part of her wanted simply to walk away, part of her needed to know what she would find here. If Rudy lied about the fee for Sweeny then he might have lied about the media billings. Lights on, Dani took the plunge. Settling herself at her partner's desk, opened the top drawer and began.

So engrossed was she in her search she didn't hear the front door of the office open. She didn't hear the person who was moving stealthily toward Rudy's office, nor was she aware that someone had hidden themselves in the dark to watch her every move: Dani finding exactly what she feared, Dani frantically turning pages of a ledger, Dani wearily leaving the office. It was only when the front door latched shut that Lora Prince emerged from the shadows.

Left behind once again, as she had been since Dani Cortland walked through the front door, Lora went to Rudy's desk and opened the top drawer just as she had seen Dani do. In moments she knew what Dani knew, and it was enough. Dani could be destroyed. Unfortunately, Rudy would have to suffer too. But he didn't mean anything to her anymore and never would again.

* * *

Polly ended up in the ladies' room. She had stood next to the bar for the longest time. She had stepped outside the ballroom and lingered in the corridor. Polly had gone everywhere the red-haired woman had gone. She hadn't let her out of her sight all evening. That had been difficult, of course, since people often came up to her to congratulate her on Alexander's success, but Polly managed to see enough to know what kind of woman this was.

She was loose and she was crass and her name was Coral. That seemed fitting for a woman like that. A slut's name. Polly saw Eric go to the woman, dance with her, only to leave and whisper in Alexander's ear when the dance was finished. Alexander caught Coral's eye while he listened. Polly saw it and saw the redhead go out the door. That was the moment Polly Grant felt sick. Her skin became clammy, her temperature rose so quickly she wanted to tear off her clothes. For a horrible instant Polly thought she might embarrass herself by throwing up. That's when she went to the ladies' room. Knowing she couldn't hide forever, Polly finally walked to the door and opened it. Eric was waiting for her.

Then Eric was beside her, holding her elbow, talking to her, steering her away from the ballroom.

". . . There's so much more to do tonight, Mrs. Grant, the Senator thinks it would be best if I saw you home . . ."

Polly shook her head adamantly. She breathed deep through her nose, struggling to keep herself from attacking this vile young man, this pimp. But Eric, that little weasel, saw everything.

"Are you all right, Mrs. Grant?" Eric sounded worried now, as he should be. Polly wanted to worry them

332

all. She was so very angry. "Let me get the Senator. He should know . . ."

"No!" Polly insisted, her voice too loud, her arm jerking out of his hold. She reached for him, patted his arm, tried to convince him all was well. "No, Eric, thanks so much, but I think I'm just tired. Please don't bother, Alexander."

"If you're sure. It wouldn't do to have you fainting with all the press around. Who knows what they'd make of that? Probably have you in the Betty Ford Clinic by the time they filed their report."

Eric laughed nervously. Polly eyed him, realizing how easy it would be to hurt these people who wanted to rule the country, who said one thing then did another, who vowed to serve the people then did everything possible to disserve them.

"I can't imagine why that should worry you, Eric. Mrs. Ford has done so many wonderful things, hasn't she?"

"Yes, sure," Eric concurred, unwilling to stand and listen to Polly Grant's babbling when there was so much willing flesh milling around the ballroom.

"Eric, are you listening?" Polly demanded, another notch of anger cutting into her. How she hated this young man. How she was beginning to hate Alexander and this political stupidity and the woman with the red hair.

"Yes, Mrs. Grant. I'm sorry. I thought I saw the CBS anchor come in."

"Is an anchor person more important than your boss's wife?" Polly's voice rose until she was shrieking.

"Certainly not," Eric acquiesced deferentially, tired of this woman, and a bit afraid that she might become a problem. "You're tired. People are staring. It wouldn't do Alexander any good to draw this kind of attention to yourself. Now I think I'll drive you home. Why don't you get your purse?"

Polly opened her mouth, her eyes hardening and a scream hovering at the base of her throat. But before she could howl, she caught herself. Though she couldn't find it in her to smile, Polly managed to modulate her voice. There were better ways, more private ways, of handling something like this.

"You're right. I'll just say good night to Alexander first, if you don't mind."

"Senator Grant has already retired to his room. He asked not to be disturbed. That's why he's asked for me to take you back home. He'll be staying over tonight. He also wanted me to thank you for all your help, and said he will see you about ten in the morning."

"He . . . he left . . . ?"

Polly's breathing slowed. Eric's eyes moved just to the left of hers. A liar's look. But Polly didn't care. She was looking for the redhead. She wanted to see the woman. But she was gone and Alexander with her. The final needle of fury dug into Polly Grant. As she pulled into herself, letting Eric Cochran lead her from the ballroom, Polly began to plan her revenge. She swore, when she figured it out, his hurt would be as deep and cutting and crippling as the hurt he had caused her.

By the time Eric dropped her off Polly had a plan. Unlocking the door to her mother-in-law's home she went directly to the study, pulled back a picture and unlocked the safe. It was still there.

For the first time in her life Polly Grant had a good thought about her deceased mother-in-law.

* * *

"It was wonderful, Rudy," Serina whispered as she reached for him. Rudy went to her, pulling the sheets over them both, covering her face with quick, happy kisses.

"It was better than wonderful. God Serina it was heaven."

"Rudy . . ." she admonished happily, sleepily.

"You're right. It was better than heaven. Can you imagine if he wins the election? We're going to have every politician in the country at our door. Green Advertising helps elect unknown. What a headline! Ah, Serina, ain't life grand?"

Rudy snuggled into her, holding the most precious thing in the world as he thought of this most recent achievement. In his wildest dreams he couldn't have envisioned this; now he wanted to share his amazement with her. But Serina was asleep, dreaming dreams that didn't include Senators or advertising or photographs or wealth. Serina was dreaming of Rudy and the day she would vow to love, honor, and obey. Serina was perfectly content with her dreams and, even in sleep, realized she was wishing tomorrow would never come.

"That you, babe?"

Blake turned and mumbled in his half-sleep, sensing rather than hearing Dani come to bed.

"Yes, go back to sleep," she whispered, sliding under the comforter, laying close to Blake, sadly in need of comfort but unable to ask for it. She felt so cold she needed his warmth. She was so scared, she needed to feel his strength. But she was so ashamed Dani couldn't bring herself to ask for either.

"Everything okay?" Blake mumbled, his voice

heavy with sleep and wine, his hand reaching back, caressing her through the silk of her gown.

Dani kissed him gently. No, everything wasn't okay. Everything was falling apart. But she said, "Go to sleep now. We've got a lot to do in the next few days. Go to sleep."

And as she stroked his long black hair, felt his muscled chest rise and fall with deep breaths, she was suddenly afraid he might do just that . . . sleep, leaving her afraid and alone. Tears formed behind her eyes then spilled over and flowed down her cheeks. She squeezed her eyes together, keeping the tears at bay, asking herself again how could Rudy have done this to her when she had given him so much? How could Rudy have been so stupid? She should have watched more carefully, paid more attention. But isn't that what she should have done all her life? Watched closer, trusted better men? Hadn't she adored the wrong ones when the right one was beside her all the time?

Scooting into Blake, cupping her body around him, she whispered, "Blake?"

He mumbled. He stirred beside her. He wanted to sleep but she couldn't let him. Her life was before her eyes and she needed him to help her focus. She tried again.

"Blake? You know how you always said I should stop listening to my father? Well you never told me whether you thought . . ." she hesitated, wondering if she even wanted to know what Blake thought. Well, now that she'd started, she'd go on and listen. What was one more hurt on top of all this? "You never told me if you thought my father loved me."

Blake's breathing stopped. Dani swore she heard his eyes open. Then he was moving and breathing again, turning on his back to lay by her side. For the first time

336

in a long while he didn't reach for her as he always did when they talked about Peter Cortland. Funny how she never realized before that that was a protective gesture. Obviously this was going to be different. This, Dani realized, was going to be the moment of truth. She waited quietly in the dark, while Blake chose the right words. Finally she felt him tense. There was no way to choose words that wouldn't hurt so he said what his heart had always known.

"No, Dani. I don't think he did."

They lay in silence, letting the words hang heavily over the bed, heavy and shroudlike.

"Not at all?" Her voice was so small Blake thought his heart would break.

"No. Not at all."

"Well. I suppose that's it then."

"I think it should be."

Dani nodded. There was something about whispering hurtful things in bed that made them seem so genuine. There could be no falsehoods between them anymore and it made Dani shiver with the intensity of it. Blake rearranged himself, propping his head on an upturned hand. He touched the tip of her hair, felt the coolness of the cotton pillowcase beneath the silkiness. But Dani lay so still he dared not touch her any further.

"Dani, life is short and we've wasted a whole lot of it because you listened to your father, believed him with all your heart . . ." Blake held up his hand, sensing she was going to defend Peter Cortland. There was no more time for that. The hour was late in more ways than one. "I'm not blaming you. I never have, and I never will. But the way you used to talk about life in that mausoleum with your father and the wife of the moment always made me shiver. The words were always perfect, but the tone . . ." Blake shook his head, remembering every time he had held his tongue against her odd remembrances of the Cortland home life. ". . . the tone of your voice was always so strange. I would hear beyond the words the loneliness, the cold beauty of things bought but never touched. You're such a smart woman yet somehow your father convinced you that the way he lived was actually life. It wasn't. I don't know how you bought into that."

Dani breathed in deeply then out slowly. In the dark Blake saw movement. She had laced her fingers together and now they moved of their own accord as if loosened they could fly away and never have to be a part of this discussion. Then he saw her lips move. It was a moment later she talked and the effort seemed great.

"When I was little—eight years old is very little don't you think—"

Blake nodded knowing she didn't need his permission to go on. Funny that they'd known each other so intimately and so long and had never really talked about Dani as a child. Perhaps she'd always seen herself as an adult, always seen herself as needing to be Peter Cortland's equal even knowing she never could be or should be.

"—Well, when I was eight my parents divorced. I remember it so clearly. One night my mother was there, the next morning she was gone. She was very nice. I loved her so much and I think it was the way a child should love a parent. I looked forward to seeing her, waited for her to come to play with me, dreamed about her at night. She made me feel safe. I really loved her. But when she disappeared like that I was so very hurt, and there's nothing like the hurt of a child. Then the only time I saw her after that was in the

338

courtroom. She didn't say much after the first few times. She even stopped looking at me after awhile. I thought she didn't care. But my father said all the right things: how he loved me, the things he would do for me, how he would die if I was taken away from him . . ."

"And did he?"

"Did he what?" Dani turned her head to look at Blake.

"Did he do all those things he said he would? Love you, die for you, give you all the things you wanted like attention and time?"

Dani turned her head back and stared at the ceiling.

"No. He didn't. But he fought so hard for me. And my mother didn't fight back. She just disappeared. She never came back. She didn't care at all . . ."

"Oh, honey, I don't think you know that. I wasn't there, I didn't see any of this, but, if I were to venture a guess, I'd say that your father fought for you because that's what he did all his life. He fought for things, he bought things, and he always won. He probably beat your mother to a pulp until she just slinked away. Not everyone can stand up to that kind of treatment no matter how much they want to. He treated you the same way he treated his wives. That's why he had so many. The problem with you was he couldn't divorce you. Once you were his, once he'd gotten rid of your mother, he didn't have any use for you. He simply had to keep you. Honey, you remember the fight and equate that with love. But that's not the way things work in the world. And given everything that's happened I suppose this is the right time to start asking those hard questions."

"What do you mean, everything that's happened?" Suddenly alert, Dani wondered if Blake knew more than she thought. But he lay back beside her, taking her hand in his as he did so and answered gently.

"Now that you have everything you've ever wanted, everything your father told you you were suppose to want and work for, it sounds like you're feeling a little empty. Maybe you're just feeling a bit betrayed?"

Dani laughed quietly, a sound so small it seemed to be only for her. How on earth did he do it? Good old Blake and the proverbial nail on the head. God she wanted to cry but her hurt was too deep, the understanding of her life too suddenly clear for her to do anything but mourn the part of herself that had been trusting and young and vulnerable.

"Yes, Blake," she said softly, "betrayed is a good word. That's exactly what I'm feeling. Betrayed. Deceived. Double-crossed."

"God I'm sorry. But maybe it's a good thing. Maybe it's . . ."

"Maybe it just is, Blake. Sometimes that's all life boils down to."

"Dani . . ." Blake began, then realized there was nothing else he could say. He lifted her hand to his lips and kissed her fingertips. Tomorrow was a big day. Tomorrow he and Serina would make photographic history. Much as he loved Dani, he was too tired for a long discussion of the mess Peter Cortland had made of Dani's values. It seemed they had been having it all their lives. It could wait until this shoot was over.

He turned on his side, too tired to continue, too aware that Dani had retreated into herself to even try. Something was obviously wrong and it was probably something more than memories gone awry. Tomorrow she'd be better. She always was.

Moments later Blake was asleep.

Faced now with more than her father's betrayal,

Dani lay her hand on Blake's waist and prayed for sleep. Tomorrow she would have to decide what to do. Strength was what she needed, a good night's sleep to add to her reserves. When it finally came, Dani tossed and turned, dreaming of being stripped naked and tied to a stake by a man in a black hood while a laughing Rudy walked away, his arm around Serina. Blake followed them taking pictures as the masked man, with eyes surprisingly like Peter Cortland's, lit the kindling at her feet.

Chapter Twenty-seven

At five A.M. Blake sleepily called a cab and he and Dani rode to the airport in silence, Blake catching a snooze, Dani hugging the window, wrapped in dark thoughts, wondering if she would be able to face Rudy without killing him. At the same time Rudy loaded Serina into the Jag without noticing she was not only wide awake but wound tighter than a spring. At that hour Lora Prince finally went to sleep after drinking herself into a happy stupor, and Polly Grant floated through the entry of the Beverly Hilton.

"May I help you ma'am?" The young girl behind the desk looked as fresh as a daisy. Polly smiled. They were the only two in the cavernous vestibule besides a bellboy. He didn't count because he was half-asleep.

"Yes, I hope so," Polly said, her voice hushed as befitted the hour. "It was such an exciting evening and I've been out celebrating, but I'm afraid I forgot my key. I'm Mrs. Alexander Grant. My husband and I had the presidential suite last evening as we waited for the election results."

"Of course Mrs. Grant. Congratulations to you and the Senator. Here it is. Shall I have Charlie see you up to the room? The hotel can be eerie so early in the morning."

Polly hitched her purse a bit closer and squared her shoulders, "That won't be necessary. I'm sure I can take care of myself."

"Good morning, then, Mrs. Grant."

"Good morning," Polly said, her voice floating behind her like a silken scarf.

The girl behind the desk looked after Polly thinking what a lucky woman she was to be married to a man like Alexander Grant.

"Alexander," Polly whispered, touching her husband's shoulder, hovering. "Wake up, Alexander. Wake up."

He moved. Turned under the sheets.

She stepped back and watched him.

His arm reached and his hand grasped; his lips moved. He tried to nestle further under the covers but was just a bit too awake to get comfortable again. Polly watched him in the grey light that came through the almost drawn curtains and spilled over the bed. She saw his silver hair and beside his head there was a tangle of gold-red waves. That made Polly angry, but she'd get to it all in due time.

"Wake up, Alexander." Polly stepped forward again, upset suddenly, anxious to have this over with. She shook his shoulder. It wasn't enough. Alexander needn't be treated with kid gloves. "You and your mistress. Wake up. I haven't much time."

Alexander yelped, angered to be disturbed. He opened his eyes and it was Polly he saw, still dressed in her evening suit, her face an oddly drawn, one-dimensional mask. He looked at her and moaned,

343

throwing one arm over his eyes in an expression of annoyance rather than shame. Beside him Coral moved. The sheets rustled, her eyes fluttered open and Polly saw that they were green. She also had the satisfaction of seeing those beautiful eyes widen in terror just before Coral scrambled toward Alexander as though his pitiful body, or the thin sheet she dragged along, could protect her. Coral crushed into Alexander, knocking his arm away from his eyes. Then he too reacted, his face slackening, his mouth opening when he saw the gun in Polly's very steady hand leveled at his head.

"That's a fine way for two grown people to act," Polly tsked. "Not even a hello for the wronged wife. Not even the decency to say how sorry you both are that I had to find out this way. Alexander? I think you're suppose to say something like, 'I wanted to tell you. I love her. I can't live without her. I'm sorry I hurt you.' See, that's how you're supposed to react. Something suave. That's how it is in the movies, Alexander. This," she waved the gun at both of them, "is a ridiculous display for two such bold people. Two people who don't care who they hurt because of their disgusting appetites. You both look like babies. Babies! You don't see me falling apart, do you? Well, do you?"

Alexander Grant found his voice and his strength at the same time. He pushed Coral away from him and turned the charm on Polly.

"I don't love her. She doesn't love me. It's just something we both enjoyed, Polly. But the rest is true. I didn't want to hurt you. I never wanted you to know. You've got to believe that, Polly. After all we've gone through . . ." Losing his voice for a moment, Alexander swallowed hard and began again, ". . . The campaign, the reconciliation. I'm weak, I admit it. But I'm not dumb. I know what a good thing I have in you . . ."

"Alexander!" Coral objected, unable to take her eyes off the gun.

"Shut up, Coral," he snapped, his eyes never leaving his wife's. "There's never been anyone for me but you."

"I suppose that's why you went to this woman's house after we shot the commercial. Or what about that woman in Washington. Allison, wasn't that her name?"

"Jesus, how did you . . ."

"Shut up, Alexander. Just shut up. And you . . ." she glared at Coral, ". . . I don't want to hear anything out of you until I'm done. Until I'm done with . . . whatever . . ." The gun wavered. Polly's free hand wandered to her forehead. She was suddenly so very tired. So tired and not really interested in any of this. But it had to be done, this had to be played out. "How many others were there, Alexander?" With a heavy sigh she looked at her husband. His eyes were bright with apprehension; hers were dead. "You can tell me. I'm your wife. We're supposed to share everything. Were there women before we separated, or was I just being a fool after you came back . . . ?"

"No! No others before this I swear." Alexander talked fast, grasping at straws. He would say anything to make her leave. Barring that, he wanted to get her to put that damn gun down. "I don't know what happened to me. The power. The prestige. Women were there, everywhere . . ." Alexander's eyes were darting around the room as he estimated the distance to the door, the phone, the bathroom where he could lock himself away. Beside him Coral whimpered. He wanted to hit her. Shut her up. She had got him into this situation. "Really, Polly, I . . ."

"Don't move, you bitch!" Polly screamed, flinging the gun to the right so quickly Coral fell back on the bed releasing the sheet. Naked, her breasts were flattened against a chest that trembled with terror. With a shaking hand she reached for the sheet, missed it, grasped it again and covered herself. The room was heavy with dread. The two people on the bed watched the woman with the gun and the woman with the gun was amused. Polly Grant began to chuckle, four fingers covering her lips as if she were embarrassed and afraid to hurt their feelings.

"I'm sorry. Did I scare you? I didn't mean to do that. You're a guest, Coral. I wouldn't want you running away before things got interesting." She kept the gun and her eyes trained on Coral but spoke to her husband.

"Did you know, Alexander, that I adored you? Did you know that every time you hurt me with a look or a word, or by the mere fact you never thought to touch me with love, that I forgave you? I did. I forgave you and forgave you and I didn't dwell on how much I was hurt. That's because I was brought up to understand the differences between men and women. I believed that you simply weren't able to express your love in a normal fashion. Yes, I did. I believed that."

"Polly, I never . . ." Alexander began, sliding up on the bed so that he could have a better chance of grabbing the gun if she should let down her defenses.

"Be quiet, Alexander and listen to me." Coral's fear no longer pleased Polly, but neither did Alexander's excuses. "I suppose women like you would tell a man when you didn't like something, wouldn't you?"

Coral whined. Polly's patience was stretched.

346

"Wouldn't you!" Polly screamed, lunging forward until, for a horrible, brutal second, the two women were nose to nose. Coral cried out, one sharp, terrified screech.

Satisfied, Polly unwound her body, pulling it back, releasing each vertebrae and willing herself to relax. She spoke softly, controlling herself beautifully. "It doesn't matter. I know you would. You'd hound him until he did exactly what you wanted. Then he'd divorce you because he couldn't stand the nagging. Well I did just the opposite. I swallowed everything—hurt, pride, loneliness—everything and he still went to someone like you. He should love me. I made it so easy for him. So damn easy."

A sob tore from Polly's throat, her hand began to shake. She looked at her hand, surprised that suddenly she should begin to fall apart. Everything had gone so well until now.

"Polly," Alexander called softly, easing himself up. "Polly, you can't want to . . ."

"Alexander," she said wearily, looking at her husband with little interest. "Don't tell me anymore what I can or cannot think or do or feel. I will tell you what I want. I want to hurt you, Alexander. I want to hurt you so terribly. I thought about that all night. Isn't that pathetic?" Polly sighed. She shrugged one shoulder. Her free hand clutched at her gown and the one that held the gun trembled. The damn thing was getting heavy and her sleeplessness was taking a toll.

"What would hurt you badly enough, Alexander, to make you remember how much pain you caused me? I'm sure you would have an answer to that right off the top of your head. It took me all night, and I was worried that I wouldn't figure it out. But finally I came up with an idea." Polly moved back a step, oddly

347

serene as her eyes looked through the two people in the bed. She had their total attention. "I know exactly what needs to be done. I want you to remember what I do so that you will never, ever again want to pain anyone else. And what's the one thing that will hurt you most? I'll tell you, Alexander. You want to be a powerful Senator and taking that away just when it's almost yours will be awful, won't it, Alexander? Won't it, darling . . . ?"

"Oh God, Polly " Alexander shrunk back against the headboard, his arms coming up to protect his chest, his hands splayed across his face.

"Please . . . don't . . . please . . ."

Coral pressed into him, trying desperately to wedge herself between him and the headboard, hoping the bullet would lodge in her lover before it came to her.

They made strange noises of protest, both whimpering as Polly pulled the hammer back. They were crying a moment later, arms and legs moving in pitiful attempts to hide themselves from this crazy woman. Polly's finger caressed the trigger. She paused. She began to pull. Coral's mouth twisted open in a silent scream. The hammer shivered, poised for its fall. Then, just before it struck, just as Alexander and Coral saw their miserable lives flash before their eyes, they witnessed a most horrible thing and their fear turned to utter terror.

"Explain this one to the voters, Senator."

With those final words Polly turned the gun to her head and let the hammer fall.

Pleading exhaustion, Dani sat far from her associates. Blake knew she wasn't sleeping. But no amount of cajoling would get her to talk about what was wrong so they managed the four-hour flight without disturbing her. Once they were settled in the hotel, once Blake and Rudy took off to check out the beach, Serina cornered Dani.

"Need an ear?"

Dani smiled at her young friend but the smile faded as she looked over Serina's shoulder. Rudy was trudging back up the beach toward them. What a mess. Rudy's idiocy would not only ruin Green Advertising, it would probably ruin his relationship with Serina. Dani's eyes flicked back to her friend. She covered Serina's hand with her own.

"Thanks, but no. Not right now. After the shoot we'll all have to talk about it. Right now all I want you and Blake to do is concentrate on this shoot. It's so important, Serina. For you especially."

"I know." She may know, Dani thought, but she doesn't care. Standing, her long legs glistening with oil, Serina shaded her eyes and looked out to sea. "I wish we were here just to relax. I don't know how you all can think about work in a place like this."

"I don't either," Dani said contemplatively, staring out at the sapphire blue expanse of water, wishing some God would rise up and tell her how she was going to handle Rudy Green and his illegal dealings.

Both women turned at the sound of Blake's voice. With a huge gesture he was beckoning them. Dani turned back. Rudy was almost upon them and Dani knew the time for questions was upon her. She tapped Serina's legs.

"You go. Blake probably wants to try you out in different places."

"Okay."

Serina was off just as Rudy came to sit beside Dani. "Where's she going?"

"To pose for Blake."

Rudy nodded. Together they sat in silence. He squinted, looked up into the blazing sun, the heat cut by the sea breeze. From where he sat he could see Blake and Serina walking toward the incredible rock formation that kept the land from falling into the sea. So high it rose, fawn colored and strong, a huge 'O' in the middle of the ocean. Impressive, but not enough that Rudy could block out the very negative vibes emanating from his companion.

"So what about you? What do you want to do? Talk?"

Dani was silent for a very long time. Rudy sat with his knees up, his arms resting atop, his hands dangling. He wore an oversized cotton shirt and baggy shorts. Very GQ yet suddenly, very clearly, Dani saw the man he had been when she first met him: a hustler, a risk-taker, a penny-ante player. Now he was screwing the world and this time it was going to hurt a lot of people. Dani dug her bare toes into the warm sand. She pressed her chest against her legs and hugged them and focused on the horizon, unable to look at him any longer.

"You keep two sets of books on the Grant account, Rudy."

Flat. Emotionless. The dispassionate imparting of this information scared Dani. She thought she was angry, she thought she was outraged. Now she found she was tired and sad. To come all this way, to have beat Sid at his own game, to have created some of her finest campaigns and built a respected agency in the process, only to have it destroyed by Rudy's greed made her feel—lonely.

"You keep two sets of books on the Grant account and Radison Chemical. Those media billings weren't incorrect. Daniel Sweeny's time wasn't free. Radison's been feeding you big money, and you've been buying time, talent, and suppliers for Alexander with it. I don't know why you've done it, but I can guess. Money. I suppose . . ." Dani dug her hands into the sand, raised her fingers, and let it filter through. "Oh, hell. It's always money with you, Rudy. It isn't legal and we can lose the agency if anybody finds out. And what about criminal charges, Rudy?" Sighing she bent her head, burying her face in the groove of her knees. Dani spoke and her voice seemed far away as she lamented. "We'll lose the agency. You'll lose Serina."

"No one will find out." Rudy said. Dani's head came up. Behind her dark glasses she eyed him.

"You don't seem surprised that I found out. You don't even seem embarrassed or worried that I know, for God's sake."

"I'm not. You're a really smart lady. I thought I was smarter, but I was lazy. Besides, this all was put in motion before we got Apache. I didn't know we'd have legitimate clients. Hell, I didn't even know you'd be around long enough to do anything for me. It happened." Rudy shrugged and let his hand fall to the sand. He dug in but was in no mood to play. "I've been caught before. I'll be caught again. At least you were the one to figure it out. I just have to be more careful and make sure no one outside you and me figures it out."

Dani lowered her head slightly, her eyes closed against the bright balls of anger behind them. She gripped her knees tighter but it didn't help. Her hands found their way to her hair, she cradled her head and when she spoke her voice was strangled with emotion. He had no idea what he was destroying—her life, her self-esteem. The child had been banished in the last

351

year, Papa put to rest, and now Rudy was just proving the old bastard right again.

"This isn't a stupid game, Rudy. This is my life you're screwing with. Mine! You're going to ruin it with your greed and your stupidity. I don't know what I was thinking when I hooked up with you. I thought there was hope, that you could grow and learn and actually figure out that an advertising agency wasn't a used car lot."

"Hey, lady," Rudy cut her off fiercely, "I may not have all the class in the world, but a year ago I told you you were screwing around with my life and you didn't give a shit." He moved, onto his knees, grabbing her hands away from her head, forcing Dani to look at him. "You think I liked feeling like a schmuck while you took over everything. You were so busy changing everything else about my life you couldn't have cared less what I did with Grant. Now that we're on top you're going to start wringing your hands and telling me it's my fault that this agency isn't everything you want it to be. Well it's everything *I* want it to be." Rudy picked up a handful of sand and threw it. Dani turned her face away. "I am sorry I got caught up in this thing with Grant. I never dreamed there would be so much to lose. But I made a deal with Grant. We shook on it and I intend to see it through. Keep it to yourself, Dani, and we're home free. Grant's campaign will be over in six months, Radison will get whatever they want out of him. Grant is happy and we've got a reputation as a fine political firm. Then I'll drop him."

Rudy pushed up and swatted at his behind to get the sand off his shorts. Only now did he dare look at her. She was still one of the most beautiful women he had ever seen but something seemed to have died in Dani

352

Cortland. When she turned her face up to him all he saw was make-up and round designer sunglasses and a great haircut. That spark was gone, that confidence that had irked him, then driven him on, had disappeared. He was sorry to see her this way. He owed her a lot, but then she had a debt too.

"Dani, when you first came to me you weren't exactly playing with a clean deck either. If I were you, I'd remember that little story about stones and glass houses."

"I never did anything illegal, Rudy," Dani said flatly.

"Yeah," Rudy laughed wryly. "Do you know what the difference is between illegal and immoral? When you do something illegal you get caught by people who can punish you. When you get caught doing something immoral you can still go home and have a drink. Think about it. Think about what you brought me all those months ago, and how you got all that information, then tell me I'm the one who ought to be ashamed of myself. At least I don't profess to love the people I'm messing with."

Rudy kicked at the sand, surveyed the beach, then headed off toward Blake and Serina. Dani watched him go. No way was he going to equate this with the trick she'd played on Blake. When they got back she would make him an offer, buy him out of Green Agency and get rid of Alexander Grant immediately. Failing that she would insist he buy her out. Ashley Cosmetics, maybe even Apache, would come with her if she opened up her own shop. Rudy deserved that at least. But for now, for Blake and Serina's sake, Dani would go along with the program. Standing up she went after Rudy ready to go along with the shoot for everyone's sake.

Dani found Blake and Rudy looking down at Serina who was laying in the sand at the edge of the shore, her eyes closed, her hair spread out behind her. For a moment Dani thought she might be ill. She had taken her first step toward Serina when the woman opened her eyes.

"What do you think?" Serina was grinning, the warm water running up and over her shoulders, across her as the pointed little white cap swelled before pulling back again caressing her beautiful body.

"I think you look wet," Dani said.

"Look, babe." Blake was by Dani's side handing her the camera. "Look at the way the foam and the clear water mesh in the sunshine. See the kind of opaque look it gives, like some weird veil around her. Kind of like we've thrown netting over her and her face is bleeding through it; like her face is rising out of the ocean. A little retouching and we can make it look as though her face and upper body are sculpted out of the sand and water. It will be fantastic. Then we'll do an insert with the new Sea Foam Colors running along the bottom of the print ad, we'll cut in on the broadcast stuff with a color chart. It's going to be dynamite."

Dani looked as she was instructed, her fingers covering Blake's as he held the heavy camera for her. Her grip tightened. How she needed him now, how she needed his steadiness and his undivided attention. But his attention wasn't hers. For the first time since she'd known him, another woman held his interest, another woman was his obsession. Lowering the camera, feeling lonely in the midst of those she had liked and loved, those she had respected and used, Dani looked at Serina laying on the sand like a beautiful beached mermaid. Serina grinned. Finally she was having fun.

Dani smiled back weakly then looked up at Rudy. He didn't even have the decency to avoid her eyes. Then her gaze lingered on Blake. Under the Mexican sun with the water at their feet and defeat at her door, Dani realized just how much she loved him and how little anything else really mattered.

Was it too late to change? Perhaps she'd already lost a part of him to his protege if she could no longer command his immediate attention or his undying loyalty. Dani wanted to cry at the thought of it. Instead she smiled gently. Once again, Blake's vision, his dream, would come true as easily as if he had conjured it up out of nothing. Thankfully there would be no envy this time, Dani's eyes were open—or was it that she was simply beaten by promises forgotten, vows broken?

"It's going to be great, Blake."

"Yes," he answered, thoughtfully, oblivious to the intensity of feeling in Dani's voice. He was lost to her because of Serina and Ashley Cosmetics. She had given him over to them in an effort to keep him for herself. How strange life was. She shook her head. Blake was still musing, standing over the prostrate Serina, his black eyes intense, his tall body shimmering in the Mexican sun. "This will be one of the most spectacular shots anyone has ever seen. Still, I think there's something we can do to make it even more sensational. Something no one has ever done before."

"What's that?" Dani asked half-heartedly, offering her hand to Serina who took it and dragged herself upright with a giggle.

"I don't know. I'll tell you all when I do." Blake answered, moving between Dani and Serina, reaching for Serina and smoothing her long, long wet hair before wandering away from the little group to contemplate the ocean and open his mind to inspiration.

Three in the morning was the hour inspiration finally visited Blake. He was out the door by five. The arrangements were made by seven and he was dressed and banging on doors, rousing the rest of the Green Agency by seven-thirty. It was time to go. It was time to make advertising history and nothing else mattered.

"Christ, I've never seen so much blood. Oh Lord, Eric, did you ever see so much blood? The whole side of her head was gone and she fell on the bed. Right between us . . . right on the bed!"

Alexander Grant sat, pulled close to the hearth, in one of his mother's crewel-work chairs that still hadn't fallen under the upholsterer's knife. A fire was blazing and the heat was also on, but still, twenty-four hours after Polly's earthly exit, Alexander couldn't seem to get warm. Eric, on the other hand, was sweating like a pig and getting damned tired of hearing about the blood and the brains.

"No, Alexander," Eric sighed, put upon. "I've never seen that much blood in my entire life. Now can we please stop with the instant replays? We've got other things to worry about."

Alexander wrung his hands, a tremor ran up his spine. His hair was unkempt, his skin pale. He looked lost and forlorn and Coral wasn't around to buck him up.

"I know. I know." Alexander's voice failed him. It weakened, as his body seemed to fall in on itself. Plaintively he asked, "Did you call Dani and Rudy? We

356

should ask them what we should tell the press. The vultures haven't been off the doorstep since this happened. Dani will know the right thing to say." Alexander's frantic, frightened eyes looked away from the fire and Eric looked away from his boss, disgusted by his lack of control.

"I already told you they're out of town. I left a message and their girl said she'd try to get a hold of them. Don't sweat it Alexander, I'm here and I know what I'm doing. This isn't about your image. It's about reality, your political life. This is out of their league."

"You're right, Eric, absolutely. Just tell me what you want me to do and I'll do it." Alexander acquiesced, giving in quickly, quietly, completely.

Eric grinned, satisfied his time had finally come. "All right, this is it. You are devastated by what Polly has done, not by the act itself but because you loved her so much. I want to see tears at the funeral. I've already gone to see Monica. She doesn't want to have a thing to do with you. She's not even going to attend the funeral because she thinks it will be a circus. That's good. That means she probably won't talk to any reporters so you're going to have to pass her off with a comment that she was just too upset to attend. Coral just wants to be left alone—with about twenty thousand dollars for 'therapist' fees."

"That's blackmail!" Alexander's senses flared briefly before deserting him just as quickly.

"Sure it is. I paid her with campaign funds. I also brought a friend along. Someone who is very scary to look at. I don't think Coral will be saying anything else. Who knows, she might even want to see you again."

Alexander shook his head. "Never."

"Never say never," Eric warned him. If he believed in that old adage he would have been out of politics long ago.

"And the cops?"

"Nothing to worry about. We told them the truth. If there's a leak and someone finds out Polly wasn't despondent, that she killed herself while you were in bed with another woman, then we don't respond. Let the information die on its own. The bereaved widower routine will buy you a ton of support in the next six months if you believe what you say about her. You'll believe that you loved her more than anyone in this world. Do that, and I promise you will be elected."

"Fine. Yes, whatever you say. I trust you, Eric. You're the only one I have left to trust. I'll do whatever you say. You know how these things work . . ."

Alexander was still babbling when Eric left him to his one-sided discussion and went to answer the doorbell. More reporters, more mutterings of horror. He loved this. Poor Polly. If only she knew how much she had helped Alexander's campaign. Giving his coat jacket a tug, Eric arranged his face in an expression of concern and opened the door, his mouth already moving to inform the reporters that Alexander would be unable to talk with them. That countenance changed quickly when two men flashed badges instead of microphones in his face. Eric let them in when they asked to see Alexander. Even he didn't mess with the FBI.

"I don't understand what the FBI has to do with the death of Mrs. Grant," Eric said, following them into the hall. "Perhaps you didn't hear it was a suicide. There is nothing political about her death."

"We're not here about Mrs. Grant's death," the taller of the two said looking around the house. It was the second man, the bulkier of the two who took it upon himself to make eye contact and convince Eric theirs was a serious visit.

"This way," Eric mumbled, knowing when to cut his losses. Thankfully, Alexander was standing. Still pale, he appeared at least somewhat Senatorial. He waited for the two men to come to him, barely glancing at their identification, controlling his chill as best he could.

"Senator Grant, we are sorry to bother you at a time like this, but we'd like to ask you some questions regarding your association with Radison Chemical Company and the specifics of your contract with Green Advertising."

Alexander sunk back into the chair he had so recently abandoned. The agents followed suit, sitting patiently while he lowered his head into his hands, tears overflowing their bounds. While they waited, Alexander Grant wept while Eric Cochran comforted the Senator from California.

"The Senator is still in shock over his wife's suicide. Perhaps I could answer your questions now, and you could talk to the Senator later."

The agents looked at one another. The taller agent gave a small nod. Eric was ready for battle.

In her apartment Lora Prince looked at the clock then switched on the seven o'clock news. Everything must have been wrapped up by now. She settled back on the sofa with a drink in her hand and was immediately gratified to hear the lead story.

"Senator Alexander Grant is under investigation for campaign funding fraud only one day after the death of his wife, Polly Grant. Our sources tell us that Senator Grant has allegedly accepted large sums of money from Radison Chemical Corporation funneled through the Senator's advertising agency, Green Advertising. Neither Mr. Green nor his partner, Dani Cortland were available for comment. We do have a clip of Eric Cochran, Senator Grant's aide, as he gave reporters a prepared statement earlier in the day . . ."

Lora pushed the button on her remote and the set went silent. Sitting alone, not caring what Eric Cochran had to say, she toasted herself.

"Here's to anonymous sources," she giggled, trying desperately to be happy now that someone had listened to her, now that Dani Cortland would soon be history.

Chapter Twenty-eight

While Serina was being made-up in a tent on the beach, Rudy, Blake, and Dani huddled in front of a fishing boat. All three were talking, giving their opinions, arguing, pleading, until nobody was sure what they were trying to accomplish any more.

"Wait," Dani snapped, "just wait a minute. We aren't getting anywhere, and I don't think it's up to us to decide this thing. As an idea it's spectacular, but the decision has to be Serina's."

"No way," Rudy said sharply, "we are not even going to ask her about it. It's insane. I've never heard of anything so ridiculous."

"It's not insane. It's perfect," Blake said dryly, disgusted that Rudy couldn't see the possibilities. Yet it was Dani's refusal to give him carte blanche that really angered him. She used to be so willing to take risks. Hell, she'd almost ruined their relationship for a risky proposition.

"Listen to me. It can be done so easily. I take Serina in full make-up and in wardrobe. We get into the water, I've got a tank on my back. We use the buddy system for breathing as we go under. All she has to do is hold her breath as long as she can while I reel off the photos. As soon as she signals I get back to her and give her the mouthpiece. Christ, we'll just be off shore, I'll be with her every moment. She doesn't even have to open her eyes if she doesn't want to. But think about it. Think about how her hair will float. Think of the background of those marvelous rocks out there, the clarity of the water, the fish . . ." Blake gestured toward a spectacular formation. "Come on, what is wrong with you guys? I've got the boat. We can shoot the campaign with her lying on the sand tomorrow. We'll get everything we need and this will be a bonus. If it works the way I think it will, we are talking unbelievable photo op."

"No . . ." Rudy growled, hands balled in fists at his side. "If we were going to do something like this we should have a diving master . . ."

Dani turned away, putting her hand on his arm as if that alone could keep him from decking Blake. In the heat of the moment even Rudy's transgressions were forgiven—for the time being.

"There isn't anything dangerous about this . . ." Blake declared, having the last word.

Serina found them as they were, not looking at each other, not speaking. Cautiously she smiled.

"Everything all right?"

"Fine, Serina. Blake's just getting a little carried away here. His inspiration is taking a very strange turn," Rudy drawled, less enamored with Blake than he ever thought possible. The guy was a nut. He wouldn't listen to anyone. He and Dani deserved each other.

"Really?" Serina raised an eyebrow, careful not to do anything that might disturb her perfectly painted face. "What's this idea that's turned Dani and Rudy into such enemies?"

"Blake . . ." Dani warned, moving toward him as if her proximity could stop him from speaking.

"It's okay, Dani. I'd like to hear it. Blake?" Serina turned her stunning, trusting eyes on him. That was all the incentive he needed. He could already see her under the ocean, his personal mermaid.

"Serina, I want to shoot you under water," Blake told her. He sounded as if he were inviting her to walk with him in the park. Dani scowled and shook back her hair, turning her face to the sun. Maybe it would burn the growing sense of unease out of her.

"Wouldn't that look a little strange if I had on a mask and one of those oxygen tanks? Nobody could see the Ashley make-up." Serina laughed but one look at the somber faces told her this was no joke. Blake had her by the shoulders.

"It can happen, Serina. I wouldn't have you under longer than ten minutes. We'd share the air. I'd just be a few feet away from you. I even asked one of the fisherman what he thought. He says to tie a bag of food at your waist and the fish will come up and nibble at it and not at you. He doesn't think it's crazy. We'll have such color, such atmosphere. This whole Sea Foam Collection screams for something out of the ordinary. So what do you say? Shall we try it?"

"Well, I don't see why not . . ." Serina was hesitant. She could see how much this meant to Blake and it didn't seem like such an awful thing to do.

"You don't see why not?" Rudy asked sarcastically, turning on her, startling her. "Because it could be dangerous, that's why not! Have you ever had a diving lesson in your life Serina?"

"Rudy, that's ridiculous. She'll be with me . . ."

"Shut up, Blake," Rudy growled. "I don't even know if you can swim. You're going to trust him just because he says it's okay? It's a stupid idea. Too many things could happen. We ought to stick with what we presented to the client. We don't have to do this just because Blake thinks he's some kind of big shot."

"Rudy!" Serina said, appalled and surprised by his meanness. Obviously something was wrong between the three of them. Afraid what was happening couldn't be repaired if it went much further, Serina did what she could to keep the peace. "Dani, what do you think?"

Dani shrugged; she shook her head. "I don't know. It wasn't in the game plan. I don't see any need for the extra effort. I think if both of you give us your best on the beach that's enough to ask."

Dani turned away. She had no reason why she didn't want this thing to happen. It was just a feeling that she wanted Blake and Serina where she could keep an eye on them. Besides, the faster they finished this shoot, the faster they could get back to L.A. where she and Rudy could try to start working through their other problems.

"Well, what if we just tried it?" Serina looked at Rudy, hopeful of keeping the peace. She laughed a little, touched him, but he didn't soften. "I'm game and I can swim. I don't see how it could be dangerous if Blake's down there with me. It won't be very far will it Blake?" She looked his way and he insisted she was right. "There, see? It might be kind of fun as long as . . ."

"Oh, do what you want," Rudy muttered, flinging himself away from her, and away from the boat. He trudged up the beach, hoping he could walk off his anger. If anything happened to Serina he would . . .

"Rudy!" Serina started after him but Blake reached

out and took her arm. Rudy was gone; there were decisions to be made.

"It's too hot to chase him. When we're done and he sees the pictures he won't be mad anymore."

"I don't know, Blake. I thought if I was up about the idea he would be too. I don't want to make him so mad."

"I know, honey. Everybody's on edge. So let's just do our work then you and Rudy can have the evening to yourselves. You can find out what's bugging him and I'll try to figure out what Dani's problem is."

"All right." Serina looked past Blake. "I just wish he was going to be on the boat with us. I'd feel better if he were on the boat."

"Well, what can we do?"

"I don't know. I feel bad. I wish I could have talked to him."

"Later, Serina. Let's get going now. The sooner we start, the sooner we'll be done."

Serina nodded. Blake handed her off the pier and onto the boat. Next he handed up his waterproof camera, his film, his duffle bag. He turned to face Dani.

"Are you coming?"

"I don't have a good feeling about this Blake. It's a waste of time and money."

"Then stay here. Figure out what's bugging you. You wanted to work together, I suggest we do it right."

Dani opened her mouth to speak but found she couldn't. Blake had never talked to her like that. Even in their worst times he had never been so cold. Finally she swung onto the boat.

"I'm coming."

"Fine."

"And I suggest you remember who's in charge here."

Blake was on deck before she finished speaking. Dani stood quietly, watching him before, together, they reached for Serina and brought her on board. The motor started a moment later and Blake went to the fisherman, pointing the way to the end of the peninsula. Dani stood silently on the bow, her eyes closed against the salty spray and the heat of the sun. Then she remembered they hadn't brought anything dry for Serina to change into. Well, the water was warm and they wouldn't be down that long. She looked over her shoulder and saw that Blake had thought of everything. Masks, oxygen tanks and the naive, willing Serina were all he needed to get the shot of his life. Turning back to the sea she let her mind wander, seeking some happy thought to latch onto until she heard the motor of the boat shut down.

Quietly she went to help Blake into his gear. She squeezed Serina's arm affectionately just before she stepped off the back of the boat and slid into the water.

The last thing Dani saw was Blake looking at Serina and Serina in a cloud of floating chiffon, her eyes laughing as she exclaimed over the warmth of the water. Then they were gone, Blake's arm wrapped protectively around the young woman as he guided her down into the crystalline depths.

Beneath the surface Blake felt Serina tense. He fixed the mouthpiece between her lips. She breathed in then gave it back. Slowly as the process was repeated she began to relax. Blake glanced at her as they went deeper into the water but not so deep that they couldn't see the sparkling surface.

Serina looked as just he had hoped she would. The waterproof make-up was in place, her hair was a stream behind her, the chiffon was so diaphanous as to be another subtle shade of the water. Finally, not too far from the boat, Blake found the place he wanted.

His arm still about her waist, Blake positioned Serina near an underwater grotto. The fish that had darted away now came tentatively back to see who had intruded into their domain. Serina grinned as she felt something brush against her thigh. She didn't open her eyes in the salt water, only motioned she needed more air. For a long while she and Blake just floated, passing the mouthpiece between them. Finally Blake squeezed her shoulder, the sign which asked if she was ready. Serina nodded. With one hand Blake took the camera from his back, the other still connected with his model. She took one more breath before Blake backed away.

For the next thirty seconds Serina gave herself up to the gentle pull and push of the underwater current. She let her head float, her hair twirl around her face. She knew Blake was shooting. Then he was beside her again, his cheek against hers under the water as he congratulated her. She was breathing again. Beautiful blessed air. How easy it was to imagine she belonged in this wet world. There was something mesmerizing about the situation, as though she would forget about air if Blake didn't remind her.

Blake moved away again, Serina moved her body, raising one arm, pulling the chiffon with her so that it drifted behind her head. She pursed her lips. She dipped her head. Her eyes were still closed. Blake was back. Now they were both feeling the lure of the sea. Serina was beginning to enjoy the little nips at her waist from the hungry fish. She moved back toward the rocks, treading as best she could with her feet to keep herself stationery.

After a few minutes Blake moved away again, taking the oxygen with him. These would be the last shots. They had promised only ten minutes. Serina thought of Rudy. He would be so proud when he saw these photos. He would love her so much. Serina let her mind wander, drifting away from her until . . .

Until she was aware of a pain deep in her chest; so deep that she thought something was ripping her chest apart. Her body stiffened she made the gesture Blake had given her. It was air she needed. She had forgotten to breath. Frantically she waved her hand then pushed herself away from the rocks. But something held her back. The chiffon wrapped so tightly about her waist had caught in a crevice. She couldn't move.

Instantly her eyes sprang open, the salt water stinging them. She half closed them as she searched for Blake. He was there. Thank God he was there. His camera was poised, pointed directly at her. She motioned, her frenzied machinations slowed by the water, seeming nothing more than the most heartfelt ballet. She was caught, she needed to breathe. She opened her mouth as if she could call to him. Her dress billowed about her, the fish nibbled at her waist and her hair floated Medusa-like in the blue green water and Blake saw it all.

Dani leaned on the boat's railing her arms spread wide, the sun beating down on her bare back. For a long while she looked at the place in the sea that had swallowed Blake and Serina. They had disappeared quickly and that surprised her. The water was clear, a sapphire blue that shimmered with diamond white points of light where the sun reflected back to the perfectly azure sky. It seemed she should have been able to see to the bottom of the ocean on a day like this. It seemed as if she should be thrilled on a day like this. All her problems with Rudy aside this shot, this campaign, was what she had lied for, schemed for, almost lost Blake for. Dani couldn't help but wonder if it had all been worth it, and she didn't know why such horrid doubt should rear its ugly head now.

Sighing, Dani pushed herself from the rail just as a speedboat shot by, halfway to the horizon. The boat in which she stood rocked a minute later as the wake broadside her. Dani steadied herself then sank to the deck, nestled her back against a load of gear, lay back her head and closed her eyes. The guide was watching, but she didn't care. This awful feeling in the pit of her stomach had nothing to do with the sway of the boat or the hungry eyes of the man on the bridge. It had to do with what Dani had seen in Blake's eyes just before he went under; what she'd seen in Serina's as she held onto him. That was what made Dani feel so strange, so uneasy . . . so frightened.

"Damn," she muttered.

Up again she fought off the nonsensical sensations that made her fingers tingle and formed a lump in her throat. She shaded her eyes once more, lacing her hands together over her eyes as she peered toward the outcropping of rock where Blake and Serina were now working, shooting the images Blake saw so clearly in his mind, images that would soon be plastered over every media in the United States. Serina was down there moving under the water, making herself into the sea godess Blake envisioned. And Dani was on a boat with a man who didn't understand. Some things a woman knew without seeing, hearing, or truly under-

369

standing the cry that came into her mind. Suddenly Dani understood. Blake was in trouble and she needed to be with him. God, if she lost him now. It was an impossible thought and it was shoved aside as Dani frantically stripped down to her black maillot just before she swung a tank of air onto her back, a mask onto her head and threw herself backwards into the warm, deadly water while the man on the bridge yelled his surprise in a language she didn't understand.

Whipping around, Serina pulled at the fabric of her costume, aware of the rock, the fish, of Blake so close yet acting as though she no longer existed. Couldn't he see what was happening to her? Snapping her head toward him, her hair floating sensuously over her face, Serina opened her mouth, trying to scream his name, trying to make him come to her with the oxygen.

But Blake didn't move.

He watched.

Through the camera he saw her and was mesmerized by the eroticism in her struggle. He recorded her fight, each expression, each new terror, each painful, panicked look. Blake saw the essence that was Serina's life as he made the camera work in the silent deep. In his marvelous delirium he lost himself in the image and forgot that the image was only a reflection of the woman, and that the woman was human.

Blake Sinclair took the last frame the moment Dani shoved life-giving air into Serina's mouth and turned, her own breath held, to look at Blake through the crystal blue and silent waters of Cancun.

Had they come to this? Was image now the reality and reality a thing to discard when it no longer amused or served them? God it wasn't just Blake who had been sorely in need, the danger wasn't his alone. It was hers and Dani knew she had brought this upon them.

Slowly, moving against the water, Dani turned away from Blake gently taking the air from Serina, breathing then giving it back to the frightened girl. In the silence of the deep she didn't hear Blake move she only knew he was upon them, his arms encircling them, holding them as they drifted toward the surface, tears streaking his face behind the mask.

Behind them the camera floated to the ocean floor and all the promise of stardom the film held was forgotten, never to be seen, the day never to be spoken of, the ambition never to be repeated.

Chapter Twenty-nine

"Ms. Cortland, may I remind you that you are under oath and that your testimony in front of this committee is as sacred as if you were in a court of law. Now, I ask you again, as a partner in Green Advertising, what was the relationship between Green Advertising, Radison Chemical, and Senator Grant?"

Dani sat at the long table in front of the senators who questioned her. She was stunningly dressed for grief in a plain black Nippon jersey, black stockings, and shoes. Only her white hair and the paleness of her skin offered relief. Her ensemble was highly appropriate. While the senators were determined to breathe life into a rather weak case of corruption, Dani was present to eulogize the death of a dream. Her lashes fluttered. It was difficult for her to tear her eyes away from the point directly in front of her. Every movement seemed to take such effort. Lately she tired so easily. Finally she did look up, directly into the faces of her inquisitors.

"I will tell you again, gentlemen, I am unaware of the particulars of the relationship between Senator Grant and Radison Chemicals. I am aware that they are clients of record of Green Advertising. I am aware that Rudy Green personally directed the distribution of those funds and that no other person within the organization known as Green Advertising was aware of the specific budget activity of either account."

Dani felt the pressure of her attorney's hand on her arm, consoling her as she fell silent again.

"And, Ms. Cortland, you would like this panel to believe you had no knowledge that Radison funds were used to purchase media for Senator Grant?"

"I did not work on either account Senator. Mr. Green and I split responsibility for the accounts in our agency. When we met we discussed bottom line, not specifics of expenditures."

"Don't you think it odd, Ms. Cortland, that the Senator would not know he was receiving more television time than his budget allowed?"

"It is entirely possible," Dani answered quietly though her eyes sparked for a moment. How good it would be to talk about something she understood rather than other things she would never understand. "The Senator is not an expert on the cost of advertising. If Mr. Green led him to believe that his budget was sufficient for the number of spots purchased, the Senator had no reason to doubt him."

The man sighed dramatically and leaned back in his leather chair. "Ms. Cortland, why would Radison Chemical funnel money into Senator Grant's campaign for election without his knowledge? It makes no sense. The only reason Radison would have donated to the Senator's campaign through Green Advertising would be to influence Senator Grant in some manner. Why on earth would they do it without telling him?"

Dani's eyes flicked toward the man. They were deep, deep blue that day; hard as flint.

"I don't know, sir. I would suggest you ask one of the two people who might know."

"We did try, Ms. Cortland, but Senator Grant disavows any knowledge of this transaction and Mr. Green . . ." the man drawled, his tone put-upon, a spoiled little boy anxious to be the center of attention.

"I know." Dani held up a hand. She didn't want to hear another word about Alexander Grant and she couldn't bear to hear this man make Rudy appear criminal or cowardly since he could not be found. Rudy was neither of those things, really. He was a man in love who had taken his woman and disappeared because she had begged him to take her away after her near-death experience. He had left everything behind because she had asked; they had gone without knowing about Alexander or the trouble they had left behind and Dani didn't have the foggiest idea where they were. But after what happened between Blake and Serina, she could only hope that they ended up somewhere peaceful, far away from the world of images and illusions.

"Dani." She looked up. Her attorney was leaning close, his arm around her shoulders. "Are you all right?"

She nodded and focused back on the panel. They were all whispering, glancing at her. She didn't care what they said anymore and she couldn't tell them what she didn't know. God, she was tired.

"Thank you, Ms. Cortland, that will be all."

Dani's attorney stood up, "Senators, will you be asking Ms. Cortland to stay on in Washington?"

"No, sir, she may leave at anytime. This committee will be reaching a decision regarding Senator Grant immediately. We have no desire to prolong an inquiry into the Senator's ethics due to the imminent elections."

So Dani was dismissed, with much less hoopla than when she had been summoned to this august body. It was finally, thankfully, time to go home.

"Alexander. Come on in, boy."

Alexander shuffled through the door. Eric remained outside. He had done what he could do to save Alexander's butt with the press but in a meeting with Basset he was useless.

"You wanted to see me, Lewis?" Alexander had lost some of his sparkle; the grey eyes didn't flash like tin in the sun anymore. Lewis had to smile at that. The pup was whipped and looking for a home—preferrably not one in a penitentiary. Well, Lewis would see what he could do about that.

"Sit down, Alexander. Rest yourself." Lewis raised a glass and drank. He didn't offer Alexander so much as a handshake. Once Alexander was settled, Lewis leaned over his wide desk. He smiled, he beamed. This felt damned good if he did say so himself. Too bad he didn't have more time, but the ethics committee was waiting for him.

"Thank you, Lewis."

"You're welcome, boy." Lewis cleared his throat. He harumphed for good measure then got right to it. "Had a bit of trouble now these last few days, boy. Bad bit of trouble, all this. In a lot of hot water, boy, and can't say I'm not happy about that. You did me real wrong, and I don't forget that easily, know what I mean?"

Alexander slid his eyes toward the old man. He was

375

grotesque. Alexander shivered. Lewis's countenance darkened.

"Know what I mean, boy?" he growled.

"Yes," Alexander said quietly.

"I didn't hear you, boy," Lewis shot back.

Alexander's head shot up, his lips clamped shut to hold back the torrent of abuse he wished he could heap on Lewis Basset. The bastard was going to drag this out and Alexander didn't know if he could stand it. Why didn't he just go to the ethics committee and tell them whatever he wanted to? Get it over with. Instead he looked Lewis in the eye and answered, "Yes, I do know what you mean."

"Good," Lewis said quietly, satisfied. "I like it when my boys are in line, Alexander. I'm assuming you still want in, is that right?" Lewis sighed and shifted his bulk. "I mean you ain't got much to go home to now, do you? No wife. Daughter probably never wants to see you again. I hear that little redhead you were sleeping with is even out of the picture now. Pity."

Lewis ruminated on Alexander's state of affairs for a moment. Lord how he was enjoying himself. A second later he pushed his chair away from the desk.

"Aw hell, Alexander, I'm not going to draw this out. You're up shit creek son and there's nothin' you can do about it. Nobody wants to hang around for fear they'll come out smellin' bad. But me, I got no reason to worry. I've been here long as anybody can remember. My word's good. I can do things other people can't. I can save your butt, boy. What I need to know is, do you want me to?"

Alexander had let his eyes wander, now his gaze snapped back to the old and ugly man, the powerful man, behind the desk. This, perhaps, was the worst of the nightmare, Lewis Basset holding the whip, waiting for him to grovel. For an instant Alexander refused. He considered attempting to fight back. His power had been growing, after all. He had made many friends, and only this one enemy. Perhaps there was a way . . .

"Met a friend of yours the other day, Alexander," Lewis purred. "Fella named Luellen. Owns some chemical company, as I recall. He's comin' to dinner tonight. Yes, indeed . . . comin' to dinner . . . So I ask again, boy. Do you need my help? Do you want my help?"

The ax had fallen, disconnecting Alexander from any hope of self-perpetrated salvation. Alexander's hands covered his face; he drew them along his cheeks as if trying to wake himself from this nightmare. But when he looked again, Lewis was still there. There was to be no escape for Alexander Grant.

"Yes, Lewis, I'd like you to help."

"No," Lewis waggled his finger, "tell me what you really want. Tell it to me the way a good old boy would. 'Cause, Alexander, you're goin' to be my good old boy from now on."

"Please, Lewis," Alexander said. "I want you to help me. I need you to help me. Please."

"Excellent, Alexander. Excellent."

Lewis Basset was gone a minute later, dragging his power after him, leaving Alexander alone and weak. Leaving him as he had found him, as he'd been all his life.

"I'll see you on the thirtieth with the layouts. Four thirty. Okay. Sure."

She hung up the phone and checked Santa Monica Bank off her list of things to do then looked at her watch. It was already five. Swiveling in her chair she flipped on the radio. The election was a runaway. Alexander Grant would be California's next Senator.

Dani flipped off the radio and began to pack her briefcase. It had been a long day, an even longer few weeks. Damage control had been enacted and all accounts but Senator Grant and Radison had remained intact. Unfortunately Ashley had cut their budget drastically after being told Serina was no longer available. But Dani could live with that. The agency would build back up again. When Serina and Rudy reappeared the agency would be solvent and aboveboard. It was the least she could do after . . .

"Dani?" From the doorway came the sound of her name and a simultaneous knock. Dani looked up. Lora waited for a nod to enter. Dani waved her in.

"I need a sign off on this schedule for Apache."

Dani flipped through the papers Lora held out, grabbed a pen and scribbled. She handed them back to Lora.

"Is there something else?" Dani asked, anxious to be away.

"Dani, I . . ." Lora, to her credit, held Dani's gaze, but it was difficult for her to talk. The two women hadn't exchanged more than three words since work had resumed. "Dani, I have to know why."

"Why what, Lora?"

"Why I'm still here."

Dani laughed, a rueful, sad sound. She threw the pen into her briefcase and latched it. "Lora, I can't figure out why any of us are still here. Let's just be grateful we are."

Lora nodded. She was looking better since she'd abandoned the bottle. Her eyes were clear, her hair starting to curl again. She'd even lost some weight.

378

And now confession, it seemed, was part of the self-improvement program.

"I told the FBI about the Radison payments."

Dani sighed. "I assumed so."

"You should have tossed me out."

"You know what they say about glass houses, Lora? Well, I think I'll leave the stones where they are."

Dani headed out, moving past Lora who touched her arm, stopping her.

"We'll never be friends."

"I know that," Dani answered. "But I also know there's a history here I can't ignore. Rudy meant a lot to both of us. When he comes back, I think he'd like to see the both of us here."

"Think he'll be back?"

Dani shrugged, smiled gently, "I don't know. If he's smart he won't. It's a whole lot nicer spending time with a woman who doesn't want anything from him, than women like us."

"Women like we used to be," Lora said quietly, courageously looking Dani in the eye. They understood one another and neither was really surprised to find they might be traveling the same track. Though Dani offered a smile, the effort seemed to be too much and it disappeared quickly. There was too much between them to settle it all in a few days, probably too much to settle ever. Dani sighed.

"We'll just see how things go, okay, Lora? No more tricks; not from me or you. If you want to work then do it here. If you want to screw around, find someplace else and I promise to do the same."

"Fair enough." Lora moved back, letting Dani pass. They'd all come such a long way. One of these days they might even start acting like adults. Impetuously Dani gave Lora's arm a squeeze and then she was gone. There were more bridges to mend.

"Hi!"

Blake lifted his head and sat away from the drawing table.

"Hi," Dani answered, gliding across the floor, her briefcase dropped without a second thought. In the next moment she was in his arms, being drawn into his lap and wondering how she could have ever wanted to be anywhere else.

"Hard day?" Blake asked.

Dani shook her head, "No harder than most these days." Dani snuggled on his shoulder, Blake's fingers wound through her hair and both let the minutes tick by. Dani's arms found their way around his waist, her lips settled on that marvelous place between the strength of his jaw and the supple flesh of his neck.

"Alexander's going to win," she murmured.

"I know. I've been listening to the returns," Blake answered. He pecked her forehead, brushed away her beautiful bright hair. "Does it make you mad?"

Dani shook her head, rearranging herself to be closer to him, thanking her lucky stars that finally she knew what it was to be comfortable with love.

"No, not really. Nothing I could do about it anyway. But I wasn't crazy about being left holding the bag in those Senate hearings, especially when I really didn't know what was going on."

"That, my love, was a blessing in disguise."

"It was." Freeing one arm Dani took Blake's hand and held tight. "You know, I honestly don't mind having had to go through that if Rudy and Serina were spared. I mean, it wasn't like they ran away. They

380

didn't have a clue what was happening back here. They chose to leave together, they chose to give up Serina's certain celebrity, Rudy's dreams of being a powerful ad man. I think that's wonderful. Their courage taught me a lot."

"Me too," Blake admitted, falling silent, thinking again of that horrible moment when he realized what he was doing to Serina. He moved, making motions as if to push Dani away, but she held on. This was no time for them to be alone, to hide their fears, or not share their secrets.

"So now we're so smart," Dani laughed, with a tinge of sadness and a good dose of optimism. She gave his hand a squeeze, lifted his fingertips to her lips. She kissed them.

"And now that we're smart," Blake murmured, "what do you think we should do?"

"I think we should put our noses to the grindstone, take care of our clients, come home on time every night, fix dinner, make love, and live like real people, Blake." Dani looked away, closing her eyes and pressing his hand to her cheek. "I think we ought to stop chasing images. You tried to tell me that when we were married, you tried to make me see that Papa's demands were as unrealistic as the photos you were taking of Serina. But we bought into it Blake, both of us, you just a little later than me. Now I want to do what I do well. I want to admire your work. I want to . . ."

She opened her eyes and considered his hand. It was so beautiful, square and competent and strong yet always so gentle. God she would die if she didn't have him to reach for, to hold . . .

"Dani?" Blake's fingers squeezed tight. She shook her head, clearing it save for one thought.

"We almost lost each other, Blake. Me with my silly games and stupid notions of what I had to have to make life worthwhile. You with your visions of Serina. Do you realize how close we came to never . . ."

Dani's voice caught. She couldn't go on. Her litanies had never brought her luck, only heartache. Her words had more often hurt than helped. Her ambitions had never brought her what they promised. How could she have been so blind?

"Forget it. I don't want to think of what we almost lost," she whispered, "but of what we can find."

"Dani, I don't think this is the time to start scheming again. Green Advertising is solid, we should work with it, accept it . . ."

"Shhh." Dani's fingers were on his lips, her blue eyes pleading with him to listen and understand. "Shh, love. That's not what I meant. Never again. No schemes, no plans. Dreams yes, but nothing that isn't attainable and real and important: dreams of doing good work, of waking in the morning and being glad I'm me, dreams of . . ."

Dani hesitated, taking time to really look at Blake. Past his beauty, through his dark eyes, and into his soul. There she saw what she wanted . . . no, what she desperately needed.

"I want my life and dreams to be one and the same, Blake. I want to put a ring on your finger. I want to take those vows again. I want to live up to them, head on and straightforward. No games, no competition."

"And what do you want from me?" Blake asked.

"From you?" Dani smiled, a beautiful smile from somewhere deep in her heart. "I want a promise to never change, to guide me back when I veer off the path. I want you to promise to love me as you did before all this happened. If you can do that, Blake,